A DIME
TO DANCE BY

A DIME
TO DANCE BY

Walter Walker

1817

HARPER & ROW, PUBLISHERS, New York
Cambridge, Philadelphia, San Francisco,
London, Mexico City, São Paulo, Sydney

FIRST EDITION

Designer: Jane Weinberger

Library of Congress Cataloging in Publication Data

Walker, Walter.
  A dime to dance by.
  I. Title.
PS3573.A52417D5 1983   813'.54   82-48688
ISBN 0-06-015145-5

---

83 84 85 86 87 10 9 8 7 6 5 4 3 2 1

To Annie, my best friend

1 We all agreed that it was very clever of Jimbo Ryder to hold his fundraiser at the Sons of Italy in America Hall. It was an obviously conciliatory gesture, but that in itself was enough for most people. A fair portion of those in attendance were under thirty-five and really did not care anyhow. We knew what Jimbo was doing and accepted it as a progressive action on his part.

But the earlier generations were also at Jimbo's fundraiser and the trepidation many of them felt was as plain as their Robert Hall suits. Not that one nationality was afraid of the other, but they were aware of essential differences between them and they were very concerned that no one think they could be manipulated by a chicken-and-canned-peas dinner for which they were paying twenty-five bucks a head. So they shook hands and exchanged words cordially when they met, and as soon as they got their drinks the Italians drifted off to one side and the Irish drifted off to the other. Later, when dinner was announced, the Italians took the rows of folding tables on the left and the Irish took the rows of folding tables on the right.

The Italians, even though it was their club, were by far the more subdued. Many were gregarious in their greetings (wide Vinnie Salvucci was stationed near the door, welcoming people as though they were entering his own living room), but they were watchful, too. They weren't interested in having anyone condescend to them and they were prepared to be resentful of any attempt to imply that the two groups were not on the exact same social level.

The Irish, for their part, boisterously established their presence from the moment they arrived. Jimbo was, after all, one of their own, and the general impression they conveyed was that of being honored guests whose very appearance was the embodiment of mirth and joviality. So they sat together on the far right and sloshed their drinks and hollered good-naturedly while their counterparts on the other side of the hall grew increasingly quiet.

Being neither Irish nor Italian, I stationed myself more or less in the neutral zone during the cocktail hour. It was a good position for seeing and being seen, and those were the only reasons I was at Jimbo's fundraiser. I was wearing my best suit, the one from Filene's that I had not bought in the basement, with my silk tie and Bally shoes. Outside the streets were filled with the slush of melting snow, but I had thought it important to wear the shoes anyway.

"Shoes," Sid Silverman once told me, "can be the most important thing in making an impression. People around here appreciate a good pair of shoes. Maybe it started when everyone used to work in the shoe factories down Brockton, I don't know, but now it's sort of intuitive. Shoes can tell a lot about a guy, and people recognize that, even if they don't put it in so many words. Like, a guy can dress up or dress down to meet whatever occasion he's going to and you can tell what his taste is and maybe you can even guess how much money he's got, but what you don't know is maybe somebody gave him those clothes for a present, or bought them for him. Or maybe he's just been to the place before and he knows what kind of clothes they wear and went out and got some just so he'd fit in—you know, like those shirts with the alligator on them. If you don't go to that place again you can always wear the shirt with the alligator someplace else, right? But shoes aren't like that. First of all, nobody ever gives anybody else a pair of shoes. Even a wife doesn't go out and buy a pair of shoes for her husband. Secondly, shoes can be real expensive, so most people aren't gonna buy a pair just for one type of occasion unless they're athletic shoes or something. It's not like a shirt, where you don't have to worry too much about getting your money's worth, and it's not like a suit, which you don't mind leaving in your closet forever because you know that sooner or later you're gonna need it again. Shoes you gotta be comfortable with. They gotta be comfortable on your feet and they gotta be useful to have around. What I'm trying to say is, they gotta be appropriate for the things you do. At least that's what everybody thinks. So the best way I know of to make a silent statement is with your shoes."

Sid Silverman is a man with very definite ideas about a great many things, one of which is my law practice. "There are two kinds of successful lawyers in this city," he used to say. "One is the parish-neighborhood lawyer. These are guys like Tommy McDonough, who get their business regardless of how good or bad they are because they're the only lawyer their clients know. They're the guys, their clients go to them and say, 'Help me, I'm in trouble. I'm in your hands—do with me what you will.'" Sid's voice would break into a high, mocking falsetto when he said this. Not being a parish-neighborhood type lawyer himself, he does not have much use for their practices and the thought of them diverting potential fees makes him very angry. "And those bastards do, too," he would add. "They may not know a writ from rye bread, but anything they say, their clients will believe. They screw up a case, they tell their clients it couldn't be won and that's all there is to it." Then Sid would shake his finger at me. "Still, it's not easy to be one of those guys. They don't get to become local institutions just by hanging out their shingles. They've gone out and worked the K of C, or they get referrals by doing favors for the priests and gaining their confidence, or they just stay around so damn long that all those poor ignoramuses who don't know the first thing about law figure they must be doing something right."

To Sid, the only other way to be a successful lawyer in Portshead is to be what he calls a specialist. "Not because you specialize in any particular area of law," he would explain, "but because people think you're somebody special. The specialist is the guy people go to when they're really in deep shit. This guy usually people don't know so well and maybe they don't even like him, but they're willing to pay him more than the guy in the neighborhood because they need him, or at least they think they do. They figure he's got a leg up on everybody else. When people say get a 'good' lawyer, this is the guy they mean—the guy who's a state rep or whose former partner is now a judge.

"You," Sid used to tell me from the other end of a stubby, pointing finger, "have a unique opportunity to combine those two types of practices. You're the only guy I know who can take the business away from those clowns out in the neighborhoods and charge specialist rates while you're doing it. For one thing, the people around here know you. Everybody who ever went to John Hancock High School feels as though he has a stake in you. And they all remember you as being somebody special. The rest is easy, Chuckie, because everybody wants to believe their lawyer is somebody special, and once they do, they're nearly always willing to pay a little extra for that feeling of confidence that the job is being done right. All Chuckie Bishop has to do to make it big in this town is to get out there and show people that he wants their business. Show them that you're still here and you're still just as special as when you were running up and down the football field."

So every now and then I would find myself at events like Jimbo's fundraiser, and whenever I went to such things I would wear my Bally shoes, brown ones with a gold buckle across the top. One hundred and twenty bucks and they pinched my feet, but they made the statement I wanted. They were, for all I know, the reason Donnie DiVito was clinging to my ear as I sat down for Jimbo's dinner.

Donnie wanted me to draw up a warehouse lease agreement for him and he wasn't going to leave me alone until he had tried out every possible idea for restricting the lessee without giving anything up himself. Donnie scrunched down onto the chair next to me and busily scribbled provisions all over a paper napkin while I engaged in a fruitless search for the shrimp that were supposed to be in my salad. By the time my chicken came he was pestering me into giving him advice on potential rights of conversion. He was, we both knew, stealing my time and I would have much preferred to join in the discussion that was going on among the rest of the table. I wanted to hear what everyone was saying about

Big Jim's future and why it was that a man who was consistently returned to his city council seat with seventy or eighty percent of the vote would hold a function like this nearly a year before the next election. I wanted to hear their comments about the abandonment of downtown Portshead now that the shopping center was completed at Coventry, and why they thought Chief Lyons had requested the city to issue submachine guns to his officers. But Donnie wouldn't back off and I missed out on everything except his chatter until Vinnie Salvucci stood up at the head table and banged his glass for silence.

Vinnie made a few opening remarks about how nice it was to see so many new faces at the Sons of Italy (laughter) and how any of those new faces interested in inquiring about membership could see him after dinner (more laughter). Then he launched into his introduction about what a great man Jim Ryder was and how he had been born right here in the Hook and had gone to John Hancock High, where he had been a star member of the basketball team.

He told us how Jim had joined the Marine Corps (cheers from all over the hall, and even Vinnie stopped to acknowledge that one with a wave and a smile), and how he had come home and married the lovely Loretta DelVecchio (more cheers from the Italian side). "Ah, you broke a lot of hearts with that one, Jimbo," Vinnie said. Everybody laughed again and Loretta, who was sitting next to Jim with her thick black hair piled high in an upsweep, blushed as her husband leaned over and kissed her on the cheek.

Vinnie beamed at them like some overfed clergyman who has just performed a marriage ceremony. Then he turned back to the audience and told us how Jimbo had taken a job at Garber's lumberyard and soon was promoted to outside sales representative. He said that for two years in a row Jim had boasted more sales than any other Garber's rep in the entire country, which brought another round of applause, but surprised me because I hadn't known that Garber's did business outside the state.

"Meanwhile," Vinnie went on, "Jimbo was active in a host of community affairs, from the Little League Umpires Association to St. Cecilia's Men's Auxiliary." Vinnie's childlike voice picked up a decidedly more formal tone as he told us how, finally, at the urging of practically everybody who knew him, Jim Ryder had thrown his hat in the ring for city councillor, Ward 5.

Suddenly Vinnie paused, and a mischievous, almost silly smile played on his fat lips. "So tell 'em," Jimbo hollered.

"So I will," Vinnie hollered back, thrusting both palms in the air while the whole hall rocked with laughter.

"The election may have gotten a little confused, but there was no doubt about one thing: Jimbo Ryder was the top living vote-getter in his first try for public office." That set everyone buzzing because there were many people who had not remembered that Jimbo had lost his first election to a man who had been dead for five days. But everyone at the head table was laughing. They knew that twelve years later the loss to a dead man was a good joke.

Vinnie resumed his serious voice. "But the people of this city weren't fooled for long. They knew that a certain past administration, which shall remain nameless, had played on their sympathies so that it could appoint its own man to the Ward 5 seat, and I'm pleased to say that in the very next election Jimbo knocked that appointee right on his you-know-what and the administration fell right along with him. Jimbo Ryder's been there ever since and I think we'll all agree that no finer job could have been done by any man—or lady, either, for all you women's libbers out there." ("Yay," shouted one lost soul, and all the others craned their necks to see who it was.) "Many's the one of you who's had the need to call Jim at all hours of the day and night, and Jim's never failed to be there to do what he could. He's helped keep our taxes down and our heads high. I'm proud to welcome him to the Sons of Italy Hall and I'm sure you'll all join me in giving a real warm round of applause to your friend and mine, City Councillor Jim Ryder."

Then, naturally, we all got to our feet, slapping our hands as loudly as we could, and a few of the Irish boys let out some shouts so that it was actually very exciting as Jim stood in six feet four inches of glory at the portable podium that someone had plunked down over his plate of melting spumoni ice cream. He grinned heartily, a man practiced in grinning, and held his hands up as if he wanted us to calm down. But we knew he didn't really want that and so we kept it going for a while and he kept standing there until the last clap had died.

Jim thanked us all for coming and then he said he had a very special guest who had taken time out of his busy schedule to drop by. He turned to his right and pointed to the end of the head table, where a smooth-skinned, cherubic-looking man now occupied what had remained an empty seat all through dinner.

"My great and good friend," Jim boomed, "State Senator Harlan Carson."

Again we all cheered and Harlan half rose out of his seat to wave and look as though he was really quite embarrassed to be stealing the limelight from Jim on his night of honor. Across the table from me, a minor official in Mayor McLaughlin's administration muttered, "That little asshole," but he had his cigarette flopping between his lips when he said it and, besides, he was standing up clapping like the rest of us.

Harlan made it seem as though he was going to sit down again, but Jim was swinging his arm at him as if he was winching in a sail and so Harlan finally, reluctantly, moved up to the portable podium. Jim stepped back so Harlan could have room to speak, but he stayed right behind him with his big grin spread all over his handsome Irish face.

• 5 •

Harlan told us how he had known and worked closely with Jim for the past eleven years. He told us what a good family man Jim was and how he was absolutely dedicated to the best interests of the people of Portshead. To show us exactly what he meant, he told us a little story about finding Jim in City Hall one day with a real worried look on his face. The story got garbled at that point and I may have missed a few essential aspects of it because the waitresses were moving around as he spoke, clearing plates and pouring coffee, but the gist of Harlan's story was that the worried look Jim wore was for the people of Portshead. He concluded by informing us that throughout the state the very name Jim Ryder was synonymous with the meaning of the word "integrity." At that we went back to our feet, clapping, and Harlan waved to us and blew kisses. "God love ya," he shouted as he sidled along behind the head table. We clapped him right out the door and then we sat down again for Jim, who had resumed his place at the podium and was patiently shuffling through his notecards.

This time when Jim started to speak he got drowned out by the noises in the kitchen at the back of the hall, where the kids who had been hired to wash the dishes were throwing pots and pans at each other. Jim stopped talking and smiled indulgently and this triggered a whole lot of people into turning around in their seats and shouting toward the kitchen, "Hey, shut up back there." Vinnie Salvucci gestured wildly at someone at the rear of the Italian section and at last Jimmy Pastore got up and went back. "Hey, keep it down in here, you guys. We can't hear ourselves think."

There were only a couple more bangs after that, the kind that could have been caused by a mistake, but were really done just to show that no one in the kitchen was intimidated.

The incident was parlayed wisely by the guest of honor. He thanked Jimmy Pastore by name and then thanked Vinnie Salvucci by name. He looked to the right, not up front where his buddies were sitting, but toward the back, and he began addressing people individually: Neil Gillis, Tommy Ferguson, Sonny Keagen, Al Kane. He swung over through the middle and called out several names, including my own—but not Donnie DeVito's and not the administration official's. He went to the left and recognized Joe Palermo and Paul Vitelli and Artie Giacomo, and he finished off by acknowledging everyone at the head table.

He let the hall go silent for a moment and then he said, "My God, it's good to see all you guys. I look out at you and my mind just bursts with memories. All the way back to the days in front of Alvie's corner store when I'd be out there with Nickie and Jack and Butchie Watson, God rest his soul, who was killed in that terrible car crash on 128 a few winters ago. We'd be out there watching all the fancy cars go by on their way to the beach, dreaming of the days when we'd have cars like that ourselves. What an impossible dream that seemed then. And

I remember taking those long walks up to Fletcher Junior High with Pat Corrigan and Gino DeStefano and John McCarthy, who's now Father McCarthy. . . ."

Jimbo Ryder took us all the way through his life, marking every step with names of people sitting right there in the hall. It was an impressive display of memory and dexterity, and by the time he brought us up to the present he had the entire audience arranged like galley slaves in the crevices of his hand. Those whom he had mentioned knew he was talking directly to them; their eyes would drop to their coffee cups when their names were spoken and they would let them hang there for a minute, maybe more, humbly proud as though they had been singled out for valor in combat. One could sense their bodies filling with camaraderie, with purpose, with meaning, even though they may have been cited for nothing more than hanging around a street corner or hiking up to the junior high with Big Jim Ryder. The important thing was that they had all come through this together. They had shared something, they had survived, they had made it this far—and they were one with Jim Ryder. His success was their success. Those whose names he did not mention, perhaps not expecting to be included, and yet listening closely to see if they would be, looked around enviously at those who sat with their eyes downcast, remembering the years gone by and the history shared.

As Jim talked on, several people got up from around the room and began distributing tiny white pledge cards. They passed up and down the aisles, slipping a card in front of everyone. Some fingered the cards, some tapped them on the table, some just let them lie. The administration official put his in his pocket.

Jimbo told us about the pain of the times we were living in, about the uncertainties that faced us on the national and international fronts and about the need for building a strong foundation of government from the local level on up. He told us that now was the time for more of us to become involved, to make a commitment, to say yes, by God, I can do something about this world I'm living in. I can and I will.

Start on your very own street, he said. Do something about those abandoned buildings at Lincoln and Beach. Take an interest in our waterfront that's being polluted by some out-of-state oil company. Speak out on property taxes and school appropriations that are being arbitrarily set by rich folks on Beacon Hill who neither know nor care about the needs of Portshead. Make sure that our workers are given a living wage by the corporate officers of the shipyard who sit in their penthouses in New York planning their vacations on the Riviera. Pass the message along to the ivory tower judges that we don't want our children bused out of the community just so somebody that we've worked all our lives to move away from can take their places. He, Jim Ryder, was going to speak out on all these things. He, Jim Ryder, was going to do something about them, and we could help because the only way to combat spiraling inflation, the high cost of living and unemployment, the only way to take back control of our own lives, was to elect competent, qualified people with roots in the community. If we were willing to make the kind of effort that was required, so, by God in heaven, was he.

The audience nearly tore the place down. People burst to their feet, stomping and cheering and clapping wildly. It was bedlam for several minutes and there were more than a few tears running down the worn faces of tough old working-men as they nodded to each other or struggled to keep Big Jim in sight among the bobbing heads. Even after the clapping broke we still had to shout to be heard as we made our way to the exits, where crowds were jamming their pledge cards through the slit tops of huge glass jars.

From everything that was said, it was clear this was thought to be the best political rally ever. The only problem was, no one yet seemed to know what Jim was running for. At the time it did not seem that important.

2 It was some six months after Jim Ryder's political fundraiser that I heard the news of Fitzy's death. It came over the radio while I was shaving—the sort of polarizing, psychologically scarring news that not only changes the color of the day but seems to shake the foundation of everything you have ever taken for granted. A childhood friend was dead. Shot and killed by a Portshead police officer while committing a burglary. I put my razor down and stared for a long time at the stranger who had suddenly appeared in my mirror.

On my way to the office I stopped off at Cubby's Corner to find out what the morning coffee crowd knew about it, but nobody there appeared to have very much information. It was mostly older guys at Cubby's that day, anyway, and they all naturally took the cop's side. "I heard this Fitzy was a drug addict," said one of them, but I did not bother staying around to find out where he had learned that.

Later in the morning I telephoned Billy Kincaid. He said he had just heard about it and had been hoping it was Fitzy's brother who had been shot. We passed a few rumors back and forth and told each other how weird the whole thing made us feel.

"To think it happened at Lanny Brandon's house, too," Billy said. "That's what's really strange."

It was, however, not the only strange thing about Fitzy's death. I went out and bought the first edition of the *Sentinel* when it hit the streets around 2 P.M. A one-column article started on the bottom half of the first page, under the headline "Local Man Slain in Burglary Attempt." The story ran for a few paragraphs and then continued in the middle of the paper somewhere. It described Fitzy as a thirty-three-year-old unemployed Vietnam veteran and said that the cop who shot him was a Portshead man who had been on the force less than eighteen months. Despite the fact that Fitzy had been caught coming out of the Brandons' Hamilton Street house at two o'clock in the morning, and despite the fact that the Brandons were not at home at the time, nothing of value had been found on his person and nothing was known to be missing. The closest thing to a weapon that was found was a small plastic flashlight.

I left the office early that day and went down to the Plough and Stars, where I knew some of the guys would be gathering. Ferrara was there. He had just backhauled an empty flatbed all the way from Buffalo or someplace and he was evidently beaned up. His white T-shirt was soaked yellow under the arms and his pupils were the size of quarters. Boyle and Ziggy Pastore were on either side of him, excitedly filling him in on all the details while he whacked the bar with his open hand and said things like "Damn!" and "No shit?"

Donovan, who was tending bar, looked up from where he was pouring a few for the cranky old Chesterfield smokers at the other end and smiled. He obviously had been through the discussion before and he interrupted Boyle to point me out. "There's your fucking lawyer," he said. "Why don't you see what he has to say?"

My say consisted of ordering a gin and tonic, but Boyle and the other guys kept pushing me as though by mere membership in the legal profession I had some great insight into the criminal intentions of a man with whom I had barely spoken in sixteen years.

"All I know," I said, trading Donovan a buck for my drink, "is that it doesn't make sense, him coming out of Lanny's empty-handed."

"Oh, he had something, all right," Donovan said knowingly. "That fucking cop who shot him ripped him off before he hit the ground."

"Lanny Brandon," Ferrara mused, with all the reflection a man whose system is traveling a thousand miles an hour can muster. "I can't believe that fucker's even back in town."

"He's got a lot of balls," Boyle said, nodding.

"I seen him a couple of times," Pastore said. "I didn't make no effort to talk with him, though." Pastore thought for a moment and then went on. "Where do you suppose the shit fell out of his sandwich, anyway? The guy practically gets run out of town and then all of a sudden he comes back after a couple a years and he's a fuckin' millionaire, for Chrissake. I'll tell you one thing: if I'd a been inside that house of his with nobody around, I wouldn't a been coming out empty-handed."

"What do you suppose that guy's into, anyhow?" said Ferrara.

"It's gotta be dope," Boyle said.

I said I thought he was a magazine writer.

"Ah," Boyle sneered, dismissing my comment with a wave of his hand. "You don't become a fuckin' millionaire writing magazine stories."

"So who said he's a millionaire?"

"Anybody's got a mansion on Hamilton Street's got to be a fucking millionaire, or close to it."

"I wouldn't exactly call it a mansion," I remarked.

"Whatever," Donovan said, laughing and looking around, "I'll take it."

"You don't like it?" Boyle asked me. "That's not good enough for you, Chuckie?"

"It's good enough. I just wouldn't call it a mansion, that's all."

"You admit it cost a few bucks, though," Boyle persisted.

I admitted that much.

"And his car," Pastore added. "Most guys, they go out, make a few bucks, they get themselves a nice Corvette or something. Maybe if they're a little older they go out and get a Cadillac or a Continental. But this asshole, for Chrissake, he's driving a fucking Mercedes-Benz."

"Those cars cost a shitload," said Ferrara, who figured to know about that sort of thing because he was on the road all the time.

"So who's ever had one around here?" Pastore demanded. "Maybe some rich bastard doctor or something . . ."

"They all drive Thunderbirds," Donovan called over his shoulder as he went down to take another order from the Chesterfield smokers.

"Fucking Mercedes-Benz," Pastore brooded.

"Must have lived in England," Boyle said cryptically.

All the rest of us slowly turned our heads to stare at him. "Mercedes are made in Germany, Boyle," Ferrara told him.

"I know," Boyle said defensively. "But that's the kind of car they drive in England." It was an interesting observation on Boyle's part. Except for the eleven months he had spent in Vietnam, Boyle had never been off the Eastern Seaboard in his life.

"England," snorted Ferrara. "You see the tan that guy's got? They don't get tans in England. There's no sun there. That guy's got a better tan than Ziggy here"—he pointed his thumb at Pastore—"and Ziggy's a wop."

"That's right," Pastore agreed. "And I ain't seen him down no Nantasket Beach trying to dodge the floating hot dogs and keep the fucking caramel corn out of his hair, neither. I ain't seen him trying to fight his way through the fucking folding chairs all those old ladies set up on the edge of the water, or trying to find a place where he can spread out his blanket and not get pissed on by a thousand little kids with yellow plastic pails."

"His tan don't come from working outside, neither, like Joey Aiello's," Ferrara said, nodding.

"You seen Joey's back lately?" Pastore asked. "He looks like a fucking nigger."

"Yeah," Ferrara said. "Well, Lanny Brandon's got a tan like that all over. His chest, his legs, his head. He's probably even got a tan on his dick. You know where you get tans like that? Florida, that's where. You know what they do for money in Florida? Dope, that's what. Weed, cocaine—anything comes up from South America goes right through Florida. Dope millionaires down there are a dime a dozen. They practically control the place. Ask Chuckie. It's like that guy from the Hook a few years ago—what was his name? Jerry something or other; used to play on my CYO team. He went down there with nothing. Nothing. Now I hear he's got an airplane, half a dozen cars, fuckin' yacht. . . ."

Donovan came back and we ordered another round. Ferrara slapped some money on the table and said he was buying. "Five hundred bucks I gross driving over a thousand miles. That faggot probably nets that much in ten minutes."

Pastore understood exactly whom he was talking about. "All I know," he repeated, "is that if I had went into that house like Fitzy did, I wouldn't a come out with nothing."

Somebody behind us at one of the tables yelled to Donovan, wanting to know what time the baseball game was coming on the tube. Donovan said they were playing in Kansas City and it wasn't starting until five-thirty "our time." The conversation drifted into the nightly discussion of what was wrong with the Red Sox. The *Herald Traveler* had been running a series in which they asked the man in the street what he would do if he managed the team. The series simply reflected a game everyone always played anyway.

"First thing I'd do if I was Zimmer," Boyle said, speaking about the real Red Sox manager, "is slit my fucking throat."

"Somebody should have done that to him the moment he traded Spaceman Lee."

"That wasn't his fault."

"Bullshit. He never once pitched Spaceman after Lee called him a gerbil."

"He pitched him a couple of times."

"What the fuck? Ten-game winner by the All Star break, best lifetime record against the Yankees on the staff, practically his only left-hander, and he still hardly ever used him. Team went right down the fucking drain."

"So Lee screwed up, too, didn't he? Remember the time he quit the team in the middle of the pennant race?"

"He quit because they traded away Bernie Carbo for nothing. I don't blame him. He said every time he got a friend, they traded him away. That was another thing they should never have done. Bernie Carbo was the glue that held that team together."

"I'll tell you what's wrong," announced Ferrara, who had been staring off into space. "They don't have enough niggers to win. How you gonna win a pennant with only one nigger on the team?"

"They got Perez."

"A Cuban nigger. They had to get him so that Rice would have somebody to talk to, keep him happy. Everybody knew that and nobody would trade them a real nigger, so they had to go buy Perez."

"I like Perez."

"I like him, too. I'm just saying the Red Sox think they're real liberal, you know, they got two black guys on their team. Not another team in baseball has so few black guys, right?"

"Not another team in any sport."

"Except hockey."

"They got French guys there instead," said Boyle.

"Right," Ferrara said. He treated Boyle's comment as though it made sense, mostly because he was anxious to get back to his own point. "So every year they get two black guys and they say, 'Whoops, that's our limit.' They trade Reggie Smith, Fergie Jenkins, Cecil Cooper, Ben Oglivie—all these guys, they're great ballplayers. The Sox don't want them 'cause they're black. But they got this trade-off thing. One black guy goes out, another one comes in. Cooper goes out, Boomer comes back. The Boomer's a fat bum, so they get rid of him. Quick now, they got to get another black guy, so they sign Bob Watson. He leaves the team, goes to the fucking Yankees at the end of the season, and they're in a panic. I'm telling you, that's why they signed Perez."

"So what are you saying, Tom? First you tell us they don't got enough black guys, now you say—"

"What I'm saying is, they got a fucking formula and they should just throw it out and go sign anybody they can."

"I don't want a bunch of spics on the team," said Boyle.

"Fuck the spics," Ferrara shouted. "I'm talking about niggers. Niggers!"

Somebody was tugging at my sleeve. I turned around and it was Davida, my secretary. She had her pocketbook over her shoulder and a newspaper under her arm and was obviously on her way home.

"Mr. Silverman is looking for you," she said, eyeing my drink. "He seemed real anxious to find you, so I said you went out to buy a paper and you'd be right back. Here." She thrust the newspaper she was carrying into my lap.

"I already have one at the office," I said, trying to give it back.

"Well, it's going to look pretty suspicious if I said you went out to get a paper and you come back without one. Especially with all that liquor on your breath. Here." This time she fumbled in her pocketbook until she came up with a piece of hard peppermint candy.

"Don't tell me I don't like niggers," Boyle was howling. "That time down Nantasket I risked my life to save that nigger who went out after his beachball and couldn't even swim—"

"All you did was get in the lifeguard's way."

"—so don't tell me I'm prejudiced."

"Nearly had to have somebody go out and save you, too, you dumb shit."

I sighed and got up. I left Davida a couple of bucks so she could have what she wanted and bid good night to the guys.

3 Another man was sitting in Sid's office when I poked my head in the door. He was dressed in the open-neck light-blue shirt and dark pants that marked the summer uniform of a Portshead police officer. From the moment I saw him I had the sinking feeling that I knew exactly what his case was going to involve.

He was a white-haired, ruddy-faced man and his forearms still showed the freckles that must have covered him when he was a kid. He smiled at me from his chair as he leaned forward, his elbows resting on his knees, his flat-top hat absently spinning between his two forefingers. Even in that position, with his thighs perfectly parallel to the floor, it was obvious that his service revolver was unnecessarily low on his hip, in the style that was so popular with Portshead cops.

"Chuckie," Sid said from deep in his leather chair, "this is Officer Monahan."

"Yes," I said, stepping forward and shaking the cop's hand. "I had you on cross in a drunk driving case not too long ago, didn't I?"

"That's right." Monahan rose to his feet, pleased that I remembered him. "And you did quite a job on me, too, I was just saying to Sid here." Monahan remained standing with his back slightly curved because he wanted to return to his seat and he wanted to finish telling Sid his story at the same time. "Chuckie says to me, 'Officer Monahan, did Mr. Foran become abusive when you pulled him over?'

"I say, 'No, sir,' and he says, 'You've had drivers become abusive to you in the past when they've been drinking, haven't you?'

" 'Sure,' I say, not knowing what he's getting at.

"Then he asks me, 'Did Mr. Foran threaten you or put up any sort of struggle?'

" 'No, sir.'

"You've been threatened in the past by drivers when they've been drinking, haven't you?'

"Now I understand, but there's nothing I can do about it, see? So I say yes and he goes on, 'Did Mr. Foran get sick at any time after you stopped him? . . . You've had drivers get sick all over you when they've been drinking, haven't you?' "

Monahan laughed. "I'll tell you, by the time this boy got done with me he had poor old Mr. Foran looking like a God-blessed saint just for the things he hadn't done."

Sid smiled politely and motioned me into a seat on his leather couch. "Did you win that one, Chuckie?"

"Reduced to a reckless," I said.

"Which was a bloody miracle," Monahan said, "considering the guy had a point two-six blood alcohol content and rightfully should have been hanging from a clothesline somewhere instead of driving a car."

Sid chuckled appreciatively. I knew that chuckle well. It meant that he was only waiting for the client to shut up so he could start talking business.

"Monnie's a good man to have impressed," Sid said. "He's the new president of the Portshead Patrolmen's Association."

"Congratulations," I said, and Monahan dipped his head modestly and replied, "Commiserations are probably more like it."

"Monnie's come to me with a little matter which I'd like to turn over to you, Chuckie. Monnie's agreed, of course, so now it's only a question of whether you can fit it into your schedule."

"What's it involve?" I said, and I sounded wary even to myself.

Monahan looked at Sid, who indicated that he could answer if he wished. Monahan said, "A patrolman named Richie DelVecchio shot a burglar last night. Maybe you read about it in the papers today. Richie hasn't been around too long and he's going to need some legal advice. I talked to him already and he seems to be pretty upset, not only because he pulled the trigger but because he don't understand all the other stuff that's going on."

"Which is what?"

"Well, the chief's suspended him with pay and now he's going to hold a departmental investigation."

"That's standard procedure anytime a cop shoots somebody, isn't it?"

"Sure. Them investigations are just whitewashes, but I think the kid would feel a whole lot better if you told him that. Advise him of his rights and all."

I nodded silently.

"Well, Chuckie?" Sid asked, his fingertips pressed together, his eyebrows raised. It was after five o'clock and Sid had put in his six hours. He was ready to go home and was just waiting for me to give the word so he could shuffle us down the hall to my office.

"I'm not sure I can do it," I said. "I may have a conflict."

Monahan smiled tentatively. He wasn't sure if I was kidding. He looked to Sid for help, but Sid barely reacted. Only the lines furrowing deeper on his brow revealed how displeased he was with my answer.

"Ah," he said after a moment, "I think I know which matter you mean.

Monnie"—he closed his fingers and pointed his now clasped hands toward the door—"can you wait outside for a minute while I discuss this with Chuckie, see if we can't somehow resolve it?"

"Sure, sure," Monahan said, getting up uncertainly.

Sid waited until he had closed the door behind him before letting loose. "You know," he said, "I have just about had it with you. This is the last time, I mean the very last time, I ever throw you one of these plums and watch you spit it back in my face. Wait a minute, Chuck. Don't you dare say another word until I'm finished."

I had been about to explain my relationship with the Fitzpatrick family, but I did as I was told. Sid, his round body so small he looked like a man sitting in the mouth of a cave, tilted back in his chair and dragged his hand over his face.

"You're a good kid, Chuckie. There isn't a guy in this city who knows you who won't say that. Whether you want to be known as a good kid at your age is something else altogether. I, personally, am tired of waiting for you to grow up." Suddenly he thrust himself forward and jabbed at the air with his finger. "You could have the world by the short hairs if you'd only try, Chuckie. Look at what Monahan just said about you. He's raving about what a great trial attorney you are. Never mind that he's talking about a technique I taught you and that's as old as the hills. The point is you had the guts and the brains and the skill to pull it off. You got talent coming out of your ears, Chuckie. You got a big name in this town and the streets are paved with potential clients for you, but you're like the man who refused to take yes for an answer. You'd rather spend your time chasing girls and drinking with your friends down the street than building up your practice. Oh, don't look so surprised—you think I don't know where you were just now? But what am I supposed to do—lead you around by the hand? I'm through with that, Chuckie. If you think I'm going to be around here forever to feed you, you're just plain wrong. You're too damn old to have anybody taking care of you, anyway."

I tried to hold Sid's gaze. It was a hard thing to do without steeling my eyes and making him think I resented what he was saying.

Sid sighed. For a moment he spoke softly. "I gave you the opportunity of a lifetime, Chuckie. I wasn't like Bernie Heifitz; I didn't give a damn that your football career had fallen apart. I also didn't need a law clerk when I hired you, especially one who was still in college and had a family to support. But Bernie said you were a good kid who'd had some tough breaks, so I took you on because Bernie asked me to and because I owed him some favors. I kept you working when your marriage was breaking up and you weren't worth two shits in a hat. I got you into Suffolk Law School when your grades weren't good enough to get you into the roller derby. I hired you when you got out and gave you the opportunity to learn from an experienced lawyer and be part of an ongoing practice. But you never seemed to really appreciate it, Chuckie. Oh, you did the work you were given and you did a good job in that respect, but that was all you did, Chuckie, and that's not all there is to being an attorney in a small office like this. As I've told you time and time again, fifty percent of everything I do is business— collecting bills, attracting clients, making office decisions. You never went out of your way to do any of that, Chuckie. Going to court is the fun stuff, but somebody's got to do the rest of the crap if you want to put food on the table."

"I joined the Kiwanis," I said softly.

"And I practically had to take you down there myself to get you to do that. No, Chuckie, you're just not hungry enough. That's why I thought it would be such a good idea to set you up in your own office, but now I see that's not working out, either. The way things are going down there, the end of the hall, I might as well have you back working for me. This thing that came in today, I figured this was it—I mean, I was going to hand over something good, something that was going to get you established on your own once and for all."

He flung his little arm out toward the door, exposing half his neatly starched, monogrammed white shirtsleeve. "This guy Monahan can do one helluva lot for you. He's just been elected president of a two-hundred-and-something-man association that's practically like a labor union. The guy's going to be in constant need of legal counsel and he wants to bring his first case to you. He comes to me, I suggest you and his eyes light up. They lit up, Chuckie. And don't forget, his prestige is riding on this, too. If he wanted to, he could have just kept on using the counsel the Association's been using, but he wants to make his own mark, get his own people in there." Sid brought his arm back, grimaced at the spot where his coat had caught on his cuff link, and shook his head.

"This is business, this is money, Chuckie. I'm giving it to you out of the goodness of my heart, taking away something that could be going to my own family, and you say no. You say no, Chuckie? My God, what am I gonna do with you?"

I looked at my shoetops. "Fitzy, the guy who got shot, was a friend of mine, Sid. We grew up together." I struggled for the right word to describe our relationship. Then I stopped. There was no right word and I was sure that any way I tried to explain what had happened between me and the Fitzpatricks would only come out sounding sick. It was nothing, I realized, that I wanted Sid to know.

Sid was leaning on his desktop, his forehead propped in the palm of his hand. He grew tired of watching me gape at him and took his hand away without lifting his elbow. "Chuckie, this has nothing to do with the victim. This is a cop, shot a burglar. Cops who shoot burglars around here do not go to trial, they get awards.

But a show has to be made, both because the public expects it and because we can't have cops going around shooting just anybody. So they hold a routine investigation, performed by the department itself. The fox looks at the damage done to the chicken coop, if you will.

"Was the victim caught in the midst of a criminal act? Yes." Bam, Sid slapped his fist down. "Was the cop discharging his revolver in the performance of his duty? Yes." Sid's fist came down again. "Case closed and all you've had to do is hold this boy DelVecchio's hand for six, ten hours plus whatever you feel like bumping it. You want it or don't you?"

There was not much left for me to argue. I apologized to Sid that I had not understood what was involved and we called Officer Monahan back into the room.

4 The light had barely turned yellow when I entered the intersection. I could have stopped in time if I had wanted, but I had Carolyn, the court reporter, leaning across the bucket seats of my Firebird and I was trying to get her back to my apartment as quickly as I could. It was therefore doubly infuriating when the arcing blue light of a police car came on behind me.

I had to push Carolyn, who was loaded with some nine dollars' worth of vodka, into a sitting position in her own seat and get myself buttoned up before the officer came up to my window. I almost made it. He bent over, looked in, and then stepped back a foot or two until I got the window rolled down.

"Chuckie?" he said, and I recognized him as a guy named Logan who used to go down to the summer cottage that Buddy Williams and Donovan and a few other people had once rented in Falmouth.

"Hey," I said.

He peered in at Carolyn again. "Hi, Carolyn," he said.

She told him "Hi," and got real busy fumbling in her pocketbook for a cigarette.

Logan said, "Listen, Chuckie, can you come back to my car for a second?"

I got out with my wallet in my hand, all set to show him my license and registration, but Logan wasn't interested. "Shit, Chuckie," he said, "I only wanted to talk to you about something. I figured that was your car going by and if it wasn't, what the hell, I would have given you a ticket. I just wanted to say that I heard you're taking Richie DelVecchio's case and a lot of the guys are real glad it's you that's doing it. You need any help, you just let us know."

"Hey, that's great," I said rather absently. "Thanks a lot." I was looking back at Carolyn, hoping the delay wasn't going to be long enough to cause her to pass out.

"Yeah, and listen, Chuckie, there's one other thing I thought you might want to know."

"What's that, Logan?" I couldn't remember his first name.

"Well," he said, "I mean, maybe you don't want to know, but maybe you do. I been thinking about it and I decided I would if it was my daughter."

The way he was speaking made me not understand at first. Then I chilled. "Candy? Oh, my God, what happened to her?"

"Nothing really happened to her, Chuckie. It's just that I had the night patrol at Wampaugh Pond last night. . . ."

"Oh, Jesus," I said. Wampaugh Pond was a shallow body of water nestled in the hills on the border between Newcastle and Portshead. It was a favorite spot for teenage neckers because it had numerous turnouts from the battered dirt road that surrounded it. The cops in Portshead called it "the fucky-sucky beat" and competed for the opportunity to patrol it.

"It was after one o'clock in the morning. Me and my partner saw this big black Chrysler, an old one, tucked under some trees and nobody was sitting up in it like they're supposed to. So my partner put the lamp on it and this guy pops up in the front seat looking all around, you know, and sort of putting himself back together. A second later this young girl comes up on the other side of the same seat. So I go up and tap on the window and get the guy's license. It says he's twenty, you know? I looked at the girl, and she's real pretty, but I knew that she wasn't anywhere near that old so I asked her for her license and she doesn't have one because, as it turns out, she's only fifteen."

"And it was Candy."

"Well, see, she wouldn't give me any ID and so I said I was going to take her in for curfew violation unless I found out who she was and unless she could prove to me that she was really seventeen like she was claiming. She didn't tell the truth until then. I asked her if she was related to you and she said you were her father and so I let her go. Made them get out of there, though."

"Thanks, Logan. I appreciate it."

"You think I did the right thing, telling you?"

"Yeah, yeah, I do. What was the kid's name she was with?"

"Marino. Glen Marino. Between you and me, Chuckie, he didn't look so hot."

5 "Put your game face on, boy." It was a favorite expression of Coach Walsh's when I was back in high school. He had a rather antiquated way of talking when it came to football, calling helmets hats and that sort of thing. "When your hat goes on, your game face goes on with it," he would say, and later Giacomini or somebody would imitate him and the team would dissolve into gales of laughter. That type of reaction had tended to obscure the meaning of what Coach was saying at the time, but some sixteen years later it was the expression that came to mind as I prepared for my first meeting with Richie DelVecchio.

My new client did not cut a particularly imposing figure. He stood a couple of inches under six feet and weighed a maximum of a hundred and fifty pounds, some of which, I could see through his green polyester shirt, could easily have been eliminated from around his waist. His hair was jet black, short on the sides and curly long in the front. His face was narrow and without distinction in its angles. His eyelashes were impossibly thick, his chin was soft and his mouth had a tendency to hang open when he relaxed. By all my powers of observation, Richie DelVecchio was a punk who would have seemed more at home behind the wire-mesh screen of a patrol car than behind the steering wheel.

"Harry Monahan says I should talk to you," Richie said as Davida escorted him into my office with a flourishing gesture that left the fat on her arm bouncing.

"That's what he told me, too," I said, holding out my hand. He offered his the way a man who is not used to shaking hands does it. He thrust it forward rapidly at the last second and his grip was wet and rather limp.

"My brother-in-law wanted me to get somebody else, but Monnie said I should speak to you first."

"Who's your brother-in-law?" I said, weighing the slight he had just dealt me.

"Jim Ryder? Councilman Ryder? He's married to my sister Loretta. He wanted me to talk to Arthur Broderick."

"Artie's a good lawyer." Artie was, in fact, no such thing. He was a former councilman himself. His partner was the city solicitor and a man who practically slept with the mayor.

"Yeah," DelVecchio said regretfully, "but Monnie says to see you, and since the Association's paying the bill . . ."

"I don't work for anybody who doesn't want me. I think maybe you'd be better off seeing Artie, that's what you want."

Bewilderment crept across Richie DelVecchio's features and it occurred to me that his thought processes were actually slow enough to watch. "Hey, I didn't mean anything. It's my brother-in-law. I don't know one lawyer from another. I don't even know what's going on, for God's sake."

"What's going on is you shot and killed an unarmed man."

"Yeah, but it was in the line of duty."

"Then you got nothing to worry about. In that case, what's going on is just standard procedure. It keeps the newspapers quiet, calms the victim's family down, that sort of thing. Your own department's going to conduct an investigation and at the end of it they'll probably give you a medal for bravery or something. Promote you to sergeant, maybe."

"Yeah, well, nobody said nothing like that to me. Nobody said nothing except Lieutenant Finucci, and all he said was that the chief had suspended me until they got done with their investigation. And Monnie. He told me to come see you." He wiped the corners of his mouth as he spoke.

"All right," I said, getting out one of the interview forms I had ordered from some legal service that was always stuffing my mail with fliers. "This visit's for free as a favor to Monnie. After this it's fifty bucks an hour for anything I do outside of court, seventy-five in court. Got that?"

"Yeah, well, I can't pay nothing anyhow, so as long as it's all right with Monnie, it's all right with me."

I grunted and penned in Richie's name, address and phone number on the interview form. Davida would use the information as a basis for setting up a file.

"How old are you, Richie?"

"Twenty-nine."

I was surprised. He seemed younger. "You from Portshead?"

"Sure. I was a couple of years behind you in high school."

I tried to place his face and could not. He understood. "You remember a broad named Linda Kilmurry?"

Images of a colorless little girl from my neighborhood floated through my mind. "Vaguely," I said.

"Yeah, well, she remembers you. She's my wife."

"She must have known Fitzy, then."

DelVecchio winced. It was not just a slight wince. It was a wince like a car had been dropped on his foot. "Look, Chuckie, I knew Fitzy, too. I just didn't know it was him crawling out that window, that was all. Honest to God, if I'd known who it was, this whole thing never would have happened. But it was dark, see, and all I saw was some big bastard coming toward me."

"He was inside the house coming out, wasn't he?"

"Yeah. That's right."

"If he was already inside, what was he doing coming out a window? Why didn't he just come out the door?"

DelVecchio seemed momentarily stunned, but I could not tell if it was perplexity or annoyance. His mouth flew open and snapped shut again and his hands twisted in his lap. "I don't know," he said finally. "I mean, I didn't ask him or anything." He looked at his palms as if inspecting for damage he might have just done. "He was already dead when I saw who it was. The funny thing, you know, I'm not even a good shot."

I put away my form and got out a sheaf of yellow legal-size paper. "You want to start from the beginning, Richie? Tell me how you happened to be where you were and all that."

Richie DelVecchio straightened himself in his chair and cleared his throat. This much he knew he could talk about. "I been on the force almost a year and a half, but I only been driving the squad car for about five, six months. I got a sector, you know? I go way down Proctor Street to the three-deckers, then go all the way to the Ashton border. Everything in between I'm supposed to patrol. Graveyard shift.

"Sunday night there wasn't nothing particular happening until I came up Hamilton Street—"

"That's part of the district, huh?"

"Oh, yeah. I got some of the best neighborhoods there is."

"You were coming up Hamilton Street . . ."

"Yeah, and then I seen what looked like a light in Lanny Brandon's house."

"So?"

"So I knew he wasn't supposed to be home for the whole week and I pulled over to check it out."

"How did you know he wasn't home?"

A comedian could make a career out of mimicking the expressions that would settle on Richie DelVecchio's face when he was stumped for an answer. "His car was gone," he said.

"How many cars he got? You know what kind they are? He the only one in your whole sector with an empty driveway?" I leaned back in my chair and threw my pen down so that it skidded across the top of my desk and landed on the floor. "Don't bullshit me, Richie. You're just wasting both our times."

Richie bent over and picked up the pen. He returned it gingerly to the desk. "I don't know how much I should tell you," he said.

"You either tell me everything or you tell me nothing. You want me to represent you, to be any help to you at all, you tell me every goddamn thing you know. That's all protected. It's confidential. Falls under attorney-client privilege and it couldn't be pried out of me with a hatchet blade."

"Really?"

"Really."

DelVecchio twisted his hands some more. "Well, Lanny told me he was going away for the week and he sort of asked me to watch the place. Look for lights, prowlers, that sort of thing."

"And you were going to do this strictly as a favor, I suppose."

DelVecchio grinned sheepishly. "It was only fifty bucks. Besides, I wasn't doing anything except what I was supposed to be doing anyhow. I figured if I had to do anything extra, I'd do it on my own time, sort of. Not take a coffee break or something." His grin disappeared and his eyes opened in wide sincerity. "I really wouldn't want this to get out, though."

"It won't come out through me. But you can't just pretend things like that didn't happen. I've got to be prepared in case Lanny or somebody talks about it. Was this the first time?"

"With Lanny, yeah. I mean, I've picked up a few bucks here and there from some other guys. But shit, I'm not the only one, Chuckie. It's done all the time. You can't hardly get by these days on the salaries they're paying."

"So you'd taken a tip and you were doing what you'd promised, checking out Lanny's house, and you saw a light come on. Did you radio for help?"

"No, because I didn't know if it was anything. You see, the light didn't really come on. What I saw was something like a flashlight. A small beam that moved around a lot and went from room to room. It could have been nothing, but I thought I should look. I parked the patrol car in front of the house next door and approached along the neighbor's property. There are a bunch of trees there that I used for camouflage, sort of, until I got to this fence leading to the backyard. It had a gate and the gate was unlocked, so I went through. By this time I had my gun out because, you know, I didn't know what I was gonna find."

He paused and took a deep breath. "You got an ashtray?" he said. I fished around in the trash bucket until I found an old coffee container and placed it in front of him. He looked grateful and set fire to a Kool. The smoke settled him down.

"I was creeping along looking for anything that might seem out of place and I sort of swung wide so I could see as much of the house as I could. I was right in front of the swimming pool when all of a sudden I noticed the open window. After that it was like it all happened so fast I didn't have time to think. I noticed the window and my heart did this little skip, you know, and before I could even think what I was gonna do this body comes through the window and I just fired at it. I mean, it all just happened at once."

Richie looked at the cigarette that was burning between his fingers. An ash dropped onto the floor and Richie went down after it. He started talking as he went. "It's like when you go duck hunting and you're squatting there ready and all of a sudden the birds lift up and you just react. That's all I did, I just reacted. I was in position, I saw the window, I saw the guy coming through and I just fired."

"How many times?"

"Twice. I fired twice. One hit him. One hit the house."

"Did you issue a warning first, or did you just fire?"

"I shouted, 'Halt, police,' and then I fired."

"Did you shout before or after you fired?"

"Sort of at the same time."

"But you gave him the opportunity to stop before you fired, didn't you?"

Richie's dull eyes flickered. "Yeah." His mouth sagged open again.

"And it was your first shot that hit the house, wasn't it? That was your warning shot."

"Yeah, I guess."

"What do you mean, you guess? You wouldn't have fired a warning shot right at somebody, would you?"

"No."

"No, of course you wouldn't. You only fired the second shot because he kept coming at you after you identified yourself, ordered him to halt and even fired a warning shot. It was dark; you couldn't tell what was in his hand—was there anything in his hand?"

"I don't know. I think so. I couldn't see."

"It was dark, you thought he had a weapon in his hand, you knew he was a burglar and that he was coming at you. . . . Isn't that the way it happened?"

"Yeah. Yeah, that's right. That's the way it happened."

I stopped and wrote it all down. Richie got up from his seat and politely stubbed out his cigarette in the bottom of the coffee container. At this point Richie DelVecchio had given himself over to me.

"Okay," I said. "So what did you do after that?"

Richie looked puzzled. "What did I do? I went up to him. Where he was laying on the ground, I went up to him."

"Did you run up?"

"Run? No. Jesus, I was half expecting him to jump up and shoot me at any second. I crept up there, in a duck walk, like. I had both hands on my gun the whole time." He held his hands out at arms' length in front of him to show me what he meant.

"Then what?"

"Then what? I dunno. Then I seen he was dead, I guess."

"How did you know he was dead?"

"The bullet, it had gone right into his head, and the blood was bubbling up in the air like a fountain. He was laying there, he wasn't moving, and he was just dead—that was all."

"Did you try to stop the bleeding?"

The young cop hesitated before he shook his head. "Some of it got on my shoe."

"Did you check for any vital signs?"

"Vital signs?"

"Pulse. Heartbeat. Anything like that."

"What I did was . . ."

I waited while Richie braced himself, his arms on the arms of the chair, his hands spread wide. "I was scared. The guy on the ground was dead and I had just shot him. For a second I didn't know what to do. I started to run for the radio and then I ran back and turned him a bit so I could see who it was because I hadn't even looked at his face yet, and then I seen and I just sorta . . . spaced out, I guess."

"What's that mean?"

"You know," Richie implored, waving his hands helplessly, begging me not to make him say it, and then finally admitting, "I sort of lost control. I ran to the gate, went into the front yard. The neighbors had come out in bathrobes and I yelled at them to call the ambulance. The guy there, though, he said he was a doctor. Dr. Maddox from the hospital, and he lives in the house right next door. So I says, 'Quick, a man's been shot,' and then I took him back to where Fitzy was laying."

"And that was when you knew for sure Fitzy was dead."

He nodded.

I got to my feet and went to the open window. Down below me the traffic on Franklin Street was sputtering up fumes that seemed to hang endlessly in the humidity of the afternoon. The noises out there were of acceleration, idling motors, clunking doors, shouted words. They all seemed flat in the stale and muggy air.

"Everything that rises," I said to myself.

"Huh?" my client said, and I was wrestled back to the immediacy of my stuffy little office.

"Nothing," I said. "It's just part of a title to a book I once read. Listen, Richie, you go home and prepare yourself to enjoy a little paid vacation. Don't talk to anybody and don't answer any questions unless I'm there. Not the police investigators, not anybody. Understand? Just take the family to the beach and enjoy yourself. It'll all be over in a few days."

6 The talk at the Plough and Stars was of the Yankees. They were pulling away from the rest of the division and it was becoming increasingly apparent that the Red Sox really might not be able to catch them after all.

"That guy Steinbrenner knows how to run a ball club," Stevie Ferris was saying. "He just goes out and buys anybody he wants. Nettles gets hurt for a fucking few weeks? Fine. Steinbrenner don't give a shit. He just goes out and buys some other team's starting third baseman. A guy busts their balls a couple of times when he plays against them? No problem. They go right out and buy him. Put him on their bench. He won't bust their balls no more. That's the way to run a team."

Boyle was not impressed. "They suck," he said.

"Well, actually, I kind of like the Yankees," Ferrara said, and everyone else looked at him to see what he meant by that. He was stroking his chin and staring up at the top of the mirror behind Donovan. "I like the concept, you know? I mean, it's nice to have somebody out there so big and powerful for us little guys to hate. It's like having the oil companies or something to root against. The fucking Yankees are the whatchamacallit of bigness. What's the word I'm trying to think of, Chuckie?"

"Epitome," I said.

"Fucking lawyer," Donovan said. "I thought 'whatchamacallit' was what he meant."

"Epitome," repeated Ferrara. "Fucking Yankees are from the biggest city, they got the biggest names, biggest salaries. Even their stadium's big. They're like what America is to the rest of the world. It makes you feel good every time they lose, and if they win you figure, so what? They're supposed to win."

"The team you gotta love is Baltimore," Stevie Ferris said. "While the fucking Yankees are out buying up everybody in sight, here's little Baltimore—nobody wants to play for Baltimore and every year they're nipping at the Yankees' heels. I love it. But I'll tell you one thing: once the Yankees get to the World Series I'm all for them. You know why? Because I hate the fucking National League more, that's why."

"I hate the National League, too," said Boyle. "All them fucking spics and coons running around stealing bases, wearing hats the wrong size so they fly off whenever they go to catch a ball."

Donovan drew us a round of beers and then he asked me if I was going to Fitzy's wake. I told him I didn't think I should.

"How come?"

"I just got hired to represent this guy DelVecchio that shot him."

Stevie Ferris looked at me for a while until I had to look back at him. "How come you're doing that?" he said.

I was glad I did not have to answer. Ferrara did it for me. "Because it's his fucking job, that's why. Someone calls you up and says fix their toilet, do you say, 'Wait a minute, I don't like the shit you stuffed down it'?"

"Yeah," Stevie said, "but this is a little different. Fitzy was your friend, wasn't he, Chuckie?"

"Jesus," Boyle said. "I ain't even gonna recognize the guy, it's been so long since I seen him. I hate fucking wakes."

We all stared into our beers.

"He wasn't a bad guy," Donovan said.

"He used to be a real good guy," Boyle declared, lifting his head up. "Me and him and Chuckie and Billy Kincaid used to hang around together all the fucking time when we were growing up."

"Fucking Billy Kincaid," Ferrara said. "We never see that asshole anymore."

Ferrara, I knew, had tried to get a job as a salesman with Billy's company and bore a grudge because Bill had told him he wasn't qualified. But I was anxious to get off the subject of Fitzy and so I said, "What do you expect, Tom? Billy's got a wife and three kids. He's got a house in Coventry, a cottage down the Cape, and he works his ass off about seventy hours a week."

"Remember the time the four of us camped out in Fitzy's backyard, Chuckie?" Boyle asked. "Remember that time? And we were playing strip poker in the tent we set up on his mother's clothesline. We were about eleven, I think. Remember that?"

"Did you lose the game, Boyle?" Ferrara asked.

"He must of," Donovan said. "Remember that time he got his first paycheck down the yard and he gambled away the entire thing before he reached his front door?"

"Yeah, well, I only lost the first game this night I'm talking about. Chuckie lost the big game."

"I thought Chuckie never lost at anything," Ferrara said, and it made me feel a little bad that he thought that way.

"Yeah, well, it was one of those things where he fell in the shit pile and came up with a rose in his mouth. You see, what happened to me was I lost all my clothes and had to jump around naked in the backyard while all these other assholes shined the flashlight on me and made loud noises to try to get Fitzy's sister Mary Ellen to come out and look at me."

"Goddamn," Stevie Ferris said. "That's no punishment. She can look at me anytime she wants. You seen her lately?"

"She works up City Hall," Donovan said. "Works for the mayor or something. She turned out to be a real piece of ass."

"Yeah," Boyle said. "Well, this time I'm talking about she must of only been ten years old because she was a year behind us up at high school and, like I said, I think we were only about eleven."

"So did she come out and see you?"

"No, she didn't see me because I dived back in the tent. Besides, the house was dark and everything, and we figured she was asleep. It was one of those times when Fitzy's mother was out for the night." He got sidetracked. "You ever see Fitzy's mother? She was like the best-looking mother there ever was. She didn't look like the rest of our mothers. She was real young and kinda small and she was always taking us places. But she was always going out at night, too, you see, and when she did she'd leave her own mother to watch the kids, and that poor old lady didn't know what the fuck was going on. What was her name, Chuckie?"

"Mrs. Conway."

"Yeah. She used to live right there in the house with Fitzy and his brother and his sister and his mother, and she almost never left the place. She'd keep the television on all the time and she'd be stretched out in front of it whenever we saw her." Boyle demonstrated, tilting back on his barstool with his hands folded across his stomach, his chin pointing up and his mouth wide open.

"What's he doing?" Donovan asked, leaning over the bar to see, and I had to explain.

"Whenever she dozed her mouth would flop open. There was something raw and unpleasant about the way she looked."

"Raw and unpleasant?" Stevie Ferris repeated, and again I tried to explain.

"It was like looking at an open wound."

Stevie Ferris laughed. "Chuckie, you should give up this law business and become a writer, you're gonna talk like that. You can be the next Louis L'A-mour."

"Fuck Louis L'Amour," shouted Boyle. "Perry Mason."

"Perry Mason's a character, Boyle, not an author," Ferrara said with exaggerated patience.

"So who's Louis L'Amour?"

"You don't know who Louis L'Amour is? Hey, Boyle, don't you ever read anything?"

"I read the sports pages," he said. "But I get bored reading. I keep thinking about all the other things I could be doing, like telling you this story. You want to hear the rest of my story or don't you?"

"I don't even remember what it was about. Fitzy's grandmother or something."

"It was about how Chuckie got caught getting jerked off by Mary Ellen Fitzpatrick."

"Oh, Jesus, I want to hear that."

"I wasn't getting jerked off," I said.

"Let Boyle tell it and stop trying to spoil the story," Donovan said, throwing a wet bar cloth at me.

"See," Boyle said, his voice dropping to a conspiratorial whisper, "when all this happened there was nobody around but the four of us guys, Mary Ellen and her grandmother."

"Where was Fitzy's brother?"

"He wasn't around."

"What was his name?" Stevie Ferris wanted to know. He had not grown up in the Hook.

"His name was Fitzy, too," Boyle said.

"His name was Bobby," I said.

"Bobby was an asshole," Boyle added.

"That so, Chuckie?"

"I guess," I said. "He was a couple of years older than we were and he used to get his kicks out of bouncing us around. He never seemed to have any friends of his own and so he was always forcing his way into our games. We'd be playing basketball and he'd do stuff like try to smack us into the garage every time we went up for a layup or something. He was a lot of fun."

"He wasn't anything like his brother," Boyle said.

"Where was the father?" asked Stevie.

"He was going to college," Boyle told him, and I snickered.

"He was away at college for eight or ten years and then nobody asked about him anymore," I said. "All the time I was growing up with Fitzy, I never once saw his father."

Boyle said, "I saw him once. He had a beard."

It seemed to me that that was the image we had of anybody going to college in those days, but I let it pass. Donovan was anxious to hear what had happened with Mary Ellen and it was inevitable that Boyle was going to tell it.

"So," he went on, "Chuckie was the loser of the last game we played and we made him run around the house without no clothes on. It was a duplex the Fitzpatricks lived in, see, and so he had to go out to the front yard where the cars would be passing on King's Road, and then he had to run all the way around the neighbor's side of the house to get back to where we were. Only by the time he got there we'd pulled down the tent and taken off with all his clothes and everything. Me and Fitz and Billy were just hiding behind the garage, but Chuckie didn't know that, and he's standing there with this real scared look on his face and his hands over his balls and he's going, 'Kevin, Michael, Billy—come on, you guys, give me my clothes back.' He didn't have no shoes or nothing on his feet, you know, so he's stumbling around, and I guess that's why he didn't come around the back of the garage. Instead he starts going toward the front of the house again. For about three minutes we don't hear nothing, and then all of a sudden there's this tremendous crash and this scream and all kinds of yelling going on and then Chuckie comes flying around the corner like he's running against Ashton High or somebody, you know? He's got his knees pumping up to his chest and this real wild look in his eyes and I thought he was gonna run right through Fitzpatrick's back fence."

Boyle was laughing so hard he had to stop to wipe the tears from his eyes. "What happened was, see, he was creeping around the front of the house looking for his clothes, you know, and old Mary Ellen saw him and pulled him right up on the front porch with her."

"She just opened the door and waved for me to come in because I was standing out there like an idiot."

"So he goes inside and they're on this little tiny porch which is like a boot room or something, you know, where everybody keeps their bicycles and old newspapers and stuff. And Mary Ellen's got nothing on but this nightgown."

"Believe me, it wasn't any slinky negligee, Boyle. It had little ballerinas or something all over it."

Boyle laughed again and the other guys were hanging there waiting for him to continue, all set to laugh themselves, and Boyle said, "So Mary Ellen reaches out and grabs his dick and starts jerking him off—"

"That wasn't what happened at all, Boyle," I complained, but it was too late. Boyle was going strong and everyone was caught up in his version.

"—and while she's in the middle of doing it, the overhead light suddenly goes on, the door opens and poor old Mrs. Conway comes out and catches them in the act."

"She wasn't jerking me off, Boyle. She was just touching it."

Donovan looked up from where he had fallen on the floor. "I think it doesn't make any difference, Chuckie," he said, and then he went back to laughing with the rest of them.

7 If ever there was a house in Portshead that was ripe for a burglary, it was Lanny Brandon's. It stood on the corner of Hamilton and Pigeon Hill Drive, in the one stylish area of town. No matter how crowded the masses were in the rest of Portshead, Hamilton Street stayed aloof and serene.

Nearly three hundred years ago it had been the carriage path that led colonists to Boston. By the late 1700s it was the post road and was lined with orchards and farms and the homes of the well-to-do. The farms were gradually broken up and the orchards sold off, but the homes remained as they were, lending the street such an air of dignity and somber tradition that no builder dared put up any structure that was not equally sonorous. Long before any legal zoning went into effect, the owners of Hamilton Street homes had self-imposed a certain area limitation on their properties on the basis of the fact that anything small simply did not fit. Hamilton Street was Portshead's answer to its snobbish neighbors in Ashton. When I was growing up, mere affiliation with Hamilton Street added a certain prestige to one's life, so that, for example, Ziggy Pastore's uncle Jimmy was thought to be quite important simply because he was the groundskeeper at the Morningbird Estate, an imposing property run by the city and open to public tours.

Lanny Brandon's house was nothing so elaborate as the Morningbird Estate, but it was a whole lot better than anything any of the rest of us lived in. It had a semicircular drive that came off Hamilton Street and trisected Lanny's huge, flat front yard. The side sections were lined with tall pines that blocked the house off from Pigeon Hill Drive on the left and the property of Dr. Maddox on the right. The structure itself had only two stories, but it was long and tastefully appointed. Black shutters and trim set off its white brick and a recessed patio area stood before a set of double front doors. The patio held an array of wrought-iron furniture which was most likely never used, except, perhaps, by peddlers waiting in line to make their sales pitches.

In the back of the house was a large, kidney-shaped swimming pool that afforded almost total privacy because it was surrounded by a vine-covered picket fence at least ten feet high. The cement deck around the pool held lounge chairs and a round plexiglass table with a large umbrella poking through the middle of it. Beyond the pool was a cabana.

"Just like in California," Lanny said to me proudly when he took me out for a poolside drink, and although I had never been to California I had to agree.

It was a long way to come for a young man who had left the city under the cloud of a boyhood scandal, and nobody knew it better than Lanny. Until he was in junior high, Lanny had always seemed like a normal enough kid. He might have been a little smarter than everyone else, but he liked to do the same things we did. He liked to go swimming at the quarries and hitchhike to the beach and build forts and play baseball. Lanny was only different from the rest of us in one significant way: he was a strikingly handsome kid. It was a fact that did not begin to take on any importance in our eyes until we started going to church dances, and even then it was something we regarded with suspicion more than anything else.

As soon as we were old enough, all of us, Lanny included, joined the Boy Scouts. Some of the kids joined the troop that met at St. Cecilia's because their parents did not want them involved in activities at a Protestant church, but most of us joined the troop that met at St. Mark's Episcopal because everyone said it was the best in the city.

We all tied into scouting with a fervor, sailing through Tenderfoot status as quickly as we could. Boyle and Fitzy and Joey Aiello got bogged down in Second Class, but I made it through there and so did some of the others, like Giacomini and Billy Kincaid and Buddy Williams. But none of us went through the way Lanny did. His rapid progress brought him to the attention of the scoutmaster.

The scoutmaster was in his mid-thirties. He was tall, blond-haired, blue-eyed, and capable of amazing feats of strength. One time he dropped down in front of the whole troop and did a hundred push-ups for us, hitting his chest on every single one. He would bend over and challenge any of us to grab him by the neck and keep his head down, and then no matter who was hanging on him, even fat Giacomini, he would straighten up without using his hands. As the troop leader, he could be very strict or very kind. A shouted word from him was enough to cow an entire assemblage, but a gift or a promotion or even a comment of praise was enough to make a boy's week. We avidly and openly curried his favor at every opportunity. Our scoutmaster was a man among men, which, unfortunately, was just the way he liked it.

Looking back, I cannot recall what was supposed to have been so great about our particular troop. I can only remember endless formations, a camping trip where I pissed in my pants because I was being held prisoner in a game of capture the flag and could not get out of jail to go to the latrine, and a constant losing struggle to master the Morse code. Unable to learn it and unwilling to practice it, I finally decided I had too many other things to do and dropped out before I earned even a single merit badge.

But for Lanny Brandon it was a different story. As with everything he attempted, he wanted to be the best. He became the scoutmaster's pet and was given one appointed post after another. While we labored over knot-tying lessons and never learned anything but the hangman's noose, Lanny was going to all kinds of special meetings and getting to do all sorts of things which seemed very exciting at the time. Painfully aware that he had succeeded where we had not, we envied Lanny from afar. We envied Lanny right up until the night the scoutmaster was caught giving him a blow job while they sat in a darkened car by the side of a seldomly used road that ran through the woods in Coventry. A Coventry cop who drove that road on his way home had noticed the same car parked in the same place several Wednesdays in a row. He had sneaked up to the car on foot and when he got there he found Lanny sitting up and the scoutmaster with his head in Lanny's lap. They were still wearing their Boy Scout uniforms.

After that Lanny was ostracized from almost every sort of activity in Portshead. His appearance in the corridors at school was enough to make the walls practically reverberate with behind-the-hand cries of "queer" and "fair-eee" and "blow job." Donovan beat him up in front of twenty or thirty people, including a dozen or so girls. He was cut from the baseball team even though everyone knew he was better than the two guys they kept at his position. Nobody wanted him around, not even the coach. The very name Lanny Brandon became a synonym in Portshead for homosexuality and merely to imply that someone was in association with Lanny was to ascribe deviant behavior to that person. Eventually Lanny stopped coming to school and his father, who was an insurance salesman and no better off than anybody else's father, took out a second mortgage on his house and got Lanny into Coventry Academy. It was, we told each other, where he belonged. Only fags went to Coventry Academy.

Beyond the immediate reach of our taunts, Lanny began to do all right by himself. Without having to cope with all the peer-group diversions that were distracting the rest of Portshead, he graduated near the top of his class at Coventry and got some incredible financial aid package to attend Cornell. It was a safe place for him in that there was no danger of anybody else from Portshead ever showing up in Ithaca.

In college Lanny got involved in creative writing and later there was an item in the *Sentinel* saying he had had an article published in one of those New York magazines that everyone had heard of but no one ever read. From then on, whenever anybody would ask what had happened to that poor bastard Lanny Brandon someone would say that he'd heard Lanny had become a writer or something, but nobody ever bothered to find out what had really happened to him.

And then one day Lanny was back in town, and not just back, but buying a house on Hamilton Street. While many of the boys from his youth had grown flabby and balding in their idle pursuit of a good job with the fire department, Lanny Brandon had grown more handsome than ever. He was a tightly packed hundred and seventy pounds and he had a full head of neatly but obviously coiffeured hair. He did not have a tattoo like Boyle, or like Ziggy Pastore or Giacomini, but he did have a gold bracelet on his wrist and a gold chain around his neck. Everyone who knew who he was had a rumor to spread about Lanny and his new wealth, but no one had any firsthand knowledge.

To the extent any of these rumors got back to Lanny, he must have been pleased with one thing: almost nobody was venturing to say he was queer anymore. Along with his Mercedes, his tan, and his gold jewelry, Lanny Brandon had brought back with him one stunningly beautiful wife. As Ziggy said, "She's the best wife I ever seen in Portshead."

Alicia Brandon was a woman out of the magazines. She was tall and willowy and her blond hair was a thick, natural yellow that fell straightly and evenly down below her shoulders. With her brilliant green eyes, golden skin, wide mouth and perfect teeth, she could have been the close-up model for half a dozen facial products at once. Her legs were good enough that she supposedly caused a traffic accident downtown when some clown was ogling her in her slit skirt, but since Donovan told that story I will not vouch for it.

Her only weakness, if one considers it a weakness, was a rather small bust, but with all the other treasures she had, it took a while for most people to notice. Not Boyle, though. To him, the fact that she did not have mammaries that hung to her knees was proof positive that Alicia Brandon was really a guy. But that was one rumor no one cared to take up and after a few days even Boyle stopped repeating it.

I first met Alicia Brandon when I went out to her house on a wretchedly humid evening when all the other guys had gone to Fitzy's wake. Lanny greeted me at the door in a yellow terry-cloth jacket and matching shorts. He was barefoot and holding a cocktail glass which was empty but for an inch of melting ice.

We stared at each other while I choked on the greeting I had practiced. "Lanny, you may not remember me, but—"

"It's good to see you, Chuckie," he said, and then there was an embarrassing moment which more or less ended with me thrusting out my hand.

He had to shift his cocktail glass, and after we shook I wondered if perhaps I had dropped his hand too quickly. I did not want him thinking I was afraid of his touch. But he gave no sign that he had noticed anything unusual.

"How are you doing?" I said, and he said, "Fine, Chuckie, or are they calling you Charles or Charlie or something like that now that you're a successful lawyer?"

I was surprised that he knew I was a lawyer. "Oh, I'm not so successful," I stammered, and for lack of anything better to say, tacked on, "I'm still here in Portshead."

"There are people who need a lawyer here just the same as anyplace else, aren't there?" He was smiling and I was a little slow on the uptake, not sure if Lanny Brandon, the man I had snubbed so many years before, was just being sociable.

"Yeah, well, there are some. That's right. Matter of fact, that's why I'm bothering you tonight. . . ."

"No bother. It's nice to see old friends."

I hesitated, wondering now if he was being sarcastic. Since I had no way of knowing, I pressed on. "I've been retained by Richie DelVecchio. He's the cop who shot Michael Fitzpatrick here the other night."

"What's he need a lawyer for? Have some sort of charges been filed against him?"

"Nothing formal. It's just a departmental investigation at this point."

"Oh, I see. You're getting paid by the hour, huh?" He laughed and so I did, too.

"There are still some things I don't understand and I wanted to check them out if I could."

"You want to come in?"

"If it wouldn't be too much trouble."

"Heck, no. I was just sitting out by the pool listening to the game with my wife. Making myself another drink when I heard you ring."

He opened the door wide for me and I stepped inside. The foyer where Lanny had been standing consisted of a few feet of flagstone. Beyond that was a thick gray carpet that spread throughout the house. In the middle of the hall behind Lanny a wide staircase with a highly burnished brown railing and lustrous white banisters spilled down from the second floor. Off to the left was a very formal living room and off to the right there was a more casual room where books lined built-in shelves, a *People* magazine lay open on a rumpled and pleasantly patterned couch, and a leather armchair was tipped back in front of a large console television set.

We entered neither of these rooms, but traversed the hallway to the rear of the house, where there was a cozy, country-style kitchen with a large butcher-block table in the middle of the floor and a big rack of hooks for hanging pots and pans. We passed through a tiny, wood-paneled breakfast nook and entered a dining room, where an ornately heavy chandelier dangled over a mahogany table around which ten spindle-back chairs were grouped like suckling kittens. Lanny went directly to a corner cabinet and opened a beveled glass door.

"What's your pleasure?" he said, pointing to an extensive wet bar.

I told him gin and tonic and he said that was a good idea because Alicia had a bowl of cut limes with her "out on the deck." Lanny poured us each a murderous drink and then pointed my way through a screened-in porch. I banged the door open at the end of the porch and stepped into the night air, which was filled with the sound of Don Coleman's radio voice theorizing as to what the Red Sox pitching coach must be saying to the battered Mike Torrez, who, I knew from having been listening in my car on the way over, had been surrendering his usual assortment of hits to the Kansas City Royals.

Alicia looked up from her seat at the plexiglass table, the smile on her face disappearing when she recognized me as being nobody she recognized. Like her husband, Alicia Brandon was wearing yellow. Hers was in the form of a sleeveless dress with a slit high up on the leg and a plunging neckline. The neckline, like the slit, teased more than it showed, and I did my best not to look. Instead I concentrated on the small poodle that was lying at her feet, its clipped fur the color of the carpet in the house. I had to concentrate on it because it was growling at me.

Lanny turned down the radio and introduced me to his wife, again asking me if it was still all right to call me Chuckie. I said it was fine with me.

"What do you prefer to be called?" Alicia asked, giving me a dainty hand that felt as if she kept it in the refrigerator and only took it out for special occasions.

"Anything but bastard." I laughed, repeating a line I thought had been particularly clever when delivered by Paul Newman in *Hombre*. Lanny gave a polite chuckle and Alicia stared uncomprehendingly at me, so I hastened to explain myself.

"There are people who know me only professionally and tend to call me Charles," I said, "but most everyone else I meet these days calls me Chuck." She didn't respond and I felt I should say something more. "On the other hand, people I know from college and law school call me Chas or Charlie and people I knew before that call me Chuckie. So it really doesn't make much difference. I answer to anything."

"And what should *I* call you?" she said coolly.

I smiled foolishly, waiting for some indication that she was putting me on. "Chuck?" I said.

We sat down and Lanny selected a lime wedge for me while Alicia patted her dog into submission. "Chuckie's a lawyer here in town, babe," Lanny said. "He's defending the cop who shot Michael Fitzpatrick."

"That awful night," she said.

• 37 •

"I have a few questions which might give me a better grip on the case," I said, watching Lanny drop his specially chosen lime wedge into my drink. In the background I heard the crowd cheer as Torrez finally got the Royals out.

"Have you known Alan long?" Alicia Brandon asked in a tone of voice that told me she was not just making conversation.

I watched the fizz spurt up from the bottom of my glass and listened to the beer advertisement on the radio. "About twenty-five years, I guess. Huh, Lanny?"

Lanny nodded. His eyes were on his wife and her eyes were on me.

"That's funny," she said. "I've never heard him mention you before."

The statement, pointed as her earlier question had been, startled me. Was she chastising me or simply being impolite? Could it be that she was unaware of her husband's past? I struggled for the right reply, knowing that almost anything I said might seem inappropriate or could be misinterpreted. Finally I mumbled, "I'm afraid I wasn't very memorable."

But I had waited so long that Lanny was already talking over me. "Honey, you remember me talking about Chuckie Bishop. He was the big football hero at John Hancock High. Scored four touchdowns against Ashton on Thanksgiving Day. Made *Sports Illustrated* or something, didn't you, Chuckie?"

In the shadows created by the light of the lawn lamp, it was impossible to tell if Alicia Brandon's eyes were mocking me. "Is that so, Chuck? Were you the big football hero?"

"Yeah," I said, and let it go at that. I could have said something self-deprecating, I could have said that I had only been in the "Faces in the Crowd" section at the back of *Sports Illustrated*, but I had the feeling that the effort would have been wasted.

"Of course, you didn't go to John Hancock, did you, Alan?" Her voice rose in a light tinkling laugh.

I quickly tried to change the tilt of the conversation. "Are you going by Alan these days?" I said. "Doesn't anybody call you Lanny anymore?"

"My family still does, but I started going by Alan when I went away to school." He didn't say whether he meant Coventry or Cornell.

"You can't blame him for that, can you?" Alicia said; and maybe she only meant that Lanny was a child's name or that it had been easier to let everyone call him by his Christian name, but that was not my immediate impression. It was not Lanny's, either.

"Alicia," he said, and his voice was a command that set her dog to growling again and left me staring into my drink while husband and wife worked things out in the looks that passed between them.

"My God," Alicia muttered, and violently crossed her legs so that she was turned in the direction of the swimming pool. Out of the corner of my eye I saw the slit in her dress expose her thigh nearly to the hip. I wondered if she could possibly be wearing anything under that dress. I wondered why she had no tan mark from a bathing suit.

"I'm sorry, Chuckie," Lanny said. "What is it you wanted to ask?"

"You and Mrs. Brandon, you weren't home the night of the break-in, were you?"

"No. We had gone down the Cape for a few days."

"Do you have a place down there?"

"No. That's one of the reasons we went. Look at some property."

"I wouldn't think summer would be the best time to do it."

Lanny took it as if I was arguing with him. "Interest rates are going up. After the election I think they're going to skyrocket and I want to catch something while I still can."

I nodded and sipped at my drink. "Lanny, I don't mean to get personal or anything, but I'm trying to help my client as best I can."

"I understand."

"Do you have any idea what Fitzy was looking for when he broke in here?"

Lanny grinned, a short, biting little grin that was wiped away when he took his next taste of booze. "Money, I suppose. Silver, television, stereo. There's plenty of stuff in there that could be fenced."

"Oh, I agree, Lanny. There are plenty of valuable things that I saw just walking through. But I don't think that's what Fitzy was after. I mean, he wouldn't have been coming out the window if he was interested in any big stuff like your stereo. And besides, he was coming out empty-handed. He didn't even have a bag or anything."

"He wouldn't need a bag if he was looking for money."

"Was any missing?"

Lanny shook his head. "There wasn't any in the house."

We sat without speaking and listened to the game for a while. Lynn and Perez had both singled and Rice had come to the plate. The crowd's roar was electrifying. Anything could happen with Rice up at bat. He could hit it clear out of Boston. We might hear the crack of his big bat and a minute later the ball conceivably could land right here in the Brandons' swimming pool. I looked at the pool and waited for it to happen. The sticky warmth of the night made it inviting. Rice drew a ball. The underwater light beamed a cozy pyramid pattern just below the surface. Rice drilled one to the third baseman, Brett, who went to second for one, and the relay nailed Rice by two steps to end the inning.

"Goddamn," said Lanny.

"He's still hitting the ball hard," I said.

"Yeah, but it's not like it used to be when he owned the plate. Maybe now that he's rich he's got other things on his mind."

"Speaking of being rich, Lanny . . ."

He raised one eyebrow.

"It looks like you've done all right."

The ice in Lanny's glass cracked. He shook it a bit and raised the glass to his lips. "Yeah, I've done all right."

"You've been the subject of a lot of speculation around town."

"I wouldn't know."

"You mind telling me what it is you do, Lanny?"

"No." He drank. "I'm a writer."

"What is it you write?"

"You ever hear of *The Fortunemaker*?"

"Sure." It was a movie that had opened with a brief run as the feature at a single theater in Boston and then had been relegated to the opening slot at a dozen different drive-ins.

"I wrote the screenplay."

"You're kidding."

He shook his head. He started to say something more and then held his pose like a pointer. Somebody on the Royals had smacked one into the screen and Torrez was coming out. "Way to go, Torrez. I never knew what anybody thought was so hot about that bum in the first place. I'll never forgive him for Bucky Dent, goddamn it."

"Lanny, this fascinates me. How did you get started as a screenwriter?"

"College. I had a creative writing teacher in college who kept insisting that the future for any writer lay in film, so I went out to SC and got in the MFA program in film."

"You did what?"

"University of Southern California. I forgot, that's not exactly on everybody's lips back here, is it? I was in their Master of Fine Arts program."

Drago came on in relief and retired the Royals before they could do any more damage.

"It would seem to me that LA would be a better place for a screenwriter to be living than Portshead."

Alicia Brandon looked up to see what her husband was going to say to that one.

"I'm not writing a screenplay," he told me after a few moments.

"A novel?" I said.

He nodded. "That's right."

"What's it about?"

"I'd rather not talk about it," he said quickly.

I felt as though I had been impudent in some way and I apologized. "It's something I'm interested in, that's all," I said.

He waved it off. "It's just that I've still got all these ideas running through my head and sometimes they're not fully worked out." There was no logical place for the conversation to go from there, and so after a moment or two had passed in silence he said, "The germ is there, maybe, but that's all, and for me to talk about that germ before its time or to try to describe it outside the natural pattern of things can make it sound so silly or inconsequential that the whole idea is killed."

"Oh," I said, anxious to show that I was not as boorish as I must have appeared.

Lanny smiled. "The thing is, Chuckie, no matter how you reacted to what I said, it would affect my own feelings about it. You'd be playing a part in what I write and I'm not ready for that yet. I don't even know my full story, but I know it's inside me someplace and if I have some outside impetus it could change my story so that the one I want, the one I know is there, will never come out."

"Oh," I said again. I didn't have the slightest idea what he was talking about.

The game went on. Pudgy Fisk doubled and Evans left him stranded when he went down on three strikes. Lanny shook his head sadly. "He's never been any good since that time he got beaned."

"Angels did that," I said. "They hit all our ballplayers. They destroyed Conigliaro, they ruined Dewey Evans. All they do is wreck our right fielders and send us second basemen."

"Who?"

"Remy, Doyle, Griffin. They all came from the Angels."

"I didn't know that."

"Sure. Anyhow, Lanny, if all you're doing is writing these days, I guess that doesn't give me much of a clue as to what Fitzy was looking for."

"I don't understand what you mean," Alicia said, speaking for the first time in a couple of innings.

I laughed. "Oh, you know—if Lanny was a coke dealer or something, we could have a pretty good idea of what Fitzy was after."

"A coke dealer?" she said incredulously. "Living in a house like this?"

"Who else can afford to?" Again I laughed, but I was laughing alone. I cleared my throat. "There are a lot of crazy rumors going around."

I stood up and looked about me. "DelVecchio said one of his bullets hit the house. Would you mind showing me where?"

Lanny led me over to a set of two conventional windows. Each window was in two parts and only the bottom parts were covered by screens.

"Kitchen's on the other side," Lanny said.

"Screens lift up?"

"That's right."

"Weren't the windows locked?"

"See, this one's been jimmied and the lock didn't hold it. I don't think it's been changed in twenty years." He covered his brow and squinted. "There's where the bullet went in, about three feet to your left."

If Fitzy had been straddling the windowsill when the bullet was fired, it had missed him only because it was wide of the mark. So much for the warning shot.

I went back to the table and thanked the Brandons for their hospitality. "Look," I said, "I'd like to leave my card if I could, so that if you think of anything later maybe you could give me a call."

Lanny picked up the card and read it. "Fair enough," he said, "but I doubt anything will come up. Still, you can never tell when you're going to need a good lawyer."

"I'll be sure to let you know if I find one," I said, and this time I got a laugh. Lanny put my card down on the table and his wife picked it up.

I turned to leave and then turned back. "Say, Lanny, I'm kind of curious about one thing. How come you don't have a burglar alarm on this house?"

Lanny spread his hands. "I don't know. I guess I didn't think I needed one."

I had expected him to say that and still I was surprised to hear it. "But you were concerned enough to ask Richie DelVecchio to come by and check the place out every night while you were gone."

Lanny did not get flustered. "Well, I do have a pretty good investment here. I figured a house like this might seem awfully inviting if nobody was home for several days in a row."

"Yeah, but don't you think it's a bit unusual to actually pay a cop to come by?"

There was a crackling noise as my card crumpled in Alicia Brandon's hand.

"Ah, yes," Lanny said, giving her a very brief over-the-shoulder glance. "I guess there are no secrets between a man and his lawyer, are there?" He shrugged. "No, I don't think it's so unusual. I mean, this is Portshead, after all. The cops here aren't exactly Eliot Ness and his Crimebusters, are they? My father has given the local boys a little something for Christmas every year that I can remember and in turn they take a little extra notice of his office down on Hancock Avenue. Anytime they see anyone there after six, seven o'clock, they stop and investigate because they know my old man doesn't work at night. So I figured I'd like the same kind of protection and I was willing to pay for it. I recognized Richie DelVecchio driving by one time in a patrol car and I made it a point to find him and tell him what I wanted."

"He says you gave him fifty bucks."

"You always give 'em extra the first time. Make sure they'll do it. Make sure it's worth their while."

"Was this the first time?"

"First and last."

I nodded and turned my back to the pool so that I could join Lanny in looking the house over. "Thing is, Lanny, it makes it tough for me to explain what Richie was doing in your backyard in the first place. We can't very well admit he was accepting gratuities on the side."

"Just say he was a good cop. Noticed the lights on or something and went around to investigate."

"DelVecchio says he came into the backyard through a gate. Fitzy must have done the same, don't you think?"

"I'd say so."

"Mind walking me out that way?"

"No, no, I'd be glad to." Lanny placed his glass on the table. "Your turn to get the drinks, honey. I'll be back in a minute."

Alicia gazed sourly at my mangled card. I stuck my hand out in front of her. "It's been a real pleasure meeting you, Alicia." Slowly, almost reluctantly, she gave me another ice-cold grip and said nothing.

"I hope you're finding Portshead to your liking," I said by means of a farewell.

Her voice was a soft, low murmur. "It's the pits."

They were wrapping up the game on the radio. The Sox had dropped another one, but Lanny let out with a boisterous laugh. "What do you expect from a Southern Californian? She doesn't feel happy unless she's buried beneath forty miles of smog."

I said goodbye and Lanny took me around the side of the house and down a cement walkway to a latch gate in the picket fence. I asked him if there was any lock on the gate.

"Just a bolt lock," he said, showing it to me. "No sense in having anything better, since anyone who wanted to could climb over."

"Richie said the gate was unlocked when he came through."

"Fitzy must have pulled back the bolt so he could get out in a hurry."

I looked it over. "Yeah, I guess. Listen, thanks very much for your time."

"Hey, thank you," Lanny said, and he sounded as though he meant it. He must have noticed my surprise because he dropped his eyes. "I—ah—I really appreciate your coming by, even if it was just on business. I've been back almost six months and you're the first one of the old gang who's been here."

It was an uncomfortable moment. I had not thought of myself as one of the old gang, but I knew what he meant. He had come back from the ashes, done something fantastic and returned home to show it off. And nobody seemed to have noticed.

I tried to break the oppression of the moment by making a bad joke. "Except Fitzy, of course."

Lanny smiled appreciatively, if not genuinely. "Except he dropped in when nobody was home."

"That's all right, Lanny." I clapped him softly on the shoulder. "You've got a beautiful place here. You should be very proud."

"Thanks," he said, and in the dark I thought I saw an unnatural wetness in his eye. I did not want the scene to get any more awkward and I made an effort to hurry off.

"Hey," he called after me, "don't worry about Alicia. She just takes a while to get to know, that's all."

I waved back without looking. I was not worried about Alicia. I simply thought she was a miserable rude bitch, that was all.

8 Taken by itself, the fact that Lieutenant Herb Finucci wore his hair in thin, semi-long strands on top and shaved nearly to the skull on the sides and in the back gave him a mischievous, youthful appearance that a man of his years had no business cultivating. When viewed in context with his pigeon chest, bandy legs and lilliputian feet, Herb's haircut simply contributed to the general slovenliness of his physical appearance. His face was narrow and his lower lip flared out unnaturally at one corner so that you half expected a stream of saliva to come flowing out the funnel it formed and dribble on down his chin whenever he talked. That deformity, combined with his disconcerting habit of looking at you out of the corner of his eyes when he talked, produced in many first-time acquaintances the conviction that he was trying to make them laugh by doing some sort of distorted mime. This was almost always a mistake. Herb Finucci did not do imitations. He did not tell jokes and he did not appreciate jokes told by others. Herb's life did not exist beyond police work, and police work was a humorless business.

This brusque, unrefined, but dedicated little man had both survived and prospered through three police administrations. His success was due almost entirely to his disinterest in making policy or pursuing personal advancement. Since the police department was Herb's family, he took pride in its achievements and he suffered from its failures, but most of all, he accepted its humanity. Whenever a new program was instituted by whoever happened to be chief at the time, Herb Finucci could be counted on to adopt that program and set about implementing it with as little commotion and imagination as possible. Consequently, whenever a new regime came in, Herb would be the one administrator held over; the one chosen to maintain continuity.

As chief of divisions, Herb was third in command of the two-hundred-and-forty-person department. This made him a rather important figure in Portshead, but, such was his charm, he made little attempt to strut his power unless he thought someone was trying to take advantage of him. I pointedly did not do that. I went out of my way never to let Herb know I thought he was an idiot.

Indeed, when Davida buzzed me on the intercom and told me Lieutenant Finucci was waiting in my outer office, I took pains to show him how flattered

I was that he had come to see me. Instead of having Davida escort him back, I went out to greet him myself. He was resplendent in a drab brown sport coat, an ornamented brown shirt and a pair of shapeless blue slacks. Not being married, Herb apparently had no one to tell him that brown and blue do not go together.

"You got a minute, Chuckie?" he said.

It was barely ten o'clock in the morning, the sun was hidden by a haze that hovered no higher than the tops of the two- and three-story buildings that made up downtown Portshead, and it was already too hot to be comfortable, but Herb wanted coffee, so I asked Davida to make him some. I showed him to the library, Sid's library, where it would be coolest and where we could have equal seating, which would spare him the impression that I was looking down on him from behind my desk. It was another one of the tricks Sid had taught me: "The only ones you want to have thinking of you as a superior being are clients and potential clients."

Herb settled himself in a chair by placing his hand in the middle of the library table and using it almost as a balancing point. "I'm here because of DelVecchio," he said. "He tells me you're representing him." He glanced around the walls at the shelves of books as though treating himself to the satisfaction of seeing the founts of all the legal rigmarole with which he found himself perpetually confronted. "That's good. I thought there might be some stuff you'd want to know."

Davida flew into the room with Herb's coffee as if she was part of a bucket brigade come to put out a barn fire. "I brought a cup for you, too, Chuckie," she said. "Can't have the lieutenant drinking alone." She put a cup in front of each of us.

Finucci slurped at his, so I slurped at mine. Davida acted as though it were normal that people made sounds like cars backfiring when they drank their coffee, and diffidently shut the door behind her.

"One thing, though, Chuckie," Finucci said when she was gone. "If anyone asks, I want you to tell 'em I was here questioning you about DelVecchio as part of my official investigation."

It was my first indication that this was not the reason Finucci was visiting. I nodded that I understood.

"You try to quote me on anything I say here and I'll make you out such a liar they'll take your ticket away and give it to Charlie Manson before they let you in another courtroom."

I nodded again.

He sighed. "I suppose you know there's some funny business going on?"

This time I shook my head.

"It ain't like me to come here and talk to you like this—you know that, don't you?"

I agreed it wasn't. I started to say something about knowing how this must be a special situation, but Finucci was not listening. "The kid's about to get screwed and I don't think I want to see it happen to one of my cops."

"You come up with something in the investigation, Herb?"

"I didn't come up with nothing," Finucci snapped. "Clean bill of health. It was dark, the kid saw suspicious movements in a house and went to investigate like a good cop should. He apprehended the suspect in the act of committing a felony, ordered him to halt, fired a warning, and then had to shoot in self-defense when the suspect kept coming."

"My defense exactly, Herb."

Finucci put his cup down and made a noise in the back of his throat. "Course, the kid was twenty yards away when he shot, and there was a bullet practically in the window frame where his warning shot missed its target, but we can take care of that if we have to. Change his angle or something. The worse thing is that the only weapon we found on the victim was a two-and-a-half-inch plastic flashlight that maybe, just maybe, could have broken a pane of glass if it hit dead center and was thrown by that big bastard on the Yankees.

"It was the kid's first experience being alone on something like this. He shoulda kept the fucking civilians away until some more cops got there. Then we could have found our weapon and there wouldn't be no problem like there is. The kid's such a simpleton. He could have used anything. He could have used a screwdriver, for Chrissake. But as it was, everybody saw the guy lying there and there wasn't even a rock nearby they could say was in his hand." Finucci swept his head back and forth sadly.

"That the problem you're referring to, Herb? About the kid getting screwed and all?"

"The problem is," he said, "the DA's gonna order an investigation. You'll probably get a copy of his letter to the district court judge tomorrow."

I was stunned. "Isn't there anything the chief can do about it?"

"The chief!" Finucci snorted disgustedly. "The fucking chief's a politician. The mayor brought him in and the mayor'll lead him out, so whiles he's here he'll do whatever the mayor wants."

I thought it somewhat ironic to hear that coming from a chameleon like Finucci, but it gave me a better understanding of the man. He may have been willing to do anything he was told by his superiors, but Herb Finucci expected a little fraternal loyalty in return and apparently he was not getting it.

"So what's the mayor's position?" I asked.

"This kid, you know whose brother-in-law he is?" Finucci raised his eyebrows over the rim of his coffee cup. "He's Jim Ryder's brother-in-law, and right now the mayor's scared shitless of Jim Ryder because he thinks Jimbo's gonna run against him. The fucking DA's the mayor's former law partner and the fucking chief don't even know the kid, so what's it to him if one patrolman goes down the tubes? He'll say he's clearing bad apples out of the department . . . and that's the other thing you got to watch out for, Chuckie."

"What's that?"

"The kid's history won't stand up to much investigation."

"I don't follow you." The coffee and the heat of the day were sending drops of perspiration raining down inside my shirt, but Finucci had not even bothered taking off his sport coat.

"DelVecchio don't really have a conviction record, you understand, but he was arrested more than once when he was a juvie. I remember him from ten, twelve, thirteen years back. He was one of those wild kids who used to like stealing cars from the downtown parking lots and taking them down Nantasket Beach. Then they'd steal one from around the amusement park down there and dump it back here. Joyriding, you know? Sometimes they'd sideswipe other cars, that sort of thing. Back when McGuinness was chief, we'd just haul the little bastards in and whack the shit out of them. Sit 'em on a metal chair in the middle of the floor, nothing but the one light over their fuckin' pointy little heads. Get 'em good and scared and then rough 'em up a little bit. Tell 'em it was going to be like that for six months if they ever stole another car again."

Finucci smacked his lips, but I could not tell whether he was relishing the memory or the last of his coffee. "We'd give a kid two chances before we'd file charges," he said. "This DelVecchio, he got his two before he smartened up— or at least stopped getting caught. We can't do that sort of thing anymore. Now we're supposed to be rehabilitating the little bastards by sending 'em down Plymouth Correctional Institute, where they learn to grow potatas, which they'll never do again, and commit new crimes, which they'll sure as shit do the minute their asses are put back on the fucking street. We can't do any of that stuff anymore because nowadays even the kids start moaning human rights and suing the department. I don't know what they teach the kids in school these days. I think they spend all their time learning how not to litter and how to smile at Japs, but they sure don't teach 'em how to respect authority."

I directed him back to the subject of my client. "Juvenile arrests without any convictions—that shouldn't keep a guy off the police force."

Finucci pushed his empty coffee cup around the table. "Nope, I guess not. In fact, those arrests, in addition to showing the kid ain't too bright all by themselves, those are what give the kid the idea he wants to be a cop. Maybe he thinks all a cop does is smack people around—I dunno. But as soon as he's old enough, he files the application, duly noting who his brother-in-law is, and takes the exam. Chuckie, he got a fucking twenty-seven on the exam. That's out of a hundred.

Jesus, we got colored guys right out of the ghettos of Boston getting higher scores than that. You need a seventy just to get on the list for consideration.

"I took a look at that exam today, Chuckie. They ask him how many days in a year, he says 180. Never mind the procedure questions, the due process stuff —he fucked up the questions they use to calm you down at the beginning. He took the exam three more times, this guy. Fifty-four, he gets; fifty-two—he actually goes down a couple a points. Then he just misses—sixty-seven or sixty-eight or something. Two years ago, finally, he passes. His score puts him . . . here . . ." Finucci paused long enough to take a piece of paper from his pocket and hold it out at the special distance reserved only for the farsighted who are without their glasses. ". . . forty-third on the list for twelve positions. He's got no veteran's preference, no college, no work experience to speak of except as a security guard, he ain't gonna wow anybody except maybe Helen Keller with his personality, and he's got forty-two guys ahead of him on the list. So how's he end up with the job, Chuckie?"

I thought he wanted me to make a suggestion, but he shook me off. "Don't try to bullshit me, Chuckie. We both know how he got the job and I ain't the one who's really asking, anyhow. I don't gotta ask because I got something else to think about. In the course of my investigation I gotta ask Captain Mowbray, who's in charge of that sort of thing, how come a guy who had been on the force less than a year got assigned to drive a patrol car in the poshest section of the city? How come he wasn't put out on the street wagging traffic or walking the Center with the rest of his class? Mowbray shrugs. He says Chief Lyons specifically told him to give DelVecchio that assignment. Now, like I told you, the chief don't know DelVecchio from DiMaggio, so how come he tells Mowbray that?"

Finucci got to his feet before I even started thinking of a reply. "Right," he said, putting his hand on the doorknob. "You got it. Chief Lyons did a favor for a political ally who's suddenly no longer an ally. Chief cuts the kid loose, announces he's shocked by what he discovered and ties into Ryder for undermining the department with nepotism and patronage. Mowbray, if he's smart, and he is, will take the bullets like a good soldier and get rewarded later."

Adjusting his lapels and craning his neck to free it from his collar, Finucci made his departure by saying, "My report comes out this week and I'll see that you get a copy, for whatever good it'll do you. I'll tell you already it's gonna exonerate the kid and the department and then the mayor will probably get the newspaper to scream cover-up." He gave a Finucci laugh: a grunt that left him seemingly in need of someplace to spit. "So what else is new?" He glanced quickly out to the corridor before adding, "But that should change my official objectivity. After that I'll have to defend what I concluded, so I'll be standing right there with you. Be sure to let me know anything you need to help the kid."

9 Meetings with my ex-wife are always held in public places. Usually we meet in a bar and that means our options are rather limited. Portshead is not the sort of city that has pickup or dating bars. It has neighborhood bars and workingmen's bars and maybe a dozen bars in the downtown area where both men and women go, but the women in those joints are usually over fifty, slump from their eyebrows to their knees, and ride the barstools as if they're glued to their rumps. One bar down by the beach plays dance music, and one on the outskirts of the Center has a live band, but the one on the beach caters to young kids and the band in the other invariably dress in matching ruffled shirts, black pants and vests.

If a guy wants to take a date for a quiet cocktail or two, the best place to go is the Holiday Inn. But even there a woman sitting alone is going to be noticed. It is because I am sometimes late that Cookie does not like to go there. Instead she likes to go to King Arthur's in the Coventry Shopping Center.

King Arthur's is a large, well—but not brightly—lighted bar that was made over from a steak and lobster house that had been the first business at the shopping center to fold. People living within bicycling distance of the Atlantic Ocean had for some reason not immediately taken to eating frozen lobster tails from Australia, and King Arthur's had been able to assume the original restaurant's lease before the shopping center was six months old. The new owners instituted an anachronistic motif, faintly medieval in nature, with imitation stained-glass windows bearing the likenesses of crusaders standing behind their shields, but they did not go overboard in sticking to any one theme. Tiffany-type lamps were hung above the lounge area, where tables and booths were purposely spaced to afford maximum viewing potential for both lookers and lookees.

The bar itself is separated from the lounge by a half-wall that bears a flourish of etched and frosted glass. At each end of the bar is a color television that is used exclusively and religiously for sporting events. Women rarely sit at the bar unless they are talking to a man they know who happens to be sitting there, and men without dates always sit at the bar. If there are no stools left they stand behind those who are sitting rather than go to one of the tables or booths. Sometimes they lean on the shelf that runs along the half-wall just below the etched and frosted glass.

But when I entered King Arthur's at about eight-fifteen I did not go to the bar, even though the game was on and I would have liked to watch the Red Sox blow another one. I took a table in the middle of the lounge, facing the door, and waited for my ex-wife. We had promised to meet at eight o'clock and she showed up at eight-thirty. She breezed through the door without breaking stride, casting her eyes to the right and to the left until, by pure chance, they fell on me. Anybody else would have stopped as soon as she entered and looked around until she found her destination, but not Catherine Maher Bishop. Cookie did not do things the way anybody else did them. It was one of the qualities that annoyed me and yet most charmed me about her.

At one time all of Cookie's little oddities had only charmed me. But that was back before we were married. Back when we were only children.

She was almost to my table when somebody else caught her attention. She gave me the one-minute signal and veered off toward the bar, leaving me foolishly suspended half out of my seat. I saw her give a quick embrace to a mustachioed young hulk in a green polo shirt, go through an introduction to his companion, have a brief conversation with the bartender—also mustachioed, but shorter and balder—and laugh a laugh that carried her head around in a semicircle until she spotted me watching her. She put her hand on the shoulder of the young hulk and smiled a few words at him. He swiveled in his seat and scanned my area until his eyes rested on me. They rested a shade too long before he turned back and said something to his friend, who also looked my way. I raised my hand to my brow in a very casual salute.

Cookie jiggled her way over to me, oblivious of the stares she was attracting. When we were in high school Cookie already had the build of a starlet. It got her nominated every year for both homecoming queen and prom queen; and every year it kept her from being elected to either one of those positions. She was cute enough, her blondish hair slightly curly, her large brown eyes open and expressive, but that was not why the boys voted for her; and the girls and the teachers and the selectors of the queens all knew that. Cookie's beauty was not and never has been the yearbook type, but it manages to draw a lot of interest wherever she goes.

She gave me a kiss on the cheek before literally flopping into the chair next to me. "Whew," she said, stretching her legs out as if she were on a couch. Immediately she bolted upright again. "I never thought I was going to get here. The traffic was so bad it was bumper to bumper and then the red light kept flashing over the speed thing in the dash because the engine was getting so hot. . . ." She prattled on in a rush of words that meant nothing until she concluded, "So, how's it going with you?"

"Who were your friends at the bar?"

"Oh, them," she said, looking back as if she'd forgotten them already. They might have been newspapers left behind on a park bench. "Just some guys I know." She paused long enough to shift gears and then demanded, "Why? What do you care who they are?"

I avoided answering by signaling the waitress. She hurried over, her red and white abbreviated wench's costume looking peculiarly appropriate on her somewhat chubby frame. She addressed Cookie by name and asked her how she was doing before turning her attention to me.

I had been drinking gin and tonic all night, but now I ordered the coldest bottle of beer she had. She listed seven or eight brand names and I said I didn't care, just so long as it was ice cold and it wasn't a light. "My guest here will have a—"

"A vodka gimlet," finished the waitress, and Cookie laughed.

"I didn't realize you were such a regular in here," I said after the waitress left.

Cookie bobbed about in her seat, dipping her left shoulder and then her right. "What are you talking about? We been in here before."

"What, a month ago? I don't see anybody calling me by my name or knowing what I want to drink before I even order it."

Cookie was looking at somebody in one of the booths. She smiled and waved. "Yeah, well, I been in here a few other times, too."

I found myself growing unavoidably unreasonable, so I refrained from saying anything more. The air conditioning had filled the room with a Freon chill, but Cookie began fanning herself anyhow.

"Listen," she said, tilting her head back and pointing her chin out toward me so she could have more of a target for the breeze she was stirring. "You don't have to worry about those guys, if that's who you're worried about."

"I'm not worried about anything."

"One of them used to play for South Shore Catholic. He says he remembers seeing you play when he was in junior high."

"What's that supposed to mean? You going out with younger guys now, is that what you're trying to tell me?"

Cookie squinted mischievously at me. "Suppose I was to tell you I've gotten myself an old man?"

"An old man," I mocked, unable to keep the sneer out of my voice. "Jesus, Cookie, whataya been watching—reruns of *Mod Squad* or something? Nobody talks like that anymore."

"I mean an *old* old man, smartie. A rich old man. A gigolo."

"A gigolo is a man who lives off women."

"Whatever." Cookie was always willing to give in to me on matters of learning. "This guy doesn't need to live off anybody. He's rich. I mean really, really rich. Super rich."

"Who is he?"

"None of your business."

The waitress brought our drinks, doing a sort of modified bunny dip as she placed them on the table. Cookie caught her by the wrist. "Terry, this is my ex-husband, Chuckie. Isn't he a doll?"

Terry looked me over as if I was a brand-new Harley-Davidson. "Hi, Chuckie," she said, and I said, "Hi, Terry," and waited for her to go away. It took a minute because she thought maybe we were going to start up a conversation.

When we were alone I said to Cookie, "So is this guy somebody I know?"

"The guy who played for South Shore Catholic? I don't know; he says he played at Springfield College after that."

"No, dummy. The old man."

"Oh, him. And don't call me dummy anymore, Chuckie." She took a sip of her drink, using the small plastic straw, and I thought she was going to answer my question, but she didn't.

"Well, do I know him or don't I?"

Cookie held one finger up close to her chin and wagged it back and forth. "I'm not going to say anything more about it."

"Well, what did you bring it up in the first place for if you didn't want to tell me?"

She looked a little hurt and stabbed at the ice cubes in her drink. "I thought you might like to know, that's all. I guess I was wrong."

"Of course I want to know who's sleeping with my wife. Why wouldn't I?"

Cookie's brown eyes flew up so fast and so hard that I was immediately filled with remorse. "You don't have to talk that way, you know," she said. "And besides, in case you don't remember, I'm not your stinking wife anymore." She threw down her straw, splattering me with its contents.

I let a few seconds pass. "I'm sorry," I said, wiping the spots of liquor from my shirt. "It's been a tough week, that's all."

"It's been tough for all of us." She was unrelenting.

"I suppose you heard about Fitzy."

"I heard. I didn't notice you at his funeral, though."

I opened my hands. "I've been hired to represent the cop who shot him. I thought it would be weird if I went."

"Oh, brother." Cookie looked away disgustedly.

"Many people there?"

"Some."

"What kind of people?"

"People people. What do you mean, what kind of people?"

"I was just wondering what kind of people Fitzy had been hanging around with recently."

Cookie stared across the table. "Is that why you wanted me to meet you here?" Her voice was querulous and challenging.

"I wanted to talk about Candy."

"What about her?" Cookie had a habit of taking any comments about our daughter as a direct affront to her methods of child-raising.

My enthusiasm and even my concern for Candy's behavior waned as I struggled to find a way to avoid further antagonizing her mother. "She's getting to be a mature young woman these days," I offered.

"What's that supposed to mean?" Cookie said. She was never one for subtleties.

Trying to be as diplomatic, trying to sound as innocent, as I could, I said, "Has she been going out a lot? With boys, I mean."

"She goes out." Again there was that personal note in her voice. Her own fitness was about to be called into question. "She's a popular girl. She has a lot of friends."

"Since I'm defending this guy DelVecchio, all of a sudden I'm a friend of every cop in town. This one guy, Logan—maybe you remember him—told me he was patrolling Wampaugh Pond the other night sometime after one o'clock and he found Candy lying down on the front seat with some twenty-year-old guy."

Cookie waited a moment before she spoke. "So?"

It was an indifference I knew she did not feel. The single word, spoken the way it was, was also a probe, a demand to know what else I was going to tell her before she decided on a defense. I knew exactly what she was doing. I knew that I needed to say nothing more to get Cookie to act on her own, and still I got angry.

"So?" I repeated, and I sat forward so suddenly I hit the table with my chest and rattled both our glasses. I glared at her and chopped the air viciously with my hand. "So she's fifteen years old, that's what. She's out with a guy five years older than she is, that's what. What's she doing out past one o'clock in the morning, anyhow? And what's she doing parking up at the pond? You know what the hell goes on up there. You want her—"

I stopped, but it was too late. Cookie knew what I had been about to say. "Do I want her to end up like me, Chuckie?"

"C'mon, Cookie, I didn't mean that."

Cookie's eyes glistened. "You're so quick to criticize. It's a good thing that's all you have to do. Why don't you try raising a teenage kid for a while?"

"C'mon, Cookie. You know that wouldn't be any good. For one thing, the kid hates me, and for another, I'm barely even able to take care of myself. I go home to my mother's once a week just so I'll have some goddamn vegetables that don't come out of a two-by-two-inch cube in a tinfoil tray. It's just, I hear stuff like this and I think, Jesus, I've got to do something. It's my kid, I've got some responsibility, some obligation to try to make sure she does things right even though I'm not around to see her every day."

"Sure," she said, her lips tight, her voice bitter. "So you yell at me."

"I'm not yelling at you. We're just talking."

"And then you go home and congratulate yourself on what a good father you been."

Suddenly we were no longer having a private discussion. The palooka from the bar had joined us, standing next to the table, his gaze on Cookie, his arms raised so that his biceps and his forearms swelled in his tight green shirt as he nervously cracked his knuckles.

"This guy bothering you, Cookie?" he said.

She buried her face in her hands and shook her head. He looked questioningly from her to me as if he sort of expected me to nod solemnly and say yes, I believe I was bothering her.

I didn't say that. Instead I looked up at him. He was in his late twenties, larger than I was, and obviously filled with a sense of self-esteem that was derived from a blissful ignorance of any world beyond a ten-step radius of his own physical being. This was a man whose idea of art was the sports drawings of LeRoy Neiman; who thought Jerry Lewis was a funny bastard; who prepped himself for picking up girls by washing in aftershave lotion. I looked up at him and I said, "Why don't you mind your own business, fuckface?"

I never moved from my chair and since it took the palooka a few seconds to overcome his apoplexy, Cookie had time to get between us. "No, Obie," she cried, in a voice so shrill that all activity in the bar came to an immediate halt.

Cookie seized Obie's massive arm and did her best to push him away. She was tearfully and angrily telling him that it was all right and that she could take care of everything. But her urgency was nothing against his strength, and he would only let her move his upper body while he snarled bizarre accusations as to my heritage and sexual preferences. All the while I continued to smile at him as if he was the moron I knew him to be.

"What's the trouble here?" the manager wanted to know. He was a wiry young man wearing a white shirt and a tie. Like everybody else in the goddamn place, he had a mustache.

I said, "The fat boy here came over and tried to bum sips of our drinks. When we refused, he got nasty and hit us up for beer money."

"You're fulla shit," Obie shouted, and he tried to wrestle himself free of the two or three people who had joined Cookie in trying to hold him back.

"I said no and so the fat boy offered to entertain us by pulling down his pants and singing 'America the Beautiful' in falsetto if we'd buy him a beer. I thought that was extremely offensive to my guest and asked him to take his repulsive ideas somewhere else. That's when he became violent."

The manager gave no indication that he was enjoying or even getting my sense of humor. "Obie, why don't you go back and sit down?" he said.

Obie was dragged away in a hail of threats as to what he was going to do to me if I dared set foot outside the door.

"I don't know what this is all about," the manager said, "but if there's any more trouble I'm throwing you both out."

He stalked away and I was left with one ex-wife watching me reprovingly. "Why do you have to do things like that?" she said.

"I didn't do anything," I protested, disappointed she was not more impressed by my cleverness. "I was sitting here having a private conversation with you and he came over and butted in."

"I don't want to talk about it," she said. She scooped up her pocketbook and headed directly for the door.

Her erstwhile protector noted her progress from his seat at the bar and got up to follow her as soon as he realized she was leaving. On his way out he fixed me with a withering sidelong glance that nearly carried him into one or two tables. I toasted his departure with the rest of my glass of beer and then I was alone.

My solitude did not last long. Terry was at my side, her tray balanced in one hand, her thick lip bent sympathetically. "Don't worry about him, Chuckie. He's nothing but a troublemaker, anyhow."

I nodded and silently contemplated the chubbiness of Terry's thighs. They were not, I decided, too chubby for me. Then something else caught my eye. An exquisite-looking blonde in a pair of eighty-dollar blue jeans was taking a seat at a table across the room. The woman was Alicia Brandon and the man seating himself next to her was not her husband.

He, instead, was a person of middle years, slimmer than Lanny and at least as well tanned. He wore his gray-black hair daringly long and carried a pair of very expensive-looking sunglasses by their stems. I wondered why he even had them; it was dark outside. The night was also very warm, and yet he wore a multipocketed safari jacket over a black and yellow paisley shirt. As soon as he had pulled his chair in close to the table, he began looking around impatiently as though he expected a waitress to appear instantaneously.

Terry saw my attention was elsewhere and moved on. I continued to dawdle over my beer and watch Alicia as she and her companion engaged in a close and apparently very earnest conversation. The moment I noticed them joining hands and fixing each other with soul-delving glances I dropped a five-dollar bill on my table and walked over to them. The irony of what I was doing in the wake of my encounter with Obie did not immediately impress me and I was very polite in waiting for them to look up.

"Alicia," I said, holding out my hand. "Chuck Bishop. We met the other night."

The connection hit and she grew flustered. Her hand came out automatically and she would have taken it back as quickly as she could if I had not held on to it.

"My, ah, my agent, Mr. Robertson," she said, introducing me to the safari-jacketed man, who made an effort to overcome his extreme unhappiness at my presence by declaring he was charmed to make my acquaintance.

"Oh, really?" I said. "What sort of agent are you, Mr. Robertson?"

"Theatrical," he grumped. He was not prepared for an interview.

"I didn't know you were an actress," I said to Alicia.

She explained that she had at one point been a model and was thinking about getting back into it. I tried to develop the subject, but it was so glaringly obvious my company was not wanted that I had no choice other than to excuse myself and leave.

The delightful Mr. Obie was not waiting for me outside the bar as he had promised. He had gone, and so had my ex-wife.

10 The receptionist at the hospital told me Dr. Maddox was too busy to see me. I told her to tell him I was the attorney representing Officer DelVecchio and that I needed to speak with him regarding the death of Michael Fitzpatrick. She relayed the message and then came back and told me I had to make an appointment. I told her to tell the doctor I was a friend of Bernie Heifitz, and this time when she came back she directed me to a hallway in the basement, where she said I could find him.

I went down a flight of stairs and through a small waiting room where an anxious-looking woman in a sundress and sneakers sat at the very edge of a plastic-form chair, clutching her pocketbook in her lap. She was staring up at a television that was chained to a shelf in one corner of the room and she jumped when I came bounding in. I smiled an apology and she gave me an annoyed grimace and went back to watching her show.

The room led out to a hallway that was made cavernous by yellow square tiles on the wall. A thin rubber runner covered the floor and I followed it until I came to a set of double doors, which suddenly blew open in front of me. A dark-complected, very self-assured little guy dressed in the green garb of the operating room came out and squinted at me.

"You the lawyer?" he said, and I told him I was. "Huh," he said, looking me over.

I asked him if he was Dr. Maddox and he answered by telling me he was extremely busy and only had a minute to speak. He dug a cigarette out from somewhere and rapped it on the tile to pack it down. He lit it with a Bic lighter and hoisted his green pants up. Dr. Maddox was about forty-five years old. He was slightly built and had the mannerisms of a man whose day is only half as long as everyone else's. He looked as if he had had his last good laugh just before he entered medical school.

"The only reason I'm talking to you at all is because you're a friend of Bernie's," he said.

I told him I appreciated it.

"I've learned better than to talk with attorneys," he said, giving me one of those I-wasn't-born-yesterday smirks. "I don't even talk with my own attorney if I can help it."

"Who is your attorney?"

"I go into Boston," he said.

"I've heard they've got some good ones in there."

Dr. Maddox looked at the cigarette he was holding between his fingers. He was bright enough to realize I had taken offense. "How did you know Bernie?" he asked.

"He tried to recruit me to his alma mater when I was in high school."

"Ah." The doctor's eyes opened. "You're a Harvard man."

"No, Northeastern." I smiled. "Work-study program."

"Oh, yeah." He had heard of it. I was probably the first one he ever met who had been in it, but he had heard of it.

"That's how I became a lawyer," I said. "Bernie got me a job as a law clerk while I was going to college."

"Not bad."

"It beat stocking shelves down the Stop & Shop, which is what I was doing when Bernie rescued me."

"He was a great guy, that Bernie. We all miss him." He turned to an ash receptacle filled with sand and tapped his cigarette. "Now what is it you want?"

"The night the shooting took place at the Brandons' house, were you asleep when it happened?"

"Yes and no. I was in bed and my eyes were shut and I might even have been dreaming, but I seemed to sense that something was going on."

"I don't follow you."

"When that gun went off it was like I was expecting it. It wasn't a case of me waking up and wondering what the hell was happening. That was the way it was for my wife, but not for me. The shots went wham, bam, and I was out of bed and running for my bathrobe."

"Weren't you afraid?"

"I didn't give it any thought."

"I see."

"I apparently made so much noise running down the stairs and out the front door that my wife and daughters came running after me."

"Did you know where you were going?"

"I could tell where the shots had come from. My first thought was one of the Brandons had killed the other."

"Why?"

"What do you mean, why? The gunshots seemed to come from their house, that's why."

"But they weren't even home."

"I didn't know that."

"Well, did they ever give you any reason to believe that either one of them might shoot the other?"

"No. Except I see him coming and going at all hours of the night. Between you and me, I don't know what business he's in, but he's got an awfully peculiar schedule."

"You ever see anybody else coming and going over there? Anybody that might give you cause to believe there would be guns in the Brandon house?"

"I don't watch them that closely. I've only met them to say hello to."

"How about the night Michael Fitzpatrick was killed—you see or hear anything that night before the gunshots?"

"Nothing, except what I told you. There was something that was keeping me from being sound asleep."

"And when you went running out into the front yard, what did you find?"

"When I got to the yard I stopped. That was the first time I thought that maybe this wasn't just a domestic quarrel after all. Then this young cop literally tore through the Brandons' gate without even seeing me. He had his gun out and he didn't appear to have any idea where he was going."

"He said he was going to his patrol car."

"That so?" the doctor reflected. "Well, maybe he was."

"What happened next?"

"He ran up to me as soon as he saw me and grabbed me by the shoulders. I remember because he had the gun in his hand and it was pointing up next to my head. He said, 'Quick, call an ambulance.' I said, 'I'm a doctor; is there anything I can do?' and he told me a man had been shot."

"Did he say he had shot him?"

"No. He just said a man had been shot. I told my wife to call the hospital—she and the kids were out there by then—and I went into the backyard with DelVecchio. We found Fitzpatrick lying on his back under an open window. He was dead before I got there."

"No possible way of reviving him?"

Dr. Maddox snorted. "You don't revive a man with a bullet in his brain."

"And Officer DelVecchio—how did he react when you told him Michael Fitzpatrick was dead?"

"There were no physical manifestations, if that's what you mean. He simply stared at the body without saying anything."

"Is it possible he was in shock?"

"Shock—what does that mean? Shock is a condition of inadequate blood flow. If you're talking about what lay people refer to as emotional shock or autonomic changes in his system, I can't give you a definite answer because I didn't examine DelVecchio."

"Well, you can give me an opinion based on what you observed, can't you?"

"Oh, no, I'm not getting involved in that."

"Look, Doctor, like it or not, you're going to be subpoenaed to appear in this case as many as three times. Anything I ask you now is just a sample of what's going to be put to you on the stand when you're under oath. It would make it a whole lot easier for both of us if we were familiar with what you're going to say."

The good doctor drew himself up as straight as he was going to get in his rubber-soled shoes. "Let me tell you something, Counselor," he said, his eyes flashing. "I have had my words twisted by you people before. If I have to testify in court I will, but I want what I say down in writing and witnessed by as many people as possible. Outside of that, I don't give opinions unless I'm paid for them, understand?"

I tried to reason with him. "But, Doctor, if I paid you to say something it would jeopardize the value of what you said."

He was not listening. He was already starting his next argument. "I also get paid for my time and I've given away enough of it already today. Goodbye, Counselor." With that, he gave a vigorous forearm shove to the swinging doors through which he had passed a few minutes earlier and disappeared from my view.

11 Jimbo Ryder strode the council chambers like a squire inspecting his estate. Everything the eye could see belonged to Big Jim. The room was his fiefdom, the people his vassals. Whatever business was going on was Big Jim's business.

The chambers (there was only one room, but it was always referred to in the plural) were official Portshead's most impressive setting. Two hundred and fifty-six seats were arranged in sixteen rows to face the Great Seal of the City of Portshead, with its historical dates of founding and incorporation emblazoned on a WPA-like picture of oversized steel-armed, craggy-faced laborers breaking quarry rock in front of a flat-colored background of sailboats billowing across an ocean inlet. Below the Great Seal was the rostrum with the city council president's seat at a slightly elevated position in the center, the city clerk's seat to the left and the committee clerk's seat to the right. Facing each other, perpendicular to the council president's rostrum, were two tables of five seats each. Five nameplates lined each table. Closest to the rostrum, the nameplates read "City Auditor" and "City Solicitor," while the remainder bore the prefix "Mr." and the last names of the eight city councillors who were not council president.

The chambers were very much like an airy courtroom, with ample space for standing in back and no barrier railing to separate participants from spectators. State and national flags draped limply but cleanly over brass-plated poles in the corners. The walls were covered with a base of wainscoting which rose to a line of molding and then gave way to dark panels of well-oiled wood which extended to the twenty-foot-high ceiling. A full-color reproduction of a painting of John Hancock, pen in hand, held a place of honor at the rear of the chambers. Head-and-shoulders pictures of the two Adamses, Coolidge and Kennedy were the only other adornments. They were of uniform size except for the picture of Kennedy, which was considerably larger.

This was Jimbo's domain. With his exceptional height, he had an advantage over everyone else in working the chambers, and he used that advantage effectively. His progress down the side aisle was a series of stops and handshakes. Issuing greetings, listening to tales, he would continually throw his head back, whether in laughter or in consternation, and then his eyes would sweep the room, acknowledging contact with a smile or an index finger held straight up in the air.

Jimbo, despite having arrived early, was the last of the councilmen to take his seat. Even Broussard, the great reformer, his disheveled hair flying, his suit a mass of wrinkles, his stack of papers flopping loosely under his arm, had managed to double-park his car, run up to the second floor, careen down the center aisle and hit his seat before Jimbo made it through the last cadre of constituents.

Council President Scurillo, perturbation flushing his already red face, slapped away with his gavel slowly, steadily and gratingly until Jim was at last settled in. "May I remind you, Councillor," Scurillo said with embroidered politeness, "that these meetings are to start promptly at seven-thirty."

Jim lifted himself an inch or two off his seat. "My apologies, Mr. President," he said humbly. He put on his eyeglasses and opened the manila folder in front of him.

But that was not enough for Mr. President. "We have many things to cover here, Councillor, and if we are going to have to cater to the schedules of individual members, we cannot hope to accomplish the tasks before us."

There was a muffled reaction from the fifty or so spectators. Very deliberately, Jimbo Ryder took off his glasses and laid them upside down on the table in front of him.

"Since you have chosen to make that remark on the record, Mr. President, and since it is most pointedly directed at me, I believe I am entitled to make a rebuttal." He adjusted his gooseneck microphone and hunched forward, his eyes fixed on Scurillo. "Let me first say that this council has never and need not now cater to this councillor's schedule. I was in this room a full twenty minutes before starting time. Certain of my constituents, I am pleased to say, took the opportunity to address me on matters important enough to them that they took time out of their own busy schedules to come down here. I am anxious as you to get down to tonight's business, Mr. President, but this council member knows who he serves and the people of this city know that when they want to talk, Jim Ryder is going to be there to listen."

There would, no doubt, have been more posturing on both sides, except that the audience suddenly burst into applause. Several of the council members exchanged startled looks, but Jim simply picked up his eyeglasses and went back to looking at the report before him. Scurillo, surprised by both Jimbo's dramatic retort and the audience's reaction, whacked his gavel angrily a few times and said, "All right, we've wasted enough time already."

I was waiting by Jimbo's big Ford station wagon when he came out of City Hall almost half an hour after the council meeting had adjourned. Jim drove a station wagon because he had lots of kids. I knew he had lots of kids because he liked to pose them in his living room for pictures that he put on his Christmas cards and used for campaign brochures. He also liked to dress them up in their most formal clothes and get them to run across the library lawn in a link of hands extending between him and Loretta. The pictures from the library runs showed that the Ryders were not only a large family but an energetic one, right down to the pudgy little two-year-old who looked petrified by the apparently demonic lurching of her bucktoothed nine-year-old brother.

Big Jim was not alone when he approached the car. I would have been surprised if he was. Although he was quite obviously thrilled to see me, I had to wait until he finished with the other people before we could speak.

"I thought that was you in there, Chuckie," he said when everyone else had left. "Don't tell me you're taking an interest in politics these days. I'll have to start looking over my shoulder, if that's the case." He laughed.

I smiled. "I sat through the ordinance report, the land conveyance report, the —what else?"

"The disposal and sanitary problems report."

"The disposal and sanitary—right. But I just couldn't sit through the public safety report. Who the hell ever put Broussard in charge of that committee?"

Jimbo looked both ways over his shoulders, just as he had promised to do with me, and then he leaned in close. "We had to. Can you imagine the shit he'd cause if he was chairman of anything else?"

We laughed together on that one and I carried my laugh right into the subject I wanted to discuss. "Listen, Jimbo, I'd like to talk with you about Richie DelVecchio."

"Oh." He made a face. "Isn't that a mess? I'm glad to hear you're representing him, though, Chuckie. I recommended you."

It was a silly lie for Jim Ryder to tell. It altered my opinion of him. "I appreciate that, Jim," I said. "How did you happen to choose me?"

Whether his claim came through glibness or dishonesty, Jimbo quickly realized he had made a mistake. "Well, actually, Richie said Monahan of the Portshead Patrolmen's Association wanted him to go to you. I told him I thought you'd do a good job. I've been meaning to talk to you about it, too, Chuckie, but I've been so damn tied up these past few days."

I told him I understood. "I kind of thought you would want to talk about it, Jim. After all, it's beginning to get a little hairy."

Jim cocked his head. "How so?"

"The DA's recommending a judicial inquest." I showed him a copy of the letter that had been hand delivered to me that afternoon. "It'll be in tomorrow's papers."

Jim unfolded the letter and read it in an audible mumble. " 'Honorable Stephen DeSantis, Acting First Justice, District Court. Dear Justice DeSantis: Pursuant to Chapter 38, Section 8 of the Mass. General Laws Annotated, I am hereby requesting your court to hold an inquest to determine the facts surrounding the death of Michael P. Fitzpatrick. I have designated Assistant District Attorney Mark Brosnahan to attend the inquest and present and examine witnesses to the Justice that you appoint to conduct the inquest. Very truly yours, John Ferguson, District Attorney.' " Jim sagged back against the door of his car, a woebegone expression on his face. "Mother of God," he said.

I took the letter from his hand and folded it up again.

"I don't know," he said. "Suppose it would do me any good to talk to Fergie about it? He owes me a few favors, you know."

"Jim," I said, "I realize you just found out about this, but think about it, will you? You think Fergie doesn't know Richie's your brother-in-law? If he wasn't doing this by choice, don't you think he would have at least called you up and told you about what he was going to do?"

Jim Ryder considered what I had said. His lower lip was lodged firmly between his teeth. His brow was furrowed. "The bastards," he concluded. "They wouldn't really do that to a kid like Richie. Hell, he stopped a burglary."

"Hey," I said, tapping my chest and throwing out my hand. "What do I know? You're the one in politics. I'm talking to you because something weird is going on and I need you to tell me about it. If they don't prosecute cops around here, like everybody keeps telling me, how come they're going after Richie? The guy he shot was a good guy, a local boy, but he was nobody. Unemployed, maybe even a drug addict. You think John Ferguson is going to go after Jim Ryder's brother-in-law the cop because he killed a guy like Fitzy in the middle of a burglary? No way. Not in a million years. Not unless Mayor McLaughlin tells him to."

The expression that settled on Jim Ryder's face was meant to tell me that I was a very perceptive young man. It would have been flattering if I had not suspected he was just covering my bottom with baby powder in an effort to find out how much I really knew and how much I was guessing. "Frannie McLaughlin wouldn't have any reason for wanting to harm me." He said it the way a good debater would, with conviction if not sincerity.

People walked by and we both went quiet. One of the people, a wide-hipped lady with a face too round for her short hair style, cast a worried glance in our direction, as if to say that our suits were not fooling her because she knew that any man on the street after dark had only one thing in mind. Then a sign of recognition flashed across the broad expanse of her forehead.

"Jimmy," she said, "is that you?"

"Of course, Clara," he answered, beaming at her.

Clara had to get her two friends to meet the councillor and then, clinging to

Jim Ryder's coat sleeve, she said, "Jimmy, I wish you could do something about my Roy." She looked at me and I dutifully began inspecting the pavement while she dropped her voice. The curious thing was that the more quietly she spoke, the easier it was to understand her because of the emphasis she placed on every word. "He's drinking again something terrible, Jimmy, and when he does his temper gets real wicked. I don't mind so much for me, you know, Jimmy, but him and my oldest boy, Paul, get to fighting, and honest to God, sometimes I think they're gonna kill each other. It don't make for a happy house, Jimmy."

Jim Ryder patted her hand. "I'll give Roy a call in the morning, Clara, how's that?"

"Oh, would you, Jimmy? If you could just talk to him . . ."

"Tell you what, Clara. I'll come by and see him. That'll be better than calling." He escorted Clara back to her friends and when they were out of hearing he shook his head and said, "What are you gonna do? The guy's fifty-seven years old, he's been working in the same machine shop since he got out of high school, and suddenly he woke up one day and realized he hates his job, hates his house, his wife's grown old on him and his kids are hoodlums. He can't afford any counseling, he makes too much for the state to pay for it and he'll be goddamned if he'll go to a clinic and let anybody else see that there's something wrong with him."

"So what can you do for him?"

Jim looked off in the direction of the three women and shrugged. "I talk to him. I try to make him feel important. Sometimes I ask his advice, ask him to do little things to help me out."

"And does he do them?"

Again Jim Ryder shrugged.

"Jimbo, four, five months ago I went to a fundraiser for you. Since then I heard you've raised thirty thousand bucks and nobody knows what for. I go to a city council meeting tonight and the mayor's little puppet, Scurillo, attacks you for no reason and you end up making what's practically a campaign speech in which you promise to do everything for the little people except make them grow tall. It doesn't take any great genius to figure out what's going on. There's a mayoral election coming up next February and everybody says you're going for it. Going after McLaughlin. If that's the case, Jimbo, then we've both got a problem and his name is Richie DelVecchio."

"I'm not running for mayor."

"Good. Tell McLaughlin. Maybe he'll call off his Doberman."

Jimbo looked off in the direction of the downtown shopping center. The traffic lights were reflecting in the darkened storefront windows and causing a sparkling effect that was mirrored along the row of buildings. It stopped only when it got to the dark space next to City Hall that marked the Revolutionary War heroes' cemetery. He folded his arms and smiled down at me from his three- or four-inch height advantage. "Ah, but it's not that simple, Chuckie. There are other things involved. Things you don't know about. Things I can't talk to you about just yet and for that reason I'd prefer that you not pass around what I've just told you."

He walked to the driver's side of the car and unlocked the door. Someone drove by and beeped at him. He waved and smiled, his eyes squinting in the dark to see who it was. "Good night, Chuckie. I think you're doing a fine job. Any way I can help you, just let me know."

12 On Friday morning when I walked into my office Davida barely even noticed me. She was busy fighting with her husband over the telephone.

"Oh, but you weren't so sick you couldn't drag your ass out of bed and get down to the Tippler as soon as I left the house. What, were you afraid they were going to give away your stool or something? You thought maybe it would be standing room only at nine o'clock in the morning?"

I shut the door to the inner office, opened the cup of coffee I had brought with me from Cubby's, and started thumbing through the day's mail. Magazines from the ABA's Section of Litigation and the Mass. Bar Association; a circular urging me to send my secretary for paralegal training; a form announcement that somebody I barely knew had left the attorney general's office and was opening her own practice; notice of an upcoming seminar on real property transactions; an advertisement for a book on how to run a small office more effectively: "A MUST for every sole practitioner!" it said.

The only thing of importance, the only thing for which I could bill time in reviewing, was a twenty-three-page set of interrogatories to be answered by a client who was a plaintiff in a five-thousand-dollar loss and damage claim. I had been expecting a settlement offer and I was disappointed. By sending me such an extensive list of fact-seeking questions, the opposing counsel was serving notice that he intended to play hardball. If he dragged the thing out long enough, I could end up billing my client for more than he wanted in reimbursement, in which case I was going to have to end up eating a good part of the bill.

Davida tapped on the door and pushed it open. She leaned a bloated arm down on my desk for support and heaved an enormous sigh of exhaustion. "Don't you dare say good morning to me," she said.

"I'm sorry," I told her. "But you were busy on the phone when I came in."

"I mean there's nothing good about this particular morning."

"Problems with Carl?"

"No," she said, clutching at her enormous bosom. "Why should there be any problems with my poor, misunderstood husband? He's only lost his job. It's not the end of the world."

I was surprised to hear Carl had lost his job mostly because I was surprised to hear he had one. The more usual situation was that he was about to get a job, or that he had been cheated out of one, or that he would have had one except that some vindictive bastard had given him an unfairly lousy letter of recommendation.

"Anything I can do?" I said. "You want the day off?"

"No," she said. "Then nobody in my apartment would be working. What you can do, I guess, is see this gorgeous creature who's sitting out in the waiting room for you."

I went out to see who could evoke such praise from a woman as seemingly ignorant of style as Davida, and found Alicia Brandon thumbing through an old copy of *Newsweek*. She looked like a temporary secretary who had told her agency that she could type ninety words a minute and was afraid I was about to give her a typing test. I told her I was surprised to see her and asked her to come back to my office.

She stood up uncertainly in her designer jeans, high heels and silk blouse. Davida, with her sense of terra firma, checked Alicia out from top to bottom and then immediately went to work banging away at her typewriter. I asked Alicia if she wanted any coffee and she said no, she'd only be staying a minute; and I was glad because I had the feeling Davida would have resented getting anything for this beautiful woman.

"Chuck," Alicia began when she was seated in my office, and then she stopped and looked at me as if I was the only one in the world who could help her.

"Yes?" I said, opening my eyes encouragingly.

"It's about the other night. At King Arthur's, I mean. I'm sorry if I was rude to you."

"You weren't rude. It was rude of me to barge over there and interrupt your conversation like that." Until she had walked into my office, I had not really felt that way.

"I was surprised, that's all. I hadn't expected to see anybody I know." Twisting the straps to the bag in her hands, she added, "We know so few people around here."

I searched for something comforting to say. "Lanny's been away a long time," I tried.

"Oh, you don't have to talk to me like that. I know what happened here, but that was so very many years ago. Don't people ever forget?"

"Sure, people forget," I said. "To tell you the truth, I think everyone forgot about Lanny altogether. That's why when he shows up again after all these years —well, people get reminded of things. It won't last, though, Alicia. As soon as you get settled in the community—"

"I don't see how we ever will. We've been here almost six months, and outside of Lanny's family you're the only person we've seen." She looked away. "We barely even know the neighbors."

"Well, it takes a while. People are a little provincial around here. It's not like in California."

But she was not listening. "Alan works in the house all day or else he's out doing research. Even at night. He goes out by himself a lot and when he's home his mind is always on that book of his. Sometimes it's almost as though he's in another world and, well, it doesn't always leave much room for me." The twisting of the straps in her hands stopped. She had reached the point she wanted to make and she turned her eyes back on me. "That's why I was so glad when Leland called me and told me he was in Boston this week."

"Leland?"

"Leland Robertson. The man you saw me with at King Arthur's. That's one of the reasons I've come here today, Chuck. I want to ask you not to say anything to Alan about Leland. There was nothing that happened between us, nothing that I'm ashamed of, but Alan doesn't always understand those things. He takes them personally, like the only reason I'd want to talk to another man is if Alan himself had failed me in some way." She laughed by exhaling quickly through her nose and lifting one corner of her mouth. It was a sardonic laugh, directed at her own silliness. "To keep him from getting upset, I made up a little white lie about going to an Oriental rug auction. I'd hate for Alan to find out that wasn't where I was. He wouldn't understand."

"Well, he won't find out from me, Alicia."

Her face brightened and I realized she had not been at all sure I would cooperate. "Oh, thank you," she said. "It's not that I'm really hiding anything from him, but right at this moment Alan's so conscious of his image—" She put her hand to her mouth, a dainty, smooth-skinned, golden-brown hand with long, slender fingers leading to graceful white nails that extended a quarter to a half inch into the air. "Oh, I don't think I should have said that."

"You needn't worry, Alicia, and neither should he. I was pretty impressed by everything I saw."

"Were you? Then will you come out again? For dinner, perhaps. How about this weekend?"

The invitation was upon me before I had time to think, and my first impulse was to say no. "Jees, I really can't this weekend. I'm caught up in this DelVecchio thing and I—"

Her eyes dropped. "Of course. I understand."

"On the other hand, I do have to eat dinner sometime, so maybe Sunday would be all right if that's okay with you."

"Sunday would be wonderful." She got up. "Sunday, then. Eight o'clock. It's late for Sunday, I know. Sunday dinner should be at seven o'clock, but it's been so darn hot at that hour of the night lately."

"It's just a heat wave. It won't last forever."

"God, I hope not." Her face suddenly clouded. "This is so stupid of me, but I don't even know. Are you married?"

"Not anymore."

"Do you have a girl friend or anything like that? Anybody you'd like to bring?"

"I can probably dig up somebody."

"Oh, that would be wonderful."

13 Richie DelVecchio lived in an untidy little house not too far from the seawall in the Lighthouse Harbor area of town. It was a two-story house, narrow and covered with aluminum siding. The front was brick, but the downstairs level was nearly obscured by an enclosed white porch which clung to the rest of the place like a gas mask. An unpaved driveway ran along one side and ended at a dilapidated garage that did not look as though it was large enough to hold either Richie's Mustang or his wife's Pinto. Both were parked in the drive, one behind the other. I could tell whose car was whose because the Pinto had a child's travel seat set up next to the driver and the Mustang had a torn bumper sticker that read "STP."

I left my Firebird at the curb and walked up the cement path, mounted two cement stairs and rapped on the aluminum of the porch door. The door fell back from its frame each time I hit it, so I pushed it all the way open and let myself into the porch. It was obviously what a visitor was supposed to do. The porch was filled with toys and stacks of newspapers and it had a dime-thin welcome mat in a slightly askew position in front of the door that led into the house. I could hear the canned laughter of daytime television as I used the yellow metal knocker and waited for somebody to respond. A man's voice yelled for me to come in.

I entered a short and uncarpeted hallway and was immediately met by a little blond boy in diapers and a food-stained shirt with snap buttons on the shoulder. He pointed something at me—it was not a gun, more like a toy soldier—and said, "Bang, bang." He laughed delightedly.

In the room to the left of the hallway, the room in which the television was on, Richie DelVecchio was getting up from the sofa. He was dressed in a white T-shirt and tight black dungarees. I watched him as he tried to make his way forward, his progress slowed by the fact that he had to step around a low coffee table, a crib and a tricycle. The expectant, questioning look on his face softened into one of tempered relief when he saw who I was.

He did not greet me with pure pleasure—he was too dependent on me to do that—but he was glad to see me. "Chuckie," he said. "Come in—if you can find your way through this mess." He pushed at the tricycle, ineffectively moving it a few turns closer to me.

"Dickie," he yelled at a second little boy, this one darker and about four years old, an unremarkable kid who was using the springs of the sofa to bounce up and down on his bottom while he sang a one-note nothing song to nobody. "Get this bike outta here, Dickie." The boy continued doing exactly what he had been doing because his father was already stepping over the tricycle to shake my hand.

Richie's eyes avoided mine when we made contact and again I was struck with the impression that this was not an act he was used to performing. "You want to talk or something?" he said.

I said I did and he looked around despairingly. "Maybe we could go in the dining room. It'd be more comfortable."

He crossed in front of me without bothering to turn off the television. I stepped back into the hallway and followed Richie into the kitchen. His wife, Linda, was sitting there at a collapsible rectangular Formica-top table. She was smoking a cigarette and had the newspaper (it was the *Sentinel,* so it had to have been at least one day old) spread out in front of her. It was opened to local news, car crashes and the like, but it was also serving as a mat for her coffee cup and beanbag ashtray. On the chair next to her was a pile of unfolded laundry.

"Look who's here, Linda," Richie said, gesturing behind him with his thumb. "Chuckie Bishop. The lawyer."

Linda had one arm bent across her chest so that her hand was tucked under the other arm, the one she was using to hold up her cigarette. Her bleached-blond hair was in curlers and over them she had a mauve-colored scarf of some sort. She took one last drag off her cigarette, exhaled it quickly and stubbed the butt into the ashtray.

"Hi, Chuckie," she said, her voice high and thin, too apprehensive to be enthusiastic. Having waited this long, she suddenly hastened to her feet, saying, "Gosh, Richie, why didn't you tell me he was coming? The place is such a mess." She gave a little smile, waiting for me to say it didn't matter, and patted her curlers into place.

I said, "Hello, Linda," and made no effort to put her at ease about the condition of her house. It was a goddamn disgrace.

Richie was speaking. He was telling Linda to get some coffee.

"You want coffee, Chuckie?" she said.

"No, it's all right."

"A beer," Richie said. "You want a beer?"

"No, nothing, Richie. I just want to talk with you for a minute."

"Get him a beer, Linda, and get me one, too."

We went into the dining room and sat down at the rectangular, early American-style pine table. Linda came scurrying in a few seconds later. She scurried to keep her feet from falling out of a pair of flattened old gray slippers. She had three bottles of Budweiser on a tray, which she set down in the middle of the table as if it was a birthday cake. She regarded the beer as it sat there, poised for our taking, and then realized she had not brought any glasses.

"Oh, my God." She giggled, holding the side of her face, and ran back into the kitchen. She reemerged a moment later, gripping three glasses from the insides with her fingers.

She plunked one glass down in front of Richie and one in front of me and then took one to her own seat, across the table from her husband.

"You want her here?" Richie said.

Linda looked anxiously at me. She could not have been more than twenty-eight or twenty-nine, but on that particular day she could have passed for forty. Despite the excruciating summer heat that we had been having, her skin was pale and wan. She was as skinny as an African poster child. The seat of her slacks was baggy over her pencil-thin buttocks and her jersey hung wide at both shoulders, exposing the narrow little straps of a bra, whose purpose, I guessed, was more traditional than functional.

"I think she's got an interest in what's going on," I said, and she looked immensely grateful.

"So," she said, her eyes wide and hopeful now that the threat of expulsion had passed, "you got any good news for us?"

Richie rolled his eyes and snapped, "How's he gonna have any good news? He just got started on the goddamn case." Turning to me as if he had just rid my path of vermin, he said, "So, Chuckie, what did you find out?"

"You get a letter from the DA today? Phone call, any contact at all?"

"Nothing. I haven't heard from nobody. Why? Why would the DA contact me?"

"He's asking for a judicial inquest into Fitzy's death."

I showed him a copy of the letter to Judge DeSantis from the district attorney. He read it out loud and when he was done he looked up in confusion.

"It means they're going to hold a hearing to determine whether there's sufficient evidence to seek a criminal indictment from a grand jury."

Resentment flooded Richie's face. "Against me?" he said, holding his hand to his chest.

"That's right, unless you can think of somebody else the district attorney might be after."

Husband and wife exchanged looks. The fear that welled up in Linda's eyes seemed to give Richie strength. It made him mad.

"But they haven't even finished the goddamn departmental investigation. Nobody's even talked to me yet."

I shrugged. "They're two different things, Richie. As far as the departmental goes, you're going to be cleared. I have that on good authority. But the inquest —well, that's something the DA can do whenever there's a death caused by external means. Usually they don't bother unless there's something suspicious involved, and in your case there's an autopsy report done by the county medical examiner. I read it yesterday afternoon and it says the bullet that killed Fitzy entered the side of his head. The implication is that he was facing away from you when you fired."

"I told you, he was coming out the window." Richie glared at me and suddenly leaped to his feet. "Jesus Christ, I was just doing my goddamn job and now they're trying to treat me like I'm the criminal."

Linda started to cry. "He was just doing his job," she sobbed.

I took a sip of beer and told them both to calm down. Richie wanted to rave on for a while and I had to say, "If this is the way you're going to act during an inquest, you can probably kiss both your job and your ass goodbye. They're going to think you're a hotheaded kid who panicked the first time he was in a crisis situation and started firing his gun at anything that moved."

Richie gripped the back of his chair. "Why they doing this to me? Can you just answer that?"

"My guess," I said, finishing the beer, "is that you're caught in the middle of a game of politics that doesn't really concern you."

"Politics? You mean my brother-in-law?"

"Yes."

"What's he got to do with it?"

"Association. Unfavorable association. His family mixed up in something unsavory, it looks bad in the papers even if he didn't have anything to do with it, which I'm not a hundred percent sure is the case."

"What do you mean by that? Jimmy didn't have nothing to do with this thing."

"Richie, you've got a lot of people working for you in a lot of different ways. You've got friends you don't even know about yet. One of those friends has been looking into your departmental file. Apparently it raises some interesting questions about how you got hired and how you happened to get the assignment you did."

Richie turned to his wife for assistance, but it was a wasted effort. The look on her face brought back my memory of her as a child, her eyes, nose and mouth pinched in abject fear that she was going to be called upon to speak, think or make a decision. Richie gave up on her so quickly that I knew his attempt to get help from her had merely been a reflex action. He sat down in his chair and brought out that sheepish grin of his, the one I had seen when I asked about the payment from Lanny.

"Sure. He helped me out. He's my brother-in-law, for God's sake."

"Richie." I spoke his name the way a schoolmaster would. I let him see I was losing patience. "I can't possibly help you, I can't even come up with a line of defense, if you keep holding things back."

"I'm not holding nothing back," he protested. "This is something you never asked me about before."

"Okay, now I'm asking. Tell me everything Jim Ryder has done to help you with respect to the police force."

Richie licked his lips. He folded his hands on the table in front of him. "I was trying to get on—you know?—and I was having trouble with the test. The written test. Jim tried to help me, but that wasn't enough. So finally he got this guy to tutor me."

"Tutor you? How?"

"Jim had the guy give me a copy of the test ahead of time. Go over the answers with me, sort of."

"That's how you passed?"

Richie DelVecchio hesitated before shaking his head. "I knew what I was supposed to say, but I just froze up."

"I don't get it, then. How did you finally pass?"

"The last test I took, every time I didn't know an answer I left it blank. The grader, he filled in all the multiple choices for me. Then after that, Jim just made sure I got one of the openings, that was all. I mean, I passed all the physical stuff beautiful."

"And the patrol car assignment you had—was that something else you asked Jim for?"

"Yeah."

"You didn't ask for it because it was easy, did you?"

Richie DelVecchio drew himself up indignantly. "Shit, no. That's not such an easy assignment. You got burglaries there, you got the hospital."

"So why did you want it?"

Richie cleared his throat. He looked at his wife and then he looked back at me. Finally he spread his hands wide. "I heard it was good for tips."

"Jees," I said. "No problem, then. Any judge will understand that."

14 City councillors in Portshead do not have individual offices. The council president does, a corner room off the council chambers, but it is of no particular quality. Outside his office is a room with four desks and eight incoming and outgoing correspondence boxes. For all that the room is used, the correspondence boxes might as well sit alone on the floor. A single secretary serves all nine members of the council. She sits in a third office, a reception area, which bears the imprint of having been inhabited for nearly thirty years by the same person. Like the offices themselves, the council secretary precludes rather than ensures privacy.

It was for that reason that I went directly to Jimbo Ryder's home for our second meeting. It was an unpretentious, fifty-year-old structure, shielded from the street by a couple of sturdy oaks that had probably been planted when the house was built. The yard could have used more grass, but then the kids would not have had such a good time playing on it. The neighborhood was the sort where everyone knows the names of everyone else's children, and toys are as likely to be left out on the sidewalks as brought home.

I arrived about eight o'clock on Friday night. The light was beginning to fade and there was the warm, almost cozy smell of simmering tomato sauce seeping from the house. When I knocked, Jim answered and I had the opportunity to watch his usual affable manner go into a distinct tailspin as he realized who was standing on his porch. Instead of inviting me in, he came outside.

"Gosh, Chuckie, is this important? Loretta's about to put dinner on the table."

"I tried to time it so that I'd be sure to catch you after you'd eaten."

Jimbo looked at his watch. "The game's on in a few minutes."

"Who's pitching?"

"I don't know."

"Good, then I guess you don't have any money on it and can spend a few minutes worrying about some other stuff."

I grinned when I said it, but Jimbo's silence gave me a good indication he did not like the way I was talking to him.

"Richie told me how he managed to make it onto the police force, Jim."

Now he decided to make a joke. Snickering, he said, "It took some doing, I'll tell you that. But so what?"

"So it was all well and good while the administration thought you were playing ball, Jim. Now that they think you're not, what's to prevent them from asking a few well-placed questions when Richie's under oath and on the stand? I'm just telling you because you could find yourself in some fairly hot water."

"How so?"

"Look, Jim, if this thing goes to hearing, one of the issues I expect to come up is whether Richie is a competent police officer who reacted the way a competent police officer should. Our defense is going to be considerably diminished if it can be established that Richie isn't even qualified to be a police officer in the first place. If the DA establishes that, Jim, it's going to show you guilty of nepotism, violation of the civil service system, maybe corruption, and certainly dishonesty. I've been thinking about this ever since I heard about the inquest, Jim, and no matter what, I just can't shake the conviction that the stuff they have on you is all they want to prove in any event. If there's no need to discredit you, there's no need to fry poor simple Richie."

Jimbo walked along the porch to a window box where a single geranium wilted in the thick evening air. He fingered its petals and they broke off into his hand. "So what can I do now? The matter's been set for inquest; you can't stop that."

"It hasn't been set yet, Jim. That's what I'm doing here. I'm convinced that if you could only explain to Mr. McLaughlin that you really don't want his chair up there in City Hall, he could find a way to get Ferguson to put his request on ice, at least until the police department completes its own internal affairs investigation. Once the department comes out with a clean report, hell, the DA could use that as a basis for backing out of the inquest altogether."

Jimbo kept looking at the red petals in his hand. "I'll think about it, Chuckie, I really will. Give me a day or so and I'll get back to you." Suddenly he threw the petals down and turned to me with his classic big grin. "Now I've got to get back inside or I'll be looking for a room to rent in some boardinghouse."

15 The woman I took to the Brandons' on Sunday night was named Gail Sanders. She was tall, dressed well and had a lovely walk, so that she gave the impression of being more attractive than her slightly elongated features would otherwise have allowed. I liked her because she screamed in bed. Not ear-piercing screams, but long, loud moans that told you if you touched her just a little bit longer, or a little bit deeper, or a little bit harder, she was going to melt like butter. She was also, I felt, the perfect date to bring to the home of Lanny Brandon. She worked for a small firm in Boston as an entertainment law attorney and was a consummate movie buff who actually cared who people like King Vidor and Raoul Walsh were. She had one other thing in her favor. She did not come from Portshead and knew nothing of Lanny's past.

The only drawback to taking Gail was that I had to go into Boston to get her, which meant that I had to get dressed in the six o'clock heat. By the time I reached the Back Bay apartment in which she lived, my shirt was plastered to my body from contact with the car seat. Gail, on the other hand, looked so absolutely ravishing that I wondered what I was doing wasting her on a dinner with people whom I had almost no interest in seeing.

She was wearing a plain black cocktail dress with a simple white silk belt that hung from one hip like a bell cord. She wore her brown hair up to expose a pair of exquisite emerald earrings, and the effect was stunning. It somehow made her profile as noble as that on an Egyptian coin.

The Brandons greeted us at the door to their house, Alicia's arms tightly about her husband's waist, and I handed over a bottle of California Cabernet. I had stopped at a package store on my way into town and, knowing very little about what I was buying, had asked the storekeeper to bring me a single bottle of his best California wine. He pulled something called Merlot out of the refrigerator and when I asked if it wasn't unusual to chill such a deep red wine, he shrugged and told me most people like their wine chilled. He said that nobody heeded the old taboos about reds and whites anymore and I believed him. It was only when Gail got in my car and found the bottle perspiring in a paper bag on the floor that I learned the packie clerk had known even less about wine than I had. Gail made me stop at a place near her apartment and picked out the Cabernet for me.

Lanny, who seemed to know about that sort of thing, assured me she had made a good choice. "It'll go perfectly with our roast," he announced, holding it up to the light admiringly.

The Brandons took us out to the pool for cocktails and I found myself in the position of feeding introductory lines to everyone. "Lanny and Alicia have just bought this house. . . . Yes, Alicia's from LA; that's where they met. . . . Gail's on one side of the movie business and, Lanny, I guess you're sort of on the other. . . ."

Lanny said it was interesting that Gail was involved in entertainment law, but he made no attempt to follow it up by asking what sort of things she did. From that point on he was polite, but he seemed almost preoccupied with his own thoughts; and since I had expected that we were going to spend the evening talking about movies and the like, I was at a loss when large gaping holes suddenly appeared in the conversation. Alicia, despite having been the instigator of this little affair, did not immediately appear to be under any compulsion to put everyone at ease, although she seemed intensely interested in Gail and several times I caught her openly studying the taller woman. For her part, Gail held up extremely well. Once she looked at me questioningly, as if to ask if she had done something wrong, but I only smiled back to indicate that I was having the time of my life.

"How's the case coming, Chuckie?" Lanny asked after we had been standing silently and shaking our glasses for some minutes.

"Oh, slowly, Lanny, slowly. It's becoming a much bigger deal than it should be and I don't quite understand why. You haven't figured out what Fitzy might have been doing here yet, have you?"

"Sure. He was trying to rip me off." He said it without humor.

"Then why didn't he, Lanny? Have you figured that one out yet?"

"Must not have found what he was looking for."

"No, I guess not."

When we went inside, the table was set with liver pâté and French bread. My wine was open and breathing next to the place where Lanny took his seat. There was also a bottle of white and I studied the label so I would remember what kind it was. It said Stony Hill Chardonnay. There were two wineglasses in front of each person's plate.

Alicia produced a large glass bowl of salad, made with a mustard dressing she said she had copied from Trader Vic's. While we made our way through the salad, Alicia brought in a first course of bluefish amandine and Lanny took the opportunity to pour us all some of his wine. When the roast came we got into the red and by that time the gathering had loosened up about as much as it was going to.

Gail tried a story about a client of hers, a concert promoter who wanted to produce a new rock-and-roll act. She had gone with the promoter to review the act in a small Cambridge nightclub with open mike auditions.

"My client hadn't told me anything about the act except that the guy was a unique talent. Well"—she started to laugh and had to pause to cover her mouth —"he came out on stage and he was just the biggest slob I've ever seen. He must have weighed two hundred and fifty pounds, with a great big fat belly that he couldn't even keep in his shirt. He was balding and the hair that he had was going every which way. He wore a print shirt that might have gone okay with a plain-colored pair of pants, but instead he had on checked pants that couldn't have gone with anything God ever made."

Lanny smiled absently, but Alicia looked interested as Gail went on. "Naturally, the audience began to stir the moment they saw him, because they couldn't imagine what he was going to be like. He had a guitar with him and he started to play and I thought he played real well. He opened with sort of a ballad and the first few chords were beautiful, but just as he started to sing, somebody suddenly shouted out, 'Nice shirt.' The singer stopped in midword and froze. Only his little beady eyes were moving and when they settled in the heckler's direction the singer said, real quietly so that everyone in the place was on edge, 'You don't like my shirt?' "

"Oh, no," said Alicia, and Gail nodded.

"I thought I was going to die with embarrassment. There must have been ten seconds that went by before the heckler yelled back, 'No.' Everybody in the crowd tittered, but my heart just went out to this poor guy up on the stage, until, all of a sudden, he ripped the shirt right off his body and shouted, 'To hell with it, then. Look at this for a while,' and, barechested, he launched into the hardest rocking number one man can possibly do with a guitar. He was bouncing and jiggling all over the stage and the audience went wild."

Alicia looked at me and shook her head in astonishment.

"At the end of the song, while he's panting so much he can barely breathe and his great big belly is heaving up and down, he says, 'You like my pants?' and everyone yells back, 'No.' So off come the pants and right into the next song he goes, wearing nothing but a pair of that bunch-'em-up underwear, black socks and black ankle boots. The third song, the boots come off. The fourth, the socks. He starts the fifth song with nothing on but those Jockey shorts and everybody in the place is yelling, 'Take 'em off,' but he keeps them on until the very end and then he suddenly spun around, pulled the shorts down with his thumb and flashed his big hairy behind before walking off the stage."

"Did your client sign him?" Alicia asked.

"No," Gail said, cutting into her potato. "It only seemed to be a five-song act."

We all laughed, and there was a moment when it looked as though the mood of the party was going to pick up, so I tried involving Lanny again. "Who does your legal work, Lanny?" I asked.

"Hmmn? Oh, well, I really haven't had much need for any."

Gail said, "Chuck tells me you wrote *The Fortunemaker.*"

"Yes. Yes, that's right. I didn't do the final treatment, though."

"That was Paramount, wasn't it? You must know Irv Wasserman."

"Irv? Ah, no, not personally."

"But that's who you must have dealt with if you sold him the rights to your property."

"Actually, my agent did all that."

We were rescued from more silence by Alicia. "What sort of work do you do with films, Gail?"

Gail held up her finger until she had finished chewing her potato enough to swallow it down. "The financing aspect of it mostly. We had a client recently who had put together a wonderful documentary about all these train derailments that have been taking place in the South. Cars filled with poison gas tipping over, that sort of thing. The client became convinced in his own mind that it's the old sixties radicals who are behind it. The Weather Underground turned environmental vigilantes, if you will. He couldn't prove it, he couldn't even come close, and so the documentary sort of wandered without an ending. We convinced him to turn the idea into fiction and created a limited partnership of investors willing to put up the money he needed. Now we're trying to negotiate a contract of sale with ABC. We're hoping they'll make it into a television movie."

"Oh, how exciting. Do you do that kind of thing often?"

Gail smiled, pleased that Alicia was interested. "We're doing a lot of work with an Australian film company right now, trying to sell their distribution rights in the U.S. The problem we're finding there is that it doesn't cost the Australians enough to make a movie. We tell people in this country we've got an Australian movie that was made for two million dollars and they think it must not be any good."

Alicia nodded. "But it must be so much cheaper to make movies in Australia," she said. "They don't have union costs, union restrictions."

Gail said that was exactly right. "Without unions they can shoot a movie in half the time it would take a studio in this country, at less than half the price; but we have a hard time convincing people of that."

The conversation went on through dessert and coffee and tulip glasses of B&B, but Lanny almost never joined in. He listened, he answered questions when they were addressed to him, but he did not volunteer any information. By the time the table talk worked itself around to a discussion of the relative merits of life in Southern California, a subject about which I knew precious little, only Gail and Alicia were speaking. I looked at my watch and announced that it was time to get Gail back in town because we both had to get up in the morning.

Later, as we were driving home, I asked Gail what she had thought. "I think," she said, leaning across the console and putting her head on my shoulder, "that she is bright, charming, beautiful and very, very nice."

"And Lanny?"

"I think," she said after a moment, "that if Lanny made all his money in Hollywood like you said, then I'm the Queen of Siam."

16 Davida tracked me down at Gail's apartment on the Monday morning following dinner at the Brandons'. "The court just called on the DelVecchio matter," she said. "The inquest has been calendared to start a week from tomorrow and Judge DeSantis himself is going to preside."

I asked her how she had found me and she said that Mrs. Brandon had called to thank Gail and me for our charming company and superb choice of wine. She said that when the call came in from the court she had gone through my address and phone list until she had found a woman whose first name was Gail. I told her she was worth her weight in gold and she pretended she was insulted.

When I hung up on Davida I called Jimbo Ryder at his sales office. The moment he came on the line he started apologizing. He said he'd been meaning to call me all weekend, but just one thing after another had come up. Without giving me a chance to speak, he said, "Listen, Chuckie, I've given this thing a great deal of thought. A great deal of consideration. It's the toughest decision I've ever had to make, I want you to know that. I spent a lot of sleepless hours the past couple of nights weighing my conscience about this whole situation. . . ."

"I guess that means you decided not to talk to McLaughlin," I interrupted.

Jimbo hesitated. "I can't do it right now, Chuck, not just yet. If you can hang in there for another month or so, everything will be different and I can do whatever you like. But right now there's too much at stake and the timing's all wrong. Can you understand me, fella?"

"It's too late anyhow, Jim. I've just learned that the inquest has been set for next week."

"Well"—and here Jim cleared his throat—"in that case, let me try running this by you. I talked to this friend of mine who's an attorney, my own attorney. Only to get a different perspective, you understand. But I thought he had some pretty good ideas. He wondered if it wouldn't be wise to go for a temporary restraining order. Try to stay the proceedings at least until the police report comes out. He felt, and I have to agree with him, that the longer we can delay this thing, the better off we are."

"Don't tell me you were talking to Artie Broderick, Jim."

"Artie? No, no—it wasn't Artie at all."

"It doesn't make any difference. It's not available."

"Ehh? What's that? What's not available?"

"The TRO. I researched it already. The inquest is a quasi-judicial hearing ordered by the court itself. I'm not going to be able to get the court to issue an order temporarily stopping itself from doing something it has already decided to do. Besides, since it's only an investigatory hearing, it's not considered as being something that alters the status quo."

"Mumbo jumbo," he said, so I tried to explain it another way.

"A temporary restraining order is designed to prevent somebody from doing something—that is, keep things exactly as they are until some subsequent determination can be made of the rights of the parties involved. In this instance, the very thing we're trying to stop is the hearing that's designed to determine those rights."

"Well, isn't there anything else you can do to keep the inquest from starting when it's supposed to?"

"I could try to go to the superior court on a writ of mandamus."

"And what's that?"

"It's an order from a higher court telling a lower court to do or not do something."

"I'd go for that, Chuckie."

"I've thought about it, Jimbo. It's pissing in the wind. I've got no good reason for asking the superior court to stop the district court from carrying out an investigation to determine if a crime has been committed."

"You've got the departmental investigation."

"They'd laugh me out of the courtroom. It's not worth it."

"You talking about the cost? Because if it's money you need . . ."

The offer surprised me. It made Jimbo Ryder's failure to cooperate a little more baffling. "Where you gonna get the money?" I said.

He paused before answering. "Let's just say I have sources I can draw upon."

"Well, I'll bear that in mind, Jim, but right now everything is being taken care of. The problem's not with money but with time and exposure."

"What kind of time frame we looking at?"

"We start a week from tomorrow and we continue straight through until finished. Depending on how many days we go—and I wouldn't expect more than one or two—and how long it takes the judge to write up his report, Richie could be before the grand jury the week after next. Once that happens it's out of everyone's hands. The only thing anyone can do after that is convince the DA to put his office imbecile on the case if it goes to trial."

"I see. And where would the stuff about—you know—how Richie got hired and all . . . where would that come up?"

"Jim, to tell you the truth, I don't know. I've never been involved in anything like this before. About all I can say at this point is that if the case goes before the grand jury, and what you did comes out, Richie may not be the only person they return an indictment against."

The councilman did not speak for so long that I had to ask him if he was still hanging on.

He said, "All right, Chuckie, I can't do what you want, but I can give you something else you might be able to use if you're willing to try a whole different approach. Are you?"

"I'm willing to try anything that will work."

"Okay. Are you free tonight?"

"You want to come by here?"

"God, no. After this I don't want to be seen with you, I don't want to be heard talking with you, I don't want any contact with you except what's absolutely necessary. Got that?"

"If you insist."

"What I want you to do is go to St. Cecilia's about ten o'clock. Park in the back, right next to the vestry door. Shut your lights and leave your passenger door unlocked. If anyone you know sees you, take off, and I'll call you tomorrow. Otherwise, wait until I get there."

I almost started to say something smart, maybe remind him that this was, after all, Portshead and not East Berlin, but then I realized he was totally serious. The thought sent a curious spasm of pain through my stomach.

17 It was unusual, I thought, that Alicia Brandon had called to thank me for coming to her house for dinner. As the guest, some form of thank you had been my responsibility, and even though I had not had a particularly good time, I had intended to drop her a note in a day or so. Actually, I probably never would have gotten around to it, but I certainly felt under no compulsion to contact her within twelve hours. And yet when I got into the office a memo of Davida's phone conversation with Alicia was lying in the middle of my desk.

Perhaps what I should have done was throw the memo in the wastebasket. But there was a phone number on it and courtesy did seem to demand that I not just accept dinner, and thanks on top of it, without some sort of showing of appreciation on my part, and so late in the morning I returned the call.

Had Alicia not answered the phone herself, I might have hung up without identifying myself. But it was she who came on the line and we had a pleasant chat for a minute or so, during which time she said that she (presumably speaking for herself alone) hoped to see us (meaning presumably Gail and me) again soon. I said that I didn't know when Gail would be out this way again but that if she, Alicia, was ever downtown around lunchtime, she should give me a call. It was only a friendly offer, like those I extend two or three times a week to friends, clients and potential clients. I expected her to say that she would be sure to do so and leave it at that.

Instead she said, "Well, as a matter of fact, I have some errands I'm going to be running in that end of town today."

I took her to the Chowder House. It was not a particularly good place to eat, but it was, at least, accommodating. The lunch places within walking distance of my office consist of counters, bars, a muffin shop, Cubby's Corner and the Chowder House. The last was the only one to which I would have felt even remotely comfortable bringing a woman like Alicia Brandon.

We were seated by request in relative privacy in the loft section, where an old-fashioned fan hung from the ceiling and spun the hot air in rapid circles. Our table was covered with red and white checked oilcloth and it featured a bowl of small hexagonal soda crackers, which was left from one customer to the next. The

Chowder House was a revelation to Alicia, who pronounced the place delightful despite the fact that she looked as though she would have felt more at home dining at the Ritz-Carlton off the Boston Public Garden.

She was wearing a purple dress cut deep in front and tapered slightly at her hips. She had on a white sun hat with a white band and lavender high heels fastened by the thinnest of straps running across her Achilles tendons. It was a stunning effect, but if Alicia Brandon noticed all the heads that turned her way she gave no sign.

I decided right then that I liked her style and her attitude, and when she followed my lead by ordering a Heineken, I decided I liked her taste as well. On an impulse I toasted her as the most gracious woman ever to grace the graceful shores of our grateful city. She looked surprised at my bit of doggerel, but accepted it with aplomb.

"I think that's very diplomatic of you to say," she told me after she had tasted her beer, "especially when you're going out with a woman as attractive as Gail Sanders."

"Ah," I said, "but Gail is not from Portshead. She lives in Boston, where fine women come with the eight-hundred-dollar-a-month rents. Besides, I'm not going out with her in any sort of formal sense. You could count the number of times I've seen her on one hand."

"That's interesting. I would have thought you two would make a perfect match."

"Why?"

"Because I was impressed with her, I suppose."

"Does that mean you're impressed with me, too?" Had I been a third party at the table, I would have given myself a most quizzical look. It had not been my intention to be so forward with this woman.

She dropped her eyes to the table and began toying with the glass ashtray, sliding her fingers in and out of the corner grooves. "I'm interested in you," she said, and then she added quickly, "interested clinically, I mean. You're different from any man I've ever met before."

"Is that good or bad?"

"It just is." Seeing that such est-ian philosophy did not satisfy me, she made another effort to explain. "Here you are, Chuck, the local football hero, the attorney, the good-looking stud with the hot car and all the women chasing after him, and you've never had enough curiosity to leave home."

I had asked for it and I had gotten it. I felt paralyzed, as if I had been stung by one of those underwater sea creatures that numb your nerve ends when you touch them. Gradually I became aware that there was someone above me. Standing poised to take our orders, her pencil tapping against her green-striped bill pad, listening to every word that Alicia had just said, was our waitress, and our waitress was Joey Aiello's wife's sister.

She smirked at me.

"What would you like?" I said to Alicia, whose green eyes were still on me.

"Hmmn? I'll just have the shrimp salad."

"Louie or sandwich?" said Joey Aiello's wife's sister.

Alicia looked momentarily confused and I pointed to the pamphlet-sized menu that was stuck between the salt and pepper shakers. Alicia took the menu out and the waitress sighed audibly and tapped her pencil harder.

"I don't want any bread," Alicia said, "and I don't want any Louie dressing."

"What's Louie dressing? You get French, Russian, blue cheese or Italian."

"I don't want any dressing."

"Okay," the waitress said, implying that it was Alicia's funeral. "What do you want, Chuckie?"

Without looking up, I ordered a salad, blue cheese, and the scrod.

"What's scrod?" Alicia said.

"It's baby haddock, I think. I don't know, maybe it's baby flounder. I get them mixed up."

The waitress gave me no help. She leaned across the table to put Alicia's menu back and when her face was only a foot or so away from mine she turned and grinned wickedly at me.

"I'm sorry," Alicia said, watching the waitress move away. "I've embarrassed you. I forgot for a second that everybody in town knows you."

"It's a big town," I said defensively. "Ninety thousand people and everybody doesn't know me."

Just then a customer squeezed by us on his way back to his table in the corner. Alicia's hand shot out and caught him by the forearm.

"Excuse me," she said as he stopped. He tensed only until he saw who was hanging on to him. "Do you know Chuckie Bishop?"

The guy looked directly into my face, polite and yet wary. "Well, I know who he is."

I did my best to smile.

"You running for something now, Chuckie?" he said.

"No," Alicia said, and let go of his arm. "Thank you very much." She gave him her own smile, which was probably reward enough for blowing up Hitler's bunker, but it left him standing in the aisle in a state of perplexity.

"See?" she said to me. "Did I prove my point?"

The interviewee continued his trek across the floor and I watched the suds of my beer make little popping motions and disappear. "What is it you want from me, Alicia?"

"Oh, we'll come right to the point, will we? All right, I want you to be Alan's friend."

"Hey, I am his friend. I came to your house for dinner last night, didn't I?"

"You came because I asked you to, and he knew it. That's why he was so taciturn. It was like I was fixing him up with a date or something. We had the most awful fight after you left and he accused me of everything under the sun, but he didn't mean it. He was just mad because he thought I was trying to create a friend for him and he has too much pride for that."

"But he was right. That's what you were trying to do."

"And I denied it." She put her hand across the table and touched my own. Her eyes sought mine out. "I want you to call on him, Chuck. Maybe invite him to go into town for a baseball game or go to a bar somewhere and have a few drinks. He's a good man, Chuck. I know you two would really like each other if you only got to know each other better . . . and right now he needs somebody, Chuck. He needs somebody desperately and I'm worried about him." Her tawny skin was strained with the effort she was making to implore me, to will me to understand.

"Alicia," I said, and her fingers closed around mine. Long, cool fingers that sent a thrill running up my arm and into my chest. "We're both grown men. We're in our mid-thirties, for Chrissake. You can't go around planning friendships for us like we're little boys."

"There's something in it for you, Chuck."

My thoughts, which had been running on, came to a complete stop. "What's that?"

"Me."

She must have felt my hand go clammy. I tried to pull it away. She squeezed it tighter. Joined across the table, we might have been utterly alone in the world. Except we weren't. "Excuse me," a voice said, "but one of these plates is very heavy."

Joey Aiello's sister-in-law put the shrimp down in front of Alicia as we separated. She placed the scrod in front of me. "Heavy," she repeated.

We ate in silence, I with my eyes on my food, Alicia watching me from a distance that was much greater than the width of the table between us. The word "me." Somehow it had not been an invitation. It had been—what? An observation? An acknowledgment? She was not asking me to befriend her husband so that she and I could start an affair. She was telling me to take a particular job because it had a good location.

I finished my fish and drained the last of my beer. Alicia put her fork down.

"Well," she said, "are we ever going to talk again or are we simply going to sit here like a couple of lions devouring their kill?"

I tapped the corners of my mouth with my napkin. "I can't be Lanny's friend."

"Oh?" She tilted her head.

"He hasn't been honest with me. How can you be friends with someone who won't even tell you what he does for a living?"

"He's writing a book."

"Really? And he told me he made all his money as a screenwriter so I introduced him to my friend who's in the business and three-quarters of the time he didn't have the slightest idea what she was talking about."

"He didn't tell you he made all his money as a screenwriter."

"He did so," I insisted. "He said he wrote the screenplay for *The Fortunemaker.*"

"He did. He wrote the original screenplay. His agent sold it to an independent producer and the producer sold it to Paramount. Maybe it wasn't quite as great as you made it seem in your own mind, and maybe what he wrote doesn't bear much resemblance to what finally appeared in the movie houses, but that's to his credit, I'd say. Once Paramount got hold of it, the whole thing was rewritten by a couple of studio hacks and then the director tore apart what they wrote and filmed whatever came to him on a day-to-day basis. So what you ended up seeing was one man's conception of other men's interpretation of what Alan wrote. Still, he's listed in the credits right up there with everybody else. 'Based on an original story by Alan Brandon.' "

"And that's how he got all the money to buy the big house on Hamilton Street?"

"No, of course it isn't. But that's how he has enough courage to come home and write the novel he's had bottled up inside him for twenty years."

"But the money, Alicia—where did that all come from?"

Alicia took her napkin off her lap and threw it down on the table. "Oh, for crying out loud. It came from sandwiches, Chuck."

"Sandwiches?"

"Sandwiches."

"What's that supposed to mean, Alicia?"

"When Alan was going to graduate school, he had most of his classes at night and he earned money by working in a sandwich shop during the day. What he noticed was that nobody sold the good submarine sandwiches that he used to get around here. You know, the kind with the soft roll and the oil and all the vegetables. Even in the place he worked, which was a real popular place for all the SC students, the closest thing they had was a poorboy that they made up the night before and covered in Saran Wrap. Somehow he managed to convince the owner of the shop that he could put out a better product. The owner loaned him some money. Alan opened his own shop, and before long he had the best place on campus. He sold an interest to his old boss and used the money he got to open another shop in Westwood, near UCLA. When that made money he bought some trucks, hired the best-looking girls he could find and paid them ridiculously high salaries to drive around making fresh subs for people."

Alicia paused. "That's how we met. I was one of the girls he recruited." She paused again. "Eventually I became manager for him and then we started living together, and pretty soon after that we got married."

"All this while he was going to school?"

"He never finished the program he was in. He had to drop out because the sandwich business was taking up so much of his time. He kept thinking it was going to be a short-term thing, but he started doing so well that it didn't seem right to stop. He opened shops in Venice, Marina del Rey, Newport Beach, and every one that opened was successful. But what he really wanted to do was write, and in six years he only got one thing finished. That was *The Fortunemaker*, and he had started that as his master's thesis. He kept saying that if he only had time to write he knew he could put out something really good, really worthwhile. That was why when he got a good offer to buy him out, I talked him into accepting it. So now, if he wants, he can spend the next ten years not having to worry about anything but writing." She did not look overjoyed at the thought.

"And that's what he's doing home again?"

She nodded.

"I don't get it, then. Why didn't he tell me that before?"

"Oh, why do you think, Chuck? Because he wanted you to admire him, can't you see that? Can't you put yourself in his place? Try to imagine why he would come back to face the shame again. Do you think I wanted to come here? Do you think all my life I was waiting to move to some godforsaken town where the most visible sign of success is getting to double-park your car in front of City Hall? I don't have a friend or relative within three thousand miles of Portshead, Chuck, but I'm here because Alan needs to be, because he's got something to prove— that the little boy everybody talked about and made fun of is as good as any of the rest of you. But he's not. He's better."

Alicia Brandon burst into tears just as Joey Aiello's sister-in-law arrived to clear away the dishes. She bent low over the table and Alicia quickly covered her face with her hands. Our waitress's eyes focused on Alicia's diamond and her platinum wedding band. She straightened up suddenly, casting a glance of surprise at me. Then she slapped down a check and turned away, her face a mold of unforgiving contempt.

18 St. Cecilia's is located on the outskirts of Portshead Center. Its parking lot is behind the church and only large enough to hold early arrivals. It is shaded by twisted elms and maples and its surface is unevenly paved, with swells that resemble those you see at the drive-in. The church building sits back from a busy through street, but the entrance to the parking lot comes off a much smaller road which leads to a winding neighborhood of double-decker houses remarkable only for the consistency of lawn statues bearing the likeness of the Virgin Mary in a half-shell. The road separates St. Cecilia's from a tire shop and leaves the church occupying its own block of land between the shop on the one side and, on the other, a restaurant that specializes in breakfast and caters almost exclusively to the after-mass doughnut crowd.

Neither the restaurant nor the tire shop was open as I bumped my Firebird into the church lot at five minutes after ten. I backed the car into the space Jimbo had designated, pulled it in as far as I could so that I would not be visible to anyone from the road, cut my engine and waited.

The first thing I noticed was that there was almost nothing in the parking lot for me to look at. The darkness was broken only by various shades of shadow created by dim lights inside the church. The setting, bleak as it was, impressed upon me once again the seriousness of Jimbo Ryder's approach to what we were about to do. It was convenient and yet hidden, and since there was almost no reason why anyone would appear in the lot at this time of night, we were virtually certain to be alone. If Jimbo ever made it. My watch told me it was nearly ten-fifteen.

The blackness made the crickets' chirping seem loud and incessant. It was not an unpleasant sound and it brought back memories of the two weeks I had once spent at a YMCA camp on Cape Cod as a kid. The nightly journeys to the camp latrine had always been accompanied by crickets.

Fitzy had been supposed to go to the camp with me. Somebody from the neighborhood had gone the year before and had come back with wonderful stories that had inspired us as early as Labor Day to start making our own plans for going. My mother skimmed from the food money all winter and spring, and when we put what she had saved together with what I had earned from my paper route we came up with just enough to pay the tuition, buy the clothes and comic books I needed, and have some change left over for the camp store. Fitzy had saved nothing. He let me know the week we had to send in our reservations that he had decided a long time before not to go and had just forgotten to tell me. The memory filled me with sadness and in an effort to shake it off I forced myself to get out of the car.

Crickets and camp and the latrine had made me want to find a bathroom, anyway. The night was filled with likely spots and although I had a moment's hesitation about urinating on church property, my body let me know it was not to be held hostage while my mind considered the alternatives.

Standing at the rear of the car, close to the bushes alongside the vestry, I was in the middle of my task when I was startled by the sound of an engine close by. Headlights swung down and then came back up and over the hood of the Firebird. I adjusted myself and returned to my still open door as the newcomer's lights went off. Without getting back in the car, I closed my door enough to shut off the inside courtesy light.

My eyes were relatively adjusted to the dark and I could see that what was approaching me at an increasingly slow rate of speed was an older-model single-color Chrysler. I had expected Ryder to be in his station wagon and so I peered closely into the front seat to see if it was indeed he.

If so, then he was bringing along a friend, because there were two heads visible. But they were spaced only a few inches apart. The passenger was blond, young, female, and I suddenly knew instinctively, before I could even make out the face, that it was my daughter. She recognized me at almost the same moment and threw up her hands. There was a muffled cry that reached all the way to where I was standing and the Chrysler braked and then leaped forward. It spun hard into a pebble-splattering one-hundred-and-eighty-degree turn that rattled debris off my Firebird, and with its lights still off, shot out the way it had come.

Shaken by the encounter, I got back behind my wheel. Jimbo had said that if anybody saw me and recognized me I was to leave immediately. Did that include my own daughter? We had made no contingency plan for anything like that. Nothing like that had been anticipated. Jimbo Ryder, for all his propagation, did not have a fifteen-year-old daughter whose entire life was apparently spent parking in dark places.

As I sat there the vestry door opened and a figure stepped softly over to my car. Jimbo Ryder opened the door and got in. The instant it took him to sit down was bathed in the courtesy light.

"Damn," he said. "I should have told you to kill that one, too."

"It's all right. There's nobody else here," I said, and I realized at that moment that I was not going to tell him about Candy and her boyfriend.

Jimbo came out of his inner pocket with a crisply folded piece of white paper in his hand. He laid it on his knee and rubbed it flat. "You think they're going after Richie to embarrass me?"

"Yes, I do."

"What would you think if I were to tell you I had something here that would cause them far more embarrassment? Something we might be able to use for a deal. Would that be what you need? Would that help you out?"

"It depends, Jim."

"My God," he muttered, half kiddingly. "I've never met a lawyer yet I could get a straight answer out of." He stared through the windshield and continued to smooth the paper on his knee. "One of the things I do, Chuckie, is try to help some of the kids get summer jobs with the city. This is legit patronage. Everybody does this sort of thing. It's when you don't that you're in trouble.

"I got my neighbor's boy a six-week appointment in the cemetery this summer. He's about eighteen, nineteen, goes away to college, and he got a jump on everybody else because he was ready to work in May and they needed people, get the place ready for Memorial Day. He'd been working there a few weeks and one day I asked him how he liked it. 'Fine,' he says, 'but you know, it's kind of strange, some of the things go on out there,' and proceeds to tell me this very funny story about digging a grave and finding bones already in it. I didn't really stop to think about how this could be at first and I said, 'What do you do in that situation?' and he said, 'Oh, they just throw the old bones into the back of a dump truck and haul them away somewheres.'

"I laughed at the time, but later I kept thinking about that, Chuckie, and it really started to bother me. I mean, what's going on over there at the cemetery, they're digging up graves where people are already buried? Supposedly the whole cemetery is already filled. I know because we just appropriated money two years ago to create an annex over there on Peach Street. Only nobody wants to be buried on Peach Street. They want to be buried where everybody else is, down at Memorial.

"I thought, maybe these bones the kid was talking about were in family plots, but then I figured, what the hell are they doing throwing the old bones away if these are families that want to be buried together? No matter how you cut it, something wasn't right there, Chuckie. Wouldn't you agree?"

"Doesn't sound right."

"Yeah, that's what I thought. Now the committee that's in charge of what goes on at the cemetery is the Council Oversight Committee. It's a committee of the whole, which means all nine of the council members sit on it, but Brian O'Keefe is the chairman. Just for fun, I went through Brian's correspondence file one night when I happened to be alone in the council offices and I found this copy of a letter from him to a Mr. Woodruff in Vermont."

He lifted the paper off his knee and handed it to me. "Don't look at it now, for God's sake, Chuckie. You'll have plenty of time to read it when you get home. I can tell you basically what it says. I've been over it enough times. It says: 'Dear Mr. Woodruff: As chairman of the appropriate committee, and so forth and so on, I have been asked to respond to your recent letter to the Portshead City Council regarding your most unfortunate experience at the Portshead Memorial Cemetery last September.' The letter was written in January, Chuckie. It goes on to say: 'Our investigation into the matter has uncovered the welcome, although regrettable, fact that a recording error in our cemetery management office caused a replacement monument ordered by another family to be incorrectly situated over the grave of your late mother.'

"There was some more bullshit in there about how it's his pleasure to report that the error has now been corrected. The new monument has been moved to its proper place and the old one has been found and put back where it belongs. The letter concludes this way: 'The stone was not badly damaged. We regret any inconvenience that may have been caused.' "

I looked at the piece of paper in my hand. I was wondering what I was supposed to do with it.

Jimbo Ryder stopped staring out the windshield and turned to face me. "Chuckie, I don't ever remember seeing that letter before. Maybe every time they brought it up I was in the men's room, but I never remember hearing about Mr. Woodruff and his complaint—and I sit on the goddamn committee that Brian says investigated the matter. If Woodruff's letter was addressed to the city council, it must have gone to our esteemed president, Alex Scurillo, who then passed it along to Brian. Alex and Brian, as you probably know, are not the worst of enemies. They only vie for the pleasure of prostrating themselves closest to the feet of their reverend mother, Mayor McLaughlin."

The clip of Jimbo's words picked up and a tight-lipped grin split his features. "Chuckie, you find out what happened to Mr. Woodruff last September, what he wrote to Alex and what Alex and Brian did after that, and we've got ourselves a juicy little scandal that will make our problems with Richie seem petty by comparison. They'll cave in faster than a three-dollar hat."

I did not want to appear ungrateful, but I was somewhat bewildered by Jimbo's enthusiasm. "It isn't quite what I was hoping for, Jim," I said.

"That's all right," he told me. "Nothing is. It's what you do with what you've got that counts." He reached over and gripped my shoulder and the guarded tone he had been using all night disappeared from his voice. "Hang in there, big fella. I'll call you when you come back to town."

"Back?"

"Sure," he said. "You'll be wanting to visit old Mr. Woodruff, won't you? Just don't tell him where you got that letter. Don't tell anybody."

I felt the letter with my fingertips. "Jimbo, this copy has punch holes in it."

"Well, of course it does. I took it right out of the file."

"Why didn't you make a Xerox and leave the file copy where it was?"

"Because there's no Xerox machine in the chambers, it was late at night, the copying room down the hallway was locked up, and I wasn't at all anxious to advertise what I was doing. But don't worry, I've made a copy since then for my own files and I expect you to return that one to me."

"Isn't anybody going to notice that it's missing?"

"Like who? You think anyone goes through these correspondence files unless they're looking for something specific? But you're right. I've been meaning to put the file copy back and I'll do it as soon as you return. When do you think that'll be?"

"Jesus, it's not going to take me more than a few hours up and back. I suppose I could try tomorrow."

"Excellent." Jimbo opened the door and started out of the car. "You're a good man, Chuckie. Pull this off and no telling what kind of things might work out."

The following morning I put in a call to Mr. Woodruff and invited myself up to see him. He was obviously an elderly gentleman and was not readily open to having a stranger come to call on him until I told him I was concerned about what was going on at the Portshead Memorial Cemetery and wanted the benefit of his experience.

"Oh," he said excitedly, "I've got plenty to say on that one," and less than an hour later I was on the road to Bellows Falls with the windows down and a tape deck full of Loggins and Messina, Jimmy Buffett, and Linda Ronstadt.

Henry O. Woodruff lived by himself in a green-shuttered cottage on twenty perfectly beautiful acres of land. The area immediately surrounding his house was a thick and closely trimmed lawn. In the back, beyond the four-sided clothesline, was a small vegetable garden, and then there was nothing but blond grass and green trees. He told me there was a stream back in a ways and seemed somewhat disturbed that I did not feel inclined to take the time to go see it. He gazed regretfully at his polished hickory walking stick as though convinced he had disappointed it.

Mr. Woodruff was a tall, exceedingly slim man with pale skin that had turned a healthy pink around his face, neck and hands from the sun. I guessed him to be in his eighties, which made his great height all the more remarkable. He must have towered over his contemporaries. His white hair was soft and fine and he wore it flicked across the top of his head in a style that had been universally popular when I was a boy.

The heat in Bellows Falls was nowhere near as oppressive as it had been in

Portshead, but it was still warm enough for me to want to keep out of the direct sunlight. Mr. Woodruff, however, came outside to meet me wearing flannel pants, a plaid wool shirt and a straw hat pulled down close to his wire-rim spectacles.

He gave me a brief tour of his house, which left me with the distinct impression that Mr. Woodruff was quite the hit of his town's senior social circle. "Take some of that," he ordered, pointing to a ring of lemon pound cake on the dining room table. "Clara Hipp made me that even though she knows darn well I don't like it."

I cut myself a piece and followed him around the house eating the cake, with one hand cupped below it to catch the crumbs I was spilling.

"She knows I don't like it, but she keeps making it because it's the one thing she does best," he said, settling into a rocker in front of his soot-scarred white brick fireplace.

"You're a lawyer down there in Portshead," he said, "and you want to know what I found when I went to visit my mother's grave."

I crammed the last of my cake into my mouth and nodded. He glowered at the yellow spots on the floor between my feet and did not resume his monologue until I had made an effort to pluck them up and toss them into the fireplace.

"Won't be long now till that gets burned," he said, and since it was only August I wondered if he was telling me to get the crumbs out of the fireplace. I chose to let the remark die.

"I was born in Portshead," Mr. Woodruff said. "My mother came over to this country with her family from England in 1892. She'd had a beau back there who was my uncle Fred, but it was my father who followed her over. They married and moved to Portshead, where I spent the first few years of my life, until my mother died giving birth to my sister, Amanda. Then my father moved us up here because he knew a widow who would take care of Amanda and me. Still, once every year we'd go down there, my sister and me—my father, too, when he was alive—and we'd visit the grave. Lately, though, my sister don't go so much because she's getting old and has the bum leg so she can't get around so good anymore, but I always go. Always visit the grave and straighten it out, like most everyone does.

"Well, sir, I went down there myself last—oh, when was it?—last September, to make sure the leaves was raked off and all because I knew winter was coming on, see, and I didn't want all that stuff just getting worn into the ground.

"I went straight to my mother's grave, as I always do, and when I got there I couldn't believe what I seen. Instead of that nice little stone that we had, there stood a much bigger stone with someone else's name on it. Mary Amalfitano, it said, and that wasn't my mother's name a-tall. I said to myself, 'My God, I can't be wrong about the location—I've been coming here nearly all my life.' I was just plain befuddled.

"So I went marching right up to the cemetery office and I started asking questions, see. Finally this chap that was the superintendent of cemeteries came in—whatever his name is, I've forgotten. Eye-talian fella.

"I said to him, 'Look here, I have a grave across the way. I don't know what number it is because I know the location, and the stone had my mother's name and so forth, so I never paid no particular attention to the number, but I just went over there and somebody else's marker is on that grave instead of my mother's.' He says to me, he says, 'Well, there's been some vandalism around here and some gravestones had to be replaced. Maybe somebody made a mistake.'

"I said, 'I don't see how that can be, because this person, this Mary Amalfitano, whose name is on the stone now, just died this year.' He sort of shrugged at me and said some new stones got vandalized along with the rest. So I said, 'Let me see your records,' because I was sure they must have some sort of records about who got buried where and I thought, how come this Mary Amalfitano's family that bought such a nice big stone don't know the stone's in the wrong place?

"Well, he brought out this stack of ledgers and they were all just a big mismatch with no order to them a-tall. I sat there for two and a half hours going through ledger after ledger and finally I come up with what I wanted. It was a lot card and it proved I was right. That was my mother's grave; it said so right on the card. I showed what I found to the superintendent and he said, 'Well, that grave's been sold to somebody else,' and he pointed out this other person's name."

The old man shook as he recalled the indignation of the moment. "I said to him, 'How can you put a grave up for sale when it's already been bought and paid for?'

"He said, 'You haven't paid for perpetual care,' and that made me really get hot under the collar because I know they don't do anything for perpetual care except cut the grass, which is what they do for all the graves anyway.

"I said, 'How much is perpetual care?' and he said, 'One hundred and twenty-five dollars.' Then I said, 'You mean if I don't pay one hundred and twenty-five dollars you can just sell my mother's grave to somebody else?' I said, 'If that isn't a hell of a note,' and I decided right then and there that I wasn't going to take this lying down. I left and I went directly to the mayor's office."

"Mayor McLaughlin?"

"That's the fella."

"Did you get in to see him?"

"I certainly did, and I raised a ruckus, too. I told him everything that had happened and he said he was sure it was all a mistake. He sent me to see the head of the cemetery board—you know who that is?"

One of the regulars at the Cubby's Corner morning coffee sessions was Jim Duffy, who was chairman of the cemetery board of managers. I suggested his name.

"He's the one," Mr. Woodruff confirmed, with a vigorous nod of his head. "I told him the story and I said, 'My mother's stone must have weighed two hundred pounds, which is too much for vandals to carry away. What do you s'pose happened to it?'

" 'Oh,' he says, 'I don't know. I don't know what could have happened to it.' He promised me he would find out, though, and he said he'd get back to me. So I came home here to Bellows Falls and I waited. When nothing happened I was stumped all over again. I remember I was thinking about it the night the first snow fell, worrying about where my poor mother's remains were if they put some other lady in her grave."

Mr. Woodruff gazed quietly into the dormant fireplace. "It's a funny thing," he said after a while. "I think of my mother as being this poor old woman, but she wasn't even twenty-eight when she died. A young person like that—hell, I think of people that age as being kids—she wouldn't be resting comfortably under the best of circumstances and I sure hated the idea of them putting somebody else in on top of her. If that's what they done."

Mr. Woodruff turned his eyes back to me. "So that very night I sat down and wrote a letter to the Portshead City Council. I figured I'd tried the mayor and I'd tried the supervisors of the cemetery, and I still didn't have any answers, so I thought I'd try just one more avenue and then I was going to the newspapers."

"Did you put that in your letter?"

"I sure did, and got a call right back on it, too."

"Who did you get a call from?"

"The Irish fella whose name you just mentioned—Duffy. He told me he'd been on the case all along and that sure enough, the Amalfitano stone had been put in the wrong place. I said to him, 'How come that fella at the cemetery told me the Amalfitano family had bought my mother's plot?' And he said, 'Oh, that was a bookkeeping error. Our workers reported to the secretary where they had put the Amalfitano stone and she thought that's where Amalfitano was supposed to be and just typed the name in on the lot card.' Duffy said I'd be getting a final response to my letter soon and by and by I got one."

"Is this the letter?" I asked, showing him what Ryder had given me.

Mr. Woodruff took his time and read it all the way through before answering affirmatively.

I said, "You wouldn't by any chance have kept a copy of the letter you wrote to them, would you?"

He got up from his chair. He did not spring up, but he rose lightly with just a little help from the chair's rocker and armrest. He left the room and when he came back he had three tissue papers of single-spaced typing on which he had chronicled all the events we had discussed. I asked him if there was a place nearby where I might be able to get a copy made and he waved his hand and told me to mail it back to him when I was done with it.

"I don't need it so much anymore now that I know my mother's where she's supposed to be and her stone's back where it belongs."

"Have you been back to Portshead to see for yourself? Find out where the stone was and how badly damaged it is?"

He was silent for a moment before he said no. He folded his hands and stared down into his lap. "I've been meaning to go all year, and I keep saying I'm going to do it, but somehow when the time comes I just can't seem to work up the enthusiasm anymore. It used to be something I looked forward to, but now . . ." His voice trailed off and he sighed. "I s'pose that one of these days I'll just have to make myself get down there again."

19 I had to wait for Sid to get off the phone and then I had to wait for him to jot down his time and a description of his conversation in the billing book. "What can I do for you, Chuckie?" he said. He had been a little cool to me ever since our initial conversation about the DelVecchio case. I, on the other hand, had scrupulously avoided discussing any aspect of it with him. Until now.

"I need some advice," I said.

He nodded and put down his pencil. He eased himself back into the confines of his chair and folded his hands over his stomach so that he was in a good listening position.

"We've got a judicial inquest into Michael Fitzpatrick's death coming up on Tuesday."

"So I hear. How's your client going to stand up?"

"Not well, I'm afraid. Richie DelVecchio appears to me to be a nervous, immature, perhaps hotheaded, less than fully bright kid who cheated his way onto the police force through the good offices of his brother-in-law the city councilman. The reason that he was at Lanny Brandon's house on the night Fitzy broke in was because he was taking gratuities from people on his beat. Lanny had paid him fifty bucks to keep an eye on his place for the week they were planning to be away.

"Richie saw a light in the house, stopped to check it out, was startled to see Fitzy coming through the window and panicked. Two shots. Fitzy bought one and the other just missed. So it looks like DelVecchio blew it. But who cares?"

"Mr. Ferguson, our esteemed district attorney, apparently cares if he's asked for an inquest."

"Sure. But why? It's not because anybody cares about Fitzy, that's for sure."

"Perhaps John Ferguson has a passion for justice." Sid's smile was sardonic. "But you think there's a political motive."

"That's what I think, Sid. You know that Fergie and the mayor are like that." I held up two fingers wrapped together. "The mayor is scared to death that Jim Ryder's coming after him, so he's trying to use DelVecchio to head him off. He's even had Chief Lyons withhold the release of the police department's own report because it exonerates DelVecchio. Finucci, who did the report, tells me he gave it to Lyons last Friday."

"How do you know it exonerates your client?"

"Because Finucci told me it does. And because Finucci didn't even bother interviewing DelVecchio. He just accepted what Richie put in his report and worked to make it stand up from there."

Sid said, "Okay, so you got yourself a political situation you didn't expect. What have you done about it?"

"I went to Jimbo Ryder and tried to get him to make an announcement that he was not going after McLaughlin's job."

Sid pressed his fingertips together and raised his eyebrows. "A good start," he said. "And what was Jimbo's answer?"

"He wouldn't do it. He gave me some information on some strange goings-on out at the cemetery and then he sent me up to Vermont to talk to a guy who discovered they'd sold his mother's grave to somebody else." I let out half a laugh. "Do you believe what he's trying to get me to do, Sid? He's trying to get me to extort the mayor of Portshead with a trade-off of scandals."

But Sid didn't laugh back. He believed it, all right. "You took the information Jim gave you, didn't you?"

"Yes."

"And you went up and you talked to that guy in Vermont?"

"I just returned this minute."

"And now you want to know what you're supposed to do next." Sid stared solemnly across his desk at me until I acknowledged that that was exactly what I wanted to know. "Sounds to me," he said, "like the obvious thing is to get yourself over to the cemetery and see if you can't learn some more about what's going on out there."

It was not what I was hoping to hear. "You think I should follow through with Jimbo's idea, then."

Sid got out his pocket watch and glanced at it. "Why not?" he said, getting to his feet, and I knew it was five o'clock. Dismissal time.

I stayed where I was. "Seems to me like a funny way of practicing law, that's all."

Sid abruptly sat back down again, perching on the very edge of his seat. He rested one arm on his desk and studied me. His bow tie, knotted as tightly now as it had been when he walked into the office in the morning, moved in and out, up and down under his chin. "Since when is the law a tangible object, Chuck? You've been hired as an advocate of your client's interests and sometimes that involves more than citing cases and filing pleadings. Sometimes it involves being a spokesman and a dispassionate representative and a compromiser. Now if you think this over and you decide that your obligation to your client can be restricted to your advocacy in the courtroom, that's fine. You do your research and examine your witnesses and make your objections and leave it at that. But there are times, Chuck, there are times when you don't want your client to go into that courtroom, and then it's your responsibility, your obligation, your duty to explore alternatives. I think this is one of those times."

I watched Sid get to his feet again and I knew that in a minute he was going to be out the office door and I was going to lose him. "Okay," I said, "suppose I explore these alternatives, Sid. Suppose I get something. How will that help me keep Richie DelVecchio out of court?"

Sid went over to the closet on the other side of the room. He got his blue seersucker suit coat down from a hanger and primped himself in the mirror on the back of the closet door. "You think your client may be technically guilty of a crime. Manslaughter, most likely. But you think he's being discriminatorily and unjustly singled out for punishment." He shut the closet door and went back to his desk, where he slid a few papers into his briefcase. "I'd say that one of the things you have to consider is whether there isn't some way that the interests of justice, as personified by the perpetrators of that concept, can be satisfied without your client unduly bearing the burden."

Sid walked to the door. He opened it, indicating he wanted me to pass through first.

"You're telling me to meet with the mayor," I said in what was really a question as I got up from my seat on the couch.

He waited until I was stepping by him and then reached up and put his hand on my shoulder. "I think that would be within the realm of good reason, Chuck. If you do meet with him, though, I'd like you to remember one thing. Your presentation of the case to the mayor is going to be considerably different from your presentation to a judge, but the principles are the same. Know your facts inside out, never ask a question to which you don't already know the answer, and always keep in mind that there's never been a client yet worth losing your ticket over. You all right?"

"All right."

"I'll see you tomorrow."

20

Were it not for the fact that it has been a cemetery for nearly two hundred years, Portshead Memorial would be a superb residential location. It is close enough to the beach to hold the smell of the ocean on any breeze out of the east, and yet it is little more than a mile from Portshead Center. One hundred and fifty-six thousand grave sites are spaced throughout its gentle green hills and nichelike valleys.

In the exact middle of Portshead Memorial are a maintenance garage and a green-roofed shed which functions as the cemetery's office. Over the door of the shed is a sign bearing a single word: "Superintendent." Next to the door is a second sign, giving the hours the office is open. On my first drive through the cemetery I noticed a big LTD standing outside the office. Its personalized license plate read "BUSTER."

The grave of Julia Woodruff, beloved wife of Charles and mother of Henry and Amanda, was easy enough to find once I figured out the numbering system. The stone was where it should be, but the top corner on one side was broken off. I ran my hand over the break and felt the uneven granite. The stone was thick enough so that it would have taken a strong blow to do anything more than chip it. It might have been hit with a hammer. Perhaps it had been dropped.

A man drove by on a sit-down mower. He was a grizzled man, slightly built, with thin, sinewy arms sticking out of a green army T-shirt. He wore sunglasses and a baseball cap without an insignia. His face was set in a half-scowl, as though he were trying to clear something caught in his back teeth.

I made an effort to flag him down, but he just stared at me. I had to step in front of his machine to get him to stop.

"Hey," he shouted over the noise of his engine. "You wanna get killed?"

"Good place for it," I said, grinning, but I guess he had heard such jokes before. He thought I was a jerk.

"Get outta the way," he said.

"Shut it off," I said, walking around the mower until I was next to him. He must have been used to taking orders because he did as I told him.

"What d'ya want?" he whined.

"I'm looking for the Amalfitano grave. It was supposed to be right here." I pointed to Julia Woodruff's grave.

The man on the mower mouthed the name on the broken stone. "That's Julia Woodruff's grave," he said.

"Yeah, and I'm darn mad about it, too. That's supposed to be where Mary Amalfitano is buried."

The man let out a breath of exasperation and dismounted by kicking his leg over the seat of the mower. "It's too fuckin' hot to do this," he said. "As soon as it hits a hundred we get to go home, but right now it's only ninety-fuckin'-six."

"You ought to move the thermometer," I said.

"Yeah." He walked up to the grave and stood on top of it. "She's not here. There's nobody here but Julia Woodruff."

I walked up next to him. "They moved the grave," I said.

To a passerby hearing our conversation, my statement would have been ludicrous. But it had no such effect on the professional cemetery worker standing next to me. He frowned and rubbed his jaw. "How long's it been since you was here last?"

"Last fall."

"Hmmn." He put his hands on his hips, raised up on his tiptoes and surveyed the area. He turned around and walked to the corresponding grave in the next aisle. "Here," he said, pointing down at the base of a much larger monument. "Here it is right here. Mary Amalfitano. Died last year. You were in the wrong aisle, mister. You shoulda went to this one."

I said, "Well, you move graves sometimes, don't you?"

He said, "Sometimes, but you was just in the wrong aisle." He got back on his seat and clattered away.

I walked over to the office, entering through a screen door. An L-shaped counter limited me to about twenty square feet of room. On the other side of the counter were two stocky men who sat facing each other over a two-sided desk. One of the men had on a short-sleeved white shirt and a tie. He was sipping coffee from a mug as he spun his chair in quarter circles. His companion was a little smaller in bulk and wore a dark gray shirt with an even hem to it. He gripped his elbows as he leaned forward onto the blotter that covered his portion of the desk.

"Hi," the smaller man said. "Can I help you?"

"I'd like to talk to somebody about buying a plot."

The man who had spoken got up and came to the counter. "I don't think we're going to be able to find anything for you at this facility, but we have many choice sites at our brand-new annex on Peach Street, if you'd be interested in considering that."

"Oh, c'mon," I said. "You must have something here. My wife and I have three generations of family scattered all over this place."

The man said he was sorry, but the Peach Street facility was all they had available. "Have you seen it since it opened? It's really very nice."

"Look, I refuse to take no for an answer. There must be some way I can get a plot here at Memorial. I'll pay extra if I have to."

The man with whom I had been speaking turned to the other. "How about it, Buster? We got anything for this gentleman?"

Buster put down his coffee cup and opened an oversized book. He scanned the first page and turned it over. "How many people?" he said.

"Just two."

"You and your wife?"

"Sure. Let the kids fend for themselves when the time comes."

He grunted and turned another page. "There may be a double you can have," he said without lifting his gaze from the page. "Check in with us tomorrow."

"Mind if I take a look at it as long as I'm out here?"

Buster raised his eyebrows. They moved considerably far because he was bald on top of his head and there was no natural border to stop the ripple of wrinkles once they started. "We're a little short on manpower today. Everybody took vacation days because of the heat wave we been having."

"Oh, hell, I don't mind going out there myself."

"Well, I'm not sure which one I can give you. There are several that we've been in the process of repurchasing from people who aren't going to use them, but it will take me a while to find out which ones have been cleared. I don't got the time today. Come by tomorrow and we'll see what we can do for you."

"You sure you'll have something, now? I don't want to waste a morning off from work if you're not going to have anything for me."

"I'll have something for you, don't worry."

"Tomorrow, then," I said, and started my retreat to the door.

Buster stopped me with one more question. "By the way, you gonna need a monument?"

I tried to remember what I had said. "Uh, no. Not yet. This is for future use."

Buster grunted and went back to thumbing through his book.

21 There was no listing for Mary Amalfitano in the Portshead phone directory. There was no listing for an Amalfitano at all.

I went to the office of the *Portshead Sentinel* and asked to look at the papers from the week following the date of Mary Amalfitano's death as it appeared on her stone. The *Sentinel* told me they did not keep copies for more than a year and sent me to the public library, the one with the lawn on which Jimbo Ryder's family liked to romp about. They were not there the day I was. If they had tried their happy gambol on that particular day they would have died of heat prostration. I pictured how that would look on a campaign brochure, all the Ryders piled up like so many war dead on the library lawn.

Strangely enough, there were a score of people in the non-air-conditioned library. I was not even the only one looking at microfilm, which turned out to be fortunate because the librarian set up a floor fan for our use. It took me about twenty minutes of hand rolling the microfilm through a viewer until I found the obituary of Mary Amalfitano. She was, it said, survived by a sister, Rosa Grasso, of the same Pringle Street address as the deceased. She was also survived by numerous nieces and nephews, only one of whom, Nicholas, was mentioned as living in Portshead.

Pringle Street is an exceedingly narrow lane which was once the center of an almost entirely Italian enclave. It had gained more notoriety than it rightly deserved when one of its denizens, a certain Buttons LaRusso, was shot dead in a Mafia-style execution in the basement of a nightclub in Providence. Since Buttons had no known source of employment, drove a Continental and had not one but two pinkie rings, everybody naturally assumed they knew who he was and what he did.

People park on both sides of Pringle Street, their cars facing in either direction. Driving the street consists of a series of spurts and brakes as you dodge the parked cars and outmaneuver the traffic coming toward you. The rule is to make the other guy relinquish the road. The corollary to that rule, at least at one time, was that if you saw Buttons's Continental coming toward you it was best to pull up on the curb as quickly as possible.

Almost all the houses on Pringle Street contain gardens and many of the yards are dominated by stakes of tomato vines. The Grasso-Amalfitano house had no tomatoes, but it had a brilliant bed of azaleas beneath the front window.

I parked the Firebird with two wheels as far up on the sidewalk as I could and went to the door. A dark, unshaven man answered my knock. He had the damaged look of someone suffering from a massive hangover, but given the afternoon hour it was possible he had just awakened from a nap.

"Yeah?" he said. He was quite a friendly fellow.

I introduced myself and handed him one of my cards. It obviously hurt him to look at the print in the light. He flipped it over and handed it back. He must have thought it was my only one.

"You wouldn't be Nicholas Grasso, would you?"

He instantly became suspicious. "Yeah," he said, waiting for more.

"I wonder if I could speak to your mother for a minute. It concerns her sister Mary."

"Mary? She's dead."

"Yes. That's what I want to talk to her about."

Nicholas made an unseemly noise and closed the door, not all the way, but almost. I remained where I was until two sets of footsteps sounded and the door was pulled open again.

Rosa Grasso was a diminutive woman. Her dress was black and so were her stockings, but she wore a full-length sleeveless apron with a fairly cheerful pattern of red and green apples. She was quite nervous about having a lawyer at her door.

"Yes," she said, wiping her hands on the corner of her apron. "I Rosa Grasso."

Since Nicholas made no effort to give my name, most likely having forgotten it, I introduced myself. She took my outstretched hand, but she gave an embarrassed little side glance to her son when she did so. Nicholas leaned heavily on the doorknob. He was having trouble remaining on his feet and was only interested in what I wanted.

"Your sister Mary died recently, is that right, Mrs. Grasso?"

"Ya, ya, that's right." Again she glanced at her son, who had now closed his eyes.

"Did you purchase a grave for her?"

"Why?" Nicholas demanded, suddenly pushing himself off the knob. "Is there something wrong with the grave?"

"Well, I don't think so, Mr. Grasso. There just appears to have been a mix-up a few months back with a plot in which a client of mine has an interest." It was roundabout, but not untruthful. We lawyers do not ever want to be untruthful. "Are you familiar with the mix-up I'm referring to?"

"What mix-up?"

"Would it be possible for me to take a look at the deed you have to Mary Amalfitano's plot?"

Nicholas Grasso thumbed his nose. I spelled trouble to him and he was doing his best to rally himself mentally enough to deal with me. "I don't know. Maybe I should have my own lawyer here."

I could have said all kinds of mean things, since the man was about as likely to have a lawyer as a yacht, but I said only, "All I want to do is check the lot number," and after mulling over the possible ramifications, Nicholas Grasso went and got the deed.

As soon as he left, his mother invited me inside the house. "You like something to eat?" she said.

I said no, thanks, and she repeated me. "No, thanks." A tangerine appeared magically in her hand. It must have come from her apron. "You want tangerine?" she asked, and I smiled and shook my head. The tangerine vanished. She showed me a tentative smile that evaporated as soon as her son came hurrying back into the room with the plot deed in his hand.

"Here," he said, thrusting it at me. "This what you want?"

The lot number listed was 247. It was the same as Julia Woodruff's.

"Did anyone from the cemetery contact you, either of you, about transferring Mary Amalfitano to another grave site?"

Mrs. Grasso began trembling and turned to her son for help.

"Hey," he said belligerently. "They can't do that. My mother paid for that grave."

"I was just asking."

"And I was just telling you. They can't do that."

Mrs. Grasso looked at her son with relief. She was clearly proud that he was handling me so well.

I said to Nicholas, "So as far as you know, this deed is correct?"

He plucked the deed from my hand. "What's wrong with it? Right here it's signed by Buster Vizarelli and he's superintendent of cemeteries, isn't he? He's the one who sold it to us."

"Is Buster a friend of yours?"

Grasso shrugged. "I know him, yeah. Matter of fact, that's how we got the lot. He only had a couple left, see?"

"Did you have to pay anything extra?"

Mother and son exchanged glances and when Mrs. Grasso began wringing her hands, Nicholas turned on me fiercely. "It's none of your damn business what we paid."

"Oh, I'm very sorry. I didn't mean to cause you any embarrassment."

"You didn't embarrass us," Nicholas said defensively.

"Then I'm sorry to have troubled you and I thank you for your time."

Mrs. Grasso nodded politely. "Thank you," she said. Nicholas nodded, but in a different way. Without speaking, he was saying okay, now get out of here.

As he was pushing the door shut behind me, I stopped. "One more thing," I said. "Was the monument in place when Mary was buried?"

Nicholas thought back. "Yeah," he said. "Yeah, of course it was. Buster saw to that himself."

"You mean he arranged for the stone?"

"He got us a deal on it. He had me and my mother meet him down at this monument dealer and he had her pick out the one she wanted. He took care of everything for us."

"What was the name of the dealer, do you remember?"

"Triple A Monuments. A-A-A."

"I guess you were satisfied, huh?"

"We were satisfied."

"Do you go out there to the cemetery often?"

"Who, me?" Nicholas said. "What would I go out there for?"

"How about you, Mrs. Grasso—do you go out there very often?"

"No." She shook her head. "No, I no like go out there." She shivered as the idea went through her mind, and promptly blessed herself with the sign of the cross.

22 At seven o'clock I closed up my office and headed down to Blanchard's Tavern for a beer. I poked my head in the door and recognized Giacomini sitting by himself. By the looks of him, he had been sitting there for some time.

"Oh, no—my favorite fuckin' lawyer," he said, and waved me over to his table. I had to sit down with him because we were friends. We were not the sort of friends who ever called each other, but we shared some history and that required acknowledgment. If I had not sat down with him he would have said it was because I thought I was too good for him.

Giacomini was in the moving business. He worked for one of the large interstate companies as a local loader and unloader. If the move was within a hundred miles of Boston he would do both. It was a good job for Giacomini because he took pride in his ability to lift things. Unfortunately, he had somehow developed the mistaken idea that the moving trade was the fount of an endless array of fascinating stories.

He spent a whole bottle of Bud telling me how easy it was for a mover who was getting paid by the pound to bump weight by loading up with everything from rocks to scrap metal before placing the moving van on the scales. "You like to catch the ones where the government or some company is paying for the move. Then the people who are moving don't give a shit what their stuff weighs."

"Sure. What would they care?"

"My company's got a lot of little tricks it uses," he said, grinning wickedly over a second bottle. "They put this provision in their tariff, says we won't be responsible for any items of extraordinary value unless the customer writes 'em all down before we load. The government said we couldn't do that. It said there wasn't no way to describe what an article of extraordinary value is and besides, the government says, what if some dumb housewife just forgets to write down she's got a diamond ring in one of the drawers of her dresser. Does that give us the right to steal it and then tell the lady to fuck off when she claims it's missing? I say, fuck, yeah, but nowadays they got all these consumer fuckin' advocates so they make us take the thing out of our tariff. You know what we do now? We give 'em this slip and we tell 'em if they *want* to write down their articles of extraordinary value they can, but that the government says they don't have to. This works out great for us—you know why? Because if they don't write nothin' down they don't got no way of provin' it was shipped. That diamond ring in the dresser ain't gonna appear on anything we write down. All we write down is 'dresser.'" Giacomini cackled. "Fuckin' government."

"That's amazing," I said, and stole a glance at my watch.

Giacomini ordered me a third Bud and enlightened me as to a dozen different ways to hide the damage done to furniture. "Sometimes it's too much even for us to hide, though. One time we had this cross-country move and the truck got in an accident. The stuff come inta Boston all busted up and me and my crew gotta make the delivery out to Belmont, you know? It was great. We pulled up to the new house these people were gonna move inta and we told the lady we couldn't start unloadin' until she paid us the full amount she owed. The lady gives us the check and I pulled open the back doors of the van. Everything they own falls into the street in a million pieces. It was classic, Chuckie. You shoulda been there to see the look on that lady's face."

"Sorry I missed it."

"Yeah, you woulda loved it. So what have you been up to?"

I mentioned the DelVecchio case.

"Oh, yeah. Poor Fitzy. I never thought he'd end up gettin' shot by a cop. You about ready for another beer?"

I told him I had to get going and Giacomini squinted at the clock above the bar. "Jesus, I suppose I gotta get home, too, see what the old lady wants to bitch about tonight. I can guess what it's gonna be. One of my kids has been screwin' up in school and she thinks he's got that disease where they can't read."

"Dyslexia."

"Yeah. I think he's just dumb. Let me get you another beer, Chuckie," and before I had a chance to stop him he had signaled to the waitress that he wanted two more. "How's your kid doin' these days?"

I told him she was doing all right.

"You see much of her?"

"I saw her the other night," I said. I didn't feel inclined to explain the circumstances.

"You know, I seen her the other night myself. She's goin' out with some big tall guy with long black hair, right? I had to take the kids down Nantasket to the amusement park and I saw this girl down there, looked just like Cookie when we were in high school. I'm sure it was your girl."

I didn't say anything. The waitress came and gave us new bottles. She scooped up the empties along with Giacomini's money. He watched her go and then looked back at me. "Hey, Chuckie, you're doing pretty good now, huh?"

"Not good enough."

"You know, I think about you sometimes. About you and me, and you know what I think, Chuckie?" He waited for an answer and when he didn't get one he went ahead and told me. "I think you're about the luckiest bastard that ever lived."

I looked up to see if he was smiling. He moved closer, crowding the table. "You know, I keep thinking about that Ashton game, Chuckie. That was the best game I ever played in my life and I didn't get shit out of it. The whole fuckin' team knocks off the state champs and you get all the credit."

"We didn't knock them off, Giac," I said wearily. "We just tied them."

"We broke their twenty-two game winning streak, didn't we?" Giacomini's voice was challenging. He stuck his jaw out when he spoke. "I blocked on all four of your touchdown runs. Twice I flattened Bobby Foley and he went on to play for Syracuse, for Chrissake. So how come nobody came knockin' on my door, get me to go to their college?"

"Giac, you were in the trade school. You didn't even want to go to college."

"So, if I had known what was gonna happen I woulda gotten in the college course like you. The only reason anybody recruited you was you got all the publicity. How many touchdowns you score the whole season long before the Ashton game?"

"Two."

"Two. See? And the *Globe* names you fuckin' All Scholastic just because you get four on the last day of the season. And the *Herald Traveler,* they named you something, too, didn't they? Player of the week, or something. You ever heard of a tackle getting named player of the week? I busted my ass as much as you did that day and here I am sitting here with blisters all over my hands and you got the fuckin' two-hundred-dollar suit on—"

"Hey, Giac, knock it off, will you? You wanted to get noticed fifteen years ago, you should have lost a hundred pounds and become a halfback. You wanted to go on to school, you should have read a couple of books instead of trying to memorize *My Three Sons,* or whatever it is you used to watch all the time. I'm not going to feel guilty over you, Giac, I got my own problems. I got problems up the yingyang."

Giacomini sat very still. "Fuck you," he said quietly.

I drained most of my beer and got up from the table. "Listen, I gotta go. I'm supposed to meet these people."

"Yeah, see ya around," he said without looking up.

I squeezed his slumping shoulder as I passed him on my way to the door. I had never particularly liked Giacomini, but I had no real reason for wanting to make him feel bad, either.

Out on the street I turned in the opposite direction from my apartment and walked to the Plough and Stars to see if Donovan was working. He was and so I ordered up another beer and a corned beef sandwich and sat down to chat with him. Almost immediately I found myself in a better mood.

There is nothing so Irish about the Plough and Stars as its name. It offers no Irish music except the occasional song on the jukebox mixed in between Frankie Valli and the Four Seasons and Tom Jones. There is no more hint of Ireland in its decor than there was when the place was called the Good Times. It does serve a corned beef sandwich, but it also serves ham and cheese, pastrami and even liverwurst. Guinness comes out of one of the taps, but it takes so long for the head to settle that it is probably the slowest seller they have. Donovan, in certain ways, is almost a paradigm of the place in which he works. He has the right name, but he is third-generation American and the closest he has ever been to Eire is Provincetown, where he used to go to beat up fags.

"Any of the guys been in tonight?" I asked when Donovan dropped my sandwich in front of me. Business was slow and he was able to lean against the sink and sip at some Jack Daniel's while I ate.

"No," he said, "but a couple of cops were in and I was talking to them about your case."

"DelVecchio?"

"Yeah. Those guys are real upset about what's happening to him. Crying about how it's bad enough they have to crawl around dark alleys after hoods; now if they try to protect themselves they get busted. Usual cop bullshit, but I can see their point. Except that it was Fitzy, you know? I mean, Fitzy wouldn'ta harmed a fly."

"Who knows? I wouldn't have expected him to be a burglar, either, but he was caught coming out of somebody's window in the middle of the night."

"Yeah, what's that all about, Chuck? You figured that one out yet?"

I shook my head because I had a mouthful of sandwich.

Donovan watched me eat for a minute. "Maybe you should talk to Buddy Williams. You done that yet?"

I swallowed what I had. "I don't think I've seen Buddy in a year. Why him?"

"That's who Fitzy was living with. They shared a house up on Fell Street, near South Shore Catholic. I guess it's Buddy's grandmother's house and she's in a nursing home. I thought you woulda checked that out by now."

I finished the sandwich, took a bite of my pickle and pushed the plate across the bar. "I started to look into it, but then it didn't seem to make much difference. Regardless of what he was looking for, he wasn't supposed to be there and he is dead. Now maybe if I could show he was stealing nuclear warheads or something . . ."

"I don't know. There's something funny about this whole thing, Chuck. Once a guy goes so far as to break inside a house, he's gonna take something even if it's not what he wants, don't you think? Like, everybody says Lanny Brandon's a big dope dealer and supposedly that's what Fitz was after. But even if he didn't find anything, don't you think he would have taken something else as long as he was there? And me . . . now you know a whole lot more about this than I do, but I'm standing around here listening to all these guys talk and I'm thinking, so what's this DelVecchio doing in Lanny's backyard in the middle of the night? Remember, I don't know shit about this, but I'll tell you what I think. . . ."

Up until this point Donovan had been speaking in his usual loud, hoarse voice. Now he turned and put his size twelve shoe up on the sink and leaned across the bar toward me. He threw a look over his shoulder to see who was in the closest hearing range and whispered, "I think DelVecchio was in on it." A smile drifted near his lips. "Am I right, or what? I mean, either DelVecchio was part of the deal from the beginning and was around the house to ride shotgun and keep the other cops away, or he just stumbled onto what was happening. But either way, he could have zapped Fitzy, gone through his pockets and kept everything for himself before he ran for help."

I put my glass down carefully.

Encouraged, Donovan snuggled in closer and began ticking things off on his fingers. "It stands to reason. Look, nobody searched DelVecchio after the shooting, did they? Also, the Brandons say nothing was taken. The only thing that could have been taken that they wouldn't admit would be dope. Right? You bet your ass. Finally, Fitzy wasn't the brightest guy in the world, but like I said before, you'd have to be a fucking idiot not to take something and just because they didn't find anything doesn't mean he didn't have anything."

"Donovan, you're dangerous. Where do you come up with these ideas?"

"Hey," he said, straightening up and using his thumbs to tuck in his shirt. "I told you, I listen. I'm a good listener. People come in here, they say things and I think about them." Without looking back, he pointed over his shoulder with his thumb. "If I can hear this asshole down here shaking his ice in his glass because he wants another, then I can hear a couple of guys carrying on a conversation, whether they're cops or lawyers or whatever. You know what I mean?" With that he crossed to the other end of the bar and refilled the asshole's glass.

"Donovan," I said when he went to the cash register.

"Yo," he said, tapping out the numbers.

"These guys you listen to—you ever get any from the cemetery?"

"Sure. I get all kinds."

"Who? You know any of them by name?"

Donovan scratched behind his ear and inspected his fingertips, just to be sure. "I got a couple of characters I'd like to put in the cemetery."

"Well, I need to talk to somebody who works there."

Donovan leaned one hand against the bar and thought about it. "Cemetery workers," he said to himself.

An old man, one of the Chesterfield smokers, who had been nursing a drink and staring at the array of bottles behind the bar ever since I had come in, rasped, "Angie DiMarco." He said it looking full-faced at me, as though it was the first in a series of questions he was going to be called upon to answer.

"Sure," Donovan said. "Angie DiMarco."

"He come in here often?"

Donovan saw a wet spot on the bar he did not like. There were many wet spots on the bar, but Donovan only went after one of them. He got out his thin white towel with the orange stripes and gave the spot a good vigorous rubbing. "Jees, I don't know, Chuckie. He comes in now and then, I guess. Wouldn't you say, Leo?"

The old man who had volunteered DiMarco's name had been anxiously waiting for the quiz to resume. "Oh, sure. He comes in now and then."

"How often, Donovan? Couple of times a week, once a week, every month? How often?"

Donovan went through an elaborate hook shot, trying to put the towel in the laundry barrel. "I don't know. What do you think, I got a little time card here or something?"

I watched him fetch the towel from the sink and drop it in the barrel. "Well, you were just telling me what a great listener you are. I figured maybe you were a great observer, too."

"I observe you're out of beer. You want another?"

I told him I did and Donovan slid back the top of the cooler and got one out for me. Friends and people who asked got the bottles. Everybody else got it out of the tap.

"This DiMarco a good guy?" I asked.

Donovan shrugged. "Good guy, you like to hear him complain for an hour about how his backhoe don't work and how the dogs at Wonderland are fuckin' him over, and then find he's left you with seventeen cents for a tip. Yeah, great fuckin' guy."

"He sounds like my man. You know where I can get hold of him?"

"I'll give you a call next time he comes in. How's that?"

It was not good enough. I pointed to the Chesterfield smoker. "Say, Leo, you know Angie very well?"

"Oh, yeah. Angie DiMarco. Sure."

"He like working at the cemetery?"

"Angie? Oh, sure. He likes it. It's a job, ain't it?"

"Oh, brother," I groaned. "Hey, Donovan, get old Leo here a drink, will you?"

Donovan poured Leo a shot of rye. Leo toasted me with it and when it was down I got out of my seat and slid a dime the length of the bar. It banged into Leo's shot glass and stopped. "How about giving him a call, Leo, and seeing if you can get him down here? Tell him there's a guy who wants to buy him a few drinks."

Panic streaked across Leo's face. Donovan saw it. He went over and put his index finger on my dime and, without picking it up, walked it all the way back to my seat. "Hey, Chuck," he said quietly, "leave the old fuck alone. You want to call Angie DiMarco, you call him yourself, but don't ask poor old Leo to do it for you. Angie'd probably tell him to stick it in his ear."

"He's a tough guy, huh?"

"No, but look at Leo, for Chrissake. Would you come down here if he called you up?"

"In a minute," I said. "As soon as I could get my nails curled and my hair polished."

Donovan took a swipe at me. The fact that it was meant to miss was very unlike Donovan. He was mellowing in his old age. "Ahh, fuckin' wiseass. How much you been drinking tonight, Chuckie?"

I drained the beer I had. "What time is it?"

"Eight-thirty."

"Hell, I just got started." I threw some money on the bar. "Call me if that guy comes in, will you?"

Donovan said he would.

One reason I went out to the Brandons' house after I left the Plough and Stars was because it was too warm to go home. The Red Sox were playing in Oakland and weren't coming on until ten-thirty and there was nothing else on television I felt like watching. I considered giving Billy Kincaid a call, but I knew he didn't go out during the week and I had the feeling his wife wouldn't appreciate my just dropping by. There was also a strong possibility that Lanny Brandon would not appreciate my dropping by, but his wife had issued me a more or less open invitation. So I went. I walked over to the parking lot outside my apartment building, the only multi-unit, high-rise apartment building within walking distance of the Center, got in my Firebird and drove straight to the Brandons'.

Lanny, as he had every right to do, looked at me in near total confusion. I told him I was just driving by and happened to see all the lights on. I wondered if they would mind some company.

Lanny glanced around at the lights, as if surprised to see that he had so many on. He was wearing tennis shorts and a T-shirt that advertised a hamburger joint with the slogan "You Can't Beat Our Buns."

"No, no," he said. "C'mon in. I was just upstairs doing my rewrites. Alicia must be—here, wait right here. She might be out by the pool and I'll have to see if she's dressed." Assured that I was staying in place, Lanny literally ran toward the back of the house. In a minute both he and Alicia appeared in the kitchen. She was wearing a blue and white kaftan and was busily drying her hair. She smiled when she saw me.

Lanny was hurrying forward. "Hey, great, she was in the pool. Yeah. Look, Chuck, you want to come in?"

"I am in."

"So you are. Right. Well, can I get you a drink? Want to go in the den? Out by the pool? You drink gin and tonic, don't you?"

"That would be fine, Lanny. How are you, Alicia?"

"I'm just fine, Chuck. I couldn't be better."

Lanny calmed down by the time we all settled into chairs around the pool. "Don't you lawyers ever take your suits off?" he joked, placing a big bottle of Bombay gin on the table.

"We just never stop working," I said. "I haven't even gotten home from the office yet."

Lanny was as gregarious this evening as he had been quiet the weekend before. He was anxious to make me feel comfortable and clearly pleased that I had come. Once he even made an oblique reference to his conduct at the dinner by saying that as a writer he often got so involved with what he was working on that he couldn't clear his mind enough to deal sociably in the real world.

"Fortunately, it's something that Alicia has learned to cope with," he said, smiling fondly at her.

"You must have had a good day at the typewriter today," I said.

"An exciting day," he admitted, "but it wasn't all spent at the typewriter. I was out and around the city a good deal."

"Hasn't changed much, has it?"

Lanny shrugged. "In some ways I guess it hasn't. In others, I can't believe how much it's changed. You know, when I was in California I had this concept of Portshead fixed in my mind. It's a little disconcerting to come back and not have things look like I remembered them or be where they're supposed to be." Lanny started to say more and then thought better of it.

We sipped our drinks and I casually let my eyes wander over to where Alicia was sitting.

"You know," Lanny said, snapping my attention back, "one thing I've been surprised at is the number of blacks who've moved into this area."

"What have you seen—five, six?"

"Still, just to see one is something. There wasn't a single black family in this town when we were growing up."

"There was Gar Pena," I said, snickering.

"Yeah, and he was what—Portuguese?" Lanny leaned forward toward Alicia. " 'Gar' was short for 'nee-gar.' Tony Pena was the darkest-skinned guy we knew."

"How clever," Alicia said. I had the feeling she did not mean it.

"He used to work down the Syrian bakery and spit in the dough," I added.

"Charming," Alicia said, and I suddenly felt as though I had been the one who had spit in the dough.

"When did the blacks first come in, Chuckie?" I heard Lanny asking.

"Jees, I don't know. A few years back, I guess. Maybe when they put the transit system out here. They're in the north end, mostly. The end closest to Dorchester."

"Yeah, I heard they're in Dorchester now."

"In? They control it. My father's time, that was all shanty Irish. Then the Italians moved in and now it's all blacks and Puerto Ricans and those few old-timers who can't get it together enough to move out. Everybody, once they get to Dorchester, Portshead's the next stop. They skip right over Ashton, of course. Hell, the Transit doesn't even stop there. Ashton selectmen refused to appropriate land or increase the tax base. It was a smart move. Now the Ashton people who want to ride in town just go to the North Portshead station and get on there."

"Typical," Lanny said.

"What are you going to do? It's a law of nature. The poor people have an obligation to support the rich."

"But the blacks—were there any problems with them when they first came out?"

"Lanny," Alicia said suddenly. The word was spoken with enough exasperation that we both turned innocently to look at her. "I don't believe you're asking such questions, as if you expect there would be problems."

Lanny grinned at me and cocked his head toward her. "California," he said.

Alicia did not see anything funny in the remark. "Well, everyone back here is always so concerned with race and nationality. It makes me sick."

"You want to know when the first time I actually encountered blacks was?" I said to her. "It was when I was seventeen years old, at the Seaside Ballroom down at Nantasket. Remember that place, Lanny?"

He nodded and I felt a twinge of discomfort when I realized that even though there had been a period when we had gone to the Seaside almost every week, Lanny would never have gone with us. His troubles had started before that. But here we were drinking and Lanny had been the one who started me on the story, so I went ahead with it. He seemed to want to hear what I had to say.

"Every Saturday it was always the same. We'd meet out in front of Alvie's store after supper and we'd hang around there until we could talk one of the older kids into buying for us and then we'd each get tanked up on a half pint of vodka. Usually straight, guzzled right from the bottle over on the rocks behind the elementary school playground. Then maybe Ferrara would get his shitbox, that's what everybody called it, if it was running, or Billy Kincaid would borrow his parents' car. If we were desperate we used to let Kenny Cramer with the harelip drive us.

"He'd pull up across the street from Alvie's and sit there in his car waiting for us to ask him. And when we would he'd look like he was thinking it over, as if maybe there was some other reason he was parked there. We'd say, 'Hey, Kenny, you wanna go to the Seaside?' and after a while he'd say, 'Ah wone know. Anybody got any gas money?'

"When I think about it now I crack up. Gas was a quarter a gallon in those days. At most it was a gallon in each direction and that little asshole would ride down and back by himself unless we all chipped in for gas money."

I got the impression that Alicia was not empathizing with the right party in my story. I told her she had to have been there to know what a turkey Kenny really was. Her polite smile took on edges of condescending tolerance.

I decided I did not need that and I spoke only to Lanny as I finished my story of the night we decided to teach the black kids to confine their dancing to the street corners of Roxbury. The story grew longer than I had intended it, as details I had not thought of in years came rushing back to me. The process of remembering was exciting as I sat there in the Brandons' yellow and white plastic-strip deck chair, refreshing my own drink from the Bombay bottle. I was thinking in terms of how I had felt at the time and I was speaking with feelings that seemed unerringly preserved. Mummified by years of inattention. I would, I knew, never be able to reflect on those times as ingenuously again because as soon as I described them, as soon as the words came out of my mouth, the protective mold was cracked, replaced by a perspective that was immediately tempered by my awareness of Alicia's disapproval.

It was for her sake, I suppose, that I made a point of saying I could not recall the blacks doing anything to provoke a fight. It was just a case of us establishing our turf, I said, something we thought we were surely tough enough to do—right up until the point where some little black kid put Tom Ferrara, our knight-errant, on his back in front of everybody on the South Shore and whacked the shit out of him in a blur of flying fists that only stopped when the kid's arms grew tired.

The story seemed to put a cap on the evening. Alicia's silence left me feeling both apologetic and vaguely aggressive. Lanny gazed out over the pool, his teeth set together and his mind far away. My glass was empty but for three or four lime wedges and a chunk of ice, and I realized that it was time for me to go.

But suddenly Lanny, his eyes still set in the distance, said, "Did you ever take part in those orgies they had at Billy Kincaid's house, Chuckie?"

I glanced over at Alicia, fully expecting her to excuse herself, but she did not. She was sitting sideways in her chair, both hands on the aluminum armrest closest to me, and she was listening for my answer.

"You heard about that, huh?" I said, and Lanny answered, "I heard stories about them, but I never heard anything from anybody who was actually there."

"Well, I was there, but I never actually took part." I spread my hands. "I was already married at the time they were going on." I stared at the limes in my drink, feeling peculiarly embarrassed.

"I find it hard to picture you married, Chuck," Alicia said softly.

I tried to smile. "I've got a daughter in high school."

Her head shook slowly in wonder. "You must have been very young."

"I was—seventeen. Eighteen when Candy was born."

"And Candy's your daughter."

"My wife was very young, too. Her family called her Cookie and she thought it would be cute for Cookie to have a candy named Baby."

"A baby named Candy."

"That's what I meant." I held up my glass and shuffled the limes in my drink again. What the hell, I thought, and poured myself some more gin. "I think even she regrets it now."

"It looks like we're out of tonic," Lanny said.

"I don't care."

Alicia was still watching me. There was noticeable concern in her green eyes. I liked it better when they flashed. "And Candy lives with her mother?" she said.

"That's right." I had stopped enjoying the conversation, but I could not just chug the gin.

"Do you see her much?" It was the second time that evening I had been asked that question.

"Not much."

"Why's that? If you don't mind my prying."

"According to her, according to her mother, or according to me?"

"Her."

"She says I'm a drunk and she thinks I abandoned her and her mother."

"Is that what her mother thinks?"

"No. Her mother thinks I'm an uptight, effete, self-centered snob. Only she wouldn't use those words."

"What words would she use?"

"She'd say I'm a jerk."

"And what do you say?"

"I don't know." The gin had melted my last bit of ice. I reached for the bucket and Alicia stood up to get it for me. She could have passed me the bucket. She could have held the bucket and used the tongs. Instead she used her bare hand. She reached into the bucket and brought out several cubes. She dropped them into my glass. One by one. Each cube sent a short spurt of liquid over the edge. Some of it got on my arm and I looked up at Alicia standing above me. Without meaning to, I shivered.

The moment should have meant nothing. Merely a woman feeding her guest's glass. The only thing out of the ordinary was the length of time it took.

Lanny, far-off Lanny, was speaking. Had he been speaking before? Had I missed something? I didn't know.

"What?" I said.

"Their names were Kitty and Bunny, weren't they?"

"Who?"

"The girls at Billy Kincaid's."

Alicia returned to her seat as I started in on the story of the infamous orgies at Billy Kincaid's.

23

"You look awful," Davida said. There was awe in her eyes as she surveyed my condition.

"I'm desperately ill and I'm going to die."

"Why are you going to die?" She followed me into my office.

I sat down gently and held my head in my hands. "Because I'm too hung over to live."

"You want coffee?"

"Get me coffee. Get me orange juice. Get me aspirin."

It was not until the early afternoon that I felt well enough to return to the cemetery. The heat was so intense and the air so still that there was hardly a soul on the streets. The cemetery could have been something out of the Twilight Zone for all the activity it showed.

The car with the "BUSTER" license plates was not outside the administration building when I arrived. I was told by a bespectacled, powder-faced woman behind the counter that Mr. Vizarelli was out of the office and she didn't know when to expect him back. When I complained that I was supposed to have an appointment, she said she would try to find Ted for me. In a few minutes she returned with the other of the two men I had met the day before. He was wearing the same even-hemmed gray shirt, but now it was streaked wet with perspiration. When he saw me, he got out a handkerchief and mopped the back of his neck.

"Ho, yes indeed. A plot for two, wasn't it? I think Buster found you a good one." He smiled at me. Sweat dripped off the end of his nose.

We drove to the northwest corner and parked by a rusted faucet with half a dozen wicker baskets of dead flowers lying around its base. The area through which we walked was almost exclusively the province of those who had died before the turn of the century. I saw only two monuments with recent death dates on them and they virtually shone in comparison with the soot-stained granite stones around them. When we passed the second of the two new monuments, Ted stopped and consulted a note he had written to himself in the office.

"This is it," he said, indicating an open grassy space which appeared more than adequate for the two bodies I was supposed to want interred.

I was disappointed. There was not the slightest sign that a headstone or a monument had been removed. I went over to the space and walked around. What was one supposed to look at in buying a grave—the view? I knelt down and felt the turf. "Very nice," I said.

Ted nodded. "It's a real beauty," he said. His skin was running like melted butter.

I stepped back to get some perspective. "I don't see a plot number," I said.

Ted wiped his forehead with the back of his arm and took a few steps along the perimeter, kicking at clumps of grass. He stared at his note and then turned and walked to the end of the aisle. "This is Lot Number 4403," he said. "You've got Graves 5 and 6 in this lot."

I went up to where Ted was standing and he showed me a cement marker in the ground. The first stone in the lot bore the name Parker. So did the second. That was when I realized that the ample space I thought was being allotted me was really for four graves. On the other side of the space was a stone for a man named James, and next to that was the new monument. It had been erected for an infant girl named Deborah Reilly, and she had been dead for only a few months.

I asked Ted if he could give me the figures on how much it was going to cost me. He said, "These two will cost you two hundred and fifty bucks per grave because we had to do some overtime work to find them. Plus there's the cost of perpetual care, which we advise you to take."

I told Ted I would think about it, which didn't do much for our friendship. He thought I should have waited for a cooler day if all I was doing was shopping around.

"Davida," I said when I got back to the office, "how would you like to get out early today?"

"There's a catch," she said. "You want me to file something, is that it? You want me to take my life in my hands and walk all the way down to the courthouse in this heat to file something."

I pretended I was hurt. "A taxi ride, Davida. You can take a taxi where you're going and a taxi back. It'll be good for you to get out in the sunshine. Once you're done with what I want, just give me a phone call and go on home. You'll even have time to get to the beach."

Davida slid her already too short skirt up another inch or so. "Look at these legs, Chuckie. You think these legs ever go to a beach? They go to bars, Chuckie. And that's exactly where they'll be going if you let me out early. A nice, air-conditioned bar that plays Chuck Mangione on the jukebox."

"Davida, you do this for me and I don't care if you go sit in a steamer trunk for the rest of the day. Here's all you have to do. I want you to go down to Portshead Memorial Cemetery and go through some records they have down there. I want you to tell them that your grandmother, Mrs. Parker—got that? Mrs. Parker—is dying and that she thinks her late husband inherited a family plot. The number of the plot is 4403. Actually, that's a lot number and it contains at least six graves, one of which they just offered to sell to me. That's the tricky part, Davida. I don't want them to know we're associated. What I want is for you to find out if they're selling me a grave that belongs to somebody else."

"You mean this isn't even legal work? It's personal stuff?"

"Do I look like the kind of guy who needs a burial plot? It's tied in with the DelVecchio case."

"I'll bet."

"It would take me too long to explain, Davida. Just see what they have under the name Parker, and if you can't do it that way, then tell them you think it's Lot Number 4403. It won't take you long."

It took her over three hours. It was well after five o'clock when the phone rang.

"It's the last time I ever do you a favor," she moaned. "You know what it's like looking through records in that dump? They've got everything on three-by-five cards in books that were put in order by chimpanzees. But I found what you wanted. Phillip Parker bought Lot 4403 for himself and his family in 1880. He buried himself, his wife, his daughter Martha James and her husband. Then somebody's written in hand on the card, 'Graves 3 through 6 and 8 through 10 reclaimed by the city in exchange for perpetual care on balance.' Does that make any sense to you, Chuckie?"

"I'll tell you what doesn't make sense. You said four people are buried in that lot, but I saw only three graves with three stones and one name on each stone."

"Well, then hold on to your hat, boss, because there's more. There's a line drawn through the name of Martha James next to where it says Grave 8 and below that line someone's written in the name Deborah Reilly, spelled R-e-i-double-l-y, and a date from June of this year."

I whistled appreciatively. "You're a good woman, Davida."

"Careful what you say. You'll turn my head and my husband might get jealous —if the sonofabitch ever comes to."

On the strength of what Davida had told me I got my car out of the lot and drove over to the quarry section of town, where Triple A Monuments was located. Business at Triple A was conducted out of a cottage that had been modified into a showroom. Gravestones of all sizes and shapes were set up around the yard, but a chain-link fence kept me out. At six o'clock Triple A was closed for the day.

I saw some activity behind the cottage and I walked around to the back, where a gate was open and a truck was standing in the driveway. Somebody was hauling something between the truck and a red shack that stood off to one side of the cottage. I avoided making myself conspicuous and slipped into the yard.

I knew absolutely nothing about rocks, stones or monuments, but I thought that what I was looking for would be easy enough to find. I was wrong. Of the monuments I saw, none had any markings on it except for the ones in the showroom window, and they had been marked only to demonstrate the various kinds of scripts that were available.

I wandered the front and side yards for nearly ten minutes before I was noticed. "Hey," a voice said, "we're closed for the day."

"That's all right," I said. "I'm just looking."

A man in his mid-twenties, wearing dungarees and a T-shirt that said "Property of Notre Dame Athletic Department," jumped down off the bed of the truck and came toward me. He had curly hair, bad skin, and massive arms and shoulders.

"You'll have to come back tomorrow. There's nobody here but me, and I'm closing up."

That gave me my clue as to what I was going to say next. "I'm looking for Buster Vizarelli. I had a private matter I needed to talk to him about."

"Well, Buster's not here right now."

"He's one of the owners, isn't he?" I tried to ask as if I couldn't have cared less, but the young guy flushed.

"My brother owns this place."

"What's your brother's name."

"Tony Bonfigleone."

"The commissioner of public works?"

"Yeah. Do you know him?"

"Sure. Hell of a guy. You and Tony do all the work yourselves?"

"Well, I do most of the cuttin' and Tony does most of the sellin', but we got a few other people like Viz who help us out. Got a sandblaster comes in on a part-time basis." He pointed in the direction of the red shack.

There were chunks of gray stone lying in the tall grass around the door of the shack. "What do you use a sandblaster for? You recycle stones sometimes?" I started walking in that direction and Tony's brother, probably because he was hoping to lead me out, walked along with me.

"Oh, yeah," he said. "You get mistakes all the time. Sometimes you get damaged stones, that sort of thing. But you gotta sandblast even the new ones to get 'em smooth. Listen, I gotta get you outta here now because I'm about to lock up."

It was not that he cared what I was looking at; the stones were just lying there in the open and anybody could have seen them during normal business hours. He was only interested in going home, and I did not keep him long. Half a dozen old stones were clumped together near the sandblaster's shack and each one was engraved. One of those stones bore the name Martha James.

I was ready now to call the mayor.

24 I was counting on Francis X. McLaughlin's being a man who respected the power of the press. It was in his history. In his first campaign for mayor he had startled all of Portshead by announcing just four days before the election that his wife and daughters had been threatened with rape if he did not drop out of the race. He was careful not to come right out and attribute the threat to his opponent, but the linkage was there.

"No man," Francis X. thundered at a carefully constructed press conference on the steps of City Hall, "is going to disrupt the democratic process which has stood this country in such good stead for two hundred years. No man is going to deprive the people of this great city of the right of free electoral choice which is their heritage, born of the blood of their forefathers. And no man is going to use fear and intimidation as a means to further his own avaricious, ungodly lust for political power—not so long as Francis X. McLaughlin still has a breath to breathe."

Francis's diatribe was timed in such a way that it made headlines in the evening edition of the Friday night paper. His stunned and bewildered opponent got a hasty denial of any connection with the alleged threat into Saturday night's paper, but the impact was diminished both by Saturday's smaller circulation and by the fact that the paper juxtaposed the denial with an article describing how McLaughlin was spending money out of his own pocket to hire bodyguards for round-the-clock protection of his family. McLaughlin himself disdained protection and boldly announced, "If there are nefarious elements out there who would seek to undermine our political system with force, then let them have at me. I'd rather have them find me than harm innocent people in their search."

On the day before the election, the *Portshead Sentinel* carried quarter-page ads reading, "Keep Our City Safe. Keep Portshead the Kind of Place Where You Want Your Children.to Grow Up. Elect Francis X. McLaughlin Mayor." A picture accompanying the ads showed Francis X. with his arms spread around the shoulders of his beleaguered but grimly determined family.

His opponent, despite being the protégé of the outgoing mayor, never had a chance. Francis X. McLaughlin was swept into office with the biggest plurality in twenty years. Four years later he easily won reelection when City Councillor

Patrick Joyce, the only man with even an outside chance at beating him, unexpectedly announced that he was going to run for state senator instead. Later, in the process of being thoroughly trounced by the incumbent, Harlan Carson, Mr. Joyce complained bitterly that he had been misled into running for the senate by the actions of a group of McLaughlin people who had obtained access to his mailing list. Francis X. vigorously disavowed any knowledge of ad hoc organizations of eager supporters and soberly accepted his seventy-seven percent of the vote as a mandate to run the city exactly as he pleased.

During his first seven years in office, Portshead had neither noticeably improved nor fallen into the ocean, but there was no doubt that it had taken on a distinctly McLaughlinian look. Every department head had changed, a multitude of new boards and committees had been created, and every appointed position had been filled with an ally. With Joyce gone, the city council was firmly behind McLaughlin. Notwithstanding the recent undeclared rift with Jimbo Ryder, the mayor's programs generally encountered opposition only from Broussard, the half-mad maverick who was always trying to get the city to do wild and unpredictable things like convert public buildings to solar heat. All in all, it was a tightly run administration and if the McLaughlin team could be faulted for being unproductive, it at least had high morale.

McLaughlin himself was capable of a certain amount of personal charm which tended to bind people to him. His enemies, whispering from the closet, liked to say he could lie with an open face. In any event, it was his talent to be able to listen to almost any story with an air of commiseration and understanding without sacrificing his ability to respond by saying the matter was out of his hands. Those who knew him well, those who knew the city well, insisted that almost nothing that took place in Portshead was out of his hands.

Prior to heeding the call of public office, Mayor McLaughlin had practiced law out of the Bank Building in the heart of Portshead Center. His reputation had him being a not particularly skilled but nevertheless highly successful advocate. He was said to be especially effective at obtaining licenses and variances from city and county boards.

On more than one occasion, Sid Silverman had pointed out the mayor's success to me. "He wasn't much different than you, Chuckie. Opened an office with nothing but a law degree and a distinguished service record from Korea. Got together with John Ferguson and John Block, who at that time were just a couple of kids hanging around the courtroom waiting to get assigned misdemeanor defendants who didn't have or couldn't afford a lawyer of their own."

Twenty-five years later, with McLaughlin ensconced as mayor and Ferguson as district attorney, Block carried on the practice with three associates. Like the firm of Ferguson, Block and McLaughlin, the Law Offices of J. L. Block were said to be very successful at obtaining licenses and variances.

Francis X. (I have never seen him referred to in print as anything else) McLaughlin enjoyed the trappings of power. He rode to and from City Hall in a chauffeur-driven Oldsmobile with a little Tensor light set up on the back shelf. This was something no official had ever done before, but Mayor McLaughlin insisted it was needed so he could work while riding back and forth.

"A minimum of fifteen minutes per day in each direction, at least twice per day, not to mention the time spent parking and going to and from my car. If my time as mayor is worth anywhere near what people paid me as a lawyer, the expense of my driver will be made up before you know it. Besides, the driver is a semidisabled city employee and we'd only have to pay him his pension early if this job wasn't available."

The city council overwhelmingly agreed. Only Broussard, who was not a lawyer and who was therefore incapable of understanding just how valuable an attorney's time can be, dissented. It was Broussard's theory, stated on the record, that all lawyers were in conspiracy with each other.

Despite the prestige Mayor McLaughlin sought to impart to his official status, he made no attempt to disassociate himself from the people of his city. Once contacted he might not do anything, but he was eminently accessible, both at City Hall and at home. His address and his phone number were public knowledge and only his wife acted as a screen against bothersome or particularly unwanted calls.

It was my good fortune not to be on the unwanted list. When on Thursday evening I telephoned his home, I merely had to tell Mrs. McLaughlin my name and occupation for her to get him to come on the line.

"Mayor here," he said.

"Mr. Mayor, this is Charles Bishop. I'm a lawyer here in Portshead."

"Sure. Football player, aren't you? How's it going, son?"

"It's going fine, Mayor. As you may know, I'm currently representing Richard DelVecchio. He's the police officer accused of shooting the burglar—"

"He's not just accused. He admits shooting him, doesn't he?"

"Yes. Yes, he does."

"Then he's not just accused."

I hesitated, anxious not to get thrown off track. "The DA has asked for an inquest, Mayor. It's to start on Tuesday in district court."

"Well, I can't help you there, son. I want to stand by our men in blue whenever I can, but if it's before the district court already, I don't see what help I can be. A pronouncement, maybe. I could issue a pronouncement of support if that would help. Maybe time it for the start of the inquest. Create a favorable atmosphere, that sort of thing."

I cleared my throat and he stopped rambling. "Mayor," I said, "being a lawyer yourself, you understand what my obligation is. I've got to defend my client to the best of my ability. At the same time, though, I've got other responsibilities —as a citizen of Portshead and so forth. I'd hate to see information come out that was going to damage my city. That's why I'm calling you, Mayor. In the course of my preparation for DelVecchio's defense, I've come across some rather disturbing matters that I think you should know about before I go sticking my nose in where it probably doesn't belong."

This was the mayor's kind of talk. He understood what I was telling him. "I don't suppose you would want to come in to the office to discuss this, would you?"

"Gee, Mayor, it's the sort of thing I think we'd better talk about tonight."

"I see. Is there someplace convenient that we might meet?"

"Maybe we could discuss this over a cocktail. How about the lounge at the Holiday Inn?"

"Anybody else who'll be there?"

"You should bring along anybody you think might have an interest, Mr. Mayor."

"Wait a minute. I don't know the subject we'll be discussing."

"Sure you do, Mr. Mayor. Richie DelVecchio."

At nine o'clock, the Holiday Inn cocktail lounge was in its usual state of somnambulism. Three or four off-duty employees were seated at the bar. A suit sat by himself in the middle of the room, both hands on his drink, staring straight ahead. I guessed he was a salesman. He had that look, that should-I-have-another-drink-or-go-watch-television look. A solitary couple snuggled under an amber light at one of the tables along the wall near the entrance.

I had arrived early and had taken a seat in a back booth so that I would have a view of the door when we talked. I ordered bourbon and water and drank it more quickly than I had intended. Instead of calming my nerves, it left me fidgety, with nothing to do but rehearse the lines I was going to deliver to the mayor.

As soon as I was able to catch the waitress's attention, I pointed to my glass for a refill. She bent over my table and gave me a look down the front of her dress as she presented my second drink, and by the time I took my eyes off her there stood the short-legged, square frame of the mayor himself. Over his shoulder loomed the gloomy countenance of Alex Scurillo. I had not expected the president of the city council and it was fairly apparent that he had not expected to be there.

"Mr. Bishop?" the mayor inquired politely. When I nodded, he smiled and held out his hand. "I see you started without us."

I got out of my seat to greet him. He introduced me to Scurillo.

"Alex was by the house on some other business, so I invited him out to wet his whistle. Hope you don't mind."

"Of course not," I said, and while I was shaking hands with the petulant Mr. Scurillo the mayor sat down in the very place where I had been sitting. He pushed my glass across the table, indicating that I was to sit on the other side, facing the wall. Scurillo sat down next to the mayor and, since the waitress was still hanging around, both men ordered immediately. The mayor asked for tea and Scurillo for a beer.

It was my intention to ease gradually into the conversation. It did not happen that way. The city's two most important men had about them an air which told me I was taking up their time and they wanted to know why. The meeting may have been my idea, but the rules were theirs. I was to bring out my starting lineup while they were to continue to pretend they were unsure as to why they were in the ball park.

"Mayor," I said, "who wants Richie DelVecchio? He's just a local kid who's spent his entire life wanting to become a policeman. Sure, his brother-in-law probably helped him get on the force, but he's got a wife, two kids and maybe enough sense to pull down his zipper when he pees."

The mayor nodded. His fleshy features were draped with concern. He spread his hands apart while he spoke and clasped them together when he finished. "I'm sure nobody's out to get the young man, Chuckie." The mayor did indeed know who I was.

"It's in everyone's best interest that the police be appreciated for the job they do," he went on, "but the mere fact that they have a license to carry a gun doesn't give them a license to kill. Other people also have rights, wouldn't you agree? If they didn't, we'd have a totalitarian state. Isn't that right, Alex?"

Alex said, "Yeah."

The mayor nodded. "Now it may be that Richie DelVecchio did exactly what he should have done in this situation. I don't know. That's what the inquest is supposed to find out. It may be that the district attorney has some other information. I don't know that, either. But I would tend to think that your boy is in pretty good shape, Chuckie. This is essentially a law-abiding community with a tradition of support for our police. As far as who this young man's brother-in-law is, well, I think that can only work in his favor. Don't you?"

It was almost a shame the mayor's performance was wasted on an audience of one. The thought tickled something in my brain and I reacted spontaneously. "Mayor," I whispered, leaning across the table, "I'm not bugged. Are you? Are you, Mr. Scurillo? Look, I'm not." I leaned back and ripped my shirt open to expose the bare skin of my chest. A button flew off, hit the wall beside us and disappeared onto the floor. The mayor and Scurillo followed it like a tennis ball and then turned back to me with surprise on their faces.

I was still holding my shirt open when the waitress returned. She looked me up and down with considerable interest as she set out a beer and a glass for

Scurillo, and a cup, saucer and a pot of tea for the mayor. Fair was fair, she might have felt, and I had, after all, tried to look at her chest. I closed my shirt, to the relief of the other two men. The waitress finished her task and moved away.

I leaned closer again. "The Holiday Inn isn't bugged, is it? I mean, that's why we're meeting here, right? What's said here, it's just my word against yours and you've got Mr. Scurillo to back yours up. So, Mayor, with all due respect, how about it if we just say what's on our minds?"

"Sure, Chuckie, sure," the mayor said, laughing softly and splattering tea as he tried to pour it into his cup. "Only, no more of these strip-teases, okay? Alex, here, isn't ready for it."

Alex looked as if the only thing he was ready for was an overdue bowel movement. His eyes protruded slightly, his face was drawn and there was an edge of irritation around his mouth.

I finished buttoning my shirt and swallowed my drink in two gulps. The bourbon burned a path all the way down to my stomach. My leg kicked out involuntarily and accidentally hit Scurillo, who spilled the beer he was pouring.

"Sorry," I said to him, and he grunted. The mayor raised his eyebrows, wondering what had happened.

"Mayor," I said to him, "as I see it, Ferguson has no interest in prosecuting Richie unless you tell him to. As DA, he doesn't really want to know what Richie did. Nobody does. I bet even the victim's mother doesn't want this kept in the papers any longer than it already has been. She knows what kind of guy Fitzy had become and this whole thing is humiliating to his family. The only reason —the only possible reason—this inquest is being held is to embarrass Jim Ryder. Now I've talked to Jim about this and he doesn't believe me. But I'm convinced of it and all I'm interested in is getting my client back in his patrol car. So if I see this battle being fought for political reasons, then I've got to get some political ammunition to fight back, don't I?"

The mayor stirred his tea thoughtfully. His spoon hit the sides of his plastic cup and made a noise that went *wok, wok, wok*. He took a long time to stir and then he said, "And you think you've got some of that, Chuckie? Some of that political ammunition? That's why you wanted to meet with me?"

I held his gaze and let everything else clear so that by the time I spoke he was intently waiting for what I had to say. "Mayor," I said, "what's going on out at the cemetery?"

For a moment there was almost a look of relief that came over their faces. Another time, another place, and my heart would have faded at their reaction. Knowing what I did, it simply indicated that worse things must have been going on in other places.

The mayor sipped at his tea. He scowled, irritated at it, and pronounced it cold to the taste. "What do you mean," he said, putting the cup back in its saucer, where his sloppy pouring had left a noticeable pool of liquid, "what's going on at the cemetery?"

"Four years ago it was announced that Memorial was filled. A new cemetery had to be created, remember? So how come graves are still being sold at Memorial? Just this week your superintendent, Mr. Vizarelli, offered to sell me a plot for only fifty bucks over standard price, plus the cost of perpetual care if I wanted it. Not such a bad deal except for the fact that somebody else already bought that same plot a hundred years ago. Still, I'd be better off than some people I found out about who have bought graves with people already in them. Of course, these people didn't know there were already people in their graves because the headstones had been removed, thanks again to Mr. Vizarelli. He takes the headstones right off the top of the poor bastards who've been lying there for fifty years and he brings them down to Triple A Monuments, which just happens to be owned by Anthony Bonfigleone, your commissioner of public works. Triple A files the name off the old stone and sells it again. Who might buy a used stone? Well, any of Mr. Vizarelli's customers at the cemetery would be likely candidates, I guess, since it appears that he's also in the habit of selling monuments for Triple A."

The mayor waited until I was done and then he turned grimly to Scurillo. "Alex," he said, "we'll have to look into that." And Scurillo nodded as though that sounded like a grand idea to him.

"You mean this is the first you guys have heard about this?" I asked.

"First for me, Chuckie. What about you, Alex?"

Alex nodded again. "First I heard about it."

"Isn't that funny?" I said. "I have at least one witness willing to swear under oath that he went right in your office, Mayor, and told you about his mother's grave being sold out from under him. The very same man wrote you a letter, Mr. Scurillo, don't you recall? You gave it to Councilman O'Keefe to respond to."

I put a copy of O'Keefe's letter to Woodruff on the table. The two officials huddled over it.

"Seems to me I do remember speaking to a Mr. Woodruff," the mayor said.

"I don't think I looked at the letter. I just gave it to O'Keefe," said Scurillo.

"I think I sent Mr. Woodruff over to see Jim Duffy at the cemetery board. Never heard anything more about it."

"I don't remember O'Keefe saying anything more to me. He must have handled this one on his own."

"Gentlemen, please," I said, taking back the letter so that they would have to pick up their heads and resume looking at me. "I'm sure neither of you would have anything to do with what's going on at the cemetery, but what's the public going to think when they find out your appointed cemetery superintendent is digging up their relatives and reselling their graves? What are they going to think when they find out Vizarelli is either working for or taking kickbacks from your appointed commissioner of public works? At the very least, Bonfigleone's competitors are going to get excited, wouldn't you say?"

The mayor was quiet for a moment. "I suppose you can prove all this, Chuckie?"

"I can prove it, Mayor."

"And just so I'm clear on this, the information you have—what do you intend to do with it?"

"What I'd like to do is turn it over to you so that you can deal with it as you see fit. But I have to say, Mayor, that while I have the greatest respect for you personally, I'd be leery of trusting your professional judgment if Richie Del-Vecchio ends up going on trial for reasons of political expediency. If I should lose faith in you, sir, I don't think I'd have any choice but to go to the newspapers."

"I see." The mayor drank his cold tea, but this time he made no face. "How will you determine if DelVecchio's trial is for political reasons?"

"Well, sir, I've researched the case quite a bit, and I'd have to say that in my professional opinion, if Richie goes on trial at all, I know it will be for political reasons."

Then the mayor said a very cryptic thing. Given what I was doing and the way I was talking, it was almost a frightening thing. He said, "I think we've heard enough, Alex," and both he and Scurillo slid out of the booth.

Standing on his feet, looking down at me, the mayor hesitated. "You're a good boy, Chuckie. You seem to have a lot of good qualities. I'm interested in you and I'll be back in touch with you. Until then I think maybe you should keep your cards close to your vest." He started to go and suddenly he turned back, bumping into Scurillo, who gave his usual grunt and stepped out of the way. The mayor said, "Thank you, by the way, for the tea."

Scurillo bent down and picked something up off the floor. "Here's your button," he said, and then he followed after McLaughlin, whose swift steps had already carried him to the door.

I motioned for another drink. I was shaking like a leaf.

25 This time when she called it was after midnight and I was already in bed. She wanted to thank me, she said, for dropping by to visit Alan.

"It meant a great deal to him, I could tell."

"I take it he's not with you at the moment."

"No. He went out for a walk."

"A walk? At twelve-whatever-it-is at night? He went for a walk?"

"He does it all the time, Chuck. Either that or he gets in the car and he drives around the city. He says between midnight and dawn is the best time for thinking and he says walking or driving is the best way to do it. He tells me there are things to see at night. People and places and thoughts and ideas that don't exist anymore." She laughed softly. "It would be spooky if I didn't know what he was talking about. But I do."

"Where the hell is there to walk in Portshead?"

"He likes to go to places he remembers as a kid. He tries to capture the detail of them. Sometimes he just goes to bars and sits by himself, listening to people talk and swap stories."

"When does he sleep?"

"Oh, he doesn't go out like that every night. Only when he gets wired up, excited about some idea that's come to him, and he's trying to get it worked out in his head before he puts it down on paper." She paused. "Either then or else he goes out when he's got no ideas at all and he's trying to get inspired. Those days, the ones when he stays up all night, he sleeps in the afternoon. I think he read someplace that all writers sleep in the afternoon."

"And you—when does he sleep with you?" It was an unconscionably bold statement, consciously made. It was not just for reasons of idle chatter that she had called me at this hour of the night.

My query had long since died an unnatural death before Alicia spoke again. "Good night, Chuck."

"Good night, babe."

26 On Friday night they broke into my office. But first they sent Jim Duffy by to talk some sense into me. He showed up at about three o'clock in the afternoon, blowing cigarette smoke and nervously thumbing the bridge of his glasses.

Jim Duffy was a weasel. If he had an actual profession or job skill it was unknown to me, but he had spent years hanging around City Hall. Politics was his passion, although he had neither the brains nor the personality to be anything more than a functionary for those in power. The key to Duffy was understanding that everything he saw, heard or did was thought by him to be of the utmost importance. He thrived on having inside information, which he willingly and indiscriminately conveyed out of the corner of his mouth. Typically, he would preface his information by saying, "Don't tell anybody where you got this, but . . ." and if you were smart, you not only would not tell anybody what Duffy had said but you would not pay too much attention to it yourself. Duffy's opinions counted for zero. His value lay solely in the fact that he was willing to do things, and his compensation was appointments to positions with grand titles and minimal responsibilities. The cemetery board of managers was but a promotion from the city dump committee, and chairmanship of the board came only because he was available to do all the work.

Duffy stormed into my office with as much bluster as one could humanly expect from a five-foot-six-inch, one-hundred-and-thirty-pound man. "Whatcha tryin' to do to me, Chuckie?" he said. "The mayor tells me you're dragging his ass out of bed with cock-and-bull stories about illegal goings-on at the cemetery. You know it ain't like that, Chuckie. What are you tryin' to do?"

"Sit down, Duff, and stop looking like you want to belt somebody in the mouth."

"Yeah, well, the thought's crossed my mind."

I tried not to laugh. "C'mon, Duff, I never once mentioned your name."

"Fat lot of good that did me," he said, taking my advice and dropping onto the edge of a chair. "Anything that goes on out there I'm supposed to know about."

"And do you?"

Duffy squinted. "Do I what?"

"Do you know everything that's going on?"

"Whoa. No you don't, pal. I'm not putting my tit in the wringer for nobody. I'm just here to see what the hell's eating you. Find out where you got all these crazy ideas about selling people's graves and throwing away their remains, that's all."

"What difference does it make, Duff? You know it's going on, the mayor knows it, at least two members of the city council know it, and nobody's put a stop to it."

"Let me explain a few facts of life to you, Chuckie." Duffy stuck his cigarette in the corner of his mouth and held out his left hand palm up, ready to count the things he was going to explain.

"Hey, Duffy, you can save yourself some time because I'm not interested. You got some defenses, some excuses, some explanations? Well, I don't want to hear them. In fact, I don't want to hear anything about the cemetery unless it's bad. You know why, Duff? Because I really don't give a damn about the cemetery. All I care about is my client. I don't want him going before the grand jury. Right now the mayor doesn't understand the extent of my concern and so I've got to convince him. And you know what I'm going to use to do it, Duff? You know what I'm going to use to convince him that it's not wise to mix politics with the courts? Right—the cemetery business."

Duffy's face got very fragile. I had the feeling it was going to crack and pieces were going to fall into his lap. "Hey, Chuckie, it's not the mayor you're going to hurt. The only one who's going to get it on this is Buster Vizarelli. A goddamned disabled vet. What's he ever done to you?"

"I didn't see anything disabled about him."

Duffy took the cigarette out of his mouth and gaped at me in astonishment. "Didn't you see his left arm? My God, the guy can't hardly use it. He's a fucking war hero, Chuckie. Also, he's got a lot of friends, which is something you should know before you go stirring up trouble."

"Whatever may be wrong with his arm, it doesn't stop him from being able to stick bucks in his wallet."

"Chuckie . . . hey, what am I gonna do with this goddamn ciggie? You don't even got any ashtrays around here."

"Most people take the hint and don't smoke."

Duffy got up and threw the cigarette out the window. He didn't bother to look to see if he had hit anybody down below. He just went back to his seat. "Chuckie, I known you a long time, right? Listen to me for a moment, will ya? This is a dangerous game you're playing. You got a big future in this city, the mayor says so himself. The mayor was very impressed by you, Chuckie, and you should know that. You don't want to go fucking it up now, getting on the wrong side of people over some guinea cop. Nothing's going to happen to that kid, anyway. Believe me. You think anybody's gonna put a cop away? You think they're even gonna pull his badge for shooting a burglar? Be realistic, Chuckie."

I suddenly had had enough. Taking guff from Sid Silverman, or the mayor, or Jimbo Ryder, was one thing. Taking it from this little turd was something else altogether. "Who the hell are you to tell me how to practice law, Duffy? You go to law school? You ever do anything besides sit around and kiss McLaughlin's fat ass?"

Duffy rose immediately to his feet. "You should talk," he said, his voice choked, his words garbled. "How you think you're gonna win this case—wear your fucking football helmet into the courtroom? That don't cut no shit anymore, asshole. You're all grown up now, you know. You're not playing games with kids anymore."

"Oh, go on and get out of here, Duffy. Get out of here so I can fumigate the room."

I was actually thinking about the odor of his cigarettes when I made that remark, but Duffy did not take it that way and the moment was not appropriate for explanation. I let him scald me with a murderous look and find his own way out.

I sat alone in my office for much of the rest of the afternoon, wondering if I had any idea what I was doing. Viewed in the abstract, the approach I was taking to this case did seem crazy. Wasn't I creating unnecessary problems for myself? Shouldn't I be concentrating all my time and energy on a strict legal defense, and wasn't there something more I could do to establish Richie's innocence? Out in San Francisco, somebody had practically gotten away with killing the mayor and a city supervisor by arguing that he had eaten too many Twinkies and that they had made him temporarily insane. Could I establish a diminished-capacity defense in Massachusetts on the basis of all the junk food Richie had eaten at the Burger Pit over the course of his life? No, it wouldn't work. Under that test all the jurors, the judge, the bailiff, the court reporter, the attorneys on both sides—everybody would prove just as demented.

Duffy was right. It was unthinkable that Richie DelVecchio would ever be convicted of anything. None of those cheeseburger-eating, cola-swilling jurors was going to convict a cop of protecting their homes. Hell, half of them had guns under the beds themselves. People in Portshead believed in shooting burglars. They wanted to shoot burglars. This was a city in which all a man had was in his home. So maybe we were going to be all right after all.

Except that conviction wasn't the only issue we had to worry about. In any public trial Richie was almost certain to be exposed as an unqualified cop, and in reality, wasn't that what McLaughlin was banking on? He would have the campaign brochures already printed: "Look What Happened When James Ryder Placed Himself and His Family Above the Great American System of Employment Based on Merit."

Even a victory in court was going to cost Richie DelVecchio the thing he wanted most in the world—his job. As Sid had told me, I was supposed not only to clear Richie of charges but to keep charges from being brought. Still, there are limits to a lawyer's responsibility to his client and I had no doubt I was trespassing well beyond those limits in the game I was playing with Mayor McLaughlin. I was laying my career on the line to save Richie DelVecchio's, and that really was crazy.

Thoroughly discouraged, I told Davida to lock up the office and went down to the Plough and Stars for a drink.

I caught the boys in the middle of a Red Sox reminiscence.

"Ike DeLock, Bob Porterfield, Frank Sullivan and Tom Brewer—that was the pitching staff they had the first time I ever saw them play," Pastore was saying. "Back in the fifties."

"Fuckin' good pitching staff, too," Boyle said.

"Yeah?" Stevie Ferris said. "Then how come they never won a pennant?"

"The rest of the guys all stunk," Boyle reasoned.

"Who?" asked Pastore. "Like Ted Williams, Jimmy Piersall, Jackie Jensen?"

Boyle was out of his element in arguing with Pastore, who probably still had all his baseball cards, but Boyle was never one to learn from defeat. "They didn't have no catching," he answered.

"No?" Pastore said. "They only had Haywood Sullivan, who now owns the fucking team, Pete Daley, who wasn't bad, and Sammy White, who was fucking great until they tried to trade him to Philadelphia and he quit to open up a bowling alley in Brighton."

Donovan walked by. "I been there," he said. "I once saw Paul Pender getting shitfaced there at the bar in Sammy White's Brighton Bowl."

"Who's Paul Pender?" Boyle asked.

Donovan looked disgusted. "He was only the fucking middleweight champion of the world."

"Oh, yeah," said Boyle, sparing the rest of the guys who could not remember who Paul Pender was.

For a while the conversation turned to tales about who had beaten up whom and then somebody started talking about all the financial killings different people were making. At one point it was decided that I must be making a bundle and I nearly had to tell them what I was bringing home in order to get them off my back. Just in time, I remembered Sid's admonition about making people think I was somebody special, and rather than disappoint everybody with the bad news I managed to keep my mouth shut.

By the time Boyle, Pastore, Ferris and I got to Capaletti's Pizza around ten-thirty, the discussion had degenerated about as far as it was going to get.

"Say, Chuckie," Boyle said, looking at me bleary-eyed as the four of us huddled together in one of Capaletti's booths over our second pitcher of beer and waited for our pizza to arrive. "Can I ask you a question? I mean a real serious question. One I've always wanted to ask you."

"Don't do it," Pastore said, apparently knowing what the question was.

Boyle had been drinking since he had gotten off work in the late afternoon. When he drank he got belligerent. "Fuck you, Ziggy," he said. "Chuckie's my oldest friend and I can ask him anything I want to. Me and him go back before anybody ever heard of you." He looked at me for confirmation. "Remember when Sandy Campbell hit you over the head with a shovel, Chuckie? And me and you waited for him in the bushes and jumped him and—and—and I beat his fucking head against the sidewalk?"

Boyle was talking about an incident that had occurred when we were five years old, and he had it screwed up. Sandy had hit me with a shovel because Boyle and I had ganged up on him in a fight that must have lasted all of twenty seconds. I told Boyle I remembered.

"And we got drunk together the first time, too. We got some fag to buy us some vodka and we drank it under this rowboat down on the beach near Black Creek and when Chuckie got sick I helped him get all the puke off his clothes so his parents wouldn't find out. Remember that, Chuckie? Remember how we kept saying we couldn't feel anything after we had killed the bottle, so we kept spinning ourselves around in circles until we were sure we were drunk? Remember how I helped you that night, Chuckie?"

I told Boyle I remembered.

He was getting maudlin and I could see tears starting to well up in his eyes. "You're all right, Chuckie," he said. "You and me been best friends all these years even though you went off and became a hot shit and all. You still hang around with all your old buddies, even though we're just a bunch of plumbers and construction workers."

Boyle himself worked in a photography studio. It was a trade he had learned in the service. But Stevie Ferris was a plumber and Ziggy worked construction. They exchanged hurt looks.

"Fuck you, Boyle," Ziggy said. "I'll match paychecks with you any day."

"Fuck you," said Boyle. "I was talking about Chuckie, anyhow. At least he's not like that asshole Kincaid, who thinks just because he puts on a white shirt when he goes to work he's too good to see any of his old friends anymore."

Boyle put his hand on my shoulder. "Seriously, Chuckie, you're all right. I mean, you can get along good with everybody. You can talk to judges and lawyers all day long and then come home at night and get along just as good with guys like us. You're a real man of the people, Chuckie. You oughta think about running for something."

This was becoming embarrassing. I tried to think of something funny to say because both Stevie and Pastore were getting worked up. "Yeah, I'm a fucking saint," I said, but nobody paid any attention.

"Kiss my ass, Boyle," Ziggy said, and I seemed to be the only one who caught the joke. "I can talk to lawyers as easy as anybody else."

"Yeah?" Boyle sneered. "I'd like to see you try. It's not just using a bunch of big words, you know. It's the way you say stuff and the kinds of things you say."

"Well, I'm talking to a lawyer right now and I'm doing okay, aren't I?"

"Who?" Boyle demanded.

"Chuckie. Isn't Chuckie a fucking lawyer?" And then both Ziggy and Stevie Ferris burst into laughter.

Boyle did not join in with them. "All I'm saying is that Chuckie could be fucking governor if he wanted to, because he's a guy can talk to anybody."

"Will you knock it off, Boyle?" I said.

Stevie put his mug down and rested his elbows on the table. "You ever thought about it, Chuckie?" he said. "I mean, everybody knows that Boyle's an asshole—"

"Fuck you, Stevie."

"—but he may have a point. It's guys like you who get elected. You could kick the shit out of some of the morons they got in office now."

Ziggy spoke up. "You should look into running for Jimbo Ryder's seat."

My head snapped back. "What makes you think it's going to be available?"

Ziggy shrugged. "My uncle Jimmy. He told me Vinnie Salvucci just rented him a storefront on Franklin Street. Three-month lease. What else is he gonna use it for except to open a campaign office, which he sure don't need to get reelected to the fucking city council."

"When did this happen?"

"Couple of days ago. Maybe you shouldn't go spreading it around, though. I don't know if anybody's supposed to know."

"He's probably gonna run for mayor," Stevie said. "And if he does, you should go after his seat. We'll get you in there working on some important stuff. Legalize marijuana, prostitution. Investigate the mysterious connection between South Korea and the 7-11 store. Find out why the Chinese can't drive. . . ."

"Let's talk about something else," I said. "What was the question you wanted to ask me, Boyle?"

Boyle thought back and slowly a smile spread over his face. "Oh, yeah. Promise you won't get pissed off now, Chuckie?"

"Hey, Boyle," Stevie said, poking Ziggy, "you just told us a minute ago you could ask him anything you want because the two of you did your first circle jerk together or something."

"Fuck you, Stevie. I said we did our first drunk together."

Stevie and Pastore giggled.

"What is it you want to know, Kevie?"

Boyle's lips stretched into a positively Rabelaisian grin. It was infectious and we began to grin along with him.

"Well?" I said.

Boyle kept his eyes on me. "I always wanted to know this, okay? And it's only 'cause I'm kinda drunk right now and we been talking about broads all night, otherwise I probably wouldn't be asking."

The buildup was tipping me off and I was beginning to lose my grin. But I nodded, anyhow.

"I hope you don't mind answering this. Do you think you will? Because if you do I won't say nothing. I just figure it's all right because it's been a long time."

"It depends, Kevin. I don't know what you're going to ask me."

"Okay," he said, grinning uncertainly at the others to get up his courage. "What's she really like in the rack, Chuckie?"

"Who?" I said.

"Cookie." He kept grinning.

Stevie Ferris and Ziggy Pastore groaned and fell back on their seat. Stevie had his hands over his eyes and Ziggy was staring incredulously, but Boyle was oblivious.

"She was okay," I said. I took a sip of beer.

"No, seriously, Chuckie. I really want to know. What was she like? You can't just say that she was okay. Not somebody like her. I mean, I used to get these wet dreams over her in high school. Those big fucking tits like rocks and that hoobie ass. Really, I used to get fuckin' hard-ons over her. Not after you were married, of course, except we all used to think what it must have been like for you to come home and have that waiting for you. But when you were going out with her, she was like this fucking movie star. You know what I mean?"

"She's a good woman, Kevin," I said.

"Yeah," he said, squirming just a little bit closer to me on the red plastic-covered seat, "but was she like the best you ever had?"

"Hey, Boyle," Ziggy suddenly said, "why don't you cut the shit? Can't you see he doesn't want to talk about it?"

"Oh." Boyle was surprised. He looked at me differently now and I continued drinking my beer. "I'm sorry, Chuckie. It's just something I always wondered about."

"God, Boyle," Pastore said disgustedly. "Don't you have any class? It's like asking somebody about your mother."

"Fuck you, Ziggy," he said, and then, fortunately, the pizza came.

I left the boys at Capaletti's and went directly to the Holiday Inn, where I ordered a stinger and looked around for the waitress who had shown such interest in me the night before. When it was clear in my mind that she was not on duty, I finished my drink and left with disappointment in my heart. She may have been an older woman and she may have looked as if she had been through a few rodeos in her time, but she had liked me, and that counted for something. Sure, her breasts hung a bit farther than they should have, but they had been large. Sure, her skin was as coarse as an avocado's, but that simply gave her face some history. Sure, her hair style was sufficiently out of date that I would not have wanted to see her in the daylight, but that was not the plan anyhow. It was that kind of attitude that made me realize I was ready for King Arthur's.

Friday night is King Arthur's time of the week. When I arrived the tables were all occupied and the bar was jammed with far too many people boisterously bantering with someone who always seemed to be just the other side of the person next to them. It was more chance than anything else that I ended up squeezed into a space next to the service area and it was quite unexpected when Cookie's friend Terry asked me to move out of the way so she could get her tray down on the rubber mat.

She wasn't from the Holiday Inn, but she was a waitress.

"Hi, Terry," I said, and it only took her a second to place me.

The phone woke me long before I would have chosen to get up if left to my own devices. Some very large hunk of flesh stirred, sighed contentedly and snuggled closer to me as I tried to reach for the receiver. I raised myself up to see who it was and nearly got swept flat on my back again by the nausea I felt as I tried to peer through a mass of black hair on the pillow beside me.

The phone kept ringing. I crawled into a straddle position on my unknown guest and picked it up.

"Chuckie," said a voice that was both familiar and yet unrecognizable. "You've got to get here right away."

"Who—me?" I said. Then some semblance of reason began to take hold in my mind. "Wait a minute—who is this?"

As I was speaking, the unknown guest lifted her face from under the covers and opened her eyes.

"Terry," I gasped.

"No," the voice on the phone said. "This is your secretary, Davida. And somebody's rifled the office."

It did not quite register. "Did what to the office?"

"Chuckie, will you get with it? We've been burglarized. I left just after you did yesterday and figured I'd come in this morning and finish up that brief you wanted for Monday. There was something wrong; I could sense it as soon as I came inside. Sure enough, somebody was in here going through the files, Chuckie."

"Is there anything missing?"

"I don't know. That's why I want you to come over. I didn't want to touch anything until you got here."

"Okay." It was all I could think of to say. Terry was lying on her back watching me. The smile she was wearing did not obscure the specks of white at the ends of her mouth or the balls of black in the corners of her eyes. I could tell by the way she looked at me that she thought we were still enjoying each other's company.

"Chuckie, do you understand what I'm saying? Are you still there?" Davida's voice was roaring in my ear.

"Yeah." I was looking at Terry. She arched her back, spreading her elbows out to the sides. Her breasts, with nipples the size of half lemons, lay flat from the position she was in, but she was pushing them up toward me. I was trying to think what I should do.

"You're coming over here, aren't you?" Davida said.

"Yeah," I said. "I'll be there in five minutes."

Below me Terry made a face.

"You sure you can make it, Chuckie? You don't sound so good."

"Uh, call Finucci at police headquarters. See if you can get him to come over."

Somehow I made it to the shower, where I used the spray to try to beat the sickness out of me. I did my best to look at things on the bright side. I told myself that at least I was not going to have to think up an excuse for getting rid of Terry. I would not even have to take her out to breakfast, something which almost seemed important at that moment.

She was standing naked by the sink brushing her teeth as I shut the water off and stepped out to dry myself. She was using my toothbrush. I tried to remember if I had any new ones packed away anywhere.

"Bad news," she said, balancing a mouthful of toothpaste liquid as she spoke.

"Huh?" Some of the liquid escaped and she bent over to plop it in the sink. Her breasts hung straight down as if they were weighted with buckshot.

"Bad news," I agreed. I patted her on the behind as I passed by. It shimmied.

"I have to get over to my office before the cops do. There's been a break-in." I pulled on a pair of Slim Guy boxer shorts and khaki-colored pants.

"Want me to come with you?" she asked, leaning against the doorway.

I looked at the sheets in total disarray on the bed. I would have to change them as soon as I got back. As soon as I felt better.

"No, Terry. I'll be going over my losses, filling out reports, that sort of thing. I'll probably be there all day."

"Oh," she said. She walked to the end of the bed and picked a pair of bikini underwear off the floor. When she bent over, her stomach divided into shelves. "You want me to make you some breakfast? I make a mean omelet."

"Terry . . ." I did not like the tone of my own voice and I took some quick deep breaths and tried again. "Terry, I appreciate it, but this is an emergency and I'm just going to grab a cup of coffee." I selected a shirt from a hanger in the closet without looking over at her.

She was beginning to get the picture. "Well, what about me? I've got to get home."

"Where did we leave your car?"

"Don't you remember? You told me to have my sister bring it home last night."

"Your sister?" I slid into my shoes and looked around for a hairbrush.

"That was after you couldn't get her to come back here with us, remember?"

I was at the point where I wasn't interested in remembering anything. I just wanted the hairbrush. That was all. Just the goddamn hairbrush. I began irritably tossing things around, and that made Terry turn away from the dresser mirror, where she was casually stroking her long black hair into place.

"Jesus, is that my brush? Can I see that for a minute?"

"My God, you don't have to get mad about it." She threw it on the bed and folded her arms across her chest.

I took the brush into the bathroom and used the mirror in there.

"What's the matter with you, anyhow?" she said, following me.

I stopped what I was doing and gripped the sides of the sink with both hands. I stared fixedly at the wet-haired, stubbly-bearded, bloodshot-eyed image in the mirror as though it belonged to a separate person. At that particular moment there was a hardness in my liquor-swollen reflection that I admired. And yet as soon as I realized how the hardness must have appeared to Terry, I no longer wanted to look that way.

I turned and gathered her into my arms. The odor of the night before came off her skin and made me queasy for an instant, but her body felt luxurious in its suppleness as it pressed against mine.

"I'm sorry, Terry. I'm a little upset and a lot hung over. You're a nice person and I really don't have any business taking it out on you."

"That's okay," she whimpered, babylike and understanding.

I had to choke back the near rage that surged through my chest. I didn't want her to be understanding; I wanted her to beat it with a smile on her face. Go off and tell my ex-wife what a great lover I was, but not ever bother me again. Yet here she was, forgiving me for my frailties as though they were just something with which she was going to have to live.

"Ah, listen," I said between clenched teeth. "You think you can get a cab home if I pay for it?"

"All the way to Randolph?" She was telling me I couldn't be serious. Randolph was a twenty-five-dollar ride if it was a dime.

I tried to imagine what I had done to get myself in such a situation. It was the drink, I knew. There were no two ways about it—I was going to have to give it up.

Suddenly things got immeasurably brighter. Terry took my hand and ran it down her side to her thigh. "Listen, don't worry about me," she said. "I can call a friend who lives near here and get him to give me a ride." She came down heavily on the pronoun.

"You sure it wouldn't be too much trouble?" I said solicitously as my heart leaped with joy.

Lieutenant Finucci stalked my office. Every now and then he would stop and pick up something, usually a document or a page of a document. He would glance at it and put it back down.

"Place looks all right to me," he said. "What makes you think something's missing?"

Davida answered. "I didn't leave my desk this way and Chuckie didn't leave his office the way it is now."

"Maybe the cleaning people sat down for a smoke."

"The file cabinets have been opened, I can tell. Look." She pulled open the cabinet that was marked "A–D." "Those are supposed to be in alphabetical order and look at them."

"I only see a couple out of order," Finucci said after a minute.

"That's enough. Neither Chuckie nor I would have done that."

Finucci nodded. "Where's your petty-cash box? You have one?"

Davida took a key and opened a cabinet next to her desk. She took out a nine-by-twelve-by-three-inch strongbox. Anyone looking for valuables could easily have forced open the door of the cabinet and walked out with the box under his arm.

"What's in it?" Finucci gave the box a shake.

"About fifty bucks, a couple of rolls of stamps and some checks," Davida told him.

"I guess that wasn't what they wanted," Finucci said, handing the strongbox back. "What do you figure?"

"This remind you of any other burglary we've had around here recently, Lieutenant?" I asked.

Finucci eyed me carefully. "I thought that's why you called me. You figure this has something to do with DelVecchio." He pushed his hands into the pockets of the checked sport coat he was wearing over his polo shirt and leaned back on his heels. "So, like I asked a minute ago, what's missing?"

"Nothing, Lieutenant. Just like at Lanny Brandon's."

"You have a file on DelVecchio, something like that?"

I took him into my office and showed where I had left the DelVecchio file buried among half a dozen others in a pile on the floor behind my desk. Someone had rearranged the pile and the DelVecchio file was now on top. It still contained my notes, scratched out in pen on yellow-lined legal paper; my research on the question of a temporary restraining order; the letters to and from Henry Woodruff; and the letter notices of suspension and inquest.

"Not much here," Finucci commented.

"But there's nothing missing, either."

"Could they have thought there was another file?"

"Maybe."

Finucci shut the file and made his customary rattling noise in the back of his throat. "So what do you want me to do?"

"Take fingerprints. Get in a photographer. Notify the newspaper. You probably won't find anything, but we'll be setting the stage. One more bit of circumstantial evidence for the public to chew on if we get to the point where we have to scream setup or something."

Finucci scowled. "Is that what it's coming down to?"

"You tell me, Lieutenant. We're three days away from the inquest and your boss still hasn't released your departmental report."

Finucci mulled over what I was saying and then went to the phone to call for an investigative team. On the other side of the desk from where he stood, Davida was cursing up a storm. "Goddamn shitty sons of bitches, crinkling up this brief I was working on. They had no reason to do that, goddamn it. They were just being mean."

I did not get home until midafternoon. The surprise I felt at discovering my office had been visited was nothing compared with what I felt when I opened the door and found a dazzlingly clean apartment. The papers and magazines that had been lying around for nearly two weeks were now neatly stacked on the coffee table. The rugs had been vacuumed, the plants watered, the dishwasher emptied and the kitchen floor had even been waxed. In the bedroom my sheets had been changed, my pillows were stacked two high and the covers were turned down invitingly on one side. Pinned to the top pillow was a note: "Anytime you need maid service, just whistle. You do know how to whistle, don't you?" Below that was a Randolph phone number.

I put the note in a drawer. I would have thrown it away except for the fact that she'd done such a nice job cleaning up.

27 It had just gotten dark when the phone rang. I was thumbing through a copy of *Sports Illustrated* and half watching a Goldie Hawn movie on television. Sorry that I had not made some arrangements for the evening, I was hoping that whoever was calling was extending an invitation to do something interesting.

The good news was that it was a woman. The bad news was that she was sobbing hysterically and could barely get my name out. It was Linda DelVecchio and that was all she could tell me as she just cried and cried and cried. I had to wait a long time before she was able to go on.

"It's Richie," she said, as I had known she would. "He's gone crazy."

Keeping my voice calm, I asked her what he had done.

"Everything. It's gotten worse and worse all week." She gasped, momentarily in better control. "Remember how he was sort of nervous about things before? And then he began blaming everybody else. The chief, Jimbo, the other guys on the force—even you. And then he began blaming me and the kids, Chuckie. He wouldn't let me help him, he wouldn't even talk to me about it. So I tried to stay out of his way, but he's around all the time and he won't even go out of the house and every time the least little thing goes wrong he starts yelling." She broke off with deep braying sounds as she tried to catch her breath.

"Tonight he got all mad about a lamp he was trying to rewire and when I offered to help him he just went wild for no reason and started screaming at me about how he could do anything he wanted and how he didn't need me or anybody else. I was only trying to defend myself, Chuckie, and he hit me. He . . . he . . . ." Her voice rose into kind of a scream that made all the words run together so that I could barely distinguish them. "Hebrokemynose . . . andhehad-meinthecorner . . . andhekepthittingme . . . Idon'twanttogethitanymore-Chuckie."

I had to wait again and while I waited I tried all the soothing things I could say. The words meant nothing, I knew. I was just Muzaking her.

"Is he there now, Linda?"

"He's gone. He ran out of the house and raced the car all the way down the street. He's gone crazy, Chuckie."

"He didn't take his gun, did he?"

"Oh, my God," she said. She dropped the phone and I could hear footsteps going away. In a few seconds she was back. "No, thank God; it's still in the cabinet."

"That's good, Linda. Now where do you think he might have gone?"

"I don't know," she wailed.

A moment like this, a man like Richie, and a mind like mine, I could only figure him going to a bar. It took me some time to get out of her a list of his favorite places. She mentioned Freddie's in Lighthouse Harbor, Babe's near the Center, the Breakers at the beach, O'Connor's and the Lucky 13 down the Hook.

We agreed that Linda would call her mother to take her to the hospital and that her mother would bring one of her sisters over to watch the kids. I told her I would do my best to find Richie and get him home before he hurt himself or someone else and I promised I would call her back. Within fifteen minutes I was in my car and on Richie's trail.

Freddie's, I guessed, would be too close to home. Babe's, although closest to me, would be out because it was a cops' bar and he would be unlikely to want to see anyone on the force. A man as upset as Richie was also not likely to head for the fun and high jinks of the Breakers. That left the Hook bars, and they were within a block of each other.

O'Connor's was the logical choice. It was large, dimly lit and rowdy. It had pool tables and electronic game machines. It also had a reputation for fights and once or twice it had even seen a shooting. So I went there first.

The parking lot was jam-packed, the green neon shamrock sign was glowing and the music from the juke was pouring out the door when I arrived. Somebody pulled out of a street space that was covering a crosswalk and I nosed the Firebird in on his bumper. I got out and walked halfway through the parking lot before I noticed the crowd that had gathered a few aisles away. There were fifteen or twenty backs between me and whatever was going on. Most of the backs were males', but there were a few women and their sharp voices could be heard rising above the guttural shouts of some of the men. I tried to push my way through and caught an elbow. I gave a shove in return and the elbower said, "Hey," and spun around real fast. But it was Cimoli, a guy who had been on the football team with me, and when he saw who it was he said, "Sorry, Chuckie. Didn't know it was you."

He let me squeeze past him and I got close enough to see Richie's Mustang standing in the middle of the aisle with the driver's door wide open. I put my head down and burst through the last line of spectators.

Two men were slugging it out on the pavement. One of them was my client and he was clearly getting the worst of it. He was in a semi-crouched position, his right hand hooked in the other man's hair and his left arm bent in front of his face as he tried to ward off the punches that were smashing into the side of his head. One punch came in particularly hard and dropped Richie onto his back.

"Get him now, Mikey," the man next to me screamed. His legs were bent at the knees, his body was tilted forward, and his hands and face were both clenched as he urged his friend on. He looked like a weightlifter about to execute a power jerk with an imaginary barbell.

I tapped him on the shoulder. "Help me break this up," I said.

"Fuck you," he told me. "That asshole's getting what he deserves."

I moved in alone. "All right, break it up, break it up," I yelled so nobody would think I was just going after the man on top. I grabbed him under the arms and around the chest and tried to pull him off. "Okay, you got him, buddy. You got him good. Let him go now, let him up."

"Let 'em fight," somebody in the crowd shouted, and the man I had tried to get to help moved forward. He was a stocky bastard in his late thirties, with thick black sideburns, receding hair and a bull neck. His eyes were locked on me and his lips were twisted. The moment I saw him draw his hand back, I decided not to wait to see if he was going to come forward with it. I let go of the fighter and slashed up in a big, arcing backhanded swing that hit my assailant far harder than I had intended. The smack that resulted as my hand made contact with the side of his face sounded like a watermelon that had been dropped from a two-story building. He pitched over into the crowd and I went back to dragging the other guy off Richie.

By this time the fighter was tired and he let me haul him up with just enough struggling and grunting to let everybody know that if left on his own he would still be whacking away. Unfortunately, Richie, who had taken eight or ten straight blows, hadn't had enough. He kicked out from where he was lying, just missing his target and connecting solidly with the man's thigh. It was a real mistake. The man had a sudden renewal of adrenaline and he broke away from my hold. He absolutely buried Richie with an avalanche of kicks to his hips and ribs and head. I tried to get in there one more time and out of nowhere a big fist blasted me in the eye.

This time I went down, but as I did I heard a voice—was it Cimoli's?—shout, "They're beatin' up on Chuckie," and then everything around me was chaos.

I was on the ground and several people were on top of me. Nobody seemed to be swinging down where I was, everyone was just trying to stand up. Somewhere there was the hint of a siren and somebody screamed "Cops" and then almost everyone started scrambling. I was kicked more than once, but it was only by feet trying to find the ground. A figure in a white T-shirt and black dungarees was the last to stir at the bottom of the pile. I seized the figure's legs. It was

Richie. He was struggling to get away and I was calling to him urgently, "Wait, Richie, wait. You *are* a cop."

By the time the first police car stopped and the blue light was rocketing around the parking lot, most of the people from inside O'Connor's had come outside and only Richie and I had stayed in place. Except for us, it was impossible to tell who had been involved in the fighting and who had not. It was, therefore, particularly fortunate that the first police car was driven by my old buddy Logan.

Logan got out with a flashlight in one hand and a billy club in the other. I was lifting Richie to his feet and Logan helped me get him sitting down on the front bumper of his Mustang.

"Looks like you got the worst of it, Rich," he said, surveying the crowd. "Can you point out who it is?"

Richie mumbled something that didn't make any sense. He did, indeed, look as if he'd gotten the worst of it. The knees were torn out of his pants. His hands and his forearms were scraped raw and trickling blood. The blood was flowing faster from his nose and his mouth and there looked to be a very large, very purplish bruise on the side of his forehead.

I told Logan I thought maybe we should try to keep things quiet. "I don't think we want the word to get around that Richie was involved here."

"The guy sucker-punched me," Richie said, covering his brow.

"Yeah, I'm sure he did, Rich, but you don't know the damage this kind of publicity can do to you."

"It was my fucking parking space. I'd been sitting here for half an hour waiting for this guy to get out and as soon as he does this bastard comes in from the other direction and takes it."

Logan looked at me and I made a face. A second police car was approaching and I suggested it would be best if we just got Richie home. Richie said he didn't want to go home, but Logan and I got him into the passenger's seat of his car and then I went around and got behind the wheel. Logan told me to take off and I did.

We had no sooner left the parking lot when Richie announced he could have beaten the motherfucker. He was slumped against the door, his eyes staring someplace around the ashtray, and he didn't look as if he could have beaten a bowl of cake batter. He was, I could see, not yet ready to go back to his wife. Trying to think of an alternative, I spied the Lucky 13 and pulled over. It was a bar I had been to many times, but had never patronized. It was the bar where my father had spent at least part of over five thousand nights.

"How about if we go nurse our wounds over a beer, Richie?"

He looked at me suspiciously. "You got some wounds?"

I flicked on the overhead light and looked in the rearview mirror. "I hope to God this isn't a shiner, Richie, or you and I are going to look like a couple of bozos walking into court on Tuesday."

He glanced out the window. "I don't want to go in there. I know people there."

That was fine with me. I turned the key in the ignition, but Richie's hand suddenly shot out and covered mine, twisting it until the engine died. "I don't want to go home," he said. "Don't take me home."

"Where do you want to go?"

He slumped back into his seat, the picture of a man adrift. "Anywheres."

"Right," I said, and started up the car again. "How about if we just go for a ride? Drive around and see if we can't get you to cool off a little."

"Yeah," Richie said, "just go anywheres. I don't care."

There are tougher jobs, I am sure, than cruising around on a Saturday night with a client like Richie DelVecchio. Washing the johns in a leper colony or cleaning up spills in nuclear reactors are two that come immediately to mind.

Richie would not have been good company on his best days, and this was not one of them. He told me he was going to find out the name of the guy who had sucker-punched him. He knew what kind of car the guy had and he would go through every motor vehicle record in the state until he found him. "Then we'll see how tough that asshole really is," he said. "I'll make his life miserable."

We drove down by the beach while Richie explained to me that he was nobody to screw around with. We passed into North Portshead while Richie wondered who it was who thought he could screw around with him on this inquest thing. "It's not me they want, it's Jimbo," he informed me, just as if I hadn't been the one to tell him that very thing.

We crossed into Ashton and drove back into Portshead along Hamilton Street. By now Richie was lecturing me on the fact that there wasn't one man in the police department with balls enough to stand up to the mayor, and he was so busy talking he did not notice when we drove past the Brandon house.

It was, at that hour of the night, ablaze in lights. Every window seemed to have at least one light burning. There might even have been a party going on, except that the only car in the driveway was Alicia's Datsun 280Z.

A hundred yards down the road I did a U-turn and drove back until I found a space under some trees across the street and down a ways from the Brandons'. The shadows hid us, but did not obscure our view of the Brandons' front door.

"What are we doing here?" Richie said.

I pointed to the house. "You have any idea what Fitzy might have been after? You given it any thought at all?"

Richie followed the direction of my finger and stared for some time. "Dope," he said finally. It was clear that he thought that was what I wanted him to say and he reacted with surprise when I groaned.

"Why do I keep hearing that? Is that the only thing that could have caused him to come out empty-handed? Couldn't he have been looking for jewels or a stamp collection or Krugerrands or something? Why, Richie, why does it have to be dope?"

Richie squirmed. "Well, everybody knows it would look better for me if drugs were involved," he said.

"Who told you that?"

"Everybody. You know. Everybody says that."

"The guys on the force?"

Richie shrugged. "People don't get so upset if they think it's just a junkie got killed. Everybody knows that."

We watched the Brandon house in silence for a few more minutes, but there was nothing more that either of us had to say. I drove Richie back to O'Connor's and picked up my car and then I followed him out to Lighthouse Harbor. He told me it wasn't necessary, but I said I had promised his wife and that I personally would feel a whole lot better if I saw that he got home safely. I told him if he weren't around I wouldn't get paid for all the work I was planning to do, and that made him accept the arrangement almost as if he was doing me a favor.

Still, I practically had to pull him out of his car when we got to his house. Then the porch light came on and Linda walked out with a comical-looking white patch across the bridge of her nose. Richie hesitated only until she put out her arms and then he walked slowly to her and bent his head onto her shoulder. When I saw that, I knew everything would be all right for the night and I got back in my Firebird and drove off, feeling just a little bit like the Lone Ranger of Portshead.

28 The traffic was already streaming past my building on its way to the beach by the time I got out of bed on Sunday morning. The cars that went by had their windows open and I could hear their radios as I stood out on my balcony. I looked down through windshields, sunroofs and rear windows in an endless procession of vehicles filled with Styrofoam toys and rubber floats, metal coolers and aluminum chairs, plaid spreads and army blankets. My ardor for the pleasures of the ocean died a sudden death and I went back inside and made myself a Bloody Mary for breakfast.

I did a little work during the day, watched part of the game on the tube, and was napping on the couch when the phone rang sometime after four o'clock. It was Donovan. He said Angie DiMarco and a buddy had just come into the bar and he thought I might want to try talking to him. I said I would be right down.

As it turned out, Angie and I had already done some talking. He was none other than the cemetery worker who had so graciously gotten off his lawnmower to help me find Julia Woodruff's grave. When I walked into the bar he was seated at a round table in the corner, his back to the door. Donovan pointed him out to me with a jerk of his head.

The fact that Angie DiMarco was inside had not caused him to take off either his sunglasses or his army-green cap. His dark blue T-shirt had a spot shaped like the continent of Africa between his shoulder blades and he was wearing a formless pair of jeans—the kind with pockets on the thighs. His companion was a ponderously bellied, swarthy man with a nose so prominent that it made his darting little eyes look like misplaced nail holes left in a plaster wall by an inexperienced carpenter. They made quite a pair, Angie slouched over his beer and the other fellow sitting open-mouthed with his small hands folded beneath his belt as though they were the only things keeping his enormous stomach from crashing to the floor.

"Say," I said, drifting by their table and pointing at DiMarco, "aren't you the fella I spoke to at the cemetery the other day?"

DiMarco looked up without answering.

"Mind if I buy you a drink?" I asked.

DiMarco glanced at his friend and shrugged. It was a shrug of surprise more than acquiescence. Not having expected the offer, he was not prepared to reject it. I signaled to Donovan by circling my finger in the air and Donovan set about drawing a round of beers. I asked DiMarco's friend if he also worked at the cemetery and he said he did. He said his name was Rizzo.

I turned a chair around so that I was sitting on it with its back to the table. Doing that allowed me to join them without appearing part of them. It made them focus on me when we talked.

"You guys look like you been working today," I said.

"Goddamn right," DiMarco said. He did not look at me, but kept his eyes on his beer.

"Usually work on Sunday?"

"You want to put food on the table you do," DiMarco answered.

By way of explanation he added, "Time and a half."

"Hot out there, I'll bet."

"Goddamn right."

The beers came. DiMarco watched Donovan put his down and then stared at it as if it was a piece moved in a chess game. Mug to Queen three. Rizzo pushed aside the not quite empty glass he had been using and picked up the fresh one. He made a slight toast to me and drained half of it in one gulp.

"You guys have to do any digging today?"

"Yeah," DiMarco said, half snorting as he exchanged looks with Rizzo. "What do you think, we went out on a fucking Sunday to cut the goddamn grass?" It was said neither humorously nor maliciously. He was tired and I was an idiot. That's all there was to it.

"You ever come across any old bones when you're digging out there?"

DiMarco shrugged. "Sure."

"Well, where do they come from?"

"Those are from old graves," said Rizzo pleasantly.

"Yeah, those are from old graves," repeated DiMarco.

"Some of them have been there for a hundred years or more," Rizzo said. "You don't want to touch them with your hands if you can help it. You get diseases. You don't know what those guys might have died from."

I was disarmed. These cemetery workers not only were not denying that they dug up old graves; they were treating the act as though it were something commonplace.

"What happens then? You sell the graves again or something?"

Rizzo shrugged. "I don't know. We just dig 'em. Somebody gives us a lot number, we get out the backhoe and go do it."

"How come you're asking?" said DiMarco, his eyebrows arching above his sunglasses.

"Oh, I don't know. Just curious. For years they've been saying the cemetery was full and now I hear you can buy a plot if you talk to Vizarelli."

"Maybe," said Rizzo. "If anybody can sell you a plot, I guess it's him."

"Well, how does he do it? Does he reclaim graves that are a certain age, or what?"

"Yeah," said DiMarco. "I guess so."

"So then it's up to you guys to get rid of the old bones, is that it? Where do you throw them?"

Rizzo said, "There's a marsh out behind the public works garage. We dump them there."

DiMarco sat forward so that the lenses of his glasses were now aimed in my direction. "What are you, some kind of ghoul or something? What do you care what we do with the bones? The other day you kept insisting a grave was in the wrong place. What gives with you, anyhow?"

"Let's just say that I'd hate to find out that a grave I bought belongs to someone else."

"So don't buy one then." He peered closer at me. "Is there something wrong with your eye?"

I fingered the slightly swollen area where I had taken the punch the night before and denied there was anything wrong with it.

"What's your name, anyhow, buddy?"

"Bishop. Chuck Bishop."

"I heard that name somewheres before. You a reporter or something?"

"I'm an attorney."

DiMarco sat back. "And you're just curious, huh? Curious, my ass. Anytime a fucking lawyer says he's just curious, we're all in big trouble. C'mon, Pete, let's get outta here."

"Wait, Ange," Rizzo said, his voice whining. "I want to drink my beer."

DiMarco, who had already risen to his feet, leaned down with one hand on the table and gestured toward me, saying, "You want to get your ass in a fucking sling talking to a lawyer, you go right ahead. Me, I'm getting outta here."

"Go ahead," I told him, spreading my hands magnanimously. "It's just as easy for me to name you in a complaint as to leave you out. You get named in a complaint, you're going to have to hire your own attorneys and then you're going to have to answer all these questions in a deposition, under oath, with some little court reporter taking down every word you say. I thought maybe you'd prefer to talk to me now, see if we can't keep you out of this whole thing."

"What whole thing?"

"Why, a possible lawsuit, of course. Desecration of graves, breach of contract, conversion, negligence, fraud . . ."

"You can't sue us," DiMarco sneered, thumbing his chest. "We work for the city."

I smiled at him. "Don't be silly, Angie. The city doesn't pay you to rob graves or sell gravestones, and even if it did, you wouldn't be entitled to any immunity. Your best bet is to sit down and talk with me now."

"Jees," Rizzo said despondently, his shoulders sagging. "I don't want to get sued."

DiMarco rapped him on the chest with the back of his hand. "You wacko, Riz? You know how long our jobs would last, we talked with this guy? About five minutes. Buster'd come after us with a fucking shotgun like he did to fuckin' Dineen, for cryin' out loud. Maybe yours ain't, but my life's too fuckin' valuable to go around talkin' about things I don't know nothing about. Now let's get outta here."

Rizzo, his coarse features twisting into a map of confusion, pressed his hands down on his knees to get the leverage he needed to hoist his distorted figure into a standing position. I put my hand on his arm.

"If I can prove what I think I can, Pete, it's not your job that's gonna be on the line. It's Buster Vizarelli's."

"Are you shitting me?" DiMarco said, bending over and grabbing the front of his own shirt. "Don't you know who Buster is? Guys like me and Pete here are a dime a fuckin' dozen, but Buster—Buster's an important man in this city. Buster and the mayor are like that." He let go of his shirt and thrust two intertwined fingers in my face. "You want to talk to somebody, slit your own throat, go talk to John Dineen. He'll tell you whatever you want to know."

"Is he the one you said Buster went after with a shotgun?"

Rizzo looked at DiMarco. "It was a two-by-four. He tried to hit him with it in front of all of us one day."

"Why would he want to do that, do you know?"

"Ah," Angie DiMarco said, waving his hand disgustedly, "for writing crap about him. Dineen's one of these guys, he's been working down there twenty years and he thinks he shoulda gotten the superintendent's job instead of Buster. He kept trying to get Buster fired by complaining about him to his councilman —Harrington, I think it was, and Harrington finally got tired of being bothered and told him just to write it all down and send it in to the Oversight Committee."

Rizzo spoke up. "I guess John thought they would hold an investigation or something and he didn't want the cemetery board of managers claiming they didn't know nothing, so he sent the board a copy of everything he wrote."

"An' one of them guys on the board told Buster that Dineen was trying to go over their heads."

"Yeah."

"And Buster went apeshit, which is what he's gonna do with us if he finds out we been talkin' to you, so you can stay if you want, Rizzo, but I'm gettin' the fuck outta here."

DiMarco's anxiety at last succeeded in getting his amiable companion out of his seat and they trotted off, one after the other, with only Rizzo throwing a backward glance. As Donovan watched them slam through the front door, he turned to me and said, "Nice going, Chuckie. You just drove off my two best customers."

Before I could answer, one of the Chesterfield smokers, a shriveled old man who had been staring morosely out the window at the passing traffic, suddenly threw back his head and in a tenor voice as clear as a bell on a windless day, sang:

> *"I asked her for credit;*
> *She answered me, 'Nay,*
> *For it's custom like yours*
> *I can get any day. . . .' "*

Donovan whirled around on the singer. "Shut up, you old Mick sonofabitch, or I'll make you drink vodka the rest of the night."

The singer looked shocked for an instant, the prospect no doubt sending his stomach into convulsions. Not until he realized that Donovan was joking did he settle into a smile of his own. "Heh, heh," he said, looking around at the rest of us, "Heh, heh," and then he went back to sucking the life out of his cigarette.

It was ten o'clock when I drove through the Brandons' neighborhood. Lanny's Mercedes was in the drive and so was the 280Z. I had a quart of Ballantine ale with me and figured that my little parking space across from the Brandons' was as good a place as any to drink it. The problem was that there was no baseball game on the radio and, it being Sunday night, most of the stations had religious programs going. After a few minutes I decided not to listen to anything and so I just sat quietly, taking occasional swigs from the bottle.

The Brandons were the light-burningest couple I had ever known. Lights were on in the den, in the hallway, in the dining room and in at least three of the upstairs rooms—and that was only the front of the house. I was reflecting on this phenomenon when I was startled by a rather constant flapping noise coming up behind me. I turned around to see a jogger nearly abreast of my car and staring curiously in at me and the big green bottle I was resting against the steering wheel. I felt caught and for lack of anything better to do lifted my hand in what amounted to half a wave. The jogger nodded and set his face grimly ahead. He was breathing heavily and probably far more concerned with his heart count than with what a guy was doing parked in the shadows with nothing but a bottle of ale for company.

I started imagining what I would tell various people I was doing if they were to stop and ask me. "I was just too tired to go home, Officer. You see, I'd been drinking a little ale and I realized I shouldn't be driving, so I pulled off to wait for assistance. Thank God you're here." "Car just overheated and I've been waiting for it to cool down. Figured I might as well have a sip or two while I sat here." "Oh, just waiting for a friend, that's all. She's never been to Portshead before, so I gave her directions to this place here in the bushes."

One of the lights went off on the second floor. A minute or two passed and then the front door opened and Lanny walked outside. He looked up at the sky, lifted on his tiptoes and stretched his arms out wide. He might have been Jay Gatsby standing at the end of his pier and reaching for his destiny, except that the stretch lasted only a few seconds and ended with a slight stumble forward, and I realized that Lanny was just working out the cramps in his muscles. Desk-sitting cramps. I knew the feeling well. An occupational hazard.

I had complained to Sid Silverman about it one time, and Sid, who thought exercise was something you did with a medicine ball or Indian clubs, nodded sagely. "The logical result of a life style spent indoors," he said. "The toll exacted by thousands of hours sequestered in the grip of your high-backed vinyl chair. You're probably still telling people those little cushions above your hips are love handles. But now they're beginning to protrude through your shirt a bit and maybe your buttocks are beginning to jiggle and your belly keeps wanting to rest on your belt. What you need is therapy, my boy, therapy. You gotta go sit in the courtroom more. Toughen yourself by doing penance on the hard chairs and the wooden benches. You'll get that body tone back in no time."

I told him he should open an athletic club. Charge people annual dues and have a big gymnasium set up for them, with nothing in it but church pews and a shower room.

Lanny was holding his elbows out to the sides and swinging his trunk back and forth. He did it only a few times and then he bent over and quickly touched his toes. When he straightened up he walked around the Mercedes and got in behind the wheel. I lost my nerve, started my own engine and drove off quickly without waiting to see if he was going to come in my direction.

29 I gave Mayor McLaughlin until Monday afternoon to get in touch with me and then I walked over to City Hall to see what this fellow Dineen had written that had gotten someone on the board of managers so upset. Since the board had no office of its own, I assumed its public records would be kept in the City Hall room euphemistically known as the Hall of Records. When I called at the Hall of Records, however, the city clerk's staff proved unable to locate the file.

"One of the board members must have it. I'm sure it hasn't vanished into thin air," I was told by the disinterested woman behind the counter. She had pointy eyeglasses and a small sliver of gum in her mouth.

"Don't people have to sign anything when they take out a file?" I asked her.

She shrugged, flipped her gum over neatly with her tongue and snapped it at me.

"There must be some way you can tell me who has the file," I persisted, undaunted by her confectionery aggression.

"I can ask Mr. Dougherty."

Mr. Dougherty was the city clerk and the beloved disciple of Mayor McLaughlin. I thought it in my best interest not to expose my mission to him if I could possibly help it, especially since I still had open the option of going to the city council office, where the copies of Dineen's letters would have been placed in the Oversight Committee file.

I told the staffer that it would not be necessary to bother Mr. Dougherty and thanked her for her assistance. She nodded absently. Ask Mr. Dougherty or don't ask Mr. Dougherty, it made no difference to her. She had to be there anyhow.

I went up to the second floor, where off to the side of the city council chambers were the three offices that served all the individual members and their various committees. In the outermost office a single secretary, a woman with close-cropped hair and blue-veined hands, sat behind an IBM Selectric and a clutter of papers. On the pine-paneled wall behind her hung the official portrait of the mayor, beaming uncertainly, like a man who has just won first prize in a hot-dog-eating contest. On the wall across from her, above the copying machine, was a framed parchment drawing of the City of Bay View, as Portshead was then known, circa 1800. There were no pictures of the city council or any city council member.

A radio was softly playing AM rock, and despite the apparent plethora of work confronting her, the secretary was thumbing through an issue of *Good Housekeeping*. She was more than willing to put down her reading, snuff out her cigarette and chitchat with me.

"Iris," she said her name was, and when she found out mine the first thing she wanted to know was if I was related to John Bishop.

"My uncle," I said, and she looked delighted.

"I went to John Hancock High with him," she told me, and then she wanted to know whatever happened to good old Johnny, because she hadn't seen him in years.

"He moved to California when I was a kid."

She smiled knowingly. "Did he strike it rich?"

"I don't know. He's still there, if that means anything."

"He was always one of the brightest kids in the class, that Johnny. What does he do for a living, if you don't mind my asking?"

"I'm not sure. Something to do with computers. Listen, Iris—"

"I've got a sister out there, too, you know. June Wallace, that's her name now; it was June Mulligan. She's living in a place called Redlands and she woulda known Johnny from the old days. Next time you see Johnny you should ask him. Tell him to look her up."

"I don't see John very often, Iris. Listen—"

"Yeah, I imagine he doesn't get back much. Who can blame him? It's paradise out there."

"Iris," I said, speaking quickly before she could get on to something else, "I was wondering if I could look at some council records."

She sighed as though I had just ruined what had all the makings of a very good friendship. "I suppose," she said, "but you'll have to promise me you won't get anything out of order. We had a man in here a couple of weeks ago going through some of our files and we've barely been able to find a thing since."

"I'll be careful."

"Anything you look at, you have to look at here." She spoke the condition as if it was a challenge.

"No problem."

"All this may be public information, but that doesn't mean we're a lending library or anything."

"I understand."

"Anything you don't put back, I have to, and anything that's not there and is supposed to be, I'm going to know who took it. I'm not having Alex Scurillo get mad at me anymore just because something's missing."

"All I want to do is look at some things, Iris."

"All right," she said, getting up from behind her desk. "As long as you understand. It was a horrible scene that last time with Alex and I don't want to have to go through anything like it again. All I did was what I was supposed to do, which is let people see records that are supposed to be public."

I followed Iris over to a walk-in closet situated next to the copying machine. "Aren't they public?" I said.

"Well, they are." She put the light on in the closet and turned around. "But Alex says, 'Look, Iris, if they're public records then we're supposed to be saving them for the public. We've only got one copy of most everything and if somebody comes along and swipes that copy, then we didn't do our job of preserving them.' I can see his point, but gosh almighty, you can't just keep everybody except city officials from seeing the records like he wants. I go to Alex, 'Look, Alex, I been doing this job since you were a little boy. I've known what it meant for something to be public information through the last four administrations and I know what it means in this one, too.' "

"Did that shut him up?"

"Hah. You never shut up Alex Scurillo—he doesn't want to get shut up. Now look, honey, they're all in here and they're all labeled. You find the book you want, you bring it out in the office where I'm sitting and look at it there. You want to copy something, it's a quarter a page. You got a lot of copying, you add two zeros, divide by four, and that's how much you owe." She patted me on the shoulder and went back to her desk.

It took me only a few seconds to find the clothbound folder that bore the label of the Oversight Committee and I dutifully hauled it back into the room. I made space for myself on the copying machine and carefully went through three years' worth of minutes, notices, reports and correspondence. It took me less than a quarter of an hour and when I was done I had not found a single derogatory reference to the Portshead Memorial Cemetery. There were no letters from John Dineen, Mr. Woodruff or anybody else.

"Iris," I said, and she said, "Hunh?" putting me on hold for a few seconds while she finished the paragraph she was reading in her magazine.

"I don't seem to be able to find what I'm looking for."

She put down her magazine and picked up a pack of Pall Malls. "I'm not surprised," she said, shaking out a cigarette and fitting it in the V of the first two fingers on her left hand. She kept her eyes focused on the end of the cigarette during the entire time it took her to light it. "Those files are a mess."

"Well, I got the impression from what you said a few minutes ago that Alex Scurillo thinks somebody took some things out of here."

"That's right. A guy said he needed some background information for a book he was writing, so—you know—I just let him look at what he wanted. Now a bunch of things are missing."

"Do you remember anything about this guy?"

She nodded, exhaling and tapping her cigarette into a glass ashtray with a single well-practiced snap of her index finger. "Sure. Nice-looking boy—man, I should say. About your age. Wore a gold necklace."

"Did he tell you his name?"

"Alan Brandon. I think his father's got an insurance company here in town. In fact, if I'm not mistaken, his mother might even be one of the Fogerty girls from down the Hook. I wouldn't swear to it, though. I just got the idea when Alex said his father has the insurance business."

"So you told Alex about Alan Brandon being in the files?"

Iris drew herself up as though she had just been criticized. "I most certainly did. I knew Alex would be interested in knowing that somebody was going to write something about Portshead, so I just happened to mention it to him. Then Alex said something was missing and he practically had a conniption. He wanted to know the names of everybody who had been through the files."

"What other names did you give him besides Alan's?"

Iris turned her head to blow a particularly heavy stream of smoke away from me. "Alan was the only one I knew about."

"Did Alex say anything about Alan?"

Iris shook her head. The directness of my questions had made her wary, but she was confident of herself and her position and she wanted to show me how much she knew. "He was just mad as hell about the whole thing, that was all. That was when we had the fight about who should be allowed into the files and who shouldn't."

"And what was it he said was missing—do you recall?"

"Sure." Iris was nobody's fool. She could recall everything that had gone on in her domain. "It was some correspondence that was supposed to be in the Oversight Committee file."

Now it was my turn to sigh. No wonder the mayor had not been afraid that I would go to the newspapers. He and Scurillo had known all along that I had nothing to bargain with, that what I was offering was already in the hands of a writer. They had stonewalled me at the Holiday Inn. They had broken into my office to make sure I had nothing more on them. And in the end they had ignored me. The message that came through as I closed up the Oversight Committee folder was as clear as if it were spelled out on the cover: the sacrifice of Richie DelVecchio was going forward and I was powerless to stop it.

30 The weather broke on Tuesday, the day the inquest hearing was to begin. The humidity disappeared with the predawn rain and it was actually chilly when I got up at seven o'clock. I showered and shaved and sprayed myself with an acrylic shield of antiperspirant under each arm. I dressed in my blue pin-stripe suit, white button-down shirt and red silk tie with the tiny white polka dots. My jousting garments. In the kitchen I had only an English muffin and a glass of orange juice. I steered clear of coffee. I was not going to need it.

Linda and Richie met me at quarter to nine, standing just inside the door of the Northumberland County Courthouse, on the edge of the parking lot behind the main street of Portshead Center. They were eagerly nervous, as though they were there to be married, or to undergo initiation rites for some secret society. Their eyes were bright and every now and then when they brushed against each other there was an extra lingering in their touch that told me they were drawing strength from each other. They would have been appealing, almost cute, if Linda had not been wearing that adhesive across her nose and if Richie's face had not been swollen, scraped and discolored. Looking at them made me self-conscious about the now faded yellow and green rim that I was still wearing around my own eye. There was no doubt about it. We were a ridiculous trio.

By himself, Richie looked dressed for the disco. He was wearing a wide-lapeled checked sport coat with brown leather piping and a useless beltlike apparatus in the back. Around his neck and exposed by his open shirt was some sort of gold chain.

"What's that?" I said, pointing.

"It's a gold cross," he said, holding it out to me.

"I gave it to him for luck," Linda said, proud that she had made such an important contribution.

"Take it off and put it in your pocket," I ordered.

Richie looked confused. "Why? Is the judge a Jew?"

"The judge's name is DeSantis and maybe he'll absolutely love your cross. But on the other hand, maybe it will remind him of some street punk he once knew and he'll hate you for it. Everything you do in that courtroom could have an effect on the judge, so my philosophy is, the less you do the better. You go in, you sit up straight. You look the judge in the eye every chance you get and you call him 'sir.' You don't say 'yeah,' and you don't say 'nah.' You say 'Yes, sir' and 'No, sir.' You answer only their questions and you don't try to explain or elaborate. Got it?"

Richie said he had it, and it was too late for me to believe otherwise.

"Linda, if they allow you in, you sit behind your husband. You don't speak and you don't distract either Richie or me. If there is something really important that you think I have to know about, you write it down and hand it to me on a slip of paper. Otherwise, you just walk in and walk out with Richie and that's all. In fact, I'd prefer that when he's on the stand you don't even look at him. You look directly at the judge. All right?"

Linda nodded anxiously. I knew she would do exactly as I said. If Richie swallowed his tongue and began to choke to death on the stand, I was convinced there was a good chance she would never even glance at him.

We went up a flight of cement stairs to the hearing room, where a bailiff stopped us at the door. "Closed inquest," he said, but when I told him who we were he apologized and let us in.

There were no other people present except a female court reporter and a broad-shouldered man in a gray suit and brown cordovan shoes. The man was standing by himself with his briefcase open on the one and only counselor's table that was arranged in front of the bench. I told the DelVecchios to take a seat and went up to say hello to him. His name was Mark Brosnahan and I was not happy to see him. He was a senior assistant district attorney and my last hope that the mayor would take a dive disappeared when I saw that Brosnahan had not been replaced as counsel.

"Bishop," he said, looking over my shoulder at the DelVecchios.

I took his hand, hoping it would be wet with perspiration, but it was not. "What does Fergie have you on this case for, Mark?"

"Gotta earn my check doing something, don't I?" That was the kind of guy Brosnahan was. That was the type of sense of humor he had. He nodded at the DelVecchios. "You gonna want them to be present?"

"That's right."

"This isn't a trial, you know, Bishop. You're not going to be able to cross-examine or offer any witnesses of your own."

Brosnahan's sententious tone of voice grated on me. "Hey, Brosnahan, lighten up, will you? This isn't Jack the Ripper, either, you know. Richie admits he shot a burglar coming out the window of somebody's house. He's a cop. He's supposed to do things like that."

"And that's all there is to it, huh?" Brosnahan said sarcastically. He watched carefully to see how I reacted. I stared back at him coldly and calculatedly.

"What's wrong with your eye?" he asked.

Before I had to answer, I heard the door at the back of the hearing room open and turned to see a slightly built woman walk in with a black mantilla tied tightly under her chin. I knew who it was as soon as I saw her, but she looked right through me and sat down in the last row on the side opposite the DelVecchios. I excused myself from Brosnahan and went back to her.

"I'm sorry, Mrs. Fitzpatrick," I said.

She raised her dark eyes to my face and I suddenly and inadvertently caught my breath. Age had come to Pauline Fitzpatrick. She had been an attractive woman when I had seen her last, but her face had not taken on the handsomeness of an attractive woman passing through her middle years. Her skin was lined and lacked the color of the season. It was pale white except for the pink color she had added to her cheeks, and that looked almost obscene, as though it were only meant to fool from a distance.

"Hello, Chuckie," she said, and her voice was so tiny, it came from so far away, that I wanted to reach out and gather her to me. I wanted to press her against my chest and tell her everything was going to be all right and that all she had to do was go home, wash off those silly color spots, brush down her hair and step out into the morning air to make things just as they had been sixteen years before. But I did none of those things. I settled for taking her hand, the one that was resting on the seat in front of her. I took it in both of mine and squeezed it.

"Is that the one who did it, Chuckie?" she whispered, inclining her head ever so slightly.

I followed her gaze. "That's Officer DelVecchio, yes, Mrs. Fitzpatrick."

"And you're his lawyer, is that right?"

"Yes, it is."

Gently she withdrew her hand. "Then you tell him for me, Chuckie, tell him for me that I hope he rots in hell."

She swiveled her head away from me just as the clerk announced the entrance of the judge. There was the bustle that only a judge's robe can make and then Stephen DeSantis took his seat at the bench and we were in session.

Judge DeSantis was a no-nonsense, rail-headed man with short black hair that was turning white on the sides. He had glasses, but he seemed to prefer waving them around by their rims rather than actually wearing them. When he spoke, his voice snapped and his eyes stared challengingly in a way that made any attorney he happened to be addressing feel as if he or she was in serious breach of decorum.

The glasses came off and he looked first at Brosnahan and then over to where I was sitting with the DelVecchios. He began speaking. "Pursuant to Chapter 38, Sections 8 through 12, of the Massachusetts General Laws, and in accordance with the Special Order of Chief Judge Whittle of this Court, issued at the request of John Ferguson, District Attorney, this Court of Inquest into the facts surrounding the death of one Michael Paul Fitzpatrick is now convened. Be it known that it is the intention of the Court to conduct the aforementioned inquest in accordance with the general principles contained in *Kennedy* v. *Justice of the District Court of Dukes County*, 356 Mass. 367, 377–78 (1969)." The glasses went back on as he inspected his notes. After a few moments he pushed the notes aside and took the glasses off again.

"The purpose of this inquest is to obtain information as to whether a crime has been committed. It is not an accusatory but an investigatory proceeding. It is within my discretion to call and question witnesses, or to assign those tasks to the office of the district attorney, as I see fit. Since it is my understanding that the district attorney has already conducted a preliminary investigation into this matter as a prelude to requesting this inquest, I am going to defer to the assistance of the representative of that office, while nevertheless reserving to myself the right to examine witnesses when I find it necessary or helpful so to do.

"I intend, when this inquest is concluded, to report when, where and by what means Mr. Fitzpatrick met his death, and all the material circumstances attendant thereto, as well as the name or names of the person or persons contributing to that death."

Once again DeSantis put the glasses on and read something on his blotter. "I have here the appearance of Senior Assistant District Attorney Mark Brosnahan. Are you ready to begin, Mr. Brosnahan?"

"Yes, Your Honor," Brosnahan said, rising like an arthritic old horse. "But before I do, I would request that Your Honor exclude from the hearing room Officer Richard DelVecchio, whom the People will call as a witness, until such time as his testimony is required."

I was immediately on my feet for an argument. "Your Honor—"

"Who are you?" the judge demanded.

"Charles T. Bishop, Your Honor, counsel for Officer DelVecchio."

"Well, whatever you've got to say, I don't want to hear it. Mr. Brosnahan has the right to have prospective witnesses excluded if he feels their attendance during the appearance of other witnesses could have any effect—and I'm not saying it would—on their testimony. You can stay, Mr. Bishop, but your client waits outside."

"But, Your Honor—"

DeSantis's glasses were suddenly being held three feet closer to me. "Let's not start off this inquest by trying my patience, Mr. Bishop."

From that point on, I felt sure we were in for a long day.

In fact, it was all over by midafternoon. Brosnahan called Officer Gilmartin, who was the first cop to arrive after the shooting. Gilmartin was a gruff ten-year veteran who spoke strongly while he was describing receiving the call, tailed off a bit as he set the scene he found in the Brandons' backyard, and practically became incoherent when Brosnahan started asking what he had found on and around the body. It took some time to establish that there had been no weapons or stolen goods.

Gilmartin was followed by Dr. Maddox, who talked to the judge as if he was trying to get him to invest in a land deal. Basically he told the same story he had told me, except that on one occasion he described Richie as "panic-stricken," and he went into great detail about the entry of the bullet into Fitzy's skull and the position of Fitzy's body beneath the window.

The coroner was called and after him came a special investigator from the DA's office. I expected there to be several more witnesses before Richie himself took the stand, but that was not Brosnahan's plan and Richie led off the afternoon session. From where I sat he appeared nervous, but credible. He leaned forward as he was testifying, his elbows resting on the arms of the chair, gripping his left wrist with his right hand. He told the judge he was cruising his regular beat when he saw a suspicious-looking light moving about inside what appeared to be an empty house. He said he stopped to investigate, noticed the gate leading to the backyard was open (he said open and not unlocked), and walked through it to the rear of the house because he immediately suspected a break-in was going on. He said his suspicion was strong enough to cause him to draw his gun, but not strong enough for him to radio for assistance. He said he circled wide of the house to get a good view and was creeping forward in a crouch position when a window opened and a large human figure started coming out. He could see something in the figure's hand, he said, and naturally assumed it was a gun. He was afraid that if he called out too soon the figure would drop back inside the house and either escape out the front door or fire at him, so he waited and when the figure was straddling the windowsill he shouted, "Halt, police."

"And did the figure halt, Officer?" Brosnahan asked.

Richie hesitated. His mouth dangled open. "It was dark. It was hard to tell."

"Is that when you shot him?"

Richie answered quickly. "I fired a warning shot."

"And that is the shot which Special Investigator Clark testified this morning resulted in a bullet being embedded in the window frame, approximately two to two and a half feet from where Mr. Fitzpatrick must have been sitting?"

"It was dark. I couldn't see too good."

"Isn't a warning shot normally fired straight up? Into the air, that sort of thing?"

"I was down low, see?" Richie got half out of his chair to demonstrate. The judge told him to remain seated. Richie apologized and in his scramble to get back in position lost his train of thought.

Brosnahan waited and when Richie said nothing more he prodded him. "You were saying you were down low, Officer."

"Yeah."

"Are you trying to say that you were firing straight up into the air when you shot the bullet that just missed Mr. Fitzpatrick by two to two and a half feet?"

Open-mouthed again, Richie gazed across the room at me.

"Officer?" Brosnahan pushed.

"No. I was kinda coming up, you see. Raising my revolver up to do it, you know, and it sort of went off before I expected."

"You're saying that the bullet which just missed Mr. Fitzpatrick by two feet was fired because your gun went off accidentally?"

"Sort of before I meant it to."

"But you were aware of Mr. Fitzpatrick's location when you fired that warning shot, weren't you?"

"I knew where he was, yeah, but it was dark."

"And how soon after your warning shot did you fire a second shot?"

"I don't know. A minute, maybe."

"A minute. Officer DelVecchio, as a means to refresh your memory, I'm going to demonstrate how long a minute is. The second hand on my watch is approaching six. I will let you know when it approaches six again."

We never even got through half a minute. As the seconds ticked interminably by, Richie began to fidget and then suddenly he burst out, "I guess it wasn't that long."

Brosnahan lowered his watch. He did it slowly and let more time pass before he spoke again. "Isn't it a fact, Officer, that your second shot followed immediately after your first?"

"Not immediately."

"There were a few seconds in between—is that what you're telling us?"

"Yeah."

"How many?"

"A few."

"And what is it that caused you to fire that second shot?"

"Well, Fitzy—the guy—Mr. Fitzpatrick made this furtive gesture, came up with something in his hand and I thought it was a weapon, you know? And I thought he was gonna shoot me—at me."

"You saw what you thought was a weapon in his hand?"

"Yeah."

"And if you thought he was going to shoot at you, then you must have thought it was a gun."

"Well, it kind of looked like a gun."

"Tell me, Officer, how is it that it was so dark that you couldn't tell if Mr. Fitzpatrick stopped when you shouted at him, but you could see well enough to believe he had a gun in his hand?"

I had kept quiet all this time, but at this point I had to divert Brosnahan. No matter how Richie answered that question, he was in trouble. "Objection," I shouted.

"Sit down," the judge commanded.

"Objection," I repeated. "Argumentative."

"You don't sit down and be quiet, Mr. Bishop, and I'm going to exclude you from this courtroom."

"But, Your Honor—"

"Mr. Bishop." The judge affected weariness. "I'm going to state this one last time for your benefit. This is an investigatory and not an accusatory hearing. I appreciate your concern for your client's interest, but so far he is merely a witness in this case and, like any other witness—"

"But, Your Honor, that's just my point. He's not being treated like any other witness. Mr. Brosnahan isn't asking factual questions like he did of Officer Gilmartin or Mr. Clark or Dr. Maddox. He's arguing with Officer DelVecchio. He's badgering him."

The judge continued his posturing, continued letting me know I was trying his patience. "All we're trying to do here, Mr. Bishop, is develop a record so that I can file my inquest report. There'll be no findings of guilt resulting from this hearing and my report won't even be admissible in any subsequent criminal proceeding that may follow. So my advice to you, Mr. Bishop, is save your objections for when they count."

"Your Honor, with all due respect, the fact is that my client is under oath and if, as I contend, he's being badgered into saying things he doesn't mean or intend to say, those things can be used against him as admissions, confessions—they can be used for impeachment purposes. The things he says don't have to come out in your report, Your Honor. They're right down there on the stenographer's machine and they can be brought out against my client if he should end up going to trial. That's why I'm objecting. He's got a privilege not to incriminate himself, Your Honor. A constitutional privilege."

Brosnahan butted in. "Are you saying that your client is about to incriminate himself by answering my question?"

I took my eyes off the judge long enough to see that Brosnahan was leering hungrily at me. "I'm saying you're trying to trick him into incriminating himself."

Brosnahan's voice rose in indignant protest, but the judge, who was tilting back in his chair and staring at the ceiling, waved him silent with a gentle pumping motion of his outstretched hand. We waited and at last the judge slid forward and folded his arms on the bench. "And what if I overrule your objection, Mr. Bishop?"

I cleared my throat in order to give myself time to think. This was not the sort of confrontation that was going to do either me or my client any good. The judge could easily find me in contempt. He also could interpret Richie's silence as meaning we had something to hide, and we already had enough going against us so that we did not need that. Still, Richie had dug himself into a hole and I did not trust his ability to crawl out.

"Mr. Bishop." The judge spoke softly. "I asked you a question."

"I would hope that the issue would not arise, Your Honor. But if it should, I would have to give some consideration to instructing my client not to answer."

"Fine, Mr. Bishop." The judge leaned back into his chair again. "Go on to something else, Mark."

The smug look Brosnahan had been wearing disappeared from his face. "Does that mean the objection's sustained, Judge?"

"It just means that I want you to go on to something else. Proceed."

It was a short-lived victory. Brosnahan went on with his questioning and by the time Richie was off the stand there was little doubt in my mind that Judge DeSantis was going to find sufficient evidence to bind him over to the grand jury. Brosnahan had established that Richie had a gun and Fitzy did not. He had established through Dr. Maddox that the shots Richie fired sounded one right after the other. Finally he established the lack of immediate threat to Richie's life.

"Now one thing I'm not sure I understand, Officer DelVecchio. You were about how far away from Mr. Fitzpatrick when you fired at him?"

"I don't know. About thirty feet."

"Ten yards?"

"Farther than that. Maybe twenty yards."

"Sixty feet?"

"I guess."

"Too far for him to jump on you, in any event?"

"I guess."

"Well, could he have jumped on you?"

"I guess not."

"For one thing, he was sitting sidesaddle on the windowsill, wasn't he?"

"Yeah."

"So he couldn't have jumped from that position—"

"No."

"—unless you were right underneath him and unless he was leaning forward."

"Well, see, he brought his arm forward when I fired the warning shot."

"But isn't it a fact that you had been waiting for him to move forward? You were afraid he might drop back inside the house when you first saw him, so you were waiting until he moved forward before you shouted at him and fired the warning shot."

"Yeah. First I shouted and then I fired the warning shot."

"But you waited until he was fully exposed."

"Until he was sort of out of the house."

"More out than in?"

"Sort of half and half."

"Well, this is what confuses me, then. Obviously, when you shot him he fell forward onto the ground. Do you have any idea why he didn't fall backward?"

The penlight battery that powered Richie's thought process surged. "I guess it was because he was still coming toward me after I ordered him to halt."

"So he was in the process of coming out of the window when you shot him?"

"That's right."

"And if had gotten out of the window he would have had to jump down to the ground, is that right?"

"Yeah."

"And he would have been sixty feet away from you, from where you stood with your gun drawn and pointed at him, and he would have been fully exposed at that point, is that right?"

"I might have been closer. Maybe forty feet."

"But not close enough for him to jump on you."

"No."

Brosnahan raised his pen to his mouth and tapped it against his lips pensively. "So from where you were standing as you watched Mr. Fitzpatrick come forward, your fear was not that he was going to attack you in any sort of hand-to-hand combat, but that he was going to shoot you."

"That's right."

"I see." Brosnahan tapped his pen again. He was not thinking; he was timing his questions for maximum effect. "And when you shot him, since he fell forward, he must have been coming down from, or at least leaning down from, the window, is that right?"

"I already said that."

"So did you think he was going to shoot you on his way between the window and the ground?"

"He might of. I thought maybe he might shoot me from where he sat."

"Is that because he brought his arm forward, as you testified earlier?"

"Yeah."

"Couldn't it be that he was simply raising his arms to surrender?"

"No. He wasn't doing it like that."

"Tell me, Mr. DelVecchio, what was it the victim could have done in that situation to prevent you from shooting him?"

Richie answered almost before the question was completed. "He coulda sat still."

"But if he was leaning forward, as he must have been, then it would have been hard for him just to stop at the precise place he was when you fired the warning shot at him. He would have had to catch his balance, wouldn't he?"

Richie stared back without answering.

Brosnahan waited only a few seconds. "And to do that he would have had to bring his arm forward, wouldn't he?"

"Objection," I called out. "Speculation."

"Overruled," the judge said, his eyes fixed on Richie. "Answer the question, Officer. Could he have been trying to catch his balance?"

Trapped, unsure himself of what really had taken place, Richie grabbed for the story he had rehearsed so many times. "It was dark, I couldn't see—" and then he stopped and stared haplessly at the judge.

"Thank you, Officer," the judge said.

"I have no further questions," Brosnahan announced.

"You may step down," the judge said, and with that the inquest was concluded. There were no questions about Richie's professional history nor was there any in-depth inquiry into the circumstances that led to Richie's being in the Brandons' backyard in the first place. None of that was needed, and yet the specter of those issues was never entirely absent from the proceeding either, for sitting out in the hallway with Linda DelVecchio, waiting for the call to testify that never came, were Captain Mowbray, Lieutenant Finucci and Lanny Brandon.

31 Donovan and some of the others were interested in learning how the hearing went, but Ziggy Pastore was intent on talking about his own problems and they soon dominated the conversation.

"Ten years of marriage, and all of a sudden she discovers this women's lib thing and wants to bust my balls," he moaned. "I goes to her, 'Denise, women's lib means you go out and get a job as a lineman for the phone company. It don't mean you get to attack your husband every time he has a few beers with the guys.' But no, she goes to me that she don't gotta take any shit anymore and quotes me some Helen Reddy song. As if I give a fuck."

Ziggy grabbed me by the arm. His grip was fierce, showing even more than his words how upset he was. "You know what started it this time, Chuckie? Friday night when me and you and Ferris and Boyle went down Capaletti's for a pizza. She accuses me of being out fucking around. Can you believe it?"

"I can believe it, Ziggy," Joey Aiello said. "You're always out fucking around."

"So if I am she's never caught me. This time I don't do nothing and she comes down on me like a ton of bricks." He turned again to me. "Seriously, Chuckie, maybe it would help if you talked to her for me. What do you think?"

"Oh, no," I said, draining my Bud. "I'm not getting involved in any domestic squabble."

"You don't have to get involved, Chuckie. Just tell her what we were doing Friday night."

"Why don't you get Boyle or Ferris to tell her?"

A look of horror came over Pastore's face. "What, are you nuts? She's not gonna believe either one of them. She thinks Boyle's a retard—"

"Fuck you, Ziggy," said Boyle.

"—and she don't trust Stevie."

Ferris laughed.

"So why's she going to trust me?"

" 'Cause she respects you, that's why, Chuckie. She thinks you're a real smart guy."

"Besides," Donovan said, "you went to law school. You can lie with a straight face."

"I'm not going to get involved, Ziggy," I said, "so you can stop blowing smoke up my ass."

Pastore's mouth twisted. He swiveled around on his stool and faced the bar. "Thanks a lot, pal."

"Hey, Ziggy, think about it, will you? What am I supposed to do? Call her up on the phone and say Ziggy was out eating pizza with me until ten-thirty Friday night?"

"You gotta say till midnight."

"Oh, great. Maybe I should go right to the house to tell her that. You think she's going to believe me, I just walk up to her out of the blue and say, 'Hey, Denise, I happened to be in the neighborhood and I thought I'd drop by and tell you Ziggy and I were out eating pizza all Friday night'?"

Ziggy sighed and rubbed his eyes. "Oh, it don't make any difference, anyhow. She's already gone down to see the priest about me. Great. Now everybody at St. Cecilia's knows all about my private life. She don't tell 'em nothing about herself, but she tells 'em what a fuckin' animal I am. I can't even show my face down there no more."

"So when was the last time you did that, anyhow?" Ferris asked.

"What difference does it make? I ain't doin' it again."

"I wouldn't worry about it, Ziggy," I said. "Anything she told the priest I'm sure was confidential."

Pastore looked at me in amazement. "What are you talking about? You ain't even Catholic."

"You don't have to be Catholic to know that they have a priest-penitent obligation."

"She's not going down as no penitent. She's going down to bullshit about me, tell 'em how wacko I am because maybe I want to go out and get a real live blow job or something every now and then. Think the priest is gonna say, 'Well, Mrs. Pastore, maybe you should be taking a little better care of him yourself?' My ass. He does anything besides get a hard-on himself, he's gonna set her up with one of them wire cages people wear when they get broken jaws and send her home with it so her husband can't bother her no more."

"Blow jobs," Boyle said reflectively. "You know what pisses me off about blow jobs?"

"Givin' 'em or gettin' 'em?" Pastore snapped.

"Fuck you, Ziggy. What pisses me off is after the broad gives you one she always wants to kiss you on the mouth. What do you suppose they want to do that for?"

Ziggy Pastore stroked his chin for a while and thought about it. Then he shook his head slowly. "Fuckin' broads. They'll do anything to bust your balls."

It was late when I left the Plough and Stars and later still when I drove past the Brandons'. Lanny's Mercedes was gone, but the Datsun was parked by the front door and, as usual, there were lights on in the house. I slowed down and wondered if the Mercedes might be in the garage. Instead of stopping under the trees, I drove by again and searched for signs that would tell me whether Lanny was home. This time I drove all the way to the Ashton line before I returned. On my third trip past, the Brandon home was still lighted and there was still only one car in the drive. I hooked a turn at the base of Pigeon Hill Drive and slid into my spot.

I killed the engine, left the switch on auxiliary and tuned in the Angels game. The Red Sox had some kid I had never heard of on the mound and I felt a twinge of resentment because there had been no announcement in the paper about him being on the roster and I wondered whose place he had taken. They were talking about the kid when a gust of wind came along and blew the day's rain off the pine branches and onto my car. Large droplets thumped the windshield and rattled the hood until it sounded as if I was sitting in the midst of a shooting gallery. It was colder than I thought it had any right to be in August and I bundled myself in a blanket that I happened to have in the car. When I glanced out the window again I was startled to see that the door to the Brandons' house was open and that Alicia Brandon was striding directly toward my little encampment.

I had a moment's panic where I reached for the keys, ready to dash up Pigeon Hill Drive with my lights off and my accelerator to the floor, but it was already too late. Alicia knew exactly where she was going.

She was wearing a powder blue jumpsuit zipped lower in the front than the cool night air required. It hugged her hips like an extra layer of skin. It accentuated the litheness of her walk. It sent little bolts of excitement shooting throughout my body.

I waited, and when she got close I rolled down the window and smiled at her. "Ran out of gas," I said. It was not one of the excuses I had practiced.

She stopped a few feet from my car and peered in, as though she did not really expect it would be me. Satisfied that it was, she stepped a little closer. "Is that why you were driving up and down in front of the house? You thought maybe there was a gas station around here?"

I laughed, feeling foolish at having been caught like a peeping Tom.

Alicia's hands were clasped and thrust between her knees as she ducked to keep her head on my level. "You still don't understand, do you, Chuck?"

I shrugged. "What's there to understand? I only wanted to see if Lanny went out at night, like you said."

Alicia waited long enough to make sure I was serious and then she straightened up and stared over the roof of my car. There was nothing for her to be looking at, just the darkness. She took a deep breath, a contemplative breath, as though making up her mind about something, and then suddenly she reached her hand through the open window and touched my shoulder.

For the first time that I could remember, Alicia's fingers felt warm to me. I crooked the tips of my fingers around hers and drew her hand next to my face. When she held it there the moment took on all sorts of unspoken meaning in my mind, and when she said, "Come, Chuck, I have something I want you to see," I dutifully got out of the car and let her lead me back across the lawn.

I asked her about Lanny, but she could have told me he was waiting inside the door with a shotgun and I probably still would have followed her.

She didn't, though. She told me he'd been gone about an hour.

"When does that mean he'll be home?" I whispered. There was no need for me to be whispering, I just was.

"I have no idea," she said, and led me into the house.

I followed her to the stairs and my heart skipped as she started up them. At the top I could see an open bedroom, but that was not where Alicia was taking me. We passed a second bedroom and then a third, and finally I saw where we were going. It was a closed door on the front side of the house, a room just like the others. While she fiddled with the handle I moved closer to her, waiting for her to turn so I could take her into my arms before we went inside. But she didn't turn. She pushed the door open cautiously and when it was wide enough she reached in and flicked on a light switch. It was like being hit by the gritty blast of a coal furnace.

It was not a bedroom. Or at least it was nothing that was being used as a bedroom. It was, instead, a study, a very cozy study, in which the walls were sloped so severely that they left just a few feet of ceiling. A blue and white print wallpaper made the room seem even closer, but there was a cushioned window seat in a little alcove and enough floor space to fit a cabinet, a sea trunk and a good-sized oak desk and chair. On the desk was an electric typewriter, a set of books between a set of inept-looking bookends, vials of Liquid Paper, erasers, lift-off sheets for type corrections, pens, pencils and sheaves of paper. There was heavy bond typing paper, long yellow legal pads, short green pads and piles of scraps made up of everything from napkins to matchbook covers; and all of it was covered with words.

Feeling very much like an invader, unsure as to what it was I was supposed to do, I mutely trailed Alicia to the desk. While she bent over a stack of typewritten pages, I stood reading the titles to Lanny's books: *Bartlett's Familiar Quotations, Writer's Market, Writing to Sell, The Elements of Style, Techniques of Modern Fiction Writing, Harper's English Grammar, Webster's Collegiate Dictionary, The Logic and Rhetoric of Exposition, Roget's Thesaurus* and Sherwood Anderson's *Winesburg, Ohio.*

"This is where he spends most of his time," Alicia said offhandedly. She continued to rummage through the pile.

I mumbled something about it looking like a good place to work, but Alicia paid the comment no attention. At last she found what she wanted and drew several pages away from the rest.

"Are you ready for this?" she said.

The question startled me. It reminded me of the way Boyle had prefaced his question about Cookie. It made me want to say no: whatever it was, I was not ready for it; but she was holding out the pages to me and I took them because she expected me to take them, because that was the reason she had brought me into this house and up to this room.

Standing where I was, I started to read.

Most everybody looked forward to the fights at the Seaside Ballroom so it never became the sort of thing where people got permanently damaged. At least not at first. Sometimes fights just developed, of course, and those were usually ones that got started on the floor and didn't last long. Off-duty cops would jump in as soon as they got started, grab the combatants, slap one of them up against the wall for long enough to blow cigarette smoke in his face and hustle the other one out the door. After a few minutes they would heave the second guy out as well.

One time the Snake was dancing and the rest of us were all gathered around him in a circle and each time Snake came around the circle he managed to bump into this one guy. About the third time around, Snake hit the guy with an elbow. Snake said later the guy was crowding him, but anyhow I saw Snake hit the guy first and I saw the guy fall back a little. So the next time Snake came around the guy was waiting for him. But I was waiting for the guy, too; not because I had anything against him, but because I knew it was coming, and as soon as he shoved Snake I whacked him one right on the side of the head.

First thing, Snake was there pushing me into the crowd because he knew the bouncers would be coming and my only chance was to get lost among the other dancers. Sure enough, no sooner had I ducked behind the first row of people than two massive characters came swimming through the crowd. One of them scooped up the poor bastard I had hit and the second one grabbed hold of Snake and had his ass out in the rain before Snake's feet ever hit the ground again.

We all laughed about it later and it became part of the folklore of Saturday night

Seaside stories. We would tell the stories over and over as we were sitting around the basketball court waiting to play winners and sometimes we would even reenact them. It didn't make any difference whether we were heroes or victims, everything became laughable after a couple of days anyway, and we would always go back down the Seaside the next week just to see what else might develop. So you can see the kind of attitude we had the night the niggers showed up.

Nobody thought too much about it that first time. There were just a couple of them: tall, very dark-skinned guys who weren't dressed too differently than the rest of us. Most of our crowd didn't even know niggers were supposed to be good dancers and it wasn't until we noticed the broads seemed to be clustering over in the niggers' area that we began talking among ourselves. Mostly, though, we were talking about the broads, wondering what would possess a broad to want to dance with a nigger. Then later on we forgot about it and went off to fight the kids from Ramtucket.

The next week there were more niggers there and a couple of the broads, a couple of the broads right from our high school, went straight over and made themselves available. It was after that second Saturday night that we started being concerned about the niggers. The problem was, none of us had ever known a nigger. Not personally, I mean. We had seen them playing sports and in singing groups and we knew that Southern hicks discriminated against them, but that was about the extent of our knowledge. Burnsie observed that they smelled, but he admitted that they couldn't help it. "It's in their skin," he informed us.

The fight with the niggers was inevitable when they showed up on the third week. This time there were more of them, maybe not more than a dozen, but they had brought along a couple of girls and that meant something. Cronin said it meant they were here for good. The girls were either chunky as tanks or real long-legged. They didn't smile much and they spent most of the night dancing with each other, but the boys, from what we could see, had their pick of anybody they wanted. This confirmed some of our worst suspicions.

Still, there was not a lot of animosity as the fight was arranged. There was not even an igniting spark, just a gradual spreading of the word that we were going to fight the niggers. It brought out an excitement different from that of any other Saturday night. Guys from Ramtucket and all the other towns sidled over to tell us they would be there if we needed them. Advice was passed around freely. "You get in trouble, man, everybody's gotta go for their leader. They can't fight without a leader." Somebody who once fought with Wilson told him he had to make sure he didn't drop his head when he punched. "If they go for their knives we're coming in with tire irons. One nigger pulls a knife and there'll be dark meat on the streets tonight."

But it didn't turn out that way at all. The fight was practically negotiated.

Before the slow dance that ended the evening was even halfway through, people had started to break for the exits. The fight was going to be in the beach parking lot and everyone wanted to get on the seawall for the best vantage point. There had never been that many people watching before and we actually had to push our way through to get to where the niggers were standing. There were only eight of them and they were formed up in a slightly bent line, not saying anything, just staring at us as we came one at a time into the open combat area. Even when we were all assembled and the crowd of white faces pushed in closer, none of the niggers moved or even looked over his shoulder. It was almost eerie.

Cronin took a step forward and started talking to them. He was wearing a plaid pullover windbreaker and light corduroys and there wasn't a nigger there who was built like Cronin. Even the tall ones couldn't have come within thirty pounds of him. We were only a few feet behind, spread out as if we were afraid the niggers might try to circle around behind us. We were cracking knuckles and flexing legs, picking out the nigger that was going to be ours. But the niggers weren't looking back. They were all watching Cronin.

He was explaining it wouldn't be him. He was on probation for hitting a kid with a bench six weeks before. The tallest nigger nodded. He understood probation.

Cronin came back and we gathered a little closer for an instant. Snake said he wanted it and moved out into the middle. He hadn't taken his second step before this black flash came flying across the open space, smashed headfirst into Snake's chest and took him flat down on his back as sixty or a hundred surprised voices screamed for Snake to get up and kick the piss out of the little bastard.

Snake did his best. He bucked and the little nigger rode him like a bull. He tried to swing up from where he was lying and the little nigger hit him in the face, both hands, one right after the other. Snake rolled to one side and took another shot around the ear. He threw his body back the other way and we all roared like he was a thoroughbred coming into the back stretch because we knew that as soon as Snake got up it would be all over. And Snake did get on top, but as he got there the nigger had hold of his shirt and kept right on pulling him over until all of a sudden they were wheeling through the parking lot, forcing the crowd to dance out of their way. Then suddenly the rolling stopped and the nigger was on top again. Snake tried to cover his face, but the nigger's hands were just one black blur, raining punch after punch down until he had hit poor Snake with so many punches that the crowd had gone silent and then he leaped to his feet with his hands in the air.

The victor's friends gathered around him, their congratulations almost soft compared to the noise we had been making a moment before. They slapped his hands, they gave him quick one-armed hugs and knowing smiles and then they closed ranks and moved out together, raking us with contemptuous side glances and strutting as they stepped.

Snake stayed on the ground, one elbow covering his face. There were no tears and there wasn't much blood, but he didn't want to get up because he had been beaten.

We looked at him, stunned. Snake was one tough sonofabitch and none of us could have done any better. The crowd moved away but we moved in closer because we didn't want everybody to see him lying there. Some of us tried to give him a hand up, but he shook us off.

Snake rode home with us in Wilson's car and nobody said a word until we were standing around the Burger Pit with our hands full of fast food. Then Snake, who was trying to get his mouth around a cheeseburger, suddenly fired what he was eating into the trash. "I guess I got my ass kicked, huh?" he said, and then he grinned and we all started talking at once about how fast the kid had been. By the time we were done everybody at the Burger Pit was laughing at the memory of how Snake looked crumpled on the ground outside the Seaside and eventually it even became one of those stories we told around the basketball court.

Thing was, we didn't go back to the Seaside much after that. We heard it had become something of a nigger hangout.

Alicia was watching me intently, studying my face. She saw me drop the story back onto Lanny's desk and she said, "Now do you understand?" But I didn't understand, at least not then.

"What did he want to write this for? It was just something that happened when we were kids, that's all."

Alicia began to rearrange the pages I had spilled. "It reveals a little bit about Portshead, don't you think? I thought it captured what you told him quite well."

"But what would he want to write it for?" I insisted. "What's it got to do with politics in Portshead?"

Alicia's green eyes flashed in surprise. "Nothing," she said. "Why should it?"

"Isn't he writing some sort of political exposé?"

She stopped her tidying and looked at me curiously, like maybe I knew something she didn't. "Whatever gave you that idea?"

"The papers he took from City Hall—the correspondence about the cemetery and all that stuff he got out of the council files. Why would he take all that if he wasn't writing an exposé?"

This time she regarded me as if I was kidding. "Chuck, he didn't take any papers out of any files. He wouldn't have any need to, not for the kind of book he's writing."

We both looked at the stack of papers on the desk. I cut into it at random and read Coach Walsh's locker room pep talk, the one where he said, "Gosh darn it to heck, fellas, losing to these guys would be worse than being nibbled to death by a pack of ducks." Lanny had laughed when I related that to him. Now he had copied it as his own.

I leafed through the rest of the manuscript and came across the story about Kitty and Bunny and the orgies at Billy Kincaid's. I flipped through the pages faster and read one familiar scene after another and suddenly Alicia's hand was on my arm and she was gently taking the manuscript from my hands.

"You're angry," she said. "I didn't think you would be or I wouldn't have shown it to you."

"Hey, why should I be angry? It's only my life he's planning on telling the world about."

"Don't be silly, Chuck," she said. "He's not writing about you, he's writing about Portshead. The time, the place, the people. He's trying to make sense out of what happened to him when he was growing up here and you're just a source for the information he needs, like those men he listens to in bars, like the twenty years of *Sentinels* he's been reading through. You don't begrudge him that, do you, Chuck? You don't begrudge him that he was interested enough in what you had to say that he wrote it down. Surely your boyhood memories aren't so precious to you that you can't share them with someone who should have been there and wasn't. Someone who can only imagine what all the rest of you were doing while he was spending night after night sitting home with his parents."

I struggled for a moment trying to remember when she had said something like that to me before. Then I knew. It had been at the Chowder House, when she had recruited me to be Lanny's friend. A sick feeling formed in the pit of my stomach. It twisted my lips into a half-smile that wouldn't come off.

"What is it, Chuck?" she said, her hand catching my sleeve. Concern etched itself in her face. It formed little tracks that did not belong in her flawless skin. It clouded the emerald color of her extraordinary eyes.

"All of a sudden it's all so clear," I said. "The come-ons, the invitations, the midnight calls. You've only been doing it to keep me feeding material to Lanny, haven't you?"

The clouds lifted. The emeralds flashed. "What did you think I wanted?"

"I thought—I thought you wanted me."

Whatever Alicia had been about to say was lost. She covered her mouth with her hand and then took it away again. "Oh, Chuck." She spoke the words like a mother who has just discovered that her favorite little boy has not made the Little League team. "You really didn't understand, did you?"

I looked away, afraid that she would see the embarrassment in my eyes and mistake what she saw.

"God," she said softly, "I've really made a mess of things, haven't I?"

"You haven't done anything, Alicia. It was just me."

"No, it wasn't just you, Chuck. I'm not so innocent as to pretend I'm not attractive to men and I played on that with you. My only excuse is that I did it for my husband and, well, if you could have seen the way he was struggling before he met you, you'd understand better."

"It doesn't make any difference, Alicia. You couldn't have led me on if I didn't let you."

"He'd just sit up here in this study of his for hours, getting nothing done, going nowhere. And he was becoming so depressed I was afraid for him. I mean that really, Chuck."

She looked up at me, compelling me to accept what she was saying. "He had expected things were going to be so different when he got back here. But then we got settled in and it was as though nobody cared he'd been away, nobody cared he'd done well, nobody cared he'd come home; and it was depressing for both of us. It affected him badly. Much worse than you can imagine."

I nodded, not sure I wanted to hear any more.

"There'd be whole days when I'd never hear that typewriter going at all. He'd come back to the house with all these notes and things and none of it ever seemed to get down on paper. I tried to get him to talk about it and all he'd say was that everything was the same and nothing was as he remembered it. But then you came along, came by our house that first night, Chuck, and it was like a godsend. That's what gave me the idea. I thought if I could get you to sit down with him a couple of times, get you to talk to him . . ." Alicia's voice faded and now when she looked at me she was no longer compelling me, she was imploring me.

"I'm sorry, Chuck. All I can say is that it worked. Basically, everything you see in that manuscript has been pounded out since he started talking to you. You've given him a framework in which to tell his story and he's been a whole different writer, a whole different man, since then."

"I'm pleased to hear it."

She caught the undertone of my voice and she hesitated. "I'm not ungrateful, Chuck."

"For helping Lanny, you mean."

She stepped closer. She touched the tips of her fingers to my cheek, forcing me to look into those exquisite eyes. "And me," she said. Her hand spread across the side of my face, gently, almost sadly, caressing it. "Meeting you, getting to know you, listening to you, Chuck—you've been the one bright spot for me in what has otherwise been a wholly miserable experience."

"Great," I muttered. "I can be replaced by an incandescent light bulb."

"Don't joke. I have too much at stake to think that any of this is funny."

Alicia hadn't moved. She was still touching my cheek, still holding my eyes with her own. Slowly, giving her every chance to pull away, I lowered my mouth to hers. For an instant our lips merely touched, suspended, barely making contact. And then her mouth, full and wet, opened beneath mine. Her arms went around me, pulling me to her. I could feel the tips of her breasts pressing through the thin cloth of her jumpsuit, the firmness of her thigh wedging between my legs.

I was holding on to her waist, a tight, incredibly narrow waist, and then her buttocks were swelling into my outstretched fingers, filling the palms of my hands. Excitement swept through me and I wanted all of her at once. "Don't," she said, as I lifted her onto Lanny's desk, but she was already spreading her legs to fit around me as I guided her down to where she wouldn't hit against the typewriter. From somewhere far off her dog was barking frantically, throwing itself again and again into some closed door, but beneath me Alicia was arching her back, hooking her legs around mine, driving herself up and into me.

The front of her suit opened and I felt her stomach, flat and smooth and golden brown. I covered her breasts with my hands and felt the hardness of her tiny dark nipples. "Don't," she said again as my hand slid down past the bottom of the zipper and touched hair as long and soft and light as feathers. "Not here," she said, "not on his desk."

But she made no effort to stop me as I peeled the jumpsuit over her hips and down the long length of her legs. The only thing she asked was that I take her into another room and the only thing she made me promise was that I not think any the less of Lanny for what we were about to do.

32 "Guess what," Cookie demanded. She was gushing with excitement and I was already wishing I had not allowed Davida to put the call through.

"What?"

"I've won a trip to Atlantic City. Oh, Chuckie, it's the first thing I've ever won and I'm so excited I can hardly stand it."

I put my pen down and leaned back in my chair. "Did you enter a contest or something?"

"No, I didn't have to do anything, that's what's so great. They just sent the notice here to the house."

"Did they say how they happened to choose you?"

"No. It just says, 'Congratulations,' and then there's an exclamation mark. 'You've been selected as one of a limited number of winners,' blah-blah-blah . . . Isn't it exciting? I'm already making plans, Chuckie, that's why I'm calling. I want to know if you'll take care of Candy while I'm gone."

"Oh, yeah, that'll be wonderful, Cookie. Won't Candy just love that?" The idea, frightening at first, was ludicrous enough to annoy me. "When are you going to get it through your head? The kid hates me. I see her, she runs away from me. It won't work, Cookie. Besides, what's wrong with your folks? Won't they watch her?"

"Oh," Cookie said, the crack in her voice belying her glibness. "I don't want to send her over there."

"Why not?"

The phone was silent for a moment. "Because they can't handle her, that's why."

"They've always handled her before."

"Until your father had to go shooting off his big mouth, Chuckie."

"What's that supposed to mean?"

"You should hear the stories he told my father about her. I'm telling you something, Chuckie—I feel like punching his teeth down his throat."

An internal alarm was singing throughout my body. Bad news was coming. "What stories, Cookie?"

"Stories—stories," she said, her voice rising in annoyance because I did not know exactly what she was talking about and because now she was going to have to spell it out for me. "He claims he saw her coming out of Eddie's Motel the other night. At two o'clock in the morning. With a boy."

"Oh, Jesus. Is it true?"

"How do I know if it's true? You think I was there? Ask your father; he's the one who's claiming he saw her."

"What was he doing at Eddie's Motel at two o'clock in the morning?"

"Him and your mother were driving by on their way home from the drive-in."

"Did you ask my mother about it?"

"You're a hot ticket, Chuckie."

"He could have been mistaken, you know. It could have been somebody else."

"That's right. So tell him to keep his big fat mouth shut for a change."

"All right, okay, just calm down for a minute, will you? Look, let me ask you something about the contest you won. Are they going to fly you down there?"

"No," she said sullenly, as though the failure to provide transportation were somehow my fault. "I have to get back and forth myself."

"But they're going to put you up in one of the casino hotels, is that right?"

"It's not a casino hotel." This time it was clear from her tone that I could not be any dumber than I was being.

"Well, how many nights are they going to put you up?"

"It's whatever I want, Chuckie. It's a discount. They give me a discount rate and they give all these coupons to buy meals and see shows with and they give me free coinlike things to spend at the casinos. All I've got to do is go down there between Labor Day and Christmas and show them my winner's letter and they'll have a whole package of stuff waiting for me."

"Oh, for God's sake."

"What's that supposed to mean?"

"Cookie, goddamn it, don't you know anything? It's a come-on. You didn't win anything. They're just trying to get people to go down there in the off-season. They're giving that shit away. What, you probably have a coupon there that says you're entitled to one egg and a slice of bacon for seventy-five cents any weekday morning between six and eight o'clock at the Lucky Shooter Café. Is that the kind of stuff you have?"

She did not answer.

"Listen, Cook." I tried to modulate my voice. "Look at the top of the letter where they have your name. Is it printed differently than the main body of the letter?"

"It says, 'Dear Winner.' "

"And who's it addressed to? It's not addressed to 'Resident,' is it?"

"Boy," she said, "you really know how to make somebody's day, don't you? I was all excited about this until I called you."

"Well, I can see why that would happen, Cook," I said, not meaning to make her unhappy. "These things are designed to get you all excited."

"It was someplace to go, you know? I haven't even been out of the state except when we went on our honeymoon."

The mention of our honeymoon caused a rock to drop in my stomach. It was surpassed in my annals of embarrassing events only by the memory of our wedding reception at the American Legion Hall, where my mother sobbed uncontrollably and Donovan busted Cookie's uncle on the jaw for cutting in front of him at the pay-for-your-own bar.

"Remember how your father gave us his car for the week and we drove to Montreal, Chuckie?"

"Yes."

It had been the week of spring vacation our senior year in high school and it had been too cold to go down the Cape or up to New Hampshire. We had chosen Montreal because Cookie didn't want to go to New York and somebody had told us Montreal was a good place.

"That was the last nice thing he ever did for us, I think." She paused, and then almost brightly said, "Remember how we didn't know what to do once we got there?"

"Yes."

"And how we snuck out of the motel after two days because we were afraid we couldn't break our reservations?"

"Yes."

"It was worth it, though, wasn't it, Chuckie? I liked going to Niagara Falls much better than Montreal. We shoulda stayed there that whole week instead of coming home early like we did."

"Look, Cookie, I've got a client waiting for me. Let me get back to you later."

"I just wanted to go someplace exciting like that. I really liked Niagara Falls, Chuckie."

"Hey, Cook, give me a break, will you?" A sudden thought occurred to me. "What about the old man you've been going out with? Can't you get him to take you anywhere?"

She laughed. As quickly as that her mood had changed. "You'd really like to know who he is, wouldn't you? C'mon, admit it."

Now that she had stopped being nostalgic, I felt myself growing exasperated. I told her I had to get off the line.

She got the message. "Anyhow," she said, signing off, "he can't take me anywhere because he's so famous everybody will know him. There'd be tons of things in all the newspapers saying what's old Mr. So-and-So doing with a sexy young thing like me." She laughed again and hung up, leaving me drowning in consternation.

33 I was late getting the news about Jimbo Ryder. Sid had asked me to cover a deposition for him down in Plymouth and I had spent the better part of the day sitting in a windowless room listening to Sid's client do his best to explain that there was an oral understanding between him and the three defendants whereby each of the defendants was going to pay him an unspecified, but readily apparent, commission fee for bringing them together in such a way that defendant A could sell an airplane to defendant B to lease to defendant C. The deal was so complicated that each of the three defense counsel had to spend from one to three hours questioning Sid's guy about it. My participation consisted of half a dozen objections to the form of the questions being asked, but it was an exhausting experience nonetheless and I was physically drained from the relentless concentration.

When it was over I went straight home instead of going back to the office. I put on a cotton shirt and a pair of dungarees and even though it was not yet five I took a hike up to the Plough and Stars to see if anything was going on.

Boyle was the only one there. He had a beer growing warm in front of him and the afternoon's *Sentinel* folded to the sports page. Donovan was off and the wife of the owner was behind the bar. I asked her for a Bud and she acted as if I had ordered a pack of rubbers, but she gave it to me and she took my money.

"It says here," Boyle said, squinting at the print, "that they're gonna lose Lynn, Fisk and Burleson next year. Says they're gonna play out their options and sign with somebody else. They all want contracts bigger than Rice's."

"Fisk won't leave. He's from New Hampshire, for God's sake; what would he want to play anyplace else for?"

"It says here they all got the same agent and the guys that own the Red Sox hate him and won't talk to him."

I could empathize; I didn't feel like talking to Boyle. I took the part of the paper he was not looking at and turned to the front page. There was a picture of Harlan Carson and next to it was a headline that read, "Carson Resigns Senate Seat." The subheading said, "Accepts Appointment as General Counsel to Mass. Legislature."

The resignation was a matter of interest but no immediate import to me. I glanced around the rest of the page and noted the articles on the presidential campaigns, the unrest in Poland, new killings in Northern Ireland, and the death of a Coventry man in a fiery car crash. Then my eye caught the name of City Councilman James Ryder and I turned back to the article on Harlan Carson.

State Senator Harlan Carson (D. Portshead) announced at a press conference this morning that he is resigning his office effective immediately in order to accept the newly created post of General Counsel to the Massachusetts Senate. The announcement came as a surprise to those who thought the press conference was being called in order to announce the appropriation of funds for a new high school vocational program in Coventry. Although Carson is known to be a very close friend of Senate President Patrick Leahy (D. Framingham), his name had not been mentioned among those of the leading candidates for the $46,000 a year General Counsel's position.

Reached at his office in the Statehouse, Leahy confirmed the appointment. "Harlan was the man we wanted right from the beginning. He has the respect and admiration of both sides of the aisle." Leahy said an official announcement would follow.

Despite Leahy's assertion that Carson has been the preferred choice all along, most local officials seemed to be caught unawares by the development. "I'm at a loss for words," admitted Mayor Francis X. McLaughlin. "We'll miss him. We'll miss him very much. Harlan Carson always served the District to the utmost of his ability and I'm sure he'll prove to be an exemplary General Counsel."

City Council President Alex Scurillo declined comment, saying he would have to review the situation further before issuing a statement. Asked if he was considering running for the now-vacant State Senate seat himself, Scurillo said it was something he would have to look into.

One politician who was not so circumspect was City Councilman James Ryder. The popular representative from Portshead Hook immediately announced his intention to enter the race to succeed Carson and complete his four-year term of office.

Scheduling of an election under these circumstances is the prerogative of the Senate, and while no dates have yet been announced, Senate President Leahy did declare that it was his intention not to leave the people of Senator Carson's district voiceless for any longer than is absolutely necessary. "With national elections coming up in ten weeks, I see no reason why we cannot avoid the costs and logistical problems of separate polling, provided we are able to get the ballots printed," he said.

Boyle was watching me curiously and I realized I was groaning out loud. "Did you see this?" I said, shaking the paper in his face.

He looked at the headline and then back at me as if I was going to play a joke on him. "Yeah. So what?"

It was not Boyle's fault. He was unaware of my involvement with Jimbo Ryder, and a lifetime of intellectual abuse had taught him to be wary of questions that did not personally pertain to him. Still, he was there and I was angry. "Hey, Boyle," I said, "don't you ever have any thoughts about anything?"

Boyle leaned closer and looked again at the headline. He read a bit of the story and then he straightened back up and eyed me with as much distance as could be put between two men sitting on adjacent barstools. "Yeah, I got a thought. I think that all politicians are crooks. So what the hell difference does it make?"

"What makes you think they're all crooks?" I said, and we both knew I was taunting him.

"'Cause they are. Look at Nixon."

"So what did Nixon do that showed us he was a crook?"

Boyle snorted and turned his head away. When he looked back his mouth was flat and his expression was hard with concentration, like someone who half expected to be hit. "What are you talking about? He broke into Watergate, didn't he?"

"And that's what made him a crook?"

"Hey, Chuckie, why don't you fuck off? I'm reading the paper here, trying to figure out what's happening to the fuckin' baseball team, and you want to give me a fuckin' politics test. I get done with this, maybe I'll look at that. For now, why don't you leave me alone."

I threw the paper at him. He knocked it to the floor and did not bother to pick it up. "What's eating you?" he said.

I started walking toward the door. "You see Ziggy, tell him to call me right away. I need to talk to him."

"Hey, where you goin', Chuckie?" Boyle yelled after me. "What the fuck, Chuckie? I swear to God, sometimes you act worse than a broad."

The owner's wife told him to watch his language. By the time I closed the door she and Boyle, the only two people in the place, were locked in an argument that had them both flinging their hands in my direction.

Tracking Jimbo down proved unexpectedly easy. I found him at his office at Garber's, where he was emptying his drawers and packing what things he could into an oversized and overstuffed briefcase.

Garber's had a huge plant and the only reason I found the office building was because Cookie had worked there recently as a receptionist. The lumberyard had its own railhead, and the parking lot, which was big enough to hold the international Jehovah's Witness convention, had half a dozen entrances and exits which acted like arteries pumping cars and trucks from every direction. In the center of the lot sat the main store, with its line of merchandise that covered anything and everything needed for home building, repairs and improvements. Beyond the store was the lumberyard itself, and next to that was a nursery, and off to one side were warehouses. Fitting sideways between the warehouses was a two-story, flat-roofed, boxlike building that gave almost no indication that it was headquarters to a multimillion-dollar empire. I walked into the end of the building, found that whoever had taken Cookie's place was gone for the day, and wandered the halls until I came across Jimbo's name on a door.

Despite the late afternoon heat, Jimbo had not taken off the coat to his light blue suit, and despite his activity the coat showed nary a wrinkle. The only thing that sagged on Jimbo was his jaw when he saw me. "Hey there, fella," he burst out, shifting a fistful of pencils from right to left hand so that he could shake with me. "What brings you to these parts?"

"C'mon, Jimbo. You know exactly what I'm doing here."

Jimbo's eyes swept fondly around the office. "Good thing you came when you did. I'm just in the process of moving out." Then, as a personal aside, he said, "And with any luck I won't be back, either." He stepped over to the window and knocked on the wood of the sill.

"You've quit?" I asked, and he shook his head.

"No. Old man Garber's being really good about it. He's letting me take a leave of absence until election day. If I make it, I'm gone. If I don't, I get my old job back."

"Keeping you on the payroll, Jim?"

"Let's put it this way," he said, speaking sotto voce as though we were such close friends that he could afford to tell me, but he didn't want the word getting around. "We're keeping the family insured."

"I can see where there would be worse things for Jerry Garber than having one of his employees become a state senator."

"Oh, it's not only that, Chuck. Mr. Garber's a great guy. Do you know him? You should; you'd really like him. Man must be close to seventy and he's in the office every single morning at nine o'clock. Active, too. He's down sailing at Martha's Vineyard every single weekend. He's out entertaining every single night of the week. I tell you, I'd like to have half his energy. Tonight, for example, he's going all the way down to the Vineyard just because his wife's having a dinner party. Tomorrow, mark my words, he'll be back here at nine o'clock. The man's amazing." Jimbo shook his head. "But the thing I've discovered, Chuckie, is that he likes his work, and things aren't half as tough as they appear when you like what you're doing."

Jimbo stopped talking and read something he had picked up. He said, "Hmmn," and crumpled it into a ball. He almost seemed surprised when he noticed I was still standing there.

• 195 •

"You know, Chuckie, you're looking at me like I owe you an apology or something."

"Jimbo," I said, "I want to talk about your announcement today."

"Who doesn't? I tell you, Chuckie, the phone's been ringing off the hook. People wanting interviews, people wanting to sell me bumper stickers, people offering me their help. It's been an exciting day, believe me."

"How long have you known this seat was going to open up, Jimbo?"

"Boy," he said, smiling and not meaning it, "that's what they all want to know. I had Alex Scurillo threaten me on that already. He's going to make a campaign issue out of it, he tells me. I said, go ahead. You think I'm going to be vilified because I happened to have enough foresight to plan ahead in case something like this happened, you're crazy. He says, 'But it wasn't just foresight, was it?' and he brings up the little fundraiser we had last winter. I said to him, 'Alex, listen. The rumors were there for everyone. We all knew the general counsel's position was being created. It's no secret that Harlan has a lot of friends in high places and if you'd bothered checking with him personally, as I did, you might have found out that Harlan was very interested in the job.' "

"And would Harlan have told him?"

Jimbo laughed. "Seeing as how Alex is part of McLaughlin's political machine, and seeing as how McLaughlin tried to drive Harlan out of office by getting Pat Joyce to run against him a few years back, I'm sure Harlan would have told him to go fly a kite. But that's not the point, Chuckie. The point is that they've got nothing they can drag out against me—"

"The point is, Jimbo," I fired back, angered at the jovial manner in which Jim Ryder was addressing me, "that you threw in your lot with Harlan Carson at least six months ago; that you built up a war chest and rented a storefront from Vinnie Salvucci because you knew exactly what you were going to run for and when. The point is, Jimbo, that I asked you to do something to save your wretched little brother-in-law and you wouldn't do it because you were afraid it might spoil your chances at walking away with what's essentially a rigged election. All I asked you to do was go to the mayor and tell him you weren't going to run against him. For about two weeks now I've been trying to get you to do that. But no, you don't want to give him even that little bit more time to figure out what's going on or to prepare a candidate to go up against you."

I advanced on him until just his desk separated us. "It's very clever, Jim. I applaud your ingenuity. The announcement's made that the election will be in ten weeks and you've already got your whole campaign under way. You probably have people out there getting your ballot signatures for you right now while everyone else is running around in a panic trying to figure out who's going to sacrifice his career by taking you on at this point. The political part of it is brilliant, Jim, but as for what you've done to Richie, it makes me sick."

I had already started for the door when Jim Ryder's voice cut through me. "You've got a very effective way of speaking, Counselor, but I think you better learn to get your facts under control before you try taking me on. Now shut that door to the hallway and come back here."

It was, of course, Jim Ryder who had the effective way of speaking. The chastisement of his words was nothing compared with the authority and conviction of his tone, and I found myself doing exactly as I was told, dragging my feet back to his desk with the dubiously defiant air of a recalcitrant schoolboy.

Jim Ryder gripped the back of his chair in both his enormous hands. "If you'll think back, Chuckie, you'll remember that I told you I was not the only one involved in making the decisions that had to be made. If the decision were mine alone to make, do you really believe for one minute that I'd sacrifice my wife's brother for my own political career?"

You're goddamn right I do, I thought. But he did not give me a chance to say anything out loud.

"From the moment you explained to me what your theory was about Frannie McLaughlin trying to get at me through Rich, I've been trying to get Harlan to make the announcement. The thing was, Chuckie, it wasn't even Harlan's decision to make. Now here I'm going to let you in on a little privileged information and you must swear to me that it won't go any further than this room."

Once again he did not wait for me to respond and it was just as well. I was not in the mood to swear to anything.

"Harlan Carson had a heart attack last Christmas. It happened while he was at home over the holidays, so not many people knew about it. The hospital and the doctors kept it quiet and Harlan more or less let the word get out that he had had a hemorrhoid operation. That way nobody ever asked too many questions and that was the way it should be. There's a very tenuous majority in the state senate, Chuckie. The party leadership is very concerned about losing even one vote and they don't want to give any of those rich Republican bastards from Ashton the chance to buy their way into a vacated seat. That's why when Harlan's doctor told him he had to get out of the stress and pressure situation of the senate it was a matter of concern to everyone. They had this idea for the general counsel on the drawing boards for a long time, but it wasn't getting anywhere until somebody figured out that it would be perfect for Harlan.

"Here you have to understand the party's strategy, Chuckie. Our senate district is essentially made up of three towns: Portshead, Coventry and Ashton. Portshead is overwhelmingly Democratic and has as many people as the other two towns combined. As long as we keep control of things in Portshead there's no problem. But let Ashton and Coventry come up with a candidate and chances are just as likely that he'll be a Republican. Then we're in trouble because Ashton and Coventry will vote town instead of party while the Republicans in Portshead will still vote party instead of town, and that's how Republicans get elected around here. So the first thing that concerns everybody is making sure the winner comes from Portshead. The way to do that is to control the election dates so you don't give any Ashton or Coventry people a chance to gear up. In this case they decided to control the election dates by controlling Harlan and the way they did that is by holding out the general counsel's job to him. Since it took some time to get that job established and funded, it would have defeated their purpose to announce Harlan right away, so they laid down some red herrings and they never mentioned his name. As late as today, nobody knew he was going to resign before his term was up. But I knew, Chuckie, because I got half the orderlies at the hospital their jobs and the moment I found out about the heart attack I went to Harlan and told him I was his boy.

"You look back, Chuckie, you'll see there's no history of Harlan and me working together, but the simple fact is that he'd rather see me in there than any of McLaughlin's crowd. My problem, Chuckie, is that I've been waiting on Harlan, who's been waiting on the senate. When you came to me a couple of weeks back I did what I could. I went right to Harlan and forced the issue. I said something had to happen immediately, and finally something did.

"You read the newspaper today, Chuckie. You're a bright young fella. Doesn't it strike you as a little funny that Harlan announced he was taking the post before the senate president even announced his appointment? Who do you think caused that to happen? Me. Leahy wanted another two weeks. Give the Republicans only eight weeks to mount a campaign. But I've got you telling me that if I don't make some announcements fast they're going to fry Richie. So what choice do I have? I piss off everybody in the Democratic party, that's what, and I hope to God I can make it up to them later."

Jimbo released his grip on the back of the chair and I saw the deep impression his fingers had made in the soft synthetic material. He hoisted his coat and put one hand on his hip while he ran his other hand through his hair. "I don't know, Chuckie. I don't know what else I could have done, except maybe drop the idea of running altogether, and believe me I've thought about it. But I've also thought about all those people who have a vested interest in getting me elected. People who've been counting on me for all these months. I've got an obligation to them, too, you know. Still, ever since I heard how the inquest went I've been lying awake at night wondering if there's any possible way I'm responsible for what's going to happen to Richie, and that thought alone made me realize that I had to do something now, before DeSantis issues his decision.

"I'll tell you, Chuckie, and I wouldn't say this to anybody else, but I've got a pretty good inkling that DeSantis can be had on this one." Jimbo held up his palm in anticipation that I was going to say something. "I just think he can be had, that's all. He's got a few political ambitions of his own, I'm told, and that's all I'm going to say, except that I think this little announcement of mine should change a lot of priorities."

Jimbo walked around the desk until we were standing face to face and then he put his hand out and he smiled as if he was somebody whom he knew I would be very pleased to meet. "All things considered, Chuckie, and given what we had to work with, I'm very pleased with the timing."

I was a good lawyer. I told him I understood what he was saying and I didn't comment one way or the other.

34 When the phone rang as I was getting into bed I was sure it would be Alicia and I said something cute into the receiver. I immediately regretted it when Ziggy Pastore asked if he had reached the right number. I was tempted to say no and hang up, but then Ziggy seemed to develop a late reading on my voice and he said, "Chuckie, is that you?"

I confessed that it was and he said that Boyle had told him I needed to speak with him right away. I had forgotten about Ziggy. I had only wanted to know if his uncle had mentioned anything about Jimbo's campaign office opening and now that was no longer important.

"That's okay, Ziggy. It's taken care of."

"Well, then, Chuckie, I gotta talk to you about something."

"Can it wait until tomorrow, Zig?"

"Not really, Chuck. You see, I need a place to crash tonight." I said nothing while he cleared his throat. "Denise threw me out."

"Not for good?"

"I don't know, Chuck, but it's either your place or I go stay in fucking Eddie's Motel."

"Where are you now?"

"Blanchard's."

"Isn't anybody else with you?"

"Everybody's gone home, Chuck. I stayed out because Boyle said you had to talk to me and I been calling you about three hours."

"I was down my mother's."

"Jesus, I thought of calling you there, but then I figured you must be out with some broad or something. Look, Chuck, the real reason . . . you know, I figure . . . well, you been through this before and I'd kinda like to get your advice."

I told him to come over and in less than ten minutes Ziggy was beating on my door with two six-packs of Michelob in his hands. He was wearing a T-shirt, dungarees and work boots and he apparently had not changed since he had gotten off work that afternoon.

"Jesus, Chuck," he said, dropping the beer in the middle of my coffee table and looking around the apartment admiringly. "You keep this place real neat, don'tcha?"

"There was a chick here who cleaned it up for me last week."

Ziggy untwisted one of the bottles of Mick and handed it to me. He opened another for himself and sat down on the couch. I didn't want to say anything, but the seat of his dungarees was all dusty and I knew it was going to mark up the cushions.

"Jees, Chuckie, that's the way to go. Get the broads in here, doing all the work for you—not have to put up with any shit from them." He glanced at me for confirmation. He wanted to know if that was the way single life was going to be. I told him it wasn't always that way.

"Yeah, well, if I can have just one day without any shit, that would be like paradise, far as I'm concerned."

"You want to tell me what happened?" I asked wearily. Sitting down in the recliner opposite Ziggy and lifting the footrest up so that my bare feet were pointed at him, I was conscious of the fact that we made an odd couple: me lounging in my bathrobe and Ziggy perched on the edge of the couch with his legs spread wide apart and his arms resting on his knees.

"Oh, you wouldn't believe it if I told you. Just a lot of stupid little things that kept happening. I told you how she was pissed at me for last Friday night? Well, she's still pissed. We ain't been talking all week, so I haven't been in no hurry to get home, you know? Like today, this guy at work says he's having trouble getting the carb off his motorcycle and the fuckin' thing's leaking all over the place. So after work I go over and help him work on his bike for a while. No big deal. But fuckin' Denise goes crazy because I'm late for dinner and didn't tell her. We weren't even talking, for Chrissakes, and she wants me to call her up and tell her I'm gonna be late for dinner? Besides, it was only fuckin' meat loaf, anyhow. I don't see what's the big deal."

Ziggy had finished his beer. He reached for another. "You know what gets me, Chuckie? I don't remember her being this way before we got married. You knew her pretty good; did you think she'd ever turn out like this?"

My eyelids had been dropping shut and I popped them open again. I took a quick sip of my beer and was surprised and a little disappointed to find that it was still almost full. I knew Denise as a slightly silly, round-bottomed little girl who chewed gum and had always been pleasant to me. She had been a peripheral member of our group in high school and my image of her was as one of those people who always showed up down the Cape on weekends to lend her giggle to the crowd without ever getting involved in the actual shenanigans. Ziggy, who was something of a clumsy lothario, had started going out with her just before he left for Vietnam. They had written the whole time he had been gone and had married a few months after he returned.

"No, Ziggy," I said. "I never thought she'd turn out like that."

"What I want to know, Chuckie, what I sorta had to talk to you about, is—

is that what happened with you and Cookie? I'm asking, see, because one of the reasons I got married when I did was because—well, you and Cookie were married and, like Boyle said the other night, it sorta seemed like you had a real good deal." Ziggy shook his beer bottle. Somehow it was empty already and he opened a third. "I'm not saying that was the reason I got married, but it sorta, you know, had an effect on me."

"Well, you should have asked me then, Ziggy. I would have told you. Being married sucked."

Ziggy looked surprised. "Even to Cookie?"

"Being married to anybody at nineteen sucks, Zig."

Ziggy Pastore spread his hands and once again he looked around as if mine was the epitome of the bachelor's existence. "This is much better, huh?"

"I'm not saying that. I wouldn't mind being married at all right now if I could find the right person. I'm just talking about when you're not even twenty-one and your friends are all going out on dates or to parties or playing hockey or something in the afternoon and you're sitting home with your wife and kid; that, Ziggy, that sucks."

Ziggy let his breath out slowly. "Jesus, I didn't know you felt that way about it, Chuckie. I mean, we always thought of you guys like the perfect couple." He held out a bottle to me. "Here, you look like you need another."

"I haven't finished this one, Zig, and I've got to go to bed."

"I know. I gotta get up in the morning myself, but I just want to know, you know? When you finally broke up with Cookie, was it like with me and Denise? Was it fighting over little stuff, like us?"

I used the wooden handle on the side of the chair to drop the recliner into a vertical position and stood up. "Look, Ziggy, it just sort of developed over a period of time. I'll talk about it with you someday, but right now I gotta go to bed. What I'll do is I'll get you some sheets and you can make up that couch for yourself, okay? The bathroom's down the hall there and anything you find in the kitchen you can have."

Ziggy got to his feet looking anxious. "Sure, Chuck, sure. I'll be all right."

It was one-fifteen when I shut off the overhead light in my bedroom and it was four o'clock when it was snapped back on again.

"You awake, Chuck?"

I flung myself up on my elbows, blinking furiously against the brightness. "What is it?"

"I didn't mean to wake you, man." Ziggy was standing in the doorway to my room in his Jockey shorts. He had a brown bottle in his hand, but it was his belly I was staring at. I wondered how it had gotten so flabby.

"Unless the building's on fire, Ziggy, you've got two seconds to shut that light off or I'm going to heave your ass out into the hallway."

The light went off. "I just wanted to know one thing, okay?"

I turned on my side and pulled the covers up to my ears. I was already halfway back to sleep. "Yeah."

"Did you ever have Denise?"

"Jesus," I moaned. "Whatever gave you that idea?"

"I wouldn't be mad, Chuckie. I just want to know. It's something I been lying there thinking about."

"No," I said, lifting my head up and looking directly into the dark shadow of Ziggy's face. "The answer is no, I have never so much as touched Denise in my entire life."

"Good, Chuckie. I'm glad." Then he said good night and closed the door behind him.

35 Piña coladas were the order of the day. Lanny came down from his afternoon nap wearing a tiny Speedo swimsuit that left me feeling as though I was wearing a pair of Archie Moore vintage boxing trunks as I spread out next to him on one of the reclining deck chairs. The clouds that had been coming and going since Tuesday's rain had cleared away for good and at two o'clock on Saturday afternoon the sky was an immense field of blue and the sun was as sharp and round as a new coin.

Alicia had her blond hair pinned up with extravagant nonchalance. She had been sunning herself all day and I sensed that she had only put on her bathing suit when I arrived. At that, it was not much of a concession to modesty. It was a smoldering raspberry color that almost seemed a backdrop to the rich cocoa shade of her skin. The top, had it been any larger, might have been mistaken for red-tinted sunglasses. The bottom consisted of two patches connected across the tops of her hips by an infinitesimal cord that made her sinful thighs seem to go on forever. I did what I could not to look at her, and I looked at her every chance I had.

Lanny arranged the stereo speakers so that they were directed out "on the deck" and he put on a slew of Jimmy Buffett albums. The Jimmy Buffett was in deference to me. Lanny had suggested Willie Nelson and Alicia had wanted Wes Montgomery, but then they both said that my choice was best, and we settled in for an afternoon of lounging.

If Alicia and I had developed a special relationship, it would not have been apparent to anyone watching her. She spread oil over her skin until it beaded. She set up her chair a few yards away from ours. She pointed herself at the sun and she immersed herself in a hardbound biography of Errol Flynn. But she never talked to me as long as Lanny was there. In fact, our only point of contact was in passing around the shaker of piña coladas and she only appeared to notice me when I would get up and dive into the water. After I had a few drinks in my stomach I began to dive in with increasing frequency. Once I swam a few laps in my very best style and even threw in a classic kick turn, but she must have missed it because when I emerged smiling and with my chest heaving she had flipped over and was lying on her stomach with the book open just below her nose.

Still, it was right after that when she reached one hand between her shoulder blades and untied the string that bound the top of her suit.

It was a natural movement and it showed nothing, only the long expanse of her back plunging deep into the tight valley of her waist. I had been over every inch of that territory and no ground had ever been more completely explored. But now it was only an indistinct memory, like something I had read in a book or seen in the movies or watched somebody else do.

I picked up the pitcher and poured everything that was left into my glass. "We're out, Lanny," I said, and Lanny, who had been lying face down with his eyes closed, cried out in horror and sprang to his feet. "We can't have that," he said, and holding the pitcher like the Olympian torch, he ran into the house to make some more.

I sat down in my chair and raised the back into an upright position so that it would be easier to see her. "I miss you," I said.

Alicia covered her brow with one hand and gazed across the top of her book at me. I might have been talking to someone else except, very deliberately, she rolled over onto her back. Her small brown breasts flattened into hand-sized swells and her tiny dark nipples pointed straight into the sky.

"Jesus, don't do that," I said between clenched teeth.

Alicia didn't answer. She raised the Errol Flynn book above her head to block the sun from her eyes. Quickly I threw a look over my shoulder. Too quickly. Lanny was standing at the kitchen window, the one in which Fitzy had been shot, and he must have seen my head turn. He smiled as our eyes met and then he shifted his glance to the rest of the yard and he stopped smiling. I got up and dove into the pool again.

I stayed there until Lanny came out of the house—which may only have seemed like a long time. By then Alicia had turned back on her stomach and Lanny and I were able to resume our places as though nothing unusual had happened. And perhaps nothing had. I thought it strange when Lanny held the pitcher of newly made drinks over my glass and said, "Oh, you haven't even touched yours yet. I guess it wasn't such a big emergency after all." But I could have been misinterpreting.

The music played out and this time nobody got up to change it. Afraid of the silence, I mentioned that the baseball game must be going on. "They got creamed last night," I said, and Lanny complained because they had Rooster and Lynn aboard with no outs in the ninth, and Rice, the Captain and Pudgy couldn't get them home.

"Oh, Lord," Alicia said, lifting her face in mock supplication. "What is it that possesses my otherwise very sophisticated and mature husband to call these guys he doesn't even know by such ridiculous little nicknames?"

And then Lanny said, "Ah, a lesson in sophistication from the woman reading Errol Flynn," and we all laughed. The danger, if there had been one, passed as we started trading sports stories. Lanny mentioned the Patriots and I said, "Now there's an intelligent football team."

We both snickered.

"Remember the time they made Dennis Byrd their number one draft choice and then cut him after only one season?"

"I remember the time they paged Bob Gladieux to come down out of the stands to the locker room and then they had him suit up and run out on the field for the opening kickoff because that crazy coach they had had just kicked a bunch of guys off the team."

"Good thing he was there. They would have had to ask for volunteers next."

"Maybe they would have paged you, Chuckie."

"Yeah. Right."

Lanny was watching me and I could see what he was going after next.

"You ever think about football anymore?" he said.

"Oh . . ."

Lanny waited. A few steps away, Alicia still had her eyes on her book, but I could sense that she had stopped reading.

"Sometimes," I said. "I try not to think about it too much, but it's always there, in the back of my mind."

Lanny let a minute pass by. Then he said, "At least you'll always have that good memory of the Ashton game."

"At least," I said, wondering how my drink had managed to disappear. It had, after all, been filled to the top.

"You do remember it, don't you, Chuckie?" Lanny asked; and I told him I remembered every single minute of that day.

It was, I knew, exactly what Lanny wanted to hear and as I sat in the lengthening afternoon shadows, I told him the story and did my best to make it as easy as I could for him.

36 The inquest report by Judge DeSantis was issued on Monday. The clerk of court called me in the early afternoon to tell me it was ready and ask if I wanted to come by and pick it up or await delivery in the mail. I dropped what I was doing and literally ran over to the court. I read it sitting on a bench in the clerk's office.

This is the report of an inquest held before the Trial Court of the Commonwealth, District Court Department–Portshead Division, sitting as a Court of Inquest and convened at the request of John Ferguson, District Attorney for the County of Northumberland, to inquire into the facts surrounding the death of one Michael Paul Fitzpatrick. A copy of the District Attorney's request letter is appended hereto.

This report is filed pursuant to Massachusetts General Laws, Chapter 38 section 12, and with it are filed the transcript (1) of the proceedings and twenty (20) exhibits offered in evidence during the course of the hearing (2).

In accordance with General Laws, Chapter 38 section 12, I, Stephen DeSantis, Magistrate in this matter, can report with reasonable certainty the following facts:

• That the deceased was a thirty-three-year-old white male named Michael Paul Fitzpatrick.

• That Michael Paul Fitzpatrick died in the rear yard of a home located at 1009 Hamilton Street, Portshead, that said home is the property of Mr. and Mrs. Alan Brandon, and that neither Mr. or Mrs. Brandon nor any other people were in the home at the time the death occurred.

• That the cause of death was a bullet wound that penetrated the brain.

• That the bullet which caused the death was fired from a revolver which was in the possession of Portshead Police Officer Richard Anthony DelVecchio.

• That if any person by his unlawful or negligent act contributed to the death of Michael Paul Fitzpatrick it was Officer DelVecchio acting alone.

The material circumstances attending the death of Michael Paul Fitzpatrick are in certain respects quite clear. There is no question that Fitzpatrick was illegally in the home of the Brandons and that he was exiting that home when he was discovered by Officer DelVecchio. It appears from the testimony that Officer DelVecchio first suspected Fitzpatrick's presence in the Brandon home when, as part of his normal duties and night routing, he passed by the Brandon home in his Portshead Police cruiser and noticed what appeared to be a flashlight moving from darkened room to darkened room. Although it is not clear why Officer DelVecchio did not radio his suspicions, request assistance or inform Police headquarters of his intended course of action, it is clear that he stopped and exited his vehicle and approached the house on foot. From his own testimony, Officer DelVecchio approached the rear of the Brandon house through an opened gate and it appears that the fact that the gate was open not only induced Officer DelVecchio to enter the rear yard, but also induced him to draw his gun as a precautionary measure.

The evidence as to what took place in the rear yard of the Brandon home is in dispute with the further testimony of Officer DelVecchio. The testimony of Dr. Maddox, who lives next door to the Brandons at 1005 Hamilton Street, and who was an aural but not eye-witness, also disputes the Officer's account of the events.

Medical testimony is quite clear. An autopsy was performed by Dr. Wiley Robins, Medical Examiner for Northumberland County. He found that the cause of death was a bullet entering the head just above and next to the left ear and embedding itself in the cerebellum. The autopsy also reveals contusions on the left and front areas of Fitzpatrick's face where it impacted the ground.

Equally clear and important for the purposes of this report are the determinations of Special Investigator Clark and Portshead Police Officer Gilmartin. According to Clark, two bullets were fired and the bullets struck within a range of two to three feet from each other. According to Gilmartin, Fitzpatrick had no gun or weapon on his person at the time of his death.

Upon all the evidence, I, Stephen DeSantis, Magistrate in this inquest, find that there is ample cause to believe that the death of Michael Paul Fitzpatrick was the result of an unlawful act or acts on the part of Richard Anthony DelVecchio and that further Judicial inquiry is required. I therefore bind Officer DelVecchio over to the Grand Jury to issue or not to issue an indictment, as it so determines, before the expiration of its current term.

By all rights I should have brought the report directly to the DelVecchios. It would not have taken me long. I could have gone over it with them. I could have pointed out the breaks the judge had given us, explained how we were going to deal with the matters he had found against us. Except at the moment I could see no breaks, I could think of no explanations, and the thought of going out to the DelVecchios' squalid little house depressed me. I did not want to see their noisy kids, step around the scattered toys, sit amid the unfolded laundry or shout to be heard over the television. I did not want to deal with Richie's anger or confront the near reverence with which Linda would greet my every word. I did not want to watch Richie lapse into self-pity or be there when Linda started to cry. So I avoided the whole scene. Instead I walked the report back to the office and sought out Sid Silverman.

The little man had his door closed, but he acknowledged my knock and put down the travel brochure he was reading. He spread the brochure out on his desk so that I could see it. It contained a picture of a boat steaming through impossibly blue waters. Three decks were visible and each deck had a pool surrounded by multicolored deck chairs, triangular pennants and fun-loving people.

"Izzie wants to go on a cruise," Sid said, looking the picture over carefully, the way a man at a candy counter might look before making his choice of bonbons or chocolate cashews. "You ever go on a cruise, Chuckie?"

I shook my head.

"No," he said, interpreting. "I'm wondering if I'd get bored."

I dropped the inquest report on top of the picture because Sid had gone back to looking at it again. Sid's eyes flickered upward behind the rims of his glasses. My rudeness had been noted.

"Jimbo's antidote didn't work," I said. "DelVecchio goes to the grand jury."

Sid took the report in his miniature hands and leaned far back in his chair. He read through the first page, licked his finger and turned to the second. "Hmmn," was all he said when he was done.

I took the seat that had not been offered and Sid and I spent a minute contemplating each other. "You talked to Ferguson yet?" Sid asked. "Find out what he's gonna do?"

"I don't see where he's got any choice. The judge himself ordered the case to the grand jury."

Sid read through the last paragraph one more time. "But he didn't order DelVecchio arrested. As I recall the state law, he could have issued an arrest warrant once he determined that there was probable cause to believe that a crime had been committed."

"Well, he didn't really say probable cause, Sid. He said ample cause."

"Is ample probable? Or probable ample? Or are they distinguishable? An interesting question." Sid's legal mind was beginning to snap into gear and I felt a sudden twinge of excitement at the thought that maybe, just maybe, he was going to become interested enough in this tar baby he had given me to provide some help instead of his usual shower of homilies.

He turned his attention to the appendices at the back of the report. "You know," he murmured after reading through the list of witnesses who had appeared, "a couple of things puzzle me. This, for instance. How does he determine that there is no question that Fitzpatrick was in the Brandon home illegally when neither of the Brandons was ever called to testify?"

My hopes for some great revelation sagged. A point, I thought, but so what?

And then Sid tucked his little chin into his little neck and peered at me over the tops of his glasses. "You know, Chuckie, I assume the reason you've come moping in here the way you have is that you need some help in devising a new strategy now that things haven't gone your way. I assume you realize that I'm only trying to lend a hand and that there are plenty of other things I could be doing besides helping another lawyer practice law."

I was getting a bit tired of the shots I had been taking from Sid lately and I thought it was time to make that clear to him. "I know how to practice law, Sid. It's just that I'm a little out of touch. You see, during the departmental investigation I was busy holding Richie's hand. And during the inquest I was busy learning how to play politics—"

Sid's chair slapped forward, a jarring, room-shaking response to my sarcasm. "And now it's a grand jury hearing, Chuckie," he said, "and through no fault of either yours or mine you got a whole new set of problems to deal with. From here on in, you stop thinking in terms of quashing investigations and start thinking of how you're going to make it seem reasonable for Richie DelVecchio to have pulled that trigger when he did. You say you know how to practice law, Chuckie? Good. Then here's an excellent opportunity for you." He tossed the inquest report into my lap. "Let's see how you're going to use that decision to win your case."

I held the report in both hands and stared silently back at him. Visibly annoyed, he snapped his fingers at me twice in rapid succession and when that got no response he said, "As I recall the story, young Fitzpatrick was seen emerging from the window, DelVecchio shot him, ran up to him and then immediately ran away."

"To the front yard," I said.

"What?" Sid scowled, turning one ear to hear me better.

"He ran to the front yard and bumped into the Maddoxes."

"Then he brought Maddox back with him, didn't he? You've been out there —how long would that take? Half a minute?" Snap, snap, went his fingers again.

I pictured the yard from memory. "At least," I concluded. "He had to run from the window back to the pool, then around the corner of the house where the porch sticks out, then along the side and through the gate. There are some trees there and he would have had to get past those to see the Maddoxes in their bathrobes, which is what he said he saw. He said he yelled at them and then he and Dr. Maddox exchanged words. Then he had to lead the doctor back with him. I'd say a minute, easy, if not more."

Sid was on me again as soon as I finished. "And all this time Fitzpatrick was lying unobserved on the ground."

I nodded, and I began to comprehend what Sid was getting at.

"And Mr. and Mrs. Brandon were not at home while all this was going on—"

"And they weren't called as witnesses, either," I added.

"Yes?" Sid said, leaning forward expectantly and waiting for me to tie it all together.

"Which makes you wonder how the judge could have determined that no other people were in the house at the time the shooting took place."

Sid smiled triumphantly and sat back in his chair, his hands splayed across his stomach, while I, still feeling the sting of his earlier remarks, tried not to look pleased at having pleased him. "There you go," he said. "An accomplice, following Fitzpatrick out of the house, hides when the shots are fired. He hears DelVecchio running off and then he jumps out of the window himself and makes his getaway." Sid mused for a moment, his brow wrinkling. "How was the ground? Was it soft?"

"It was grass. I think it all got trampled between DelVecchio, Maddox and everybody else who arrived after them. Anyway, there was no mention of footprints in the report from the DA's inspector."

"Who's that? Clark?"

"Yeah."

"Don Clark?"

"Yeah."

"He's a drunk. He can be discredited." Sid did not elaborate and I did not pursue the matter. I was more interested in trying to find out how we were going to locate this missing accomplice. But when I asked that question, the fond looks Sid had been bestowing on me disappeared and he acted as though it was the strangest thing he had ever heard.

"C'mon, Chuckie, we don't actually have to find an accomplice, you know that. It's just one theory we can use to keep the prosecution from meeting its burden of proof if this case goes to trial. Okay. What else have you got?"

Sid got tired of waiting for a response and slid his hands behind his head. It was a pose most men could not get away with, but most men were not so overmatched by their chairs. "Tell me, Chuckie, did your client see Fitzpatrick open the window himself?"

I said I didn't remember.

"Sure you do, Chuckie," he urged. "How did he say he first noticed Fitzpatrick? If the window was shut he probably heard him opening it. If it was open he probably saw him first. Which was it?"

"I think he first noticed the window was open. Then he saw Fitzy start to come through it."

Sid lowered his arms to his desk, beaming with satisfaction. "So there's another possibility. Maybe Fitzy wasn't even the first one out, huh? Maybe there was somebody else in the shadows already. Maybe that's why Fitzy had no booty and no weapon. He could have been picked clean by his accomplice while Richie was running for help." Sid grinned at me as if he had solved the mystery, as if he was challenging me to find a flaw in his reasoning.

I tried. "But look, Sid, even the Brandons say that nothing was taken from their house. Without evidence of something missing, all you've got is a phantom accomplice who didn't steal anything except Fitzy's weapon."

Sid's smile faded and he looked faintly irked. "Maybe the Brandons are lying," he said.

I started to rise to their defense and then I thought better of it. My reaction had not been lost on the little man, however. He folded his hands together and pointed his two forefingers at me. "We're talking about keeping the prosecution from meeting its burden, remember. If they base their case on the presumptions that come out of this inquest report, then it's up to you to knock those presumptions down whenever and wherever you can. If you're going to show that Fitzpatrick wasn't the harmless victim that the report makes him out to be, then you may have to show why it only looks like he didn't take anything and that may involve challenging the credibility of these people, the Brandons. If that offends your sensibilities, then you've got to come up with something else that's going to raise reasonable doubt in the jurors' minds."

Suddenly Sid grinned. "Fortunately, this report is fertile ground for planting the seeds you need. I mean, look at it. Here's the judge getting only one side of the story and he's still got no more idea of what happened than I do. All he's done is expose the other side's strategy and give you carte blanche to tear it apart." Sid's grin grew wider. "I'll tell you, Chuckie, the more I think about it, the more pleased I am with the turn events have taken."

Buoyed by Sid's enthusiasm at my deftness in getting Richie bound over to the grand jury, I went back to my own office to plot out my next move. Notwithstanding my respect for Sid, the glow began to wear off once I was sitting by myself, sipping at a cup of instant coffee. What Sid had told me was good advice, but it was trial strategy and it was not going to help keep Richie from being indicted. At the grand jury proceeding I was not going to be able to get away with concocting fantastic defenses, or, indeed, any defenses at all. As with the inquest, I was not going to be able to put on any evidence. The state rules of criminal procedure specifically prohibit an attorney from being present during the presentation of evidence except when his own client is being examined—and even then the attorney isn't allowed to object, argue or otherwise address the grand jury.

While I was pondering this the phone buzzed and Davida put through a call from Mark Brosnahan. The senior assistant district attorney apparently had interpreted the inquest report a little differently than Sid had because he was all cheer and accommodation as he blithely informed me that Richie was going to be called first thing next Monday morning.

"That's great," I said, filling my voice with enthusiasm.

Brosnahan seemed surprised at my reaction. Then he laughed. I laughed harder and hung up.

37 It was with some disappointment that I found Ziggy Pastore still in my living room when I got home from work. We had yet to discuss his tenure, but it had been my expectation that every night he stayed would be his last. Little things about him were already beginning to drive me crazy. He smoked cigarettes, he liked to keep the television on all the time, he didn't brush his teeth before he went to bed, he went through a ritual of flatulence every morning ("To clear out my system," he explained), and he constantly left his shoes in the middle of the floor.

Yet in his own way Ziggy was doing what he could to be helpful. When I had arrived home from the Brandons' on Saturday there had been a stoveful of Ziggy's special chili waiting amid a kitchen that looked as if its walls had been daubed in chili sauce by Jackson Pollock. We ate it together in front of the television and on Sunday, since he had made enough for forty, we ate it again. I was not looking forward ever to eating it a third time, and yet there was Ziggy with another bowl when I walked in the door on Monday night. He also had a bag of Fritos spilled on the coffee table, a beer opened and the television tuned in to a gangster movie.

"Hey, buddy," he said, picking a half-smoked joint out of the ashtray and extending it in my direction. "You look like you could use this."

I told him I didn't want it and, sidestepping his work boots, went straight to my bedroom and shut the door behind me. I took off my coat and tie and threw myself onto the bed so that I could search the ceiling for ways to save Richie DelVecchio.

There was a knock on the door and I reluctantly told Zig to open it. He had the bag of Fritos with him and he was also dangling a couple of beers from the rings of a plastic six-pack holder. The joint was wedged between his teeth, but it did not seem to be going.

"Hey," he said, "you tired?"

I told him I was resting.

"Jees, I don't know what you're so tired for; you probably sat in a chair all day long." He took the unlit joint out of his mouth, looked at it and dropped it into the pocket of his T-shirt. "I been waiting for you to get home. You want to go do something?"

I told him I was doing something.

"What, resting?"

"Thinking."

"Oh," Ziggy said. He came over and sat down on the edge of my bed. He broke off one of the beers and held it out to me. He said he had been thinking, too.

I took the beer and pushed myself into a sitting position against the wall behind my bed so that I could drink without slobbering all over myself. Ziggy offered me the Fritos and I declined them. I didn't particularly like Fritos to begin with and I especially did not want their crumbs in my bed.

Ziggy apparently did not realize this. He filled his mouth with chips and began talking. "I been thinking about me and Denise. I been thinking that maybe her throwing me out's a pretty good thing after all." Ziggy reached down to the floor and picked up a beer with one Frito-speckled hand. "I was just remembering the first date I had with her. I took her to the Howard Johnson's on the highway. The good one, you know? My brother told me the broads really suck that up, you take 'em to someplace nice. So I fuckin' blew about ten bucks on dinner that night and after that, boy, I thought I was in love." He took a long, long slug of his beer and crunched the aluminum can when he was done. He tucked his chin and belched silently. "Thing is, I can't ever imagine feeling that way again. Now it's like this thing I gotta drag around with me. Instead of being real proud, like, I'm sorta always hopin' nobody sees me with her. It's not that I don't love her anymore or nothing like that; it's just sorta different. That's all." He cocked his head and squinted with one eye at me. "You know what I'm trying to say, Chuckie?"

I deliberately stared at the top of my beer can and made no attempt to answer.

"Besides," Ziggy said, "it's like we're always pissed off at each other. It's been so bad I even been thinking about having a baby, you know, because I figure maybe that's part of the problem, her not having any kids to keep her occupied; but now I think this thing's even better. I think it's better we split up." Suddenly Ziggy brightened. "And this is what I decided to do, Chuckie. I decided I ought to go to California."

Ziggy sat at the end of my bed, grinning at me, waiting for my reaction; waiting, more specifically, for me to congratulate him. "The way I figure it, Chuckie, is I belong to a pretty good union and there's lots of places I could go out there to get jobs. Seriously, Chuckie, I want your honest opinion: what do you think?"

I gave him an answer by snorting, and when that did not seem to make sufficient impact I said, "I think you ought to make damn sure you and Denise are all through before you go making a crazy move like that."

Ziggy raised his eyebrows in surprise. "I don't know it's so crazy, Chuckie. I been thinking about it a long time. Not just since Denise threw me out. I mean, what's there for me here? Sitting around, always doin' the same old thing, goin' the same old places, seein' the same old people. No offense, Chuckie, because you're not like the rest and I don't mean nothing about you, but I been thinking, there must be something better out there." Ziggy shook the bag of Fritos and searched around for the last big pieces. "I'd like to go to California and get me a nice little beach house somewheres."

"You have any idea how much a house on the beach costs in California, Zig?"

"Hey, California's huge. Los Angeles, San Francisco, Oakland, San Diego, Sacramento, San Jose. They got beaches all over the place out there. It's not just Malibu, you know. Besides, I'm not expecting to get no movie star's place or nothing. I mean just some kind of shack I can live in, mind my own business." He finished the last of the Fritos, crumpled up the bag and tossed it on the bureau. The bag rolled onto my tie. "Oh, sorry," he said, and went over and dropped the bag into the wastebasket. He waited until he got back and sat down on the edge of the bed again before he said, "You know what else I was thinking, Chuck? I was thinking maybe I'd go back to school when I got out there. I don't mean nothing big. Start off in junior college—"

"Ziggy, listen to yourself, for God's sake. How are you going to support your house on the beach if you're going to junior college?"

Ziggy smiled. He had already thought about that. "They're free out there, Chuckie. This guy I know told me that all colleges are free in California, so I won't need much. Besides, I can get by real good on not much money. Really. I done it before, when I been laid off and stuff. I figure I can go to college during the day and maybe pick up a little rock 'n roll gig during the night. Earn some money that way."

I choked on my beer. I was expecting Ziggy to laugh and tell me this was all a big joke. Instead he looked hurt that I was not treating him more respectfully.

"Hey, I used to be pretty good at the guitar, Chuckie. Course, I don't know this punk shit they're playing now, but that won't last, and I been in some pretty good bands in my time. I was on *Community Auditions* when I was fourteen." He said it seriously. As if it was more than just a fun memory. As if it was something a grown man could still be proud of.

"Ziggy, you haven't even picked up the guitar since high school."

"So I'm planning on getting back into it. I just need to practice, that's all."

"Okay, Zig. So you're going to move out to California and get a house on the beach. Then you're either going to get a construction job through your union or you're going to go to college and play in a rock 'n' roll band at night—"

"When I first get there I'm gonna get a construction job. Get settled, you know? After that's when I'm gonna go to college."

"Anything else you're going to do when you get to the land of milk and honey?"

I asked the question sarcastically, but Ziggy did not notice. "Well," he said, contemplatively, "I think the change will be good for me." He pushed the curls out of his eyes and held his hair straight back. "Look," he said. "Have you seen how I been losing my hair lately? Look at how it's going back up on top there." He pointed to two half-moons of scalp. I tried to remember if it had ever looked any different and decided that maybe it was receding after all. "I know what's causing that," Ziggy declared, letting his hair flop forward over his forehead again. "I think that as soon as I get away from Denise and all the problems she's been causing me, I won't have to worry about that no more."

"Oh, brother," I said, swinging my feet over the bed and standing up. "Ziggy, I think that if you can prove that all a person has to do to get his hair back is move to California, you'll be in line for the Nobel Prize."

Ziggy followed me to the bathroom and stood outside the open door talking until I was done. "Sure, go ahead, cut me down, Chuckie. That's easy for you because you got nothing to worry about." He followed me into the kitchen and leaned against the counter while I got ice cream out of the freezer, scooped some into a bowl, put the container back and carried the bowl to the kitchen table.

"Hey, Chuck," he said, speaking as though the idea had just come to him. "Why don't you come with me? I got a friend I used to work with who lives out there and he could put us up until we get a place of our own."

"No, thanks."

Ziggy sat down across the table from me and watched me eat. "You could get a job as a lawyer out there. Get away from that fat little Jew you work for."

"I've got more than enough to keep me busy right here."

"Yeah," Zig said thoughtfully, as if he was sorry that my life was just so much more empty of opportunity than his own; as if he was coming to grips with the realization that some people simply lived more interestingly and adventurously than others.

My patience with Ziggy Pastore was beginning to ebb and he must have noticed that because he suddenly said, "You think I'm nuts, don'tcha?" and I told him, "Sometimes."

Ziggy's expression reflected his profound disappointment. He reached between his legs and pulled his chair in closer to me. "Chuckie, I'm gonna tell you something I never told anybody before." He waited until he was sure that I was giving him the attention he deserved, and then he said, "I got this theory, see, and the theory is that none of this"—he swept the room with one hand—"really exists." He paused to let the enormity of the idea sink in. It would have been inappropriate for me to smile and so I filled my mouth with ice cream instead. Ziggy, I saw, was completely in earnest.

"Everything that's happened to me is just part of my dream," he said, "just like everything that's happened to you is part of yours. We all create our own reality, Chuckie, and the only way you can change that reality is by doing it yourself." He seemed to recognize from the way I was looking at him with my spoon suspended between my mouth and the bowl that I was not grasping the concept, and so he explained further. "If I get up and walk out of this room, Chuckie, how do you know I exist?"

He got up and demonstrated. I watched him disappear around the corner and into the living room. "You don't," he called back, answering himself. A moment later he reappeared, spreading his hands and smiling faintly, certain that he had just proved an incontrovertible fact of nature.

"How do I know, Zig?" I said, plunging the spoon into the last ball of ice cream and leaving it there so that I could have both hands free to confront this latest inanity. "How do I know? I know because all I have to do is look around and see the cigarette butts you've left in every ashtray in the place. All I have to do is look in the sink and see the dishes you've piled there; or look in the bathroom and see the shit stains you've left in the toilet bowl. All I have to do is look at the dirt you've left on the couch or trip over the goddamn shoes you're always leaving around." I started to mention the chili sauce stains in the kitchen and then thought better of it and shut up. I had said enough as it was and the chili had been something of a gift.

Stunned by the viciousness of my onslaught, Ziggy searched my face for signs that I was kidding. Finding none, he let out his breath in a long, slow exhale. "Jesus, Chuckie, I didn't know you minded me being here that much."

Feeling almost, but not quite, contrite, I got up and washed the last vestige of ice cream down the drain. It gave me a moment to calm down. "Ah, it's not that, Zig."

"What, am I cramping your style, or what?"

"I just like living alone, Zig. I do it on purpose and I wasn't really planning on having anybody move in with me."

"I wasn't moving in," he said, and even though our backs were to each other I knew his mouth was twisting when he said it.

I returned to the table and sat down in front of him again. "The place really isn't big enough for two guys, Zig."

"So what am I gonna do?" he said softly. "I can't just pack up and move to California tomorrow."

I had a suggestion ready for him. "How about Ferrara's? His place would be perfect. It's big and Ferrara himself is usually on the road about three days a week."

Ziggy blew his cheeks out with distaste. "Ferrara lives with Boyle. Would you want to live with Boyle?"

I smiled sympathetically.

"Every time Ferrara went away I'd be stuck with that little . . ." He did not finish the sentence, perhaps realizing that Boyle had not yet issued an invitation.

"How about Stevie Ferris?"

"Stevie lives with his folks."

"You're kidding," I said, surprised. "What's a guy his age doing still living at home?"

"He just moved back there when his brother Tommy got married. Him and Tommy used to have a place together up in North Portshead."

"I didn't know Tommy got married. Who to?"

"You know, that broad from Weymouth he was always goin' out with. The one with the big nose and the mustache."

"Tina? I always liked Tina. I thought she was a nice kid."

"Yeah, nice nice. Nice like a nun. How would you like to slap the make on her and end up spitting out hairs?"

"Well, Tommy must have liked her or he wouldn't have married her."

"Who knows with Tommy? I figure he married her because he thinks she's an intellectual or something. She teaches school, you know, and I think Tommy was real impressed with that. He's a weird guy, Tommy. He's nothing like his brother."

We were getting off the one-way track that led out of my apartment, so I broke the conversation about Tommy Ferris. I asked if there wasn't anybody else he could move in with for a while and Ziggy shook his head.

"Who? Everybody else is married. Joey Aiello, Giacomini, Howie White, Billy Kincaid—wherever he is."

"How about Donovan?"

"Donovan? What—are you kidding me? Who knows if that guy even has a place to live? I think he sleeps in his car or something."

I was running out of possibilities. "How about Buddy Williams?" I tried. "He's got a whole house to himself now."

"What—and take Fitzy's old room? I ain't doing that." The idea seemed to incense Ziggy, but he might just have been taking a jab at me. "Besides," he added, "Buddy Williams has been kind of strange for a long time. Ever since he fucked up his leg that night and didn't get to Nam with the rest of us he's been a little weird as far as I'm concerned. Listen to this—it'll give you an idea what I mean. A couple of weeks ago me and Denise was driving through Kenmore Square about two o'clock in the fucking morning coming back from Denise's brother's in Brookline. I seen this guy hurrying down the street, you know, limping along like Buddy does when he's in a hurry. So I pull over and sure enough, it's Buddy. I goes to him, 'Hey, Buddy, where you going?' and he looks at me like he don't even recognize me. So I'm driving along beside him and I'm goin', 'C'mon, Buddy, get in the car.' He goes, no, he's got some business to take care of and he practically runs away from me. Two o'clock in the fuckin' morning and he's got some business to take care of in the middle of Boston? What the fuck? Next time I see him, I don't even have to ask what that was all about."

"What was it all about?"

Ziggy, who had been finishing off yet another beer, waited until he had crunched the can before he answered. "Dope, of course."

"Oh." Of course Buddy Williams, scurrying around in the dark of Kenmore Square, would be on his way to or from some kind of dope deal. That's what Buddy Williams did. And Buddy Williams was Fitzy's old roommate, and Fitzy was coming out of a house that half of Portshead thought had been purchased with dope money. If I were to suppose, just to suppose, that there really had been an accomplice, as Sid had suggested, who would know more about it than weird Buddy Williams?

Ziggy was talking to me. "Huh?" I said. He wanted to know if I was interested in going down the bowling alley to play pool.

I told him I was too tired.

Ziggy nodded and got up and stretched. He said he thought he would go down Blanchard's and play the new Space Invaders game.

Ziggy started to leave the room and then slapped his forehead. "Oh, by the way, Chuckie, I almost forgot. A chick called just before you came home. She sounded wicked nice." He did not mean nice nice the way he had when talking about Tommy Ferris's wife.

"Who was it?" I said.

Ziggy didn't know. "She wouldn't give me her name or nothing. Just told me to tell you that the story's finished if you want to see it. Does that make any sense to you?"

I told him it did.

"Yeah," he said. "I figured it had something to do with one of your cases." Then he laughed. "Either that or it was some broad kissing you off."

It was not until I heard the apartment door shut that I remembered we had not resolved what we were going to do about Ziggy's living arrangements.

38 I was there the night Buddy Williams shattered his leg. It was at the end of the summer, the year we graduated from high school, and Buddy was going into the marines the next day along with Fitzy, Ferrara and Pastore. They were going in on the buddy system, and parties, in one form or another, were being held all around town in their honor.

Ziggy's parents started the evening with a cookout and a tin basin filled with beer. Plump-armed mothers with sharp-rimmed glasses stood on crossed legs in Ziggy's backyard and told each other how unbelievable it was that the little boys who used to go sliding down Bolen's Hill were now going off to war. Their round-shouldered, strong-handed husbands clustered about the grill swigging beer, fondly remembering their own service experiences and wondering aloud why it was that every boy didn't want to fight for his country. Sons who ventured over to pick up a hot dog or hamburger were grabbed around the neck or shoulders and commanded to eat as much as they could because they wouldn't be getting anything as good for a long time to come. And in the far back, Buddy Williams stripped to his Jockey shorts, climbed to the roof of the garage and jumped into Pastore's aboveground circular five-foot-deep swimming pool with a scream of "U.S. Marine Corps." He tore the vinyl liner in the pool, but Mr. Pastore was not as mad as he might have been and we all admitted that Buddy had been the first to go nuts.

As Buddy climbed out of the pool, somebody, I think it might have been Ferrara's father, started singing the "U.S. Marines' Song." Then, even though it was not a Marine Corps song, we followed with "The Caisson Song" because everybody knew it and because it seemed appropriate. This sent Mr. Boyle, who might have started drinking a day or so before the rest of us, into a rollicking, leg-flailing dance that was part Irish jig and part Jimmy Cagney soft shoe. When he was done, we sang the John Hancock fight song:

> ". . . for it's fight, fight, fight,
> 'Cause we know we're right
> As we cheer on Hancock Hi-eye-eye."

And then one of the fathers started:

> *"Nothing could be finer*
> *than to be in her vagina*
> *in the mor-or-ning"*

and that was the signal for all the mothers and aunts and sisters to go in the house and make coffee.

The boys, of course, did not want coffee. We were, after all, celebrating, and we did not want any unnecessary interference with our ritual observance of the fact that for four of our buddies everything in life was going to change with the coming of the morning sun. We left the Pastores' in a caravan of cars and stopped first at the Harbor Street tennis courts, where a bunch of the guys from West Portshead had gathered to meet us. One of the people who was there was Pat Frazier, who was the catcher on the John Hancock High baseball team and who ended up coming home from Vietnam in a box. Another one was fat Giacomini, who had already received his draft notice from the army and who was as anxious to go nuts as anyone. He drove his car onto the ball field next to the tennis courts and fishtailed it around the bases until there was a cloud of dust twenty-five feet high. He brought the car to rest on the pitcher's mound and climbed up on its roof, where he lay screaming obscenities at the darkening sky.

We stood around watching him, leaning against the fence and drinking beer or warm Bali Hai or Gallo Vin Rosé. Some people had showered and washed their hair and put on fresh clothes because, later, they were supposed to meet up with the cheerleaders and that whole group. But those of us who were working still bore the grime of the day under our nails and in the creases of our knuckles. The guys who were going in, Pastore and Ferrara, Buddy Williams, Fitzy and Pat Frazier, started talking about how they hoped the whole thing wasn't over before they got there. Every one of them was anxious to tear through basic training and get to Nam while there was still somebody left to shoot at. Buddy Williams explained that as far as he was concerned, one good company of marines should be able to clean up the entire country and he didn't understand why that hadn't happened already. He said it was the army that was fucking things up and Pat Frazier said fuck him and everybody started trading insults. After a while they began picking on Boyle until Boyle announced that in the morning he was going down and enlist in the marines himself, which brought him into the fold with Pastore and those guys, but made Pat denounce him as an asshole. Then everybody started picking on Joey Aiello because he was only going into the navy and therefore obviously had to be a fag. Joey defended himself by pointing at Billy Kincaid and me and saying we weren't going anywhere. We were going to be sleeping in nice warm college beds and probably would be smoking pot and wearing bell-bottom pants with stripes on them and carrying peace signs before long. Joey said if anybody was a fag it was us, but Donovan, who wasn't going in, either (he had failed his physical because of asthma), pointed out that I couldn't possibly be a fag since I already had a wife and a kid. That left Billy, and everyone concentrated on attacking him. But Billy, who had been working out with weights all summer, got tired of hearing it and said that he was going to flatten the next one who called him a fag. Buddy was drunk enough to think he could get away with saying it one more time and Billy threw him into the fence. The two of them would have gone at it, and Buddy would most likely have gotten destroyed, except that a bunch of us jumped in between them.

That took the fun out of the Harbor Street tennis courts and we all got in our cars and drove over to the bowling alley parking lot on Presidents Boulevard, where some of the girls who weren't in the cheerleaders' crowd had promised to join us. It was at this stop that the Marine Corps lost the services of Buddy Williams before they had even begun. Still smarting from being roughed up by Billy, and remembering the success of his garage roof leap into Pastore's swimming pool, he decided to take advantage of the overhang that stuck out about fifteen to twenty feet above the glass doors of the main entrance to the bowling alley. While the rest of us stood and cheered him on, Buddy shinnied up a drainpipe to the roof, made his way along the parapet and dropped down onto the overhang. Whoever was the first person to come out of the bowling alley door was going to get the full Buddy Williams Marine Corps treatment.

Unfortunately for Buddy, his intended victim turned out to be a hefty thirty-year-old who carried his bowling ball in a double-handled canvas bag. He was locked in an animated conversation with a priggish-looking woman in a pastel sweater and he was already waving the bag about in an effort to make his point when he noticed the group of us watching him. He looked up just as there was a cry of "U.S. Marine Corps," and Buddy Williams came hurtling out of the air toward him. Reacting in an instant, the man swung the bowling ball. He slung it up from below his hip and across his body and the ball, hard as a cannon shot, hit Buddy in the knee. Buddy's jumping cry became a scream of terror and he crashed onto the blacktop on his side.

Buddy spent nearly ten weeks in the hospital and underwent three different operations. When he got out, one leg was an inch and a half shorter than the other and he couldn't get it to bend the way it was supposed to. Most of the guys were pretty good about going to visit him for the first month or so, but then everybody started talking about the changes in his personality. At one point he told a group of visitors that if he could ever walk again he was going to join every peace march there was. He said he had a lot of time to read and it was making him think differently about some of the things that were going on in the world.

He started growing a beard and he grew his hair and he didn't cut either for years. When he got out of the hospital he began going into Cambridge and those of us who remained in Portshead did not see much of him for a long time after that.

We heard he was hitchhiking around Europe and then we heard he got arrested during an antiwar demonstration in Washington, D.C. Later he got an apartment in Boston, where he gave strange parties at which everyone sat around in the dark, watching the Lava Lites and listening to rock music that was not meant for dancing. He had a motorcycle for a while and then he got a van and customized it with rugs and stereo speakers. He did all this without going to school and without having a trade and I think even Boyle realized what he was doing for money before I caught on.

Over the years I had pretty much lost contact with Buddy. I still considered him a friend because we had never stopped being friends, but outside of occasionally running into him on the street, my appearance on his doorstep in the bright near-noon light of Tuesday morning was the first time either of us had sought the other out in over a decade. Still, he did not seem surprised. He greeted me in his underwear and held the door open.

"Hey," I said, surveying his condition, "you just getting up or just getting home?"

"Oh, brother, don't ask." He left me to shut the door and limped toward the back of the house. I followed and we went to the kitchen, where he filled a saucepan with water and put it on one of the gas burners.

I sat down at a table that was loaded with half a dozen Miller beer cans, a bottle of catsup, a jar of jelly and some plates that still carried the remnants of a Chinese dinner. Neither of us said anything while Buddy thumped around on his too short left leg looking for clean coffee cups.

In the end he washed a couple out. Turning on the faucet and running them under the water without waiting for it to get warm, he didn't bother with soap or a dishcloth. He got some instant coffee out of a cabinet and shook some into each of the cups. He asked me how I wanted it and I said I wanted it regular, so he shook some sugar into mine and then hauled some milk out of the refrigerator for me. The refrigerator light was a pale blue and I commented on it.

"Oh, that," he said. "The one that came with it was too fucking bright."

When the coffee was ready we drank it and when Buddy was halfway through he dropped his head onto his folded arms and said, "Sheeitt."

I asked him if he was okay and he sat back up and said it took him a while to get cranking in the morning. After another sip or two of coffee he began to make some progress.

He looked me up and down, apparently noticing for the first time that I was wearing a suit. "What are you doing in those clothes?" he said.

I explained I had just come from the office.

Buddy stroked his beard. "You probably freaked out the neighbors," he said. "They must think I'm getting busted or something."

I started to apologize, but then Buddy burst into laughter and reached across the table to shake my shoulder. "Hey, it's good to see you anyway, man."

I told him it was good to see him, too, and felt just slightly embarrassed by the exchange. I was trying to think of the best way to reveal the business nature of my visit when Buddy made things easy for me.

"You here to talk about Fitzy?" he asked.

"How'd you guess?"

"Hey, I'm not exactly a hermit, you know." Buddy used the palm of his hand to rub his whole face: his hair, his forehead, his eyes, his beard. "I was talking with some of the guys at the wake. They told me you were working for Del-Vecchio."

Considering the source, that sounded better than saying I was working for the Portshead Patrolmen's Association. "You mind then if I ask you a few questions?"

Buddy shrugged. "Do I mind? Yeah, of course I mind. I mean, I don't like to go messing around in nobody else's affairs. Anybody knows me knows that. But with Fitzy dead, what choice do I got? I could end up with a whole lot of people messing around in my affairs if I'm not careful. So I figure I'm gonna have to talk to somebody and it might as well be you. If I tell you what little bit I know, maybe you can help keep the rest of them assholes away from me."

I was surprised. "Haven't the cops been by to see you already?"

"Some lieutenant guy was here for about five minutes, but I wouldn't let him in the house and he didn't push it. He mostly just wanted to know what I thought Fitzy was doing inside there that night."

"What did you tell him?"

"I said I didn't know. I said Fitzy just rented part of the house from me and that I didn't know anything about him breaking in anywheres."

"You know what the rumors are, don't you? Rumors are he was after dope."

"Yeah, well, that's what I figured the guy was trying to get me to say, the way he was asking questions. But I'll tell you, Chuckie, the one thing I know he wasn't after was dope." Buddy Williams snorted, chuckled, and then started to laugh. He sat back in his kitchen chair and spread out his arms. "I mean, why would he want to break in anywhere for dope? Shit, anything he wants is right here, man. I got whatever he needs."

"I don't want to piss you off or anything, Buddy, but let me just try thinking like a cop. . . ."

"That's easy. Two plus two equals twelve. You can do it with any equals you want, just as long as it's not four."

"All the more reason you gotta worry about them, Buddy. They're thinking who's a more likely candidate to steal dope than a guy who's going to sell it?"

Buddy shook his head. "Fitzy wasn't really in the business."

I held up my hand. "You're still not thinking like a cop, Buddy. They think he wasn't alone. They think there might have been somebody else in the house with him."

The import of what I was saying sank in. "Me?" Buddy said, pointing his thumb at his chest. As I watched his eyes pop wide, I knew that Buddy Williams had not been Fitzy's accomplice. But Buddy was going to make absolutely sure I knew. His voice rose and split with outrage at the very idea that a pegleg like him could be crawling in and out of anybody's window. He stood up and showed me the leg, showed me the operation scar, showed me how it wouldn't bend.

It took me some time to convince him that I had never had any thought that he was there, that I was only concerned because that was one of the theories being tossed around. "You know cops," I said. "They're trying to clear one of their own and they'll do whatever they can get away with doing. That's why if it wasn't you, I gotta have an idea who else might have broken into that house with Fitzy."

Buddy sat down as if he had been dropped from a crane onto the seat of his underwear. He folded his arms across his chest and shook his head. "Chuckie, if he was in there with anybody else, I don't know about it. And as far as this whole dope thing goes, believe me, if he'd been doing anything that had anything to do with any kind of dope, I would have known about it."

Again I knew he was telling the truth, and the knowledge made me frustrated. "Well, he wasn't just a common burglar, was he?"

Buddy glanced at me out of the corner of his eyes. "You hadn't really seen him in a long time, had you?" He knew the answer. He gave it himself. "Fitzy hated you."

I looked at the remnants of food scattered across the top of Buddy's table and I wondered how much Fitzy had told him.

Buddy said, "He was never really the same after what you did, you know."

"We were in high school, Buddy. Everybody's life changed after that. . . ."

"I guess you'd know as well as anybody."

Buddy had pushed me. I pushed back. "Maybe he got changed in the marines."

"Sure. Vietnam did it to a lot of guys. But how come people like Ferrara and Boyle and Pastore were all able to come home and fit back into the so-called mainstream and Fitzy wasn't?"

"What did he do after he got out?"

"Oh, he went to computer school or something like that. Then he dropped out and went to California and bummed around for a year or so. Came home again and was working as a security guard down the shipyard until he fell asleep one too many times and got fired. Then I think he was a night watchman for a heavy-machinery company out on 128 for a while, but some stuff turned up missing and he got fired again. Begin to get the picture, Chuckie? By the time I hooked up with him again he was collecting unemployment and living at home. I said he could move in here because I needed to have somebody around I could trust more than I needed somebody who could pay the rent every month."

"Were you supporting him?"

"C'mon, Chuckie. What d'you think we were, a couple of queers?"

"What was he doing for money? He wasn't still collecting unemployment, was he?"

"Nah, that ran out a long time ago." Buddy poked at his empty coffee cup. "He'd do odd jobs mostly." Buddy was no rat; he wanted that understood. But he had more to say and we both knew it.

"What sort of odd jobs?" I persisted.

"Well, his sister works up City Hall, you know. She'd get him stuff to do every now and then."

"Mary Ellen."

"Yeah, Mary Ellen Cotati—that's her married name. She's in charge of handing out permits for the Park and Recreation Department, but her office is right next to the mayor's and he's always using her for other things—like going to lunch."

"What sort of stuff would she get Fitzy to do?"

The coffee cup spun in a semicircle as Buddy softly slapped it from one palm to another. "Oh, you know, during a couple of the big storms last winter she got him jobs running the snowplows, he helped decorate City Hall for Christmas, worked the fireworks for the Fourth of July, that sort of thing." The movement of the coffee cup came to a halt as Buddy gripped it with both hands. "Then there was some stuff he did for the mayor personally."

"Like breaking into places?"

"Like, the mayor wanted something done, Fitzy would do it."

"Give me an example."

"Like, the mayor wanted to keep somebody from doing something, Fitzy might find a way to leave a message for him."

"Or if the mayor wanted to know what information a certain writer might have about certain goings-on in the administration, Fitzy might pay a visit to the writer's home when nobody was there?"

"I don't know that's exactly what was happening out at Lanny Brandon's that night, Chuckie, but yeah, that's the sort of thing he used to do."

"When was the last time you talked to Fitzy?"

"Well, I talked to him the day he got shot and he didn't mention anything about what he was doing that night, but that doesn't mean much. He could get calls at any time and sometimes he'd tell me about them and sometimes he wouldn't. Just like sometimes he'd have money and sometimes he wouldn't."

I was not sure that Buddy Williams had told me everything he knew, but he had told me enough. I thanked him and promised I would try not to involve him any further. We talked about how it was too bad we didn't get together more often and agreed to call each other real soon.

39 Jimbo Ryder's campaign headquarters was in the storefront Vinnie Salvucci had rented him on Franklin Street, a few blocks from my office. It had once been a driving school and some of the stickers from the previous tenant were still plastered to the windows. Paper bunting proclaimed Jim Ryder's candidacy and small pennants urged people to vote without saying when, where, why or for whom.

On the door to the headquarters was a two-color poster with a picture of Jimbo smiling from an official-looking seat strategically placed in front of an official-looking American flag. The picture was captioned, "Elect the Man Who Knows How," and beneath that another line read, "Jim Ryder for State Senate." I suspected an opponent could have a field day with that kind of slogan. If an opponent could be located. The primaries had been announced for the third week in September and no other candidate had yet stepped forward in either party.

There were two desks in the front room of the headquarters and both were occupied by women in extravagant hairdos conversing intently on the phones. The pattern of their conversations was such that they might have been talking with each other. Half a dozen young kids, each holding a pile of papers, ran this way and that and tried not to run into one another. Some senior citizens sat on the window benches drinking coffee. They might have been there to work or they might have just come in to get out of the afternoon heat.

Since nobody seemed to be in charge, I simply followed some of the scurrying kids down the hallway that led to the back of the building, where I could hear the whir of a photocopying machine. Along the way I passed a room where a gaunt young man was gnawing at his fingernails as he huddled over his typewriter. He glanced up at me with such suspicion that I immediately proceeded to the next room, where I found Jimbo doing his best to convince a very noisy group of four or five people that he really would do everything in his power to ban truck traffic from their street.

He caught sight of me in the doorway and practically burst with happiness. "Oops, here's my attorney. Oh, my heavens, I must be running late. Is it that time already, Chuckie? Everybody, do you know Chuckie Bishop, Portshead's finest young lawyer? Chuckie, these folks are all from Drury Street, down in the

Hook. That's your neck of the woods, you know what it's like. Lovely street, beautiful street, and Portshead Oil trucks rolling up and down it at all hours of the day and night. There's no reason in the world they should have to put up with that. No reason in the world those damn oil trucks can't go around Presidents Boulevard and I'm going to take care of that in the very next city council meeting if it's the last thing I do. My gosh, that's a family neighborhood. Those oil trucks have no business being there. Good to see you folks. Good of you to come by. Thank you, Bob, thank you, Jenny, Norman. Don't you worry about a thing. . . ."

And suddenly Jimbo Ryder and I were alone in the room and he had closed the door to keep it that way. "Whew," he said, loosening his tie and slumping into his chair. "Boy, this is something, isn't it? The train never stops." He remembered that he had not shaken my hand and got up from his chair again to do so. "Good to see you, fella, and glad you came along when you did, too. You saved my bacon, I'll tell you. I would have been stuck all day."

We chatted briefly and I asked him where he had come up with all the campaign workers.

"Friends and neighbors, Chuckie, just friends and neighbors. People that believe in us and what we're trying to do. Democratic party's always been the party of the people, you know." He chuckled.

"Right," I said. I thought he was making a joke.

"No, really. It's true. Look at history."

"Sure, like Abraham Lincoln," I said. This time I was joking, but maybe he did not hear me.

"Like FDR. Like Jack Kennedy."

"Guys who fought their way up from the bottom, you mean."

Jimbo hesitated. He seemed to be trying to decide if I was spoofing him. "It takes all kinds, you know, Chuckie. We should be damn glad we've had men like them."

"I agree. What if the Communists had gotten them first?"

Jimbo looked perplexed.

By this time I was weary of being the only one to play my little game and I abruptly changed the conversation. "You've heard Richie's been bound over, haven't you?"

Jimbo sighed. He got up from behind the desk, opened the door and stuck his head out into the hallway. "Somebody get me coffee, will you?" He looked back at me. "Chuckie, you want some?"

"Regular," I told him.

"A regular and a black," he hollered. Then he came back and sat down again. He rubbed his eyes. "Yeah, I heard. I don't know what to tell you, Chuckie. I was sure my announcement would do the trick, but it sort of backfired on me, if you know what I mean." He stopped rubbing and sat forward. "I've got that whole goddamned McLaughlin machine so pissed off—"

The door opened and a nervous young girl in a sundress practically tiptoed into the room, trying to balance two paper cups on a metal tray. She had come so quickly that I thought she must have been poised with the order.

"Thank you, darling," Jimbo said, bestowing a big smile on her and taking the coffee from the tray. The girl looked thrilled with herself.

"Shut the door on your way out now, sweetie. That's a girl." Jimbo waited until she was gone before handing me my coffee. "They're so damned pissed off because they think I pulled a fast one on them that it looks like they're not going to change their minds about Richie."

"They wanted Scurillo to run, is that it?"

"They never had any idea the seat was going to be open. But as long as it is, they want one of their own in there. They know if I take it I'm not going to owe them anything, and that thought scares them. Here was their golden opportunity to get a direct line into the Statehouse and pad their pockets with money from state sources, and they've gone and blown it. At this point, Chuckie, it's no longer business. It's spite."

"Is Scurillo still threatening to run?"

"Hey, Alex Scurillo is dumb, but he's not stupid. No, what they'll do is they'll get somebody like O'Keefe to lay his body on the line. Somebody who needs the exposure and can stand the loss." There was a great deal of sadness in Jimbo's eyes as he added, "They don't care about the Democratic party, Chuckie. If they did, they wouldn't be so anxious to try to hurt me in the election."

"What do you think they really care about, Jim?"

"They only care about themselves, Chuckie."

"You think they care enough to want to keep their asses out of prison?"

"You mean that grave-stealing business? As much as I deplore it, Chuckie, I don't think it's exactly prison material."

"How about breaking and entering, conspiracy to commit burglary, maybe even felony murder for causing a burglary in which somebody got killed?"

Jimbo sat forward, giving me his complete attention. "I don't think I follow you."

"What if I were to tell you that McLaughlin and Scurillo were the ones who sent Fitzy out to the Brandons' that night—would you follow me then?"

Jimbo had missed the little jokes I had made earlier. Now he was sure he had caught one. A smile played tentatively at the corners of his mouth. "You're kidding," he said.

"Not even a little bit."

But Jimbo wasn't convinced. He was still ready to smile when he said, "Why the hell would they want anybody to break into the Brandons' house, of all places?"

"Because they thought Lanny Brandon had some information that could hurt them politically. They knew he had been going through city council files doing research for a book he's writing, and when some correspondence turned up missing from those files they naturally assumed he had taken it. I don't know if it was just this particular correspondence that had them worried, or what, but I suspect they wanted to know how much Lanny had on them and what he was going to do with it. If you'll remember, they did the same thing at my office after I showed McLaughlin and Scurillo that letter you gave me, and nobody would even have known they had been there if I hadn't had a sharp-eyed secretary. I think that was what was supposed to happen at the Brandons'. Fitzy was just supposed to get in the house, find out what Lanny had and report back without anybody being the wiser—which not only explains why he was empty-handed, but what he was doing coming out the window instead of the door."

Jimbo spoke quickly, cutting me off before I said anything further. "Now let me get this straight. You think the mayor hired Fitzy to sneak into the Brandon house because he was afraid of what Lanny might be writing about him. . . ."

"Him or the administration. He didn't know what kind of book Lanny was working on. Nobody did. I think everyone who heard Lanny was going through the council files just naturally assumed he was writing some sort of exposé."

Jimbo stopped me again, his big right hand bobbing up and down. "But even if that was the case, why would McLaughlin send a monkey like Fitzy to do a job like that? He could reach out and tap twenty guys in this town who are professional thieves, for heaven's sake. He's got guys on his own payroll."

"Fitzy's sister is on his payroll."

"Who's that?"

"Mary Ellen Cotati."

"Oh." Jimbo's counterargument came to an abrupt halt. "Park and Rec?"

I nodded. "And if Fitzy himself wasn't a professional, I'd like to know what the hell he was doing to support himself."

That surprised him. "My God, I remember Michael Fitzpatrick when he was a little boy."

"So do I."

"He always seemed like such a nice kid."

"He was the nicest kid I knew."

"Funny what happens to people, isn't it?" Jimbo tilted his head to one side. He seemed really to want to know my opinion.

"Yeah, it's a riot."

Jimbo's expression dissolved into a grimace. "And to think they would have gotten away with it, too, if Richie hadn't shown up when he did."

"That's the irony of it, Jim. They wouldn't have gotten away with anything, because Lanny didn't have what they were looking for. He hadn't been the one who had taken the correspondence at all. The thing of it is, though, the mayor and Scurillo still don't know that, because Fitzy never got a chance to tell them. So they're still sitting on pins and needles waiting to see what Lanny's going to do with the information. That means I could get put right back into a real good bargaining position if I had the correspondence they were looking for. That correspondence could be the key to convincing them that it's in everybody's best interest to see that this whole sordid affair just goes away."

Jimbo nodded cautiously.

"How about it, Jim?"

He raised his eyebrows.

"Will you give it to me?"

"Give it?" he asked sweetly.

"The correspondence, the letters you took from the Oversight Committee file, the stuff you've been saving as an insurance policy in case McLaughlin manages to put up a half-decent candidate to run against you. Oh, c'mon, Jim, don't look so shocked. If it wasn't Lanny that took those papers then it had to be you. You're the only other person who's ever admitted going through the file. Hell, you gave me the Woodruff letter with the punch holes still in it. What did you think, I was just going to forget about that?"

I answered the question for him. "Oh, I know. You never thought anybody would discover the cemetery correspondence was missing. How could you guess Lanny would just happen to go browsing through the files looking for background material and that Scurillo would get all bent out of shape just because Lanny was a writer? I'm sure you never even dreamed anybody would know if that stuff was there or not. So you took all the letters and replies yourself and you hid them, knowing that if rigging the timing of the election didn't work to keep the opposition away then all you'd have to do is hand everything over to a couple of reporters and they'd blow McLaughlin and his candidate right out of the water. It was a hell of a good idea, Jim, because they were all public records and you, being a city councilman, had every right in the world to bring them to the public's attention. But now you've gotta make a choice. Either you can hang on to your insurance policy and leave your wretched brother-in-law to take his chances that the grand jury will be made up of deaf-and-dumb police widows, or you can turn it over to me and I'll see if I can't work a trade that can save his worthless ass."

Jimbo Ryder sat very, very still. Somebody knocked on the door, but neither of us moved and Jimbo told the knocker to go away. That was all he said, just "Go away." For a long time there was no other sound in the room, and then Jimbo reached down and picked up a briefcase from the floor. A moment later he handed me a large manila envelope. "It's all there," he said. "Everything I have."

40 The mayor scanned the letters one after another. He did not look up until he had reviewed them all and then he shook his head sadly. He poked a forefinger into the corner of one eye and a thumb in the corner of the other and painstakingly massaged the bridge of his nose.

"I had no idea, Chuckie. In fact, the whole thing comes as a complete shock to me. Oh, I had heard there were complaints, sure. But you get complaints in every department and I assumed that they were being taken care of. That's the reason we have a cemetery board of managers, for God's sake, to take care of problems like this."

We were seated in the mayor's living room and it was very late for either of us to be doing business. But I had been waiting on his porch when he and his wife had gotten home from some meeting they were attending at the high school, and he had had no choice but to invite me in.

"You see how it looks, Mayor, this many complaints and nobody even following up on them. That's the sort of thing that could be misunderstood by people in a place like Portshead. They see what these letters say and they might get the idea someone's been trying to hide the fact that their mothers and fathers and sisters and brothers are being dug up from their graves and dumped in the swamp behind the public works garage."

"Well, I hope you don't think I had anything to do with such things, Chuckie."

"Absolutely not, Mayor. But when people get angry they sometimes act irrationally. They could conceivably blame you just because you appointed the board of cemetery managers and the cemetery superintendent and the commissioner of public works."

"I can see your point, Chuckie, and I'm extremely grateful to you for being considerate enough to bring this to my attention. I just can't tell you how dismayed I am to find this sort of behavior has been going on amongst men I trusted."

"I'm sure you are, Mayor." I arose from my chair and I reached my hand out to take the letters back.

The mayor looked up, startled. Instinctively, he pulled the letters away from me.

"I'm sorry, Mr. McLaughlin. I'm going to need those for the trial of Richie DelVecchio." I continued standing in front of him with my hand out.

Slowly the mayor brought the letters down to his lap. But he still did not give them to me. "What is this, some sort of game you're playing? When I talked with you before, you told me you had evidence about the cemetery that you were going to take to the newspapers. Now you bring me that evidence, it turns out to consist of public records, and you try to tell me that as the chief officer of this city I can't have them because you're going to use them at some trial? Who are you kidding? There's nothing here you can use at trial."

"I didn't say I was going to use the letters at trial. I said I needed them for the trial. And I am going to take them to the *Sentinel* just like I told you I'd do. The only difference is that now I'm going to use them to set the stage for my defense of Richie DelVecchio. Now please, Mayor, give them back to me."

But Francis X. McLaughlin clung to the stack of papers. "I'm beginning to think you have a hole in your head. There's nothing here even remotely related to Richie DelVecchio."

"Mayor, those letters are what Michael Fitzpatrick was after on the night Richie shot him to death."

The mayor did not so much as blink. I walked back to my chair and sat down again. "I guess Alex didn't tell you," I said. "I'm not really surprised. You never would have let him get away with it."

The mayor took the cue. "I'm sure I don't know what you're talking about, Chuckie."

"Alex discovered these letters had been taken from the Oversight Committee file. He knew what could happen if they fell into the wrong hands, and when he learned from the council secretary that the last person who had been in the files was a writer named Lanny Brandon, he went into some sort of panic and sent Michael Fitzpatrick to break into Brandon's house. It's as simple as that."

The mayor thrust himself forward. "You can't be serious," he said.

I rocked forward in my own chair. "It's clear to me that somebody from City Hall sent Fitzy out there, and since the break-in occurred right after Alex's discovery, I'd say he's the most likely candidate, wouldn't you?"

The mayor looked down at the letters in his lap to see if he had missed something. "And just why is it so clear that the boy was sent out by somebody from City Hall?"

"Because that's who Fitzy did this kind of work for, Mayor."

The edge dropped from the mayor's voice. "What makes you say that?"

We were leaning so close that our heads were barely two feet apart. I could see the veins in the mayor's cheeks. I could see the saliva on his teeth, scent the smells of the day on his breath. "Mr. McLaughlin, I've spent the whole of my life in this city. I grew up on the same block as the Fitzpatricks. We knew each other before we knew schools or jobs or spouses or anything else. I know when Mary Ellen gets her brother to run the snowplows in the winter and I know when her brother suddenly gets some cash to spend when he's not working during the summer. I know other people like I know the Fitzpatricks. I know them so well I wouldn't even call them friends because the concept is too transient. There are things people tell each other when they share an intimacy like that. If I had to, I could put at least two such people on the stand and they could testify to the fact that Michael Fitzpatrick had been making his living, such as it was, by doing just this kind of work for people in City Hall. The same two people, if they were under oath and faced with perjury charges, would testify that Fitzy was on assignment the night he was killed."

The mayor slipped back into the cushions of his chair and thought about what I had just told him. "You talk about testifying and putting people under oath, Chuckie. I hope you don't think you're going to be able to use this information you claim to have at the trial of your policeman. Because if you do—take it from somebody with a little experience with our local courts—you'll never get it into evidence."

"Sure I will, Mayor. It's going to be the basis of my defense to show that DelVecchio knew who Fitzy was and what he was doing. By asking him, 'Did you know Michael Fitzpatrick? . . . Did you know what kind of work he did?' I'll be able to get the facts about City Hall's involvement before the jury. The jury's going to believe those facts, too, because by then the story about the cemetery scandal will have been all over the newspapers. Once the connection is made, I suspect the jurors are going to be so outraged that hoodlums are being used to burglarize the homes of the citizenry that DelVecchio will become a hero and they'll let him off on principle alone. And if that doesn't happen, well, then at least I'll have given Richie a good excuse for believing Fitzy was armed, which is all I really need to justify the shooting, anyway."

"And in the process, you'll have besmirched my administration."

"That's true, Mayor, and I'm sorry about it because I know that you personally wouldn't have anything to do with any of this, but as long as I'm stuck for a defense, I don't see where I have any choice." I paused, watching him, making him watch me. "That's why I'm out here tonight, to see if you have any other suggestions."

The mayor looked at the letters for what must have been the eleventh time. "How much time do I have?"

"Well, sir, Richie goes before the grand jury on Monday."

"And if he's not indicted he's not going to need a defense, is that it?"

I nodded.

"The case is in the hands of the DA now, Chuckie." He looked at me as if he half expected me to concede that the situation was hopeless.

I waited, not moving.

The mayor put the letters down on the side of his chair farthest from me and sighed. "I suppose you've made copies of these."

I nodded again.

"Don't do anything with them before Monday," he said.

"You think there's something you can do?"

"Let's put it this way, Chuckie—I'll think of something."

41 On Wednesday, Anthony Bonfigleone was placed on administrative leave. The news was not released in time to make the evening paper, but everybody at Cubby's Corner knew about it on Thursday morning. I munched on some raisin toast and listened while half a dozen of the coffee crowd kicked it around. Nobody saw anything particularly significant in the action, but it was August and any political developments coming out of City Hall were unusual in August. It gave the boys a welcome respite from having to talk about Jimbo's campaign or the state and federal elections that were coming up in November. Somebody who allegedly knew Bonfigleone ventured that his business was going so well that he probably requested the leave himself so that he could devote more time to it. Somebody else said that there had been rumors floating around the Department of Public Works about improprieties in awarding contracts. They mulled over that possibility and then decided that Tony was a good guy and if there was any real trouble he'd get out of it.

I was not there to get the coffee crowd's reaction when the announcement came out of City Hall on Friday that Buster Vizarelli had resigned as superintendent of cemeteries. But Sid Silverman thought it noteworthy enough to justify one of his rare ventures down the hall to my office.

Despite the fact that Sid knew nothing of my latest round of negotiations with the mayor, he was convinced that the two terminations meant the string was about to be pulled on the DelVecchio case. "Frannie McLaughlin didn't get where he is today by being anybody's fool. He's got to know that he's opened the door for you to go to the newspapers with proof of what Vizarelli and Bonfigleone have been up to and I can't believe he's going to take a chance on you doing that. The kind of explaining that would be involved would cost him a whole lot more than he's going to gain by continuing to screw around with somebody's brother-in-law, so you know what I'm thinking, Chuckie? I'm thinking you haven't heard the last from the mayor on this DelVecchio business."

But not even Sid's perspicacity was enough to prepare me for the mayor's next move. At quarter past five, just minutes after Davida had departed for the day, the door to my office opened and Big Jim Ryder came in and filled one of the chairs opposite my desk.

"I had a nice long meeting with Frannie McLaughlin last night, Chuckie," he announced. "We decided to see what we could do about burying the hatchet, so to speak. Naturally, your name came up in the conversation." Jimbo grinned handsomely and let the suspense build. "He's very impressed with you."

"So I've been told."

Jimbo hiked his chair nearer to my desk and licked his lips. "I assume we can talk candidly."

I spread my hands and glanced around the room. "It's not the parking lot at St. Cecilia's," I said, "but we're alone."

Jimbo paid his respects to my little witticism and got up to close the door just in case the cleaning lady should happen to amble in an hour or two early. He waited until he returned to his seat and then he said, "We decided, Frannie and I, that there's no sense us butting our heads any longer over this senate thing. He acknowledges I've got the inside track and he doesn't want to have Republicans sneaking in there any more than I do. So he's decided to support me. He'll make his endorsement as soon as we iron out a few last details, and that should just about wrap up this election for me. The big thing is, my term on the council doesn't expire until after the city elections in February. He's worried about the effect I'll have, holding down both jobs at once. So I've given in to him on that point. We've agreed that I'll resign my city council seat in order to give the mayor the opportunity to appoint someone to finish out my term." Jimbo grinned again. It was his broadest grin by far. "He'd like to appoint you, Chuckie."

The impact of Jimbo's words was not unlike walking into a sliding glass door. I had to regroup before I could respond.

"Is there something going on that I don't know about, Jimbo?"

"Like I said, the mayor's impressed with you. He thinks you'd be a natural for the job."

"Are we all joining up to sell Richie down the river? Is that it?"

"Not at all. In fact, our whole agreement is contingent upon Richie being cleared. I made that understood right from the very beginning."

"And is that going to happen? Is Richie going to be cleared?"

"The mayor told me he's working on it. The problem is he can't just get the DA's office to take a dive because of that damned inquest report. They've got to get around that somehow without making it too obvious what they're doing. At least that's the impression I get."

"So then the idea will be to give everybody a stake in the arrangement. Richie gets off, you get the senate seat, I get the city council seat, and the mayor gets to keep everyone quiet."

Jimbo wearily shifted his weight onto one hip and crossed his legs right over left. "It's a complicated situation we've got here, Chuckie. I prefer to think of it as providing an opportunity for everyone. What's the matter? You wouldn't like to have a city council seat handed to you?"

"Of course I would. I'm just trying to figure out what's involved, that's all."

"C'mon, Chuckie. The fact is the mayor liked the way you handled yourself and he thinks you've got some potential. Besides, the truth of the matter is, I'm all for it. I'd like to have you on that council if only to provide a link between the mayor and me. And think about yourself. At your age an appointment like this would make your career. As the incumbent you'll have a lock on the seat when it comes up for grabs again next winter; and even if you don't decide to stay with it, the fact that you've been a councilman will never hurt your law business, I can guarantee you that. So what do you say? What have you got to lose?"

When Jimbo saw that there was nothing that came immediately to my mind he stood up and with a big warm handshake welcomed me to the wonderful world of politics.

42 I celebrated with a clam roll. I went by the Clam Shack on my way home from work and I picked up a roll and some onion rings and an orange tonic and I brought them all back to my apartment to eat in front of the television.

It wasn't that I was unimpressed by my impending appointment. It wasn't even that I was disinterested or ungrateful. It was just that I was worried. So far everybody seemed to have been covered except Richie, and despite Jimbo's assurances, I still had no indication of what the mayor's plans were for him. Besides, I had no reason particularly to trust Jimbo at this point. On the other hand, things did seem to be going my way lately and maybe if I pulled this DelVecchio case off I deserved that council seat. These were the thoughts that were going through my mind when the door to the apartment flew open and Ziggy came running in to tell me that Buddy Williams had been taken out of his house in handcuffs and hauled away in a paddy wagon.

It was plain that Ziggy was of the idea that there was something I could do to put an end to this injustice. So I swallowed the rest of my clam bellies and tartar sauce and toasted bread and I went down to the police station to see what I could find out.

The desk sergeant recognized my name and was more than cooperative. He gave me the largest interview room and he told me he would bring Buddy in to see me in no time. But no time became ten minutes and then fifteen, and finally a patrolman came in and told me that Mr. Williams did not wish to speak with me. I went storming back to the desk sergeant, knowing that this couldn't possibly be true, and the sergeant promised me that he would check out the problem himself.

The next time the interview door opened Buddy Williams was practically thrown over the threshold. He stumbled, caught himself, and limped to a halt. I got out of my chair to greet him and froze on my feet. Buddy Williams, it was obvious, was not glad to see me.

"You must be a pretty important guy," he said, "the way you get the cops to do anything you want."

"What are you talking about, Buddy? Some guy came in here and claimed you didn't want to see me, so I went over his head, that's all. I didn't know what they might be doing to you back there."

"What the fuck did you expect they were going to be doing to me?"

"Expect?" I said, still unsure why he was treating me this way. "I didn't expect anything. I just heard you were in some trouble and I got down here as fast as I could to see if I could help. Why? You got another lawyer you want to call? Because if you do, I can—"

But Buddy wasn't listening. He was shaking his head disgustedly, looking at me as if I was day-old dog food that somebody had put in his sneaker. "How could you do this to me, man? I just don't understand it."

"What, Buddy?" I said softly. "What is it you think I did to you?"

Buddy turned to face me full on. His skin flushed deep red on his neck and on his forehead and beneath his beard. "You got me busted, you prick."

Sometimes it is as difficult to know how to act when you are innocent as when you are guilty. I could only think to deny it, to tell him I hadn't had anything to do with getting him busted.

"Oh, no, man," he sneered. "I only talk to you one day, tell you everything that's in my house, and two days later your fuckin' pal Finucci shows up with a warrant to search the place for everything I told you about. Why didn't you just go all out and say I was a heroin dealer, Chuckie? Why didn't you really try to fuck me over?" Buddy's shoulders shook with emotion.

"Buddy," I said, wanting to reach out and touch him and knowing that was the last thing he wanted me to do. "Listen to what you're saying, will you? It's crazy. Why would I want to get you busted?"

"How do I know? Maybe you worked a trade, me for that cop of yours."

"I wouldn't do that, Buddy. I wouldn't set up anyone, especially not a friend."

"Friend?" The word rolled scornfully off Buddy's tongue. "Yeah, I heard what you do to friends, man. I know all about it. You wouldn't fuck a friend or anything like that, would you? Only a friend's mother."

My skin turned to wax. For a moment I felt as though I couldn't move. "Don't say that," I said.

But Buddy's eyes flashed with the malignant joy of having succeeded at hurting me. "Why not? It's true, isn't it? Isn't that why you and Fitzy stopped talking in high school?"

"It was a misunderstanding, Buddy. It doesn't concern you."

"But Fitzy told me about it. He told me about the party Mary Ellen and him had, about how you snuck off with his mother, about how he caught you coming out of her bedroom long after everyone else had gone home."

"It wasn't like that, Buddy. Nothing happened. I just passed out."

"Bullshit. You were fucking Fitzy's mother and Fitzy knew it."

"All right," I snapped, suddenly angry at the way he was pursuing me. "You want to go around laying guilt trips on somebody, you should start with Fitzy's mother. I was a goddamned kid, for Chrissake. She was an adult, somebody I had known all my life, somebody I thought was like a goddess, and she came home drunk while the party was going and started fooling around. I just bumped into her coming out of the upstairs bathroom and she was all over me, kissing me on the mouth, rubbing up against me, undoing my belt. The bedroom was right there, it was dark, I let her take me in it because it was better than being out in the hall where everybody could see us. . . ." I stopped. "There's no need for me to be telling you all this."

Buddy Williams agreed. "It just tells me what kind of guy you are, that's all."

"Jesus, Buddy, I was sixteen years old and half scared to death."

"And now you're in your thirties and you've gone from fucking Fitzy's mother to defending his murderer. You've really made some progress, Chuckie. I wouldn't put anything past you."

"Hey, c'mon, Buddy—defending DelVecchio's just my job. It has nothing to do with my personal feelings."

"Your job? Boy, you've got an excuse for everything, don't you, Chuckie?"

I didn't answer; Buddy didn't give me a chance. He moved up until he was within a few inches of my face, until I could smell the jailhouse odor of his breath. "A job's just something you do to make money, man. You work on this job for a couple of weeks and then it's all over and you say fine and you go work on some other job. Doing a job's no excuse when you're messing with friends. You ruin their lives and they stay ruined and they don't get no better just because you came around later saying sorry, man, I was just doing my job. Fuck that, Chuckie. Fuck that and fuck you."

Buddy kept his face directly in front of mine. He was not as tall as I was and so he had to bull his neck to do it. His arms had dropped to his sides and his hands were clenched. It was the same old Buddy I remembered, always ready to go on the attack.

I put my hand on his chest and held him away from me. "Pretty easy for you to talk, isn't it, Buddy? What the hell, you don't pay rent. You're a hippie or something, aren't you? You don't believe in that stuff. Or did somebody give you the house you're living in? And you know all about working, too, don't you? I mean, you've got other people depending on you for support every month, don't you? And I'm sure you've got plenty of time to worry about your friends. I mean, you can worry whether they can pay you for your dope or not, but that's about it, isn't it? Tell me, you're such a great guy, Buddy, how come you don't give your dope away? How come you don't just sell it to your friends for what you pay for it instead of profiting off them?"

Buddy's eyes seemed to widen as I spoke. Slowly and deliberately he leaned his weight into my hand. "I see what's going down now, man. You're jealous, aren't you? Here you were, the big hot shit in high school while I was just another nobody. And now we're all grown up and you're the one who's a nobody, just some guy slaving away for a living. You only had one dime to put in the jukebox, didn't you, man? When your song ended you had to start dancing to somebody else's music. And now you look at me, living the way I want to live and doing the things I want to do, and it pisses you off. This bust, this coming down here pretending you want to help, it's just your way of cutting me down to size again, isn't it?"

I pushed Buddy Williams away. He was crowding me and I pushed him away. He slipped, his leg went out from under him and he fell to the floor. He started to scramble back to his feet, but I held him off with one pointing finger. "Don't go flattering yourself with comparisons to me, Buddy. Because as far as I'm concerned, you've never even been in the competition."

"Maybe not in your competition, asshole. But your competition don't extend beyond Portshead and there's a whole world out there who don't give two shits about that. There's a whole other competition going on out there, Bishop, and you washed out on that one a long time ago."

I asked myself what I was doing arguing with a jerk like this. It was a rhetorical question and I left the interview room before either one of us said anything more.

43 The desk sergeant laughed when I asked where Lieutenant Finucci's office was. He pointed at his watch. "It's nine o'clock," he said. "Even Herb Finucci don't live here, for crying out loud." But he told me how to get there nonetheless.

I ascended a flight of stairs, made a left-hand turn and entered a big room where a group of officers, both uniformed and plainclothes, were lounging around. There was something expectant about the way they were sitting on the edges of desks, about the way they stopped speaking when I came in; but I paid them little attention because beyond them was Herb Finucci's office and there was Herb seated behind a big mug of coffee and looking resplendent in a gray sport coat with little sailboats all over it. He was rapidly filling out papers and he was about as happy to see me as Buddy had been.

"What do you want?" he said.

"I've just been to see Buddy Williams."

"He make bail?"

"I don't think he's tried."

"That what you're here for?"

"He doesn't want me to help him. He thinks I gave you the information that got him busted."

Finucci went back to writing. "Well, you didn't."

"You're goddamned right I didn't."

Finucci regarded me out of the corner of his eye and continued with his paperwork.

"He thinks the bust might have something to do with the case against Richie DelVecchio. Does it, Herb? Or is this whole thing just a coincidence?"

Finucci picked up his coffee and slurped it.

"I just want to know what's going on, that's all."

Finucci leaned back in his chair. This time when he took a sip of his coffee a brown bubble formed at the funnel of his lower lip. "It's police business, Chuckie. I can't talk to you about it."

"You can't or you won't?"

The bubble danced, spiderlike. Herb wiped it away. "What difference does it make?"

"Hey, Herb, I thought you told me to let you know anything you could do to help Richie DelVecchio."

"That was DelVecchio. This is Williams."

"And the two things aren't related? Williams was only the roommate of the guy DelVecchio shot, but one thing has nothing to do with the other?"

Finucci was silent.

"There had to be some reason why you chose to bust him now."

"Look, Chuckie, I do what I'm told. All right?"

It was clear from the look on his face that I was going to get no further with Herb Finucci, but I continued to stand where I was until he waved his arm at me and said, "Now go on and get outta here. I've got a whole 'nother thing to get to before the night's over."

I slipped out silently, making my way past a squad room of men who seemed to have nothing better to do than monitor my retreat.

44 Alicia Brandon made it a hat trick. The third person in a row to be not glad to see me. She didn't say it in so many words, but I could sense it in the way she met me at the door, the way she looked over my shoulder as though she thought somebody else might be there with me. She told me it was because it was early and because she hadn't been expecting me. I told her I was there because I'd been driving by and because I saw that Lanny's car was gone. Neither of us was telling the complete truth.

We went upstairs to the guest bedroom, the one we had used that first night, the one we had used when I had come on Monday to see the story Lanny had made out of the Ashton game. But it was not the same as it had been on those other nights. This time we undressed quickly and made love quietly and unspectacularly. Afterwards we lay in the cool darkness, the bedclothes rumpled around us, she with her thoughts and I with mine; and when it seemed that mine were at least in an order I could talk about I got up on one elbow and tried to tell her what had happened between Buddy Williams and me that night.

She listened, her back to me, her blond hair almost translucent in the darkness. She waited until I was done and then she asked me why I was so upset by what he had said.

"I don't know," I told her. "I guess it was that dime-to-dance-by stuff, as if I've never had anything going for me except football. Hell, I'm about to be made a city councilman. That's something, isn't it?"

Apparently it wasn't to Alicia, the Southern Californian. She said only, "Why?"

Slightly miffed that she was not more impressed, I made no effort to explain. I said simply, "The mayor asked me, that's all."

"So it's just something that's happening to you; is that why you're doing it?"

I had been dragging my hand along her body while we talked. I had taken it over her stomach, across her hard little breasts and down the bow of her ribs. But now I stopped. "What's that supposed to mean?"

"It means I'm beginning to see you as a man who only makes easy choices, Chuck." Alicia threw herself onto her back and grabbed my wrist when I tried to pull away. "Look at me," she demanded. "Isn't that what you did with me?

• 248 •

Isn't that what we both did when it came to Alan? I started off trying to do something good for my husband and the moment something I wanted comes along I sacrifice him. What's my excuse, Chuck? That I can't control myself? That I didn't have a choice? Is that what I'm supposed to tell Alan when he asks me why I've done this to him?"

Fear clutched my heart, squeezed it, left it pounding furiously in my chest. "Does he know?"

"He suspects, Chuck, I can feel it. I don't know what he's going to do, Chuck, but I'm afraid."

The dog started barking before I could answer, fast and furiously, so that we instantly knew someone was there. We both sat bolt upright, our ears straining to hear the sound of a car in the driveway, a door opening, a foot on the stairs. The dog's sharp continuous yap drowned out everything but the distinct feeling of movement outside the house. In the shadows I could see Alicia's eyes wide with fright. I reached for her, but she held up her hand to keep me away. We were both listening so intently that it sounded like a fire alarm when the doorbell went off.

"It's Alan," she said.

"Ringing the doorbell?"

"Maybe he forgot his key."

"Alicia, it's nobody you want to see. Don't go down."

But she was out of bed, hurriedly slipping back into her clothes. "I've got to find out who it is."

"What about me?"

"Stay here."

"But what if it's Lanny?"

"Quick," she said, pulling me to my feet, "straighten out the bed."

The doorbell sounded again, longer this time, more insistent. "Oh, that's got to be Alan. Pull up the spread, Chuck, and get into the closet."

"My clothes," I said, as she pushed me in among the empty coat hangers.

Some of them got to me. The rest were kicked under the bed just before she closed the door and ran from the room. I dashed out long enough to get the things that had gone under the bed and before I was back in my hiding place I could hear voices at the front door.

There was a man's voice, terse and authoritative, and then a second voice, and then the sound of many feet. In the darkness of the closet I fumbled with my clothes, searching for my underwear, trying to get it on fly front. There were footsteps on the stairs and then in the hallway outside the room. I had the underwear in place. I found my pants and hopped as silently as I could into one leg. Someone came into the room and a light went on.

The footsteps came toward me. I kicked my other leg in and jerked the pants to my waist. My hands were still on the zipper when the door was flung open.

"Freeze, cocksucker."

The face of the man confronting me was obscured by the light behind him, but I wasn't looking at his face. I was looking at the gun in his hand.

True fear shredded my stomach and loosened my bladder. I remembered stories I had heard of people letting everything go when they were frightened and I squeezed my insides together. Perversely, it seemed as important not to soil myself as not to get shot.

"Peter," the man shouted, but he was not shouting at me. "I got him."

A second man came running into the room, but I was afraid to glance at him. I was afraid to take my eyes off that gun.

"Holy shit," the second man said. "That's not Alan Brandon. That's what's-his-name, DelVecchio's lawyer."

The first man took hold of my shoulder and pulled me into the room. I knew then that they were cops and when I looked at them closely I recognized them as two of the men who had been waiting outside Finucci's office earlier that evening.

"Chuckie Bishop," my captor said. He poked me with the barrel of the gun. "Hey, you been sticking the bitch, haven't you?"

The second man gazed at me in wonder. "Holy shit," he repeated. "What are we gonna do with him?"

"Go get Finucci. Don't say nothing, just get him to come up here."

The one called Peter ran off and his companion lowered his gun. "How the hell did you ever get into that, Chuckie?" he said, but I stood mute, admitting nothing that was not already being given testimony by my state of undress.

More footsteps sounded on the stairs and in the hall and then Finucci was puffing his way into the room. "Oh, my God," he said, drawing up short. "I don't fuckin' believe it."

The cop who had been holding the gun on me started to laugh. The second one, who was now behind Finucci, joined in tentatively, his eyes on his boss to see if it was all right. But of course it was not all right. Finucci silenced them both with a snarl.

"You're a fuckin' walkin' disaster," he said, jabbing me in the chest. "What the fuck am I supposed to do now? Bust you, too, because you can't keep your thing in your pants?" Finucci grabbed his stringy hair and pushed it back across the top of his head. He opened his sailboat-covered sport coat and planted a hand on his hip. "Go on, put your clothes on," he said irritably, and he began parading around the room.

"I've got a fucking warrant to bust this place for narcotics, Chuckie. If I carry it out I gotta bring you in along with your gorgeous little friend and I'm sure as hell I wasn't supposed to be doing that. Where the fuck is her husband, for Chrissake? It's eleven o'clock in the fucking night, he ain't here and you are. What the fuck's going on?"

By this time I had my shirt buttoned and I was pulling up my socks. "There's nothing to bust here, Herb. Whoever told you that gave you a bum tip."

"You just let me worry about what there is to bust and what there isn't," Finucci said. "I gotta call somebody." He looked around. "There must be a phone in this dump," he said, and he stalked out of the room.

The two cops who were left behind looked at each other and shrugged. The one who had been showing me his gun put it away and sat down on the edge of the bed. He ran his hand over the spread and gazed up in the direction of the pillows. "Gee, this where you been getting her, Chuckie?"

I went over to the mirror that hung above the room's sole dresser and began wrapping my tie. It wasn't necessary to put it on. My shirt was a mass of wrinkles and at this hour there was no need for a tie, but it helped me disassociate myself from what had happened.

"I'd give my right nut for a few minutes with her," the cop on the bed said, continuing his ruminations.

The other cop, Peter, said, "I ever got my pecker in her, you could cut it off and bronze it for all I'd care after that. Hang it on the wall, over the fireplace or something, with a little plaque for meritorious service that says, 'I have been to the mountaintop,' with the date underneath it."

"You'd have to cut it off," the first cop said. "You wouldn't be good enough to hang around with it anymore."

There was some commotion downstairs. Voices were raised and there was a lot of movement. Thinking something might have happened to Alicia, I started for the door, but Peter, who was closest to me, blocked my way. "I think you better stay here," he said.

A minute later the door opened and Finucci burst back into the room. "There a way outta here without going down the front stairs?" he asked.

I pointed to the window.

"Funny," he said. "You wanna jump? The husband just came home."

I ran to the window. From what I could see, there appeared to be a bit of a sloping roof and then a drop-off which I suspected was about twenty feet from the ground. "I'll try it," I said.

"Yeah, you break your fucking leg, you'll probably sue the department. No way. Peter, you go down and get that guy Brandon into some room where you can close up the doors. Tell him you're gonna interrogate him or something, but don't lay a hand on him. And be polite, understand?"

"What about the bust, Herb?"

"It's off. Forget it. Just ask him about his drug associations and all that. Ask him how well he knew Fitzpatrick, how many times he been over, if he ever had any business dealings with him, that sort of thing."

"What about the broad?"

"Get her in there, too. But first tell her not to say anything about Chuckie, you follow me? And make sure nobody lays a fuckin' hand on her, either."

Peter disappeared and Finucci walked around the room some more, shaking his head. "I don't know how you do it, Chuckie. . . ."

"He's a stud." The remaining cop laughed from his position on the bed.

Finucci whirled on him. "I'm talking about he manages to cause so much trouble for himself."

I looked up in alarm. "You're not saying this is being done for me, are you, Herb? You're not telling me that this is part of the mayor's plan for clearing Richie DelVecchio—to set up these people and Buddy Williams and God knows who else. What was the idea, Herb—to make it look like Richie had foiled a big dope ripoff? To make it seem Richie was on a dangerous mission? Or was it just to create a motive for Fitzy being in the house? Because if it's just to create a motive, Herb, this little operation isn't being done for me and it's not being done for Richie, either—it's being done to cover up the mayor's connections with the burglary that took place here."

Finucci shrugged, unfazed. "Not everything is black and white, Chuckie. My departmental report was released today. You'll want to read it." He looked at his watch. "Now come on; they've had enough time to do something about Brandon. Let's see if we can't get you outta here before he starts screaming about human rights violations or some such crap. Oh, and one more thing. I wouldn't talk to anybody about any of this, I was you. I think I'm doing you a big favor and I'm expecting you to remember that."

We descended the stairs and went outside past a couple of uniforms who gawked at me but didn't say anything. The semicircular driveway was filled with cars. There were a few police cruisers and one of them had its blue lights on, its doors open and its radio belching words into the night. It had succeeded in attracting most of the neighbors and they were lined up all along the sidewalk. I could see the Maddoxes in their bathrobes, standing on their own property. I could see Lanny's car parked out in the street, not more than a hundred feet from my own.

I told Finucci I'd remember.

45 The lights were still on in my living room when I got home. The turntable on the stereo was spinning round and round and the needle was slipping frantically back and forth across the slick centerpiece of an old Moody Blues album, but there was no sign of my roommate.

I shut everything off and walked into the bedroom. I found the switch for the lamp on the table next to my bed and flicked it on. A woman named Darlene Ghilotti smiled up at me from between my sheets. She had been there once before, shortly after she had gotten divorced from a guy named Tony Ghilotti who had been a year or so ahead of me at John Hancock, but now she was there with Ziggy Pastore.

Ziggy was dead to the world. He was curled up in the fetal position, facing Darlene's back. His mouth was open wide enough to catch a baseball and his curly hair was spread all over one of my pillows. "Good God almighty," I said.

"Shh," Darlene said, putting her finger to her lips and looking fondly at him. She smiled and sat up, pulling the sheet around her. "So, how you been?"

I looked down at her incredulously. "Darlene, what are you talking about? What are you doing in my bed?"

Ziggy stirred and looked at me with uncaring surprise before flopping over onto his back.

"Ziggy, you asshole, what the hell's going on here?"

"Hey, Chuckie," Darlene said, drawing her knees up under the sheet, "don't be a jerk."

But I was tired and on edge and determined not to follow Darlene's advice. I lunged across her and grabbed Ziggy by the shoulder. He shook himself awake and covered his eyes. "Shut that fuckin' light off," he ordered, and I responded by saying, "Get the fuck out of my bed."

With his hand over his brow, Ziggy managed to focus on who was talking to him. "Oh, hi, Chuckie," he said, and rolled over, pulling the sheet from Darlene, so that she had to grab quickly to pull it back. "Cookie called you," he yawned. "She said it was real important. I meant to leave you a note, but I forgot."

Nothing that I could imagine Cookie wanting at that hour seemed as important as getting my bed back, but no one else seemed to realize that. Darlene was glaring at me, Ziggy was facing away from me, and neither seemed the least inclined to get up. "What did she want?" I said.

"She was pissed off about something. She said for you to call no matter what time you got in."

I looked toward the living room, where the couch contained the only other prospect for a night's sleep. "I guess I'll go call her, then," I said.

"Shut off the light," Ziggy said.

Darlene's high-pitched voice ripped into Ziggy the moment I closed the door behind me, but I didn't stop to listen. I went straight to the phone and dialed Cookie's number.

She answered on the first ring. "Chuckie?" she said hopefully.

"Yeah."

"Oh, great. Nice of you to come home."

"What is it, Cookie? What do you want?"

"Oh, nothing. Just your daughter's ran off, that's all."

"Ran off? Run off? Cookie, is this something serious?"

"Oh, no, nothing like that. What do you think, I been calling you just to pass the time? Tell you, by the way, your daughter ran off to Maryland to get married?"

"Maryland? What the hell did she go to Maryland for?"

"What do you care? You never paid any attention to her all the time she was here."

"Cookie, she hates me." But this wasn't the time to argue. "Never mind. Stay right where you are and I'll be there in ten minutes."

"You don't need to bother coming by here, stupid. Just go get her."

"Go get her? In Maryland? I don't even know where she is."

"She got up early this morning and drove down there with Glen."

"The greaser?"

"The shit."

"Did she leave you a note? Why didn't you call me sooner?"

"She didn't leave me a note. I thought she was at the beach and I been waiting for her to get home. A couple of hours ago I got a call from some guy who said he was a justice of the peace in a place called Aberdeen—"

"Aberdeen's in Scotland."

"Yeah? Well, now it's in Maryland because that's where Mr. Golden is, who called me, and that's where your daughter is and that's where that juvenile delinquent who took her there is."

"How did this Mr. Golden happen to call you?"

"Because he's a nice guy, that's why. He said Candy and Glen showed up at his house this afternoon and said they wanted to get married. He said they hadn't had any blood tests or anything. For some reason they just thought they could drive down there and get married. He says he's seen it before. He says he made them fill out questionnaires and told them they'd have to come back in twenty-four hours. That means you have to get down there right now, Chuckie."

"Cookie—"

"Right now."

I got the name and address of the motel where Candy was staying in Aberdeen and hung up the phone. It was midnight Friday night. I had a case going before the grand jury in less than sixty hours, a lover and her husband undergoing police interrogation, a bedroom full of unwanted visitors, and now I was being sent off to Maryland to save my teenage daughter from elopement. I must have looked like a man who had been run over by a train.

46 I spent the predawn hours in the parking lot of Mitch's Motor Inn on the outskirts of Aberdeen, Maryland. It was a desperate-looking place in the dark and it depressed me to think that my daughter was shacked up in one of its meager little units. I wondered where she had gotten such bad taste and blamed it on her mother.

Although it was just off the highway, it had taken me an extraordinary amount of time to locate first Aberdeen and then Mitch's. When I at last arrived, the manager's office was locked up, without any sign of life. I had found the big black Chrysler that I had seen in the churchyard at St. Cecilia's, but it was in a stall that did not seem to be the exclusive province of any particular room. At another time in my life—a few days, maybe even a few hours, earlier—I might have started banging on some doors, but my recent experiences with that kind of confrontation kept me from doing that. So I waited instead. I parked my Firebird behind the Chrysler, I scrunched up in the front seat, and I waited.

The first stirrings of the morning came from one of the units that I suspected might have belonged to Candy. The door opened and a single male slipped out carrying his shoes and socks in his hand. He came to a dead stop when he noticed me watching him, and then he quickly stepped around my car and climbed into a little Gremlin. He was gone as soon as the engine caught hold.

Later, an enormous couple emerged from an end room that did not seem big enough to hold them and I watched them haul several armloads of luggage out to their car. The sky was still slate gray and already they were arguing with each other.

At seven o'clock a car drove by and chucked a newspaper at the manager's door. I went out and got it and by the time I was done reading it enough activity had taken place around Mitch's Motor Inn to make me ninety percent sure I knew where Candy was. At that point I figured the odds were sufficiently in my favor and I went up and knocked on the door I had selected.

It was obvious that Candy's boyfriend did not immediately know who I was. He stuck his tousle-haired, sleepy face into the crack and stared uncomprehendingly at me, like maybe I was a train conductor come to collect a ticket he had already surrendered.

I had spent several hours rehearsing what I was going to do when I confronted the two of them, but all my plans for suave persuasion evaporated at my first glimpse of this pimply-faced, stubbly-bearded, bat-eared boy who had the temerity to think he could run off with my fifteen-year-old daughter. I jammed my foot in the door.

"Hey," he said, his reaction coming a bit late. "What is this?"

"Candy Bishop in there?"

Again the kid was slow. He was holding the door closed against my foot, but he wasn't trying to shut it. He was trying to think of something clever to say as he looked from me out to his car and then beyond it to where my Firebird was blocking it off.

"Nah," he said. "She's not here."

He showed no indication that he realized how silly such a simple denial sounded in Aberdeen, Maryland. But somebody in the room behind him knew. There was a sound of scrambling movement and running feet that he pretended not to hear. I gave the door a shove and the boy fell back. "Hey," he said again as I entered the room. He took one step toward me and walked his forehead right into the palm of my hand. Somehow he lost his balance and went tumbling back over the room's one and only chair.

The bed was empty and my eyes went immediately to the closed door of the bathroom. "Candy, come out here," I ordered. "I'm taking you home."

The only answer I got came from the corner where Candy's boyfriend sprawled between the overturned chair and the wall radiator. "It's too late," he said. "We're getting married this afternoon."

There was a certain part of me that wanted very much to kick this boy in the teeth. I turned, ready to take him on if he came out of the corner, but he wasn't moving. It was just as well. He was taller than I was, but his naked chest was thin and underdeveloped, and I knew he was no real threat to me. The tenseness went out of me and I sat down on the end of the bed. All I wanted was my little girl out of that room and I was not going to make it any easier by beating up her boyfriend.

"Glen," I said to him, and when he looked startled I said, "That's your name, isn't it?"

When I got no response I told him who I was and he nodded, awkward and wary in his squatting position, but still managing to be half polite to his fiancée's father.

"You can't get married, Glen. That's how come I'm here."

Glen's eyes flicked uncertainly to the closed door of the bathroom. He wanted some help, that was clear. Meeting your fiancée's father was one thing. Squatting bare-balled in front of him was something else altogether.

"I don't know if you know anything about me, Glen," I said, trying to be soothing and friendly and unchallenging all at once, "but I'm a lawyer. You might think that's no big deal, and you'd probably be right, but the fact is that I may be able to help you with some of the trouble you've gotten yourself into."

"I'm not in no trouble," he said defiantly, and I winced. Not only was my daughter's boyfriend ugly; he couldn't speak English.

"Hey," I said, still keeping my voice even. "What do you think I'm doing here? How do you think I got here?" In asking him to think, I was being optimistic. I was assuming that if the kid had charmed Candy he must have something on the ball. But he held out on me.

"I dunno," he said.

"Maryland authorities called up Candy's mother. She had to get Candy's personal attorney, which is me, down here right away."

Glen hesitated. "You're shittin' me." His lips parted, ready to break into a grin if I would only give him the sign that it was okay, that my being there was all a big joke.

I thought maybe my friendly tone had been a mistake and I picked up the cadence of my speech, cutting my words off a little more crisply as I told him, "Think about it, Glen. Candy's only fifteen years old. That makes her a minor. You know what that means. You saw what happened that time up at Wampaugh Pond when Officer Logan found you. He was just a local cop and a friend of mine, so nothing came of it that time. But now you've gone and broken a federal law by taking a girl under the age of eighteen across state lines for immoral purposes. You know whose jurisdiction that is, Glen? The FBI's. And in case you're wondering what they mean by immoral purposes, let me just say that what you did last night can get you five years in a federal penitentiary. But that's not the only thing you've got to worry about. They've got a separate law here in Maryland, and that's statutory rape. Sleeping with a girl under eighteen will get you fifteen years in the state prison. Another law they've got is fraud. You represented yourself to this motel owner as being anything other than an unmarried couple and you've broken that one. Depending on how you signed the register, you may have committed forgery as well. Now what do you think, Glen? You think I'm shitting you now?"

Glen didn't think anything of the kind. What he thought was that he needed some advice, some support, some guidance on how to deal with a semi-maniacal father who was spouting legal conclusions at him with all the authority of a Supreme Court justice. He gazed fretfully around the room, skipping past the still closed bathroom door and then skipping back to it again.

"Glen."

His head snapped forward as if he had been caught doing something he should not be doing.

"Glen, I think the best thing for you is to get out of here as quickly as you can. I want you to gather up your things, walk out to your car and go on home. C'mon now. Candy will see you back there."

The boy made an effort to sneer, but he was too uncertain to carry it off. I saw his black pants and a blue T-shirt draped across the bureau and I tossed them to him. I found a pair of black ankle boots with socks sticking out of the tops and I brought them over.

"If you've got a toothbrush or anything in the bathroom you can just leave them there and Candy will bring them back to Portshead with her. That's good, Glen; hurry up now. This your suitcase? Jesus, Glen, you really should get something else, you're going to go traveling around like this. All right, that's good enough. You can finish dressing in the car. Got your keys? Good, good."

I led the boy outside, my hand lightly on his elbow, escorting him directly to his Chrysler. "You got any money?" I said. "Here—here's twenty bucks. That'll help you get home. Now you get in there and start up and I'll just move my car out from behind you. Don't you be waiting around for us, either, Glen."

Glen was out of the parking lot with his old blue suitcase that he had probably taken from his mother, his big black dinosaur of a car and my crisp green twenty-dollar bill before he even knew what hit him. I waited to make sure he didn't circle the block and come back and then I returned to the motel room. The bathroom door was still closed, but when I knocked on it Candy came out. She was dressed in a Mexican peasant blouse and a dungaree skirt. It was, I saw, her way of dressing up and it made my heart ache to see what a little girl she was in so many ways.

She didn't look at me at first. She hung her head and her long blond hair cascaded down to cover most of her face.

I tried to think of something appropriate to say, but all that came out was a plaintive little cry of "Oh, Candy" that escaped from my throat before I even knew it was there.

"What?" she said. It was a semi-defiant response; an I-wasn't-doing-anything statement.

"Candy, what were you doing coming down here with that guy?"

And now I got it: "I wasn't doing anything."

"What were you thinking of, Candy?"

"I wasn't thinking of anything."

"Getting married? You weren't thinking of doing anything but getting married at fifteen?"

"I turned sixteen last week, Dad."

Guilt swept through me. "Oh, my God. That's right."

"Yeah, that's right," my little girl said. "A lot of difference it made to you."

"Candy, everything that happens to you means a world of difference to me."

"Yeah, well, you got a great way of showing it, Dad."

"Don't say that." My voice, which had been so strong and so confident when I was railroading Glen, was beginning to falter. I tried to clear it. "People . . ." It didn't come out right and I had to start again. "People show affection in different way—"

"What way did you ever show me?"

"Well, I came down here to get you, didn't I?"

"Sure, so you could belt Glen around and make us both look stupid and then drag me back home like I'm some dumb little kid or something."

"You don't want to go back home?"

"What's for me there?"

"Well, school . . ."

"I hate school."

"Oh, Candy, someday in your life you're going to remember you said that and you're going to laugh about it. School's the easiest thing you'll ever do. Where else are you ever going to have so many people of your own age to meet and talk to and do things with?"

"They're all assholes," she said summarily.

"There's not a single person in that high school you like?"

"They're all immature. They're all interested in stupid things."

"And what are you interested in?"

"Glen."

"But Glen doesn't go to school, right?"

"That's right."

"Is that what you like about him, the fact that he's older? Do you think that's cool?"

"Dad, I don't think that's 'cool.' " Candy wagged her jaw resentfully at me.

I reacted childishly and mocked her. "Well, Candy, what is so fascinating about the guy? He's a cretin, for God's sake. Didn't you hear what was going on out here a minute ago?"

For the first time since she had come out of the bathroom she looked up at me. Her eyes, small to begin with, puffed into little slits. "So you're smarter than him, so what? What does that prove?" Then, baiting me, she added, "Not everyone can be as smart as you are, Dad."

Slipping down on the bed, I reached out and took my daughter's hand. She made no effort to pull away, but let me hold it as if it was a bridle or a rein, something attached to her but not part of her. "Candy, you're throwing your life away." As soon as I said that I shuddered. It was the same thing my mother had told me when I was not too much older than Candy was now. An idea burned horridly through my mind. "You don't have to get married, do you?"

She twisted her face in exasperation and I wondered if anybody *had* to get married these days. Quickly, I tried to steer the conversation back to some firmer ground. "Let me give you an example. You remember how many years ago it was when you were in kindergarten? A lot, right? Well, in that many more years you're only going to be in your mid-twenties and, believe me, that's young. People I work with think I'm young and look at me, I'm your father. You're a bright kid, Candy, but one thing you don't understand and that's how long life is. Life is a long, long time. Too long to have to spend the whole thing with a guy like Glen."

"Too long to have to spend with someone like Ma?"

There it was. I had not been cautious enough. I had exposed myself to the little bitch and she had uncorked one right on my chin.

"Your mother is a wonderful person, Candy," I said carefully, letting her draw her hand away from mine. "But that's a good example of what can happen. Your mother and I will always like each other and for a while we loved each other very much. But people change with the passage of time and with the experiences they have. Your mother and I are not the same people we were when we got married. We don't think the same and we don't act the same. Just like you don't think and act the way you did when you were in grade school."

"Can't people change together?"

"Yes, of course, they can—" I wanted to add that people who change together usually have a base to build on, but she cut me off.

"Then what makes you think Glen and I won't change together?"

"Because," I snapped, frustrated that she was still arguing with me and that I had no foolproof, slam-dunk, obvious-to-everyone answer, "he's a loser. Can't you see that?"

Candy recoiled, horrified that I could even think of her boyfriend in such terms. She shook her head adamantly. "That's not true. He's going to amount to something."

"Yeah. An old loser." My smart mouth was running off on its own and I groped for some better way of communicating to this sixteen-year-old girl that life shouldn't peak with a summer's ride in an old black Chrysler. Hadn't that very thing happened to her mother? But what could I say about her mother that wouldn't make Candy think badly of her? I settled for asking her what she thought was going to happen once she and Glen got married.

She shrugged. "Live, I guess."

"On what? Does Glen have a job?"

"I'll get a job," she said.

"You mean he doesn't even work? What is it he's been doing all these years?"

"He's only twenty and he's had plenty of jobs. He's fixed boats. He's worked for a janitorial service—"

"Oh, well then, he must have plenty of money to take care of you."

"I don't care about money, Dad."

"Well, care about it or not, it's something you have to consider."

"So maybe you think I should be like Ma and go around sleeping with rich guys all the time."

I stared coldly at Candy and she stared defiantly back. "Don't talk that way about your mother."

"Why not? It's true. You should see the guys she fucks."

The obscenity raked over me. "Your mother is a grown woman," I told her in measured words. "She's entitled to have a social life of her own."

"Yeah?" Candy taunted. "With married guys? With old, old married guys who just happen to be rich as anything?"

"I don't know who you're talking about."

"I'm talking about old man Garber who owns the lumberyard, that's who. You think she's interested in him just for social life, Dad?"

The information about old Mr. Garber was meant to hurt and yet somehow it did not. Cookie had hinted to me that something like that was going on, and had I bothered to give the matter any extensive consideration, Mr. Garber would not have been an illogical choice. Of more concern to me was the effect the situation obviously was having on Candy. Watching her from where I sat, I was struck by how much my daughter was like her mother: attractive, headstrong, self-reliant, innocently ignorant of everything except what was directly in front of her; and I wondered again how I could relate Cookie's experiences without reducing her in Candy's eyes. And then I knew that it could not be done, and what was more, I did not want it done. If she was to learn anything from the lives of the people closest to her, it was going to have to come from mine.

I took a deep breath. "Candy," I said, "I think we've got a lot of catching up to do."

47 "I once did a very great thing for our town." We were on the New Jersey Turnpike, somewhere north of Cherry Hill, when I said this. The rain, which had started as a few sprinkles in Delaware, was coming down in sheets by this time and I was hunched over the wheel and squinting through the windshield at the taillights of the car immediately in front of us. I could not see the look Candy gave me, but I knew it was the look children reserve for bragging fathers.

"What I did was, I scored four touchdowns to help John Hancock tie Ashton High in the annual Thanksgiving Day football game."

Candy sighed. I might as well have been telling her how many Ping-Pong balls I could stuff in my mouth at once.

"Maybe it doesn't sound like much to you, but it meant a great deal to a lot of people at the time. Ashton had won twenty-two games in a row and to Portshead it was almost a matter of civic vindication when we ended their winning streak. It paid Ashton back for all the years it had been looking down on us."

Candy said nothing. She stared out the window like someone doing time.

"I nearly got to go to Harvard as a result of that game, did you know that?"

There were no squeals of delight coming out of the bucket seat on my right.

"Then the coaches in there found out I was getting married and they dropped me from their recruiting list. One of them said to me, 'We didn't really expect that your main contribution to the school was going to be in the field of academics,' which I guess meant they weren't sure how valuable I was going to be to them if I had a family to support.

"Anyhow, that's how I happened to go to Northeastern. They had a program that let me go to school six months and work six months, and the coaches there were real happy to have me. At least at first. But after a couple of weeks it became obvious that Harvard had been right. It was just about impossible for me to commute back and forth to Portshead and be a student and a father and a husband and take care of the house and play good football all at the same time. By the end of my freshman season I was sitting on the bench watching some kid from Waltham make a name for himself at my position and by the next year I

• 263 •

was buried so deep on the varsity that I never even got to go to any of the away games. I started skipping a few practices and when nobody said anything to me I went up and told the coaches I was quitting. That was the most humiliating part of all—they didn't even try to talk me out of it."

The car I had been following braked suddenly for no apparent reason and I had to swerve to avoid running into it. We had a lane to ourselves now and visibility was no more than about fifty feet. I gave a quick glance over at Candy, just to make sure she was still with me.

She saw me looking and turned her head away. "I'm sorry I screwed up your football career, Dad. I'll try to remember not to be born next time."

Startled by her reaction to what had been meant, essentially, as a confession, I said, "I was only trying to show you the kinds of things that can happen when you make a mistake like you were going to make today."

"Well, I'm not a football player, Dad, and I wasn't exactly planning on going to Harvard, so you don't need to worry."

"It doesn't make any difference what your opportunities are, Candy, as long as you have them. They're what give you control over your life. Hopefully, as you go along, you'll choose the right ones and they'll open up even more opportunities to you. But if you choose the wrong ones, if you get married too early or you quit school, you're going to find yourself stuck like I was, having to do certain things and not being able to do others, and never knowing what you could have done if you'd only had the chance."

Candy's head tilted back. Her chin pointed out. "And if you hadn't been stuck, you would have been a football player, is that it, Dad?"

Stated so bluntly, the idea seemed foolish. But we were all alone, just the two of us in our metal shell hurtling along the turnpike in fifty-foot increments, and there was nobody on earth more worth the risk of making a fool of myself for.

"Maybe," I said. "Maybe not a professional, because I wasn't fast enough. But maybe a good solid college player whose accomplishments would seem a little more significant than what I've got to live with now. As it is, I dream about it sometimes. I wake up drenched in sweat from dreaming I've been given one more chance." I hesitated, my eyes still on the little bit of road I could see ahead of me. "They're pretty strange, those dreams. I'm usually aware that I've been given a reprieve and I know exactly where I went wrong and exactly what I have to do to make it right this time." My hands started aching and I realized how tightly I had been gripping the wheel as I talked. I felt slightly embarrassed and tried to ease off with a laugh. "The only problem is, I'm always a lot older than everybody else in these dreams."

Candy was studying me, peering intently at me until I had to turn my face to see what she wanted.

• 264 •

"And where you went wrong, that was having me, wasn't it, Dad?"

"Of course it wasn't," I said sharply.

"All these things, you being stuck and all that, they never would have happened if it wasn't for me."

"It wasn't like that."

"Isn't that what you've always thought? Isn't that why you left Ma and me?"

"Is that what your mother told you?"

"She didn't have to. I got eyes, Dad. I can see when you're around and when you're not."

"I've been around," I snapped. "I'm there often enough when it's bill time and somebody has to make sure you have a roof over your head and clothes to wear and food to eat. You didn't think your mother was doing all that, did you? Not on the measly salaries she brings home from whatever crummy job she happens to have this week."

As soon as I said it I wanted the words back. I wanted to stuff them back into whatever vile hole they had leaked out of, but it was too late. Candy turned away from me.

A big tractor-trailer drove by on our left, oblivious of the conditions. It splattered us in its wake, covering our windshield with road water that looked as if it had been thrown from a bucket. Candy waited until the windshield wipers gave us something to see again and then she said, "At least I see her once in a while, Dad."

Chastened, anxious to redeem myself, I said the wrong thing again. "It's not my idea we never see each other, Candy."

"Whose idea was it?"

Gently, I said, "I thought it was yours."

Candy's elbow fit into the armrest of the door and her chin dropped into the palm of her hand. "I don't even know you."

It was like being slapped in the face; the message continued to sting long after it had been delivered. I kept looking over, waiting for her to say something more, but nothing came.

"You know, Candy, it wasn't always that way. When your mother and I first split up you and I would spend every Wednesday night and every Saturday together."

"I don't remember."

"We stopped the Wednesdays when you started school. Your mother said it was too disruptive and I went along with it. I didn't realize it at the time, but when I only started seeing you on Saturdays we lost the continuity we had. Instead of being a father, I became a guy who'd come to take you places. As you got older it got more and more difficult to think of places to go. You had Brownies and things of your own to do and we began missing a few weekends here and there until all of a sudden getting together seemed to be almost a chore for everybody concerned. One day I arrived to get you and there you were in stockings and makeup, with boys on your mind and nothing to talk about with your old man. What was worse, I didn't seem to know how to act around you anymore. Then it was almost like what happened with football. I stopped coming around and nobody complained."

"You can't blame me for that."

"I'm not blaming anybody. It just sort of happened."

"How was it ever going to be any different unless you made it, Dad?"

If she had been a trial counsel she might have said, "No further questions," and sat down. But she didn't do that. She continued staring at me long after it was obvious to both of us that I had no answer to give.

"I can try to make it different now," I offered.

Her mouthed twitched. "Don't bother."

She bit her lower lip and I knew she was trying to keep from crying. I tried to put my arm around her and she pulled away. Her hand went to her face, quickly, wiping at her eyes. A car roared by us, its horn screaming, and I knew we were drifting all over the road.

A sign hovered overhead. An exit unexpectedly appeared and on an impulse I shot off in the direction of the Holland Tunnel.

48 We spent the better part of the afternoon in New York City. Neither of us had ever seen it before, and we didn't get to see all that much in the few hours we were there, but we had fun, and that was something we had not had together in a long time. By the time we found a parking garage it had stopped raining and the first thing we did was go to the top of the Empire State Building. From there we went to Radio City Music Hall and then we took a walk along Fifth Avenue.

We ate a late lunch at the Plaza because it was one of the few places in New York I had heard of and because I wanted to take Candy to a nice place. In the back of my mind, I suppose, was the idea that I wanted to show her a whole different style of life, but I may not have done a very good job of it. Once inside the Plaza I tried to lead her to Trader Vic's and we ended up seated in some place called the Oak Room. We decided we didn't want Trader Vic's anyhow and chose instead a garden restaurant in the hotel lobby where we had spied luscious-looking pastries being pushed around on a cart. We ate enough to keep Candy full for the whole rest of the ride home. It didn't all go smoothly, but we were no longer the strangers we had been, either.

It was dark by the time we rolled into Portshead. I had been awake for more than thirty-six hours and was pretty much driving on instinct by the time I steered into Cookie's driveway. I was hoping that there wouldn't be a scene on our arrival, but I needn't have worried. Cookie was there to hold open Candy's door almost before I had the engine shut off. She called Candy a little snot, but she meant it lovingly and she took her into her arms when she said it.

Where I went wrong was in assuming that when I left Cookie's I was just going to be able to go back to my own place and flop into bed. Given everything else I had been through, it was a ridiculous assumption. I did not realize that, however, until I stepped off the elevator on my floor and discovered that the blare of Bruce Springsteen music which had followed me up from the parking lot was coming from my own stereo.

Opening the door to my apartment meant walking into a fog of marijuana smoke. A voice shouted my name and another cheered. I peered through the haze at Ferrara, who was toasting me with a long-necked Budweiser, and Boyle, who was sitting next to him and twisting his hands to his lips to make duck sounds. Beyond them I could see Donovan and Stevie Ferris in the kitchen. Howie White was coming over to shake my hand and Joey Aiello was popping open a can of Miller. Even Giacomini was there, his fatness overflowing my La-Z-Boy recliner. Ziggy, it seemed, had decided to throw a party in my absence.

"Look who's here," Howie White called out, hanging on to me with his handshake grip and leading me into the center of the activities.

"I know who that is," Ferrara announced, "that's Billy Kincaid."

Howie White looked at me in confusion, like maybe there was a possibility I really was Billy Kincaid. "What are you talking about? This here is Chuckie."

"No," Ferrara said, hooting at him. "That has to be Billy Kincaid. He looks familiar, but we never see him no more, so it can't be Chuckie Bishop. Chuckie Bishop was a good guy who used to come around and see his friends once in a while. This guy here acts like a stranger. It's gotta be Billy Kincaid."

Boyle scrambled to his feet, not without some difficulty, and started pawing at my clothes. "Take off his shirt. We'll see if it's Billy Kincaid."

Howie White helped me push him away. "What are you talking about?" he said again. "What do you want to take off his shirt for?"

"Remember that time in high school when Kincaid started working out with weights and he said he wasn't gonna take his shirt off until he had the perfect build? Remember we'd all go down the beach and he'd be there in his cut-off sweat shirt?"

"Billy Kincaid's an asshole," intoned Giacomini from the bowels of my chair.

"Yeah, well, long before he got around to taking the sweat shirt off he beat the shit out of you," said Stevie Ferris, who had arrived from the kitchen and was holding out his hand to greet me. "Long time no see, buddy," he said, smiling.

"I was drunk," Giacomini said, but nobody paid him any attention. A few seconds later he added, "I'd like to see him try it now."

That was too much for Ferris. He wheeled on Giacomini and said, "Who are you shitting, Giaco? Billy Kincaid still works out with weights and he could still kick your ass blindfolded."

"Yeah? Well, get him up here and let's see him try."

The boys, I saw, had been partying for some time. I extricated myself from the circle in which I was standing and set off in search of Ziggy. I found him in the kitchen, engaged in an exceptionally earnest conversation with Donovan. He was saying, "You see who they got pitching for 'em now? Some guy from Norway, for Chrissakes. Norway. I didn't even know they played baseball over there."

"The guy's from Holland," Donovan corrected.

"Great. He grew up playing in wooden baseball shoes." Ziggy noticed me and turned happily. "Chuckie. Where have you been, boy? We've been drinking all the beer and smoking all the dope without you."

"Ziggy, I want to talk to you."

"Uh-oh," Donovan trumpeted. "Watch out. Chuckie's pissed."

"I'm not pissed. I just want to talk to Ziggy for a minute."

"Hey, Chuckie." Ziggy slapped the lapel on my coat with the back of his hand. "What are you so pissed off for all the time?" Stevie Ferris wandered back into the room and Joey Aiello was tagging along behind him. Ziggy turned so that he could address everyone at once. "Last night—right?—the first time since I told Denise to fuck off, I get myself a little piece of ass and bring her home."

"Who was it?" Joey asked.

Ziggy shook his hips and moved his arms back and forth like pistons. "Dar-lene Ghi-lotti."

"All right," Stevie said, slapping Ziggy's outstretched palm. "Ferrara got her one time in the sand dunes down Hyannis."

"Everybody's got her one time," Donovan said.

"Did you ever get her?" Ziggy asked him.

"I didn't want her." Donovan made a noise like a pig. "What was I gonna get? A little snout job?"

"What are you talking about?" Stevie said. "She's built like the perfect woman, I heard."

"What's so perfect about her?"

"Well, she's waist high, her mouth makes a circle, and she's got this little flat spot on her head where you can rest your beer."

"Hey, listen," Ziggy shouted, holding out his hands to quiet everyone down. "You want to hear about what happened with Darlene last night?"

"Same old thing that always happens with Darlene, I imagine."

"Does she still wear that girdle with the flowers on it? She used to wear that all the time in high school."

"Hey, she don't need no girdle. She's got a great body."

"She used to wear it in high school."

"Well, she didn't have it on last night. I bring her home here and Chuckie's not around, so I figure, what the heck?, the bed's just lying there, and I bring her into Chuckie's room. We're going at it, you know, hot and heavy, and all of a sudden Chuckie here walks in and turns all the lights on and tells us to get the fuck out of his room."

"No!"

"That's cold."

"Not that I give a shit, but you shoulda seen Darlene. The minute Chuckie leaves she starts reading me the fuckin' riot act. 'Why did you let him get away with that?' she goes. I go, 'Hey, it's his fuckin' apartment,' and she acts like I just shat in the bed or something. She jumps up and starts yelling, 'All you Portshead boys are the same. You think just because a girl's been married before that makes her a whore and you can do anything you want to her.'" Ziggy had his wrists on his hips and his eyes trained obliquely on the floor while he imitated the way Darlene had looked. "She goes, 'Well, I'm no whore. I'm assistant branch manager of a bank and I'm no whore.'"

Ziggy fell onto Donovan's shoulder, laughing. Joey Aiello was laughing with him, but I wasn't sure it was over the same thing since he kept repeating, "'All you Portshead guys are the same,'" and it was clear he liked that line the best.

Stevie Ferris spoke up. "Seriously, though, Chuckie, you didn't really try to kick them outta your bed, did you?"

"Sure, he's all uptight about us putting stains on his sheets or something," Ziggy said.

"Jesus, Chuckie." Stevie Ferris looked disgusted.

"Hey, it wasn't like I been taking his bed every night or nothing. This was the first fuckin' time. You know, I figure here's Chuckie, the big fuckin' bachelor with all the broads in the world. I figured they'd be cookin' him dinner, doin' the laundry. I figured they'd be parading in here night and day and I'd be getting all the spillovers. You know, they'd be introducing me to all their sisters, their roommates, their horny friends. But no, since I been living here he hasn't brought a broad home once."

"What about that broad today?" Joey Aiello asked.

In slow motion, almost in stages, Ziggy's eyes lit up. "Oh, yeah, Chuckie, you didn't tell me about that."

Instantly I was on my guard. "Tell you about what?"

"That you knew Lanny Brandon's wife. What's her name—Alicia?"

Finucci and his detectives went through my mind. Someone must have talked. "What makes you think I do?" I said.

"She came by here this afternoon looking for you. Me and Joey and Ferrara were all hanging around, getting a little crazy, and all of a sudden there she was, standing right in front of us."

"Alicia Brandon came here?"

Ziggy smiled. "I never seen her before that close and, Jesus, she's beautiful, Chuckie."

"Not too beautiful for you, though, huh, Zig?" Joey poked him in the ribs.

"What's he mean, Ziggy?"

"Ferrara had some coke. You know how you get on coke, Chuckie."

I had Ziggy by the front of the shirt and the conversations around me came to a standstill. "What did you do to her?"

Ziggy's hands were on my arms, trying to push me away. "I was just fooling around with her, Chuckie. It was dumb stuff; we didn't hurt her or nothing."

"What kind of dumb stuff?"

"We told her you'd be back in a few minutes and we got her to sit down and wait for you. Then we started making little jokes, that's all. We figured, being married to that queer-bait and everything, maybe she was looking for a little action, we didn't know. But she wouldn't talk to us. I thought maybe she was real stuck-up or something. So I left the room and came back with my dick out, that's all. Just to see what she'd do. And she got all bullshit and left."

"You did that to Alicia Brandon?"

"Well, it wasn't like it was anybody else's wife, Chuckie."

I flung Ziggy Pastore aside and ran to the living room. The phone was practically buried under bags of potato chips and empty beer cans, but I found it. I had the Brandons' number ringing when Howie White obsequiously appeared at my elbow. "What's so important, Chuckie?"

"Oh"—Ferrara waved his hand—"it's the fuckin' DelVecchio thing, I'm sure. The guy that killed Fitzy."

From behind me, Giacomini said, "Hey, Chuckie, how come you're representing that guy, anyhow?"

Joey Aiello had followed me out of the kitchen. He said, "I been wondering the same thing, Chuckie. I remember that guy from dances down the Congregational Church. Remember them? And all the worms who thought they were so tough would go into the boys' room to smoke cigarettes? He was one of them, Richie DelVecchio."

"He was on my Little League team," said Boyle. "He sucked."

"Anyhow," Joey pressed, "how come you're defending that guy? I always thought he was worthless."

"How did he ever get to become a cop, anyhow?"

"His sister's married to Jimbo Ryder."

"Are you shittin' me? I didn't know that."

"But seriously, Chuckie, what about Fitzy? Don't you got no respect for the dead?"

"I guess that doesn't figure into it when you're a lawyer."

"One thing I got, that's respect for the dead."

There was no answer. I hung up the phone and cornered Ferrara. "Was she upset?" I said. "Did she act like she was frightened?"

"Who?"

"Alicia Brandon."

"She was freaked out before she ever got here, Chuckie."

"Did she say anything about Lanny? Anything that made you think she was in any danger?"

"All she said was that she wanted to see you."

"Do you know why?"

"No, but I can guess." Ferrara panned our audience with a smirk.

Boyle howled with laughter and some of the others joined in, but I didn't have time to laugh with them. I was already on my way out the door.

49 This time there were no lights on. It made the house look different somehow. It made it look larger, more aloof. I thought it looked more forbidding, too, but that might only have been my own projection. Both the cars were in the driveway, lined up one behind the other, but nobody answered the doorbell when I rang. I rang a second time and a third, and then I just left my finger on the bell while it rang over and over again. There was still no answer.

I tried the door and it was locked. I went around to the side gate and opened it by reaching over the top. I walked into the backyard and tried the door of the screen porch and then the door that led into the kitchen. They were both locked and I knew of no others.

Standing back by the swimming pool, I surveyed the house for any signs of life. I kept focusing on the window in which Fitzy had been shot. He had been able to climb up there and Lanny himself had said the bolts on the window were no good. I wondered if they had been replaced or repaired. I wondered if it was worth trying.

The sill was over my head and I had to grab on to it and kick my toes into the side of the house in order to boost myself up. The screen that covered the lower half of the window slid easily, and the window itself moved when I hit the frame with the heel of my hand. Forcing it bit by bit, I managed to get the window to a point where something snapped and after that it was only a matter of holding it high enough to get my body through. I was halfway inside when I heard Lanny Brandon speak to me.

"Do you think it would be terribly ironic if I were to shoot you now?"

I couldn't see him. It was too dark and there were too many shadows. I stayed where I was, not moving, my arms bunched beneath me as I balanced on my stomach and tried not to think about the target I was making. "I was worried about you," I said. My voice was small and reed thin. "I tried calling. I tried ringing the doorbell."

"I wonder if Fitzy did the same thing before he came visiting. I wonder if he was coming to call on Alicia when he came squirming through the window like that? Well, don't just hang there on my account. It'd be just as easy for me to shoot you once you're inside."

I hauled myself in over the kitchen sink and tumbled to the floor, narrowly missing the butcher-block table that sat in the middle of the floor. I started to get up and Lanny told me to stay where I was.

"I should make you crawl first, don't you think, Chuckie? Don't you think that would be fitting for all the crawling you've made me do over the years?"

I still couldn't see him. I only knew he was in the corner of the room. "I never made you crawl, Lanny."

"No?" Lanny's voice strained with surprise. "You mean you never thought I was a fairy? You never felt that way when you heard what happened between me and the scoutmaster? You were right there to stand by me, the good friend that I needed? Well, jees, Chuckie, my parents must not have told me you called. I must have been at the store every time you came by to see me. I must not have noticed you standing up for me when everyone else in the junior high was harassing me."

My arms and legs, already brittle from lack of sleep, were beginning to cramp under the tension with which I was holding them to the tiled floor. "Lanny," I said, "you're talking about something that happened twenty years ago."

"And you haven't changed a bit, have you, Chuckie? I wanted to believe you had, you know. I really did. Even when all the signs pointed to the fact that you were only interested in Alicia, I still refused to read them. I didn't ask you how come we never got together outside my house or how come you never brought anybody else from Portshead over with you. I accepted you exactly as you presented yourself—right up until last night. Right up until I found your flashy little Firebird parked under the neighbor's trees and half the police department pulling their hair out over something they hadn't expected inside my house. What do you suppose that could have been, Chuckie?"

From the center of the floor, on all fours like a donkey, I said, "It was me, Lanny," and he said, "Yes," and stepped away from the corner. There was something in his hand, something he held lightly. He was nearly on top of me before I realized that it was a bottle.

Slowly I released myself from my position and leaned back against the butcher-block table. Just as slowly Lanny let himself down onto the floor next to me.

"Here." He offered the bottle to me. When I hesitated he got angry. "Go on, drink it," he said. "What do you think, I put Drano in it? Or hair bleach, maybe? Or female hormones?"

It was a quart bottle and it smelled of bourbon, the same as Lanny did. "What are we drinking to, Lanny?"

"To Alicia, of course. To her departure."

I put the bottle to my lips without tasting it. "Where did she go?"

"She's left. Left me. Left you, too. Took the big silver bird to LA at six o'clock this evening. So drink up. Drink good riddance to bad rubbish."

I handed the bottle back. "Why did she do that?"

Lanny brought his chin around very slowly until it pointed directly at me. "I confronted her with your scummy little affair and then I threw her ass out."

"She tell you we were having an affair?"

"That's right." Lanny took a quarter inch out of the bottle and handed it to me.

This time I filled my mouth with bourbon and let it seep down into my throat. "You're lying, Lanny," I said. "Either that or she is, because there was no affair, scummy or otherwise."

Lanny's face loomed close to mine. His hand wrapped around the neck of the bottle just above where mine was holding the body. "I know what I saw."

"You saw my car under the trees. If you'd come home early on Monday night you would have seen the same thing, and it was there one time last week as well. I've been here three times without you, Lanny, and there hasn't been any affair yet. She's just been leading me on, Lanny, milking me for everything she could."

Lanny pulled the bottle away and squinted at me. He took a quick drink and squinted again. "What's she got to milk from you?"

"My help."

"In what?"

"In getting your book written."

The bottle shook in Lanny's hand and bourbon flew all over both of us. "It's my book," he said, "and I damn well don't need help from you or anyone else. I'm the only one who knows what I have to say."

"I've seen the manuscript, Lanny. I've seen what you've written."

Angrily Lanny said, "She had no right to show it to you."

I shrugged. "It was part of her plan. She knew how you had been struggling ever since you got back here, how you hadn't been able to get the material you needed, and she hit on me as a way of getting it for you. The manuscript was just one more way of doing it. She'd tried the dinner party and when you saw through that she tried convincing me to come around on my own. A look here, a word there, and she had me thinking she wanted me. So I hung around until you went out one night last week and then I tried to force the matter. That's when she got out the manuscript and showed me what was really going on."

I needed the bourbon and Lanny put up a little struggle before releasing his grip on it. I took a swallow that burned a hole in my belly. "I pretended I was interested, Lanny. I came over twice to read what you did with the stories I told you, but the truth was, I was only here for her. She knew it, too, and she played me for the perfect sucker. She had me tell everything I know for a couple of promises and a glimpse of her tits last Saturday afternoon." Another sip, another swallow. "But in terms of an affair, Lanny, it never happened, and if she told you it did, I can only guess it was because she knew how important the book is to you and she was even more afraid of what would happen if you found out she had been manipulating it."

The two of us sat shoulder to shoulder in the darkness, our backs against the hard, even side of the butcher-block table, while I held my breath and hoped that I had guessed right that Alicia really had not confessed. Lanny took the bottle once more and I could hear the liquor sloshing as he tilted it up to his lips and down again.

"Why don't you go after her?" I said.

"I can't." Lanny's tongue was thick. He coughed and sucked air up his nose, throwing his shoulders back to get it all in. "I've got to finish my book."

"To hell with the book. That woman's worth a hundred books."

Lanny shook his head. He drew his hand along the side of his face and across his upper lip. "It's something I've got to do. If I don't, none of what happened to me will have any meaning."

"Of course it will. It got you out of Portshead, didn't it? It made your father send you to Coventry Academy when he never would have done that in a million years. It got you in Hollywood while the rest of us were still trying to scrape together enough money to buy a GTO or something important like that."

Lanny snorted. Quickly he swiped at his nose again with the heel of his hand. "How many of the guys you've talked to think about me that way, Chuckie?"

"Oh, Jesus. Who cares? Here you are a goddamn walking success story and you're trying to justify yourself to a bunch of guys who in twenty years have managed to make it from Alvie's Corner to the Plough and Stars. They're still having the same conversations as when you left, Lanny, and the only difference is that most of them have given up any hope of ever doing the things they talk about. You're worried because of what they might think about you? You're nuts."

Lanny stared into his lap. His thumb scraped at the label of the bottle. "That's easy for you to say. You've never had to prove yourself to anyone."

The room was entirely still. Sitting in the darkened kitchen in the back of his large old house, I thought of all the things that had been said to me since I had last been to bed and, perversely, I started to laugh. My whole body was filled with sadness and the tears were rolling down my face, but Lanny couldn't see either of those things. He could only hear the laughter.

"Get out of here," he gritted. "Get out of here, you miserable sonofabitch, before I really do shoot you."

"C'mon, Lanny," I said, trying to get myself under control. "You don't even have a gun, remember?" I reached across my body for the bottle and my fingers closed around a cold tubular piece of metal. I let go of it as if it had burned me.

"Just leave, Chuckie," Lanny said softly. "Leave me before I blow your fucking head off and all the fun goes out of this conversation."

• 276 •

50 The Northumberland County Grand Jury's inquiry into the death of Michael Paul Fitzpatrick lasted two days. Eighteen of the county's most upstanding citizens, eleven men and seven women culled from the voter registration records, listened to the testimony selected for presentation by Senior Assistant District Attorney Mark Brosnahan. Under the laws of the Commonwealth, the grand jury sat as an accusatory body, advised of the law by Mr. Brosnahan and hearing such evidence as Mr. Brosnahan chose to produce before it in support of the charge against Officer Richard Anthony DelVecchio. Right from the beginning, Mr. Brosnahan's choice was faultless.

The first witness called was Lieutenent Herbert Finucci. He entered the grand jury room carrying a copy of the Departmental Investigation Report and he came out empty-handed. The report made for interesting reading. It went to great length to discuss Michael Fitzpatrick's lack of known employment as well as his suspected drug connections and associations. It identified his roommate by name and similarly described him as being without known employment. It referred to the Brandon home as "a house under investigation for suspected illegal activities" and noted that Richie had been aroused by "highly unusual activity" in a place "marked for observation."

Finucci was before the grand jury for nearly the entire morning. He was followed by an unexpected witness who tried to slip quietly through the hallway but whose leg-shortened gait denied him anonymity. I would have said hello to Buddy Williams when he emerged from the hearing room at the conclusion of his testimony, but he was moving a little too fast for me to catch his eye.

Richie himself was the very last witness called. That surprised Sid Silverman. "It's not often the potential defendant is allowed to testify before a grand jury," he said, "not around here," and he looked at me curiously, as though he suspected I knew something more about what was going on than he did.

What I knew was that by the time Richie took the stand in his wide-legged European-cut suit purchased specially for the occasion, he was as well prepared as he was ever going to be. What I also knew was that the moment Richie entered the grand jury room he was on his own; alone except for Brosnahan, the official stenographer, the grand jurors themselves, and me, voiceless and powerless in the back of the room. He was unprotected except for his rights to refuse to answer under the Fifth Amendment and to leave the proceeding to consult with me. And I knew that neither of those rights was going to do Richie much good if Brosnahan really wanted to get him. And so I worried. And even after Richie emerged unscathed and slightly bewildered by the gentleness of the examination he had undergone, I continued to worry that the grand jury hadn't believed that the danger of his situation justified his firing his weapon when he did.

I worried right up until Wednesday afternoon, when, just fifty-five hours after their investigation had begun, the Northumberland County Grand Jury rose from their folding chairs and declared a no-bill against Officer Richard DelVecchio for the shooting death of Michael Paul Fitzpatrick. They had found insufficient evidence to warrant returning a criminal indictment against him.

I was not at the courthouse to get the news, but Jimbo Ryder was. He granted interviews with reporters from the *Sentinel* and one of the Boston dailies, both of which quoted him as declaring the decision to be a total and complete vindication of his brother-in-law and a resounding manifestation of the fact that the legal system in this country really does work. Jimbo was further quoted as saying that the courage and intelligence shown by the grand jurors made him proud to be a representative of their community. But he did not tell me that. When he called me on the telephone to relate the decision he told me that he had given me a good plug and that I was about to become a hero.

I buzzed Davida and told her not to take any calls from the press. Then I telephoned Richie and gave him the good news. He listened without comment as I explained that the grand jury had found no probable cause for charges to be filed against him and that he was, in effect, in the clear. I told him that in all probability he would be returning to work in a few days. He said, "Good," and asked if there was anybody he could sue for defamation of character or anything like that. I told him he might try praying to God Mrs. Fitzpatrick didn't institute a civil suit against him for wrongful death. "Jesus, she couldn't do that," he said, and because I was feeling a little bit spiteful I said she very well might. He turned the phone over to his wife.

Linda was ecstatic. She shouted thank yous into the phone and kept telling me how wonderful I was and how grateful she and Richie really were for all I had done for them. She knew I could do it, she said, she knew I was the only one who could have.

She was starting to cry when Davida came over the intercom and told me the mayor was on the other line. I broke away from Linda and took the call. His Honor was purring.

"Well, Chuckie, what do you say?"

I said I was very pleased.

"Very pleased?" the mayor repeated good-humoredly, as if I must be pulling his leg. "Your man got off scot-free and that's all you are is very pleased? What more is it you wanted? Personally, I'm delighted. Something like this gives the concept of order a little support. It bolsters the whole city structure and that's important to all of us involved. It should be important to you, too, Chuckie, since you're going to have a stake in the structure of things yourself in a few more weeks. We play it right, this kind of victory can work to everyone's advantage, if you know what I mean."

I told him I thought I did.

"Thing is, though, it's got to be presented right. You know how the media can twist things around. You remember what they did last winter when I let Chief Lyons go through with that fool idea about issuing submachine guns to his officers."

I told the mayor not to worry. I said I wasn't planning on talking to the media myself. He said, "Attaboy." He knew he could count on me.

As soon as the mayor hung up Davida came over the intercom again and told me the lines were flooded with calls from reporters. I instructed her to tell all of them I had gone out and then I took a single packet of papers from my briefcase and I left the office.

Without its lights, the house appeared dark even at six o'clock on a late-summer evening. The shadows from the pine trees accounted for some of it, but the house itself had taken on a somber, unused look. The Mercedes and the 280Z were in the exact spots I had seen them in three days before. The shades in the front windows were in the same positions as I remembered them. The only thing that was different was the front door. It was unlocked, and even that might have been the way I left it.

He didn't answer the doorbell when I rang and he didn't answer my calls when I entered the foyer. I tried the kitchen. I went through the breakfast room and the dining room and looked out into the backyard, just in case he was in the pool. I checked the living room and the den and then I went upstairs.

The door at the top was ajar and I pushed it open. The bed had been slept in. It hadn't been made. A bathrobe was thrown across the foot of the bed. Clothes were piled haphazardly on a chair. There was a noise, a whirring noise, coming from behind the door to an inner room, but when I opened it I found it was an untuned radio on the shelf of an empty bathroom.

I went along the hallway, past the room Alicia and I had used. The door there was shut tight, but I did not try it. He would have no reason for being in that room. None that I wanted to find. Far more likely that he would be in the study. That was where I found him. He was seated at his desk, his back to me, and all around him, on the desk, on the floor, on the windowseat, were balls of crumpled white typing paper. In front of him, partially obscured by his back, was a stack of typed papers only a quarter as high as the one Alicia had once shown me.

"Hello, Lanny," I said.

There was no response. No movement.

I stepped into the room and hesitated. "Lanny?" I had moved closer, I was reaching out to touch him, when he finally turned his head.

Lanny Brandon's eyes were bloodshot, his hair was tangled and unwashed, his beard was unshaven, but he was alive and conscious and he knew who I was. I laid the packet of papers I had brought from my office on the desk next to his arm and backed slowly from the room.

Outside again, the encroaching evening had spread the darkness of the house across the lawn. I stood facing the street, listening to the sounds of someone laying out plates and silverware in the Maddox house next door. Suddenly a light appeared on the second floor behind me, in the study I had just left. It shone down onto the cars in the driveway, reflecting off their chrome bumpers and glass windshields and high-gloss paint jobs. They might have been newly washed, the way they glistened, except that even my Firebird looked good and it had seen nothing but rainwater since the beginning of the summer.

I glanced at my watch and saw that it was not as late as it seemed. I was glad. The sounds from the Maddoxes' had made me hungry and it occurred to me that if I hurried I just might be able to catch Candy in time for dinner.

Epilogue

The information I provided Lanny Brandon never appeared in his book. To the best of my knowledge, the book itself never appeared.

The information did, however, form the basis for the lead article in the November issue of *Boston Monthly Magazine*. Entitled "Who's Buried in Your Mother's Grave?" it rocked the very foundations of the City of Portshead with its detailed treatment of everything from the initial discoveries by old Mr. Woodruff to the sudden resignation of Buster Vizarelli.

Lanny had done his homework. He had interviewed each of the people who had written letters of complaint and he had done all the substantiating research in the cemetery files. Where he left off, the *Sentinel* began. Incensed that it had been scooped in its own backyard, it unleashed a team of reporters on investigative assignments which soon had almost every city official pointing fingers at everybody else. The only one to escape untainted was Jimbo Ryder, and he shook his head despairingly all the way to the November polls, where in the race for state senator he trounced some twenty-one-year-old kid who was just out of college and looking for a job.

I myself did not get appointed to fill Jimbo's city council seat, but that was due first and foremost to the fact that once accusations of mayoral misconduct began flying Jimbo decided it was no longer necessary for him to resign. He apologized to me, of course, but as he pointed out, the mayor was no longer of a mind to appoint me anyway, and, since the mayor's bargaining chips weren't worth much at this point, there was no sense in handing him one. Jimbo offered to make it up to me by delivering me his ward in the upcoming city election in February. He told me if I chose to run I could be part of a coalition of people who would shake off the shame of the McLaughlin machine and make Portshead proud again. To demonstrate what we could do together he showed me a whole list of facts and figures that he had compiled. "Do you know," he said, waving his notes in front of me, "that Moody's Investor Service has just dropped Portshead's credit rating from A to Ba? Do you know what that means in these days of tight money? It means it will be virtually impossible to sell city bonds this year. That means no upgrading of the sewer system." He told me Moody's had done this to us because of the budget deficit McLaughlin had given us. "There's waste in that budget, Chuckie," he promised, "and I've got it all sorted out for you. All you have to do is say you're with us and I've got your whole platform laid out for you."

I told him I wasn't interested. I told him my practice had just gotten too busy for me to take on a responsibility like that, and Jimbo, while expressing his disappointment, looked as if he was pleased to hear it.

In truth, the practice *had* gotten good. Not only had the publicity from the DelVecchio case brought in new business, but Sid suddenly announced that the cruise he and his wife had been planning had escalated into a one-year round-the-world tour and that he was turning over all his files to me. It was, I had the feeling, not a totally sudden decision on his part.

Sid left in December, heading west, the same direction Ziggy Pastore had taken a few weeks earlier. I got a card from Ziggy at Christmas. He was living in an apartment in a place called El Segundo and looking for work. He said he had tracked down Alicia Brandon in LA, but when he called her up "to apologize," Lanny had answered the phone. I was not altogether surprised by that, either. I hadn't seen Lanny since the evening of my delivery and his house had gone up for sale just about the time his article had appeared in *Boston Monthly*.

In February, the city elections turned Francis X. McLaughlin, Alex Scurillo, Brian O'Keefe and Dan Harrington out of office. There had been talk of criminal indictments, but nothing ever came of it and for most people it was enough that the culprits were gone. The new mayor was Robert Broussard, who rode in on a platform of sweeping reform. The new councilman from down the Hook, Ward 5, Jimbo's old district, was wide Vinnie Salvucci. He came in on a platform of fiscal conservatism, lamenting the fact that Moody's had just dropped our credit rating two notches and warning everyone that the past administration's budget deficits meant that our sewer system could not be upgraded.

84808